SIESTA

Books by Berry Fleming

THE CONQUEROR'S STONE
VISA TO FRANCE
THE SQUARE ROOT OF VALENTINE
SIESTA
TO THE MARKET PLACE
COLONEL EFFINGHAM'S RAID
THE LIGHTWOOD TREE
THE FORTUNE TELLERS
CARNIVAL
THE WINTER RIDER
LUCINDERELLA
THE MAKE BELIEVERS
TWO TALES FOR AUTUMN
THE AFFAIR AT HONEY HILL
COUNTRY WEDDING
ONCE THERE WAS A FISHERMAN
THE BOOKMAN'S TALE & OTHERS

SIESTA

BY BERRY FLEMING

THENCE for nine whole days was I borne by ruinous winds over the teeming deep, but on the tenth day we set foot on the land of the lotus-eaters, who eat a flowery food. So we stepped ashore and drew water, and straightway my company took their midday meal by the swift ships. Now when we had tasted meat and drink I sent forth certain of my company to go and make search what manner of men they were who live here upon the earth by bread, and I chose out two of my fellows, and sent a third with them as herald. Then straightway they went and mixed with the men of the lotus-eaters, and so it was that the lotus-eaters devised not death for our fellows, but gave them of the lotus to taste. Now whosoever of them did eat the honey-sweet fruit of the lotus, had no more wish to bring tidings, nor to come back, but there he chose to abide with the lotus-eating men, ever feeding on the lotus and forgetful of his homeward way. Therefore I led them back to the ships weeping, and sore against their will, and dragged them beneath the benches, and bound them in the hollow barques. But I commanded the rest of my well-loved company to make speed and go on board the swift ships, lest haply any should eat of the lotus and be forgetful of returning. Right soon they embarked, and sat upon the benches, and sitting orderly they smote the grey sea water with their oars. . . THE ODYSSEY, BOOK IX

SECOND CHANCE PRESS
Noyac Road, Sag Harbor, NY 11963

*The quotation on the title page is re-
printed, by permission of the Macmillan
Company, from the Butcher and Lang
translation of* The Odyssey.

Copyright © 1935, 1962 by Berry Fleming
Originally published by Harcourt, Brace and Company

First republication 1987 by
SECOND CHANCE PRESS
RD2, Sag Harbor, New York

Library of Congress Catalogue Card Number: 87-060785
ISBN: 0-933256-66-3

Typography by Robert Josephy

PRINTED IN THE UNITED STATES OF AMERICA

There will probably be a few very gentle readers who will need to be reminded that this book is not intended to be a likeness of any real place or of any real group of people or of any real series of incidents; that it is intended to be, in a word, fiction.

SIESTA

CHAPTER ONE

1. Isobaric

IT was dry that summer. Mr. Estill, the weather man, up in the top of the Post Office Building, drew a daily red circle of high pressure over the South Atlantic States for two months almost without change. The pink roads round Georgetown were powdery from the lack of rain, and on nearly any day you could look about the low rim of hills and see one of those little white puffs of still smoke somewhere on the horizon from a fire in the pine trees. The river sank to three feet at the Sand Bar Ferry Bridge and some people began to be afraid that soon there wouldn't be enough water to fill the power canal and run the cotton mills. Up above the railroad bridge The Georgetown Manufacturing Company played a famous baseball game on the red river bottom and Chris Troupe, the dentist, took his little nephew across to the narrow channel on the other side and waded through the shallow water to the Georgia bank with the boy in his arms: "Now you can tell your grandchildren," he said, "you've walked across The Congaree River. . . . Wave your hand at the train!"

The golf course was burned almost khaki and you could drive three hundred yards if you were any good at all; boys like young "Dub" Meigs, who were very good, sometimes drove the eighteenth which was three hundred and forty-five yards long. After the drought had continued for four weeks the congregation of the Sanctified Church on the hill above the golf course opened a series of prayer meetings in the afternoon and as you passed along the third fairway you could hear them over beyond the chinaberry trees wailing for rain with a syncopated cadence and

3

an ecstatic slapping of palm upon palm that gave you a peculiar feeling at the back of your neck; Austin, anyhow, felt that way, though of course, as people were fond of pointing out, that was Austin. Anyhow, you couldn't fail to hear the thin tunes all over the parched golf course, drifting about on the warm wind.

Once in early August a storm blew up out of the gulf and passed inland, cooling it off for a few hours. But the next morning the dust was rising up again in whirling flesh-colored clouds behind the old motor cars rattling in from the country, and September came with hardly a hint of fall.

Some people don't believe there is any connection between the weather and the socially dramatic, but the boys down at the *Daily News* believe it and in July when the drought had gone on for about a month they began to notice a little increase of tension in their world, like a ʼabbit hunter walking up closer and closer to his brier patch.

In the meantime, simple people drove out over the hills after the sun had set to cool off, talked of the heat and the fluctuating decline of the cotton market, and prayed nightly for the salvation of their immortal souls.

2. Country Doctor

Thursday, June 4

DR. ABERCORN was a little blue. He paid only a minimum amount of attention to it, it being nothing more than some temporary maladjustment of chemicals, probably an excess of one of those that made you contented. First you purred with well-being, then you ordered up another jigger from the laboratory and positively radiated, then you ordered up another and things began to go a little bad.

4

Yesterday life had been, in a quiet way, rather good; he couldn't quite remember what had shaken his balance. The world was full of millions of very sensitive scales, moving round, butting into things, butting into each other, blindfolded they were, like the Justice on top of the courthouse. That was it: millions of Justices, blindfolded, moving about with their chemicals held out in front of them poised in a nice scale, a sword in the other hand with which they laid about them when something upset the equilibrium. He couldn't quite remember at the moment. Austin Toombs, whom he hadn't seen for ten years, had come in suffering with acute idleness, but nothing else had happened. He had read *Tristram Shandy* most of the afternoon —oh, yes, it was Lucian; of course. His son, Lucian, wasn't coming home right yet.

He had left his six-year-old Packard coupé at the iron hitching-post on his curb and walked into the cool cement areaway under his front steps, his stethoscope in his coat pocket, his white suit beginning to lose some of its starch and get comfortable, and life had seemed in a quiet way rather good. He was expecting a telegram from Lucian saying when he would arrive, expecting to find it either in the bar across his screen door or on the stone-topped table in the hall. And it hadn't been in the screen door. If Miss Cope had been there she would have put it on the wide arm of his leather chair and meticulously weighted it down with his prescription pad.

But Miss Cope was on the Atlantic. She had been wanting to go to Europe all her life; when *Travel* and *The Geographic* came she practically met them at the door. She had been saving toward the trip for years; he didn't know how much she had accumulated, but when Lucian wrote him he would be home in May and Dr. Abercorn decided that Lucian could do her work and at the same time perhaps pick up an elementary knowledge of some of the local customs and that now was the best possible time for her to go to Europe and get it off her mind, she bought a first-class ticket on the *Majestic* and he thought she must have saved up a good deal.

5

Ten days later Lucian had written him from New York saying that his boat had just docked (he had been studying medicine in Paris) and that he would probably be down on the first of June, but would telegraph him definitely. So he told Miss Cope to go on the first. Yesterday had been the third, and he had heard nothing further from Lucian. He was a little sorry about that; not that it made a great deal of difference, two or three days one way or another, but he felt that such carelessness didn't speak particularly well for the boy.

He had counted on Lucian quite a lot, too. When the boy was just a child, before his mother died, twenty years ago—God! nearer thirty—they used to wander sometimes about the basement office, he telling the boy about that future time when he should grow up and they would open a private office for him on the other side of the hall. They could share the examining room at the back. He would come home from Baltimore and they would talk medicine in the stone-floored office, and the town would say *sotto voce,* not wanting it to get back to the old man, that young Abercorn was a better doctor than his daddy. And now that future time had become the present and Lucian was returning; he had been a little careless in saying he was coming on the first and then neither coming nor telegraphing, but it was a small matter; he would probably get there tomorrow or the next day.

Then he had gone into the dim hall with the cool floor of blue and white octagonal stones, and seen the letter on the table; he knew as he touched it, even before he had tilted it to the light, that it was from Lucian. He had carried it in his fingers through the empty waiting room and laid it on his chair arm while he hung up his hat and washed his hands under the high spigot in the examining room; then he had turned on an oscillating fan and sat down.

Dear Governor,

Sorry about the delay. Had expected to entrain Saturday but got tied up. Now have a bid to go up to Boston for a couple of weeks that is too good to pass by. We are going up tonight. I'm sure this will be O.K. with you. You can definitely count on me two weeks from today—

And his chemicals had begun to get a little out of whack. Now, twenty-four hours later, they seemed about as disorganized as ever.

A short hesitant ring from the doorbell interrupted him, though he heard it only half consciously, having become used to paying no attention to it; patients obeyed the sign on the door, "Ring and Walk In," and Miss Cope notified him.

He turned his eyes with some weariness out of the window at his elbow, gazing across the dusty joint-grass almost at a level of his head beneath the low-drooping boughs of the magnolia tree. The points of some of the long leaves had begun to turn from the dry weather. He took a small pouch from his coat pocket, inserted a ruminative finger and thumb, and pulled out a pinch of finely-shredded tobacco. Sometimes it seemed to ease his teeth. He must go to a dentist. Chris Troupe would do. These God damned infirmities!

The bell rang again, and he remembered that Miss Cope had gone to Europe. He went out into the waiting room.

It was a mulatto girl and she was standing almost invisible in the shade of the hall. She seemed to be cheaply dressed but clean.

"Come in," said the doctor in a resigned way. He sometimes 'took a look' at a friend's servant, though the friend usually telephoned him in advance or came too.

"Dr. Abercorn, sir?"

"Come in the office," said the doctor, leading the way; the girl didn't seem exactly like a servant, like a 'white-folks' nigger.'

He sat down in the dry sweep of his fan.

"Well, what seems to be the matter?" He supposed it was the usual thing and he wondered how she would act when he put the needle into her arm vein; some of them were so scared they almost fainted.

"I heard you needed a nurse, sir."

"A nurse?"

"Yes, sir."

"No, I don't need a nurse."

She looked away at the revolving fan, shifting her weight from one foot to the other.

"My regular nurse has gone away on her vacation, but she's coming back next month."

"Yes, sir. . . . And I don't reckon you need anybody while she's gone."

"No. No, I don't."

"Yes, sir. I've been goin' out here to the colored college and I wanted to get some kind of a place during the vacation time. I saw in *The News* where Miss Cope had gone to New York and I was thinking maybe you might could use somebody while she was gone."

"Have you ever worked in a doctor's office?"

"No, sir. But last summer I did some work in the colored wing at the hospital."

"What's your name?" He wondered if maybe it wouldn't be just as well to have somebody until Lucian got home.

"Laney Shields, sir."

"My son is coming back in a couple of weeks. I probably wouldn't need anybody after that."

"If I could just get something for two weeks."

The doctor looked at her slowly from head to foot; "Are you married?" he said.

She hesitated a minute, flexing her fingers.

"Yes, sir."

"I'll tell you, er—er, what did you say your name was?"

"Laney Shields."

"I'll tell you, Laney, I really don't need anybody, but if you'd like to come and look after things round here until Mr. Lucian gets home I might be able to use you."

"Yes, sir. Thank you very much, sir."

"I could pay you seven dollars a week."

8

"Yes, sir. That'd be all right, sir. I have some uniforms that I had at the hospital."

The doctor nodded. "All right. . . . You'll find a place to change back there in the examination room; there's a closet over in the corner you can keep your things in. Come about quarter to nine and you can go home about six. The cook upstairs will fix you some dinner. You keep the place straight and answer the telephone and—and that kind of thing." When he stopped to think just what it was Julia Cope did all day he couldn't quite say. Of course, though, she took letters and handled the bills, which this girl couldn't do. But perhaps it would be just as well to have her after all. She seemed clean. White blood,—as usual.

"My hours are twelve to two. Write down all messages. You can write, can't you?"

"Yes, sir."

When she had gone he read the letter again and put it in his pocket. It had been over a year and a half since he had seen Lucian; sometimes he felt that he had not really seen him since that day he took him up to Lawrenceville when he was thirteen. He wondered if it had ever been quite the same after that. The boy's center of interest had shifted. But he felt that it was temporary; he felt that when the time came for Lucian to return for good, a year's residence would change things. He had the right stuff in him. They spoke well of him at Saint Luke's in New York, where he had done his interne job; Lucian had thought the experience would be broader than if he chose the Georgetown Hospital and the doctor had felt that he was probably right. Good for a young man to go to a big city, anyhow; he still sometimes saw in the blue flames of his coal fire a different Dr. Abercorn, different primarily from having served his interneship in a big city. He might not have come back to Georgetown at all. He was really, at heart, a little surprised that Lucian was coming back. In fact, he suspected that, at heart, he still felt a slight doubt that Lucian would get there. And if he got there, would he stay? Would he be satisfied with the old office? Except

9

for an occasional coat of white paint, nothing had been done to it for twenty years.

He liked the room, himself, with the shallow coal grate and the black marble mantel and the wide glassed-in shelves of heavy books forming a base for ink drawings by Charles Dana Gibson and the famous picture of the dark-haired young woman sitting before a round mirror which upon second glance became a skull with her head and its reflection the eye sockets, the racks with pipes, the stiff sofa, the leather chair by the window. It was a human friendly room into which you felt that only simple ailments had ever ventured. It seemed to be a secure room, definitely in communication with some panacea, a room of remedies, hiding almost from the doctor himself the slightly-discomforting knowledge that with the exception of quinine for malaria and the heavy metals for syphilis (and, he usually added, water for inebriation) there were practically no medicines of real efficacy. The room also still contained those moments with a slightly-faded purple halo round them when he had, with all degrees of reception, cheerfully done what he could to smirch the fair name of Southern Womanhood.

He wondered, though, if the room might not seem to Lucian a little drab. If Lucian wanted it changed, it would be changed; he thought he would do almost anything in return for having Lucian's warm vitality under the roof again.

3. Homeward Passage

Monday, June 15

THE tropical disturbance is central tonight in the Gulf of Mexico about seventy-five miles southwest of Tampa, Fla., moving eastward about six miles an hour, attended by strong shifting winds and probably by gales over a very small area near its center. Pressure is high over the greater part of Alaska and western Canada, and remains high from the Carolinas eastward beyond Bermuda—

Mr. Estill leaned over his map table in the top of the Post Office Building, picked a blue pencil from behind his ear, and drew twenty-five hundred miles of isothermic line in a single winding sweep.

Four hundred miles of it circled through "The South": down the red foothills of northern South Carolina, down the long weak slope of the sandhills, over the pine barrens, over the flats of southern Georgia, through the tropical tangles of the swamp lands along the nigger-black rivers,—four hundred miles of cotton and pine, of share-croppers and sun-blackened tenant houses, of red land, showing, where the white taut stretches of Highway No. 1 slashed through a hilltop, like a section of underdone roast beef,—four hundred miles of red land spotted and streaked bright green from the crops and the forests with the same banal discord of coloring as the interiors of the Pullman cars that glided in their sticky dust down from "The North."

The little fan at the end of the Pullman droned away into the dusty air above Mr. Applewhite's thin-haired head while the perspiration rolled in shining streamlets down his round cheeks and disappeared into his wilted collar. It tickled him as it passed in front of his ears and now and then he drew an already damp handkerchief down his pale newly-shaved stubble. He hadn't dreamed it would be so hot, so deadly hot. He had never been South before in summer; one spring in his youth he had visited a friend in Augusta, across the state. It had been warm then, but nothing like this. And just the middle of June too.

It was an empty bloodless sort of heat, timeless, as if that part of the world had ceased to move and were lying out there motionless under the sun. The woods running indolently by his window were almost nauseatingly lush; the warm light fell on their drooping leaves with an almost palpable weight. He felt that

11

that sunshine was something to be reckoned with; it was not to be lightly put aside. He wondered if it didn't do for the South what snow did for his New England, if it wasn't the music-teacher of his far-off childhood blowing on her pitchpipe, setting the key. He had finally, at Atlanta, brought himself to the point of imitating the young man with the clipped black mustache in Lower 7 and taking off his coat.

The other young man in the car, however, continued to defy this informality. He was a dark-skinned chap of twenty-five or so, with well-kept black hair in thick waves above his ears and at the back of his head. He looked a little like a foreigner; he was dressed with a good deal more care than most Americans and the pale mauve of his soft collar harmonized fastidiously with the echoing blue of his silk handkerchief. But at the time when Mr. Applewhite had met him in the narrow corridor by the smoking room and they had squeezed past each other, apologizing, his tone had seemed unquestionably American. Anyhow, he was certainly not a Southerner, Mr. Applewhite had thought.

He turned away to the disheveled little town slowing down beyond his window screen. The train halted with an imperceptible glide; he hardly knew it had stopped until it emitted a profoundly weary suspiration and the little fan over the door took up its hot drone. He shifted his head until he could see the sign on the end of the blistered station:

Atlanta 171.6 miles   DUE WEST   *Georgetown 26.7 miles*

Not long now, he said to himself, and pulled his shirt sleeves up from his damp wrists with two or three little tugs at the elbow. Though he didn't really care; he was uncomfortable, but after all summer was summer and trains were trains. It was worth no further consideration.

What he was really concerned about was his sister Martha's child, Nora. Nora needed a hand. He wasn't sure but that his concern carried with it quite a heavy coating of sentimentality, but this possibility didn't bother him; he was fifty-eight and used to going his own way sentimental or not.

12

Nora, according to his calculations, was twenty-four. She believed. He knew by her eyes, even before she had said a word; he knew the very moment that she walked into the door of his apartment. He hadn't seen her since she was ten; he loved his relations with a good deal of old-fashioned affection but he could never seem to make himself take the slightest interest in them. Even his sister in Georgetown he had never visited and he thought he would probably hardly have seen her at all if he had not lived so conveniently close to the shops on Fifth Avenue; she stopped in once or twice a year on her way between Georgetown and Lord & Taylor's. He had intermittent news of Nora, whom he pictured now as an enlarged ten; she was at school in Connecticut, then at Smith, then at a music school in Boston. She passed through New York going to and fro for some eight or nine years and never even called her uncle on the telephone; which, however, he thought he understood perfectly, that being more or less what he would have done under the same circumstances.

Then one morning a little after twelve she rang his bell and was shown in. He was in a velvet jacket, twirling the black ribbon of his glasses round his first finger as he moiled about his library dictating to his crisp amanuensis (a patient young woman of thirty-five who had taken down some nine hundred thousand words on the Christian religion as observed by her employer). He looked at the girl in the library door, tapping the glasses against one of the flares of his wing collar.

He took her to lunch at the Plaza and to a matinée at the Metropolitan of the *Coq d'Or;* then he gave her tea and put her on a seven o'clock train for Georgetown. That was in the early spring and she had just finished her last year at the music school. Piano. He left his taxi at Forty-second Street and walked up the avenue in the twilight, wondering about her, about youth and ashy age, about his fifty-eighth birthday next September, about her expectant eyes, her believing eyes,—about how she should have happened to come to see him now. He still didn't quite understand that. He went up to the library in the Uni-

13

versity Club and drew letters close round him again as if he had been enticed out beyond them and found it a little uncomfortable; the wind always seemed to be blowing out there.

He wondered if perhaps she had been somewhat at loose ends, school finished, nothing else begun, the dead center sort of thing; it wasn't quite clear. He somehow got the idea, though, that she needed a hand. She had said she wanted to go to Vienna.

"Good," said Mr. Applewhite.

"Oh, but I don't think I can."

"Why not?"

She looked at the cigarette in her fingers, moving the lighted end pensively over the edge of the ash tray. She had been away a long time; her brother John was married now; she was the only one left; her mother wanted her at home—

"Oh, good Lord!" said Mr. Applewhite. "That's no reason."

"Well, after all," she said with a little smile, "we do owe something to our parents, don't we?"

"Well, I wonder about that. I wonder."

"I don't see how you can deny that," she said, the smile gone.

"I don't deny there is a debt," said Mr. Applewhite, lifting his pink chin out of the V of his collar. "But I sometimes wonder if you oughtn't to pay it to your children instead of to your parents. Pay it to them by letting them not owe *you* anything."

She tilted her head slightly to one side.

"All I mean is that if you *want* to go to Vienna you *ought* to go to Vienna."

He thought, remembering her, that her beauty was not the obvious kind. All the swift loveliness of twenty-four she had, the eager ear, the quick smile, but you looked twice before you saw the harmony in her face. Then you saw it, a delayed quality, a quietude, like some of the early mosaics he had seen in Roman churches. He thought she was almost too thin, though; maybe she hadn't been idle enough. He was in favor of judiciously wasting a good deal of time.

He thought she liked him, which pleased him tremendously.

14

Several times she had looked straight in his eyes and laughed, as if she could see his picture of the world reflected there and found it entertaining. He told her in the Pennsylvania Station that four weeks in Georgetown would be enough; she could even sail the first week in June. "The first Friday midnight," he said with a sentimental glance backward over three decades; "the whistles then have something of immortality in them."

"Maybe I'll do it," she said.

He opened a letter from her two weeks later, thinking she would be setting the date and he would go down to the Bowling Green himself and make the reservation for her personally. She said how much she had enjoyed seeing him, spoke of the heat in Georgetown, of the white flowers spotting the magnolias "like the things you stand candles in on a Christmas tree," and ended her very polite note without a word about the trip. He hardly knew what to say.

He wrote her immediately, asking her with some urgency when she was planning to sail. She answered ten days later that it looked as if the trip were off; she wanted to go, she said, but she didn't feel that she could leave her parents now. . . . So he had his Filipino pack two Gladstone bags and buy a ticket to Georgetown; he felt very strongly about young people's hopping off on their own wings, following that perhaps slightly-shady inclination,—making their trip to Vienna.

He had started out on his own pilgrimage when he was twenty-six, shortly after his sister Martha had married George Fenwick, a Southerner who had been a classmate of his at Harvard, leaving his parents in their snug little low-ceilinged house on the verdant outskirts of Concord to get along as well as they could. For several years after leaving college he had taught English grammar in the Concord High School, then his maternal grandfather, a ship owner in Salem whose father's fortune had been acquired largely through the importation of slaves for the South and who had himself been one of New England's most rabid abolitionists, left him some two hundred thousand dollars and young Applewhite bade his classes farewell and set out. For the

15

next thirty-two years he was never once, to all intents and purposes, in contact with the world; he moved round over most of
it, observing its inhabitants and their manners, but wherever
he went he carried with him a kind of hermit's cell, a kind of
diver's helmet, through which certain essential aspects of the
world penetrated to him, but by which many other essential
aspects were held safely at bay. The great trunk line of communication which connected most of humanity, the necessity
of working for a living, was down in his case and the best he
could do was observe. He had written several rather long books
on minor points of religion, not one of which would have sold
five hundred copies if it had ever been published, which of
course none of them ever was. They were neither scholarly nor
popular and were shot through with myriads of sidelights on
the author himself, so that, though a reader perusing them for
some knowledge of Mr. Applewhite might have found them
highly amusing, someone going through them for instruction in
their ostensible subject would more than likely have declared
them completely worthless; it would have been somewhat the
same if Evelyn had called his journal, "A History of the Great
London Fire."

There were four large volumes of bound typescript on Mr.
Applewhite's library shelves, and he spent an hour every morning
or so adding to what would eventually make the fifth. This was
more or less a study of the effect of the Christian religion on
modern American life, and he hoped to show, before he got
through, that the country had received from it a setback amount-
ing, in the evolution of reasonable human beings, to some three
or four centuries; it opened with this sentence:

Though Christianity has undoubtedly a great many practical uses,
it is very deleterious to man's moral and spiritual life.

A further reason for his going South was connected with this
fifth opus, in that he saw clearly to attempt a treatise on the
American religion without visiting Georgia and Alabama was

about on a par with trying to understand the Renaissance without considering Italy.

But he had a good many friends in New York and in spite of his being a bachelor of no conceivable interest to any daughter's mother, he went round a good deal in the social world and found relatively little time for his work.

Being possessed of considerable money and a sound constitution, he looked upon himself as a happy man. He attributed it all, however, to his having gone on his "pilgrimage to Vienna," and he was as determined that Nora should go on hers as if he had again been talking to himself at twenty-six.

He disliked profoundly the 'making yourself light' sensation of staying in somebody else's house, particularly his own sister's, and without saying anything further either to her or to Nora, he secured from a wire to the Georgetown Chamber of Commerce the name of a gentlewoman who took boarders (a Mrs. Eubanks on Davis Road), had himself and his bags put into an open taxi one warm June morning and went to the Pennsylvania Station. He followed his long-armed porter down the iron stairs and back to the last car; here he paused a minute on the platform by the door to give an indulgent smile at a lighthearted group of young men and women at the end of the train cheerfully submitting to the cameras and pencils of the press. He thought then it must be a wedding party, but later, when the train started, the young man with the black hair came into the coach from the rear door alone. He was tucking a large handkerchief into his pocket with his first finger and a smile still glimmered on his face.

Mr. Applewhite gave no further thought to him until night, down in Virginia, when, returning to the smoking compartment in his car after dinner, he found him bending over a basin with his sleeves rolled up, his suspenders making a black cross below his shoulders against his pastel shirt. He sat down on the hard divan by the window and carefully pinched the end of a cigar. In the pocket of the coat hanging on what he had often thought must have been the nearest thing to a nail that the

Pullman Company engineers could devise at the time, he saw the top of a green fountain pen. He smiled inwardly; it was the kind of inconsequential little detail that the author in him enjoyed thinking he had not overlooked.

The young man nodded in a friendly way. "Warm," he said with a rueful smile, not as if he thought the remark mattered but as even a good chess player will not disdain the conventionality of opening with his pawn to king four.

"It really is, isn't it?" said Mr. Applewhite. "But I suppose it'll be worse tomorrow."

"You must be going all the way to New Orleans."

"No," said Mr. Applewhite, "I'm going to Georgetown. It's a little town on the Georgia border of Alabama."

"*I* know," he laughed. "I was born there."

"Were you really!"

"I haven't lived there in years. But it remains," he smiled, "the home town." He put on his coat, glancing at the green pen in his pocket; then he said, wiping the perspiration off his upper lip with his silk handkerchief, "This isn't the best time of year for Georgetown."

"The heat, you mean."

"It's hot and dull. Nothing happens. Everybody goes away who can. It's really quite deadly. I think of the summer burying the South like the ashes burying Pompeii." He laughed. "They say it's very nice in winter, though."

"I think, as a matter of fact, I'd rather see it in the summer."

"Maybe you like hot weather. I don't."

"Not so much that, but I think a place has its formative season. In New England it's winter; it's the cold weather that has built the houses, the cold weather that's so marked on the people's instincts."

The other gave him the kind of look that is equivalent to the drawing of a finer focus.

"It's their uphill season, their pulling season. In the South it's the opposite. . . . Theoretically. I've never really been South before."

18

"I don't know, maybe you're right. I just find it hot and dry and dull." He put both hands deep into his trousers pockets, took two steps toward the door, swaying with the motion of the train, and paused. "Do you remember in *The Wizard of Oz* how they got lost in the field of poppies and were all overcome with sleep? All but two very significant exceptions: the Scarecrow and the Tin Woodman, who couldn't smell." He laughed and pulled aside the green curtain. "It's like that. You're taking your life in your hands. . . ."

The next morning Mr. Applewhite was looking through the smoke-caked mesh of his window screen at the town of Due West, Georgia. Across a broad space of gray sand his eye was just sweeping the weather-stained wooden shed with the rust-streaked corrugated iron roof in front of the store of Ben Gray & Co.; on one upright was a blue tin rectangle advertising The Georgetown Chemical Company, Makers of Acid Phosphate and High Grade Fertilizers. Under an old Ford a dusty hound lay in the shade, his nose lifted in languid indifference at the arrival of the mail bag. A lean man with a brown straw hat forward over his eyes sauntered toward the head of the train, his hands stuffed in the waist of his khaki trousers.

Mr. Applewhite looked out with a slight contracting of his eyebrows, running his thumb and finger pensively down the black cord of his pendent glasses.

"Good morning."

"Oh, hello," said Mr. Applewhite. The young man was standing in the aisle, his damp fingers spread apart gingerly on his hips; he was still wearing his coat. "I looked for you at breakfast."

"I'm always late for breakfast." He sat down sociably on the rough cushion across from Mr. Applewhite. When the train almost imperceptibly began to roll, he said, "It's funny the things you remember from when you were a child. Down here they always seem to start the trains quietly. It's probably because the trains are light, but it will always be one of the little things that remind me I'm not far from home."

"You're going back now to live."

"Oh, no. My mother has been sick. I think she's going to have to have an operation. There's nobody there but my sister. I'll probably be down a month, maybe six weeks. I don't like it."

"There's just your mother and your sister?" Mr. Applewhite asked him paternally.

"Yes." He paused, then added, "My sister has the distinction of being the only woman stenographer on Cotton Row."

Mr. Applewhite smiled at him sympathetically. "Cotton Row?"

"It's where the Cotton Exchange is and the warehouses and the offices, the sky-blue offices."

He spoke out with much the ingenuousness of a child. He gave the impression of having lived among people who understood him; he seemed to make no allowance at all for being misinterpreted. He seemed artless, but Mr. Applewhite could not decide whether it was the artlessness of the simple or the great.

"Are the offices blue?" said Mr. Applewhite; he somehow felt attracted to the boy.

"Sky blue. It seems almost ironical to me that people so absolutely lacking in a sense of beauty should have been tricked by a commercial necessity into painting their offices a lovely color." He looked at Mr. Applewhite. "It's as if even in their ignorance God wouldn't let them starve,—sending the ravens into the desert to feed them."

Mr. Applewhite sat up.

"The blue sets off the cotton samples, you see. But it really makes them look like balls of cloud against a summer sky."

"You haven't a very Southern accent," said Mr. Applewhite, referring in his own mind more to the substance of what the boy was saying.

"I haven't been in Georgetown in four years. It seems a little odd sometimes, not being there any more than I am, that I still think of it as home."

"A man needs to think of some place as home," said Mr. Applewhite. "You need to have some place in the world where you know you will be accepted without question for what you

20

are, where you can give your name and have people know all about you."

He smiled. "Well, I don't know. . . . I mean I don't find I am taken for what I am. Home, to me, is just where I become once more the shoemaker's boy. Elsewhere I am Sergey Pavinovsky; in Georgetown I am the shoemaker's boy. So I don't come back often." He laughed. "I don't mind so much being thought of as the shoemaker's boy, you understand, but they make it color everything I say or do. After a few weeks of it I wake up one morning and find I am *becoming* the shoemaker's boy—"

"Excuse me, but did you say your name was Sergey Pavinovsky?"

"Yes."

"But don't you dance in The Metropolitan Ballet?"

"Oh, yes."

"I saw you in the *Coq d'Or!*"

"Oh, did you?"

"But you are very, very good!"

Pavinovsky laughed. "That's very kind of you to say so."

"I was there with my niece. We were both charmed."

"I have been offered something very good for next year. Nikelief saw me and liked me and he offered me a very good thing in Paris. He has promised me a *pas seul*. Of course I am extremely pleased."

"I should think you would be," said Mr. Applewhite in blind sympathy, somewhat amazed at the simplicity with which Pavinovsky spoke of himself and his plans; there was something a little unaccountable in his face and in the graceful angles that his fingers assumed, even in the light of his being a dancer, but Mr. Applewhite thought of it only half-consciously. "You must have lived away from Georgetown a long time."

"I was sixteen when I went away," said Pavinovsky. "I had to go. I was very unhappy. I have never been so unhappy since. Never. Now I live and life is exciting and I am well thought of in the profession and already my name is on the bills outside and on the street people are beginning to know who I am. It is very thrilling." He laughed again.

"You had quite a send off too," said Mr. Applewhite, remembering the scene on the platform at the end of the train.

"They are all so good to me. . . . I don't think I shall ever get tired of being photographed."

Mr. Applewhite smiled, a little embarrassed at such frankness.

"Did you notice the boy in the gray hat?"

"No, I didn't," said Mr. Applewhite.

"He was *The Times* photographer. His name's Bertonelli." Pavinovsky paused and looked away. "No, I shan't be home long. I can't feel it is as desirable as you do."

"Oh, I shouldn't advise you to stay there," said Mr. Applewhite quickly. "As a matter of fact, I am on my way now to rescue my niece from—well, the horrors of home. . . . But she's young; you don't need a home when you're young. But as you get older—well, I call Concord, Massachusetts, home and I feel it is probably the only place in the world where people can be really sure that I'm all right, can know who I am, know who my father was—"

"But my father was a Russian Jew, you see, a Russian Jew shoemaker. It makes a good deal of difference in valuing home."

"But you oughtn't to mind that, really."

"I don't mind it, except when I'm home. Away, I feel, on the contrary, if he hadn't been what he was I should probably be living in Georgetown today, never having realized that it is possible to be occasionally beautifully happy. It is like the hot summers; I was sixteen years old before I discovered that there are places in the world where the summer is delightful. All my life I had gone to school as the shoemaker's boy; perhaps if I had been a little different it wouldn't have mattered so much, but things like baseball and football terrified me. I was scared. I don't mind saying I was scared; it is just a detail of how I am made. I was scared of football but I wasn't scared of running away to New York alone. You're afraid of one thing, I'm afraid

22

of another. I'm afraid of violence, but I once put my head in an oven and turned on the gas and—"

"Good God!"

"Wasn't afraid."

"But you oughtn't to—"

"It was a little silly, perhaps, under the circumstances, though I was very unhappy."

"I'm not sure I think anybody ought to kill himself," said Mr. Applewhite, looping his black ribbon bewilderedly round his forefinger.

Pavinovsky laughed. "Oh, I can't agree with you. I have always felt since the days of Grimm and Hans Andersen that no possible equipment could be as valuable to a man as a Vanishing Cloak. When things get too bad, you just disappear—"

"Brush you off, sir?" said the porter.

"After you," said Pavinovsky. . . .

When Mr. Applewhite returned to his seat he saw Pavinovsky down at the other end of the car closing his suitcase; he sat down and looked out the window. Strange fellow. Introversion. These artists!

Tall, bulb-rooted swamp trees raising their tropical foliage out of a jungle of dry bushes and brushwood along the base of the railroad embankment; strong sunlight and shade moving richly past the window amidst the retarding click of the wheels over the rail-joints as the train slowed down. When it stopped, the fan became smoothly audible again in the sudden silence, like the hot buzzing of summer flies.

"Vanishing Cloak," said Mr. Applewhite, frowning. "When things get too bad you just disappear—"

Two shrill blasts from the whistle echoed down the lane of trees and in a minute they began to roll again. The woods thinned out and the embankment disappeared; on a trestle over a baked, mud-stained wasteland they crept toward the bridge, high over all that was left of the river. He looked down at some figures on the pink river-bottom; a man and a boy were waving at the train.

"Georgetown!" said the porter. "This way out."

"Perhaps you will be good enough to have dinner with me some evening," Mr. Applewhite said to Pavinovsky, waiting in the corridor while the porter handed down the luggage from the car platform.

Pavinovsky looked at him with an equivocal smile; "That's very kind—," he began, when a round voice behind them interrupted him.

"Isn't this Pavi!"

It was the young man with the clipped black mustache in Lower 7; he was holding an unlighted cigarette in one corner of his mouth and smiling with the other.

Pavinovsky changed color, scrutinizing him. Then he smiled and held out his hand.

"I'm Lucian Abercorn."

"I remember," said Pavinovsky. "How are you?"

"I hardly knew you, Pavi. I've been wondering all the way down if it could be you. Good old Pavi!" He patted him on the shoulder, laughing. "What are you doing now?"

"I've been living up in New York."

"Are you going to be home for good now?"

"Just a couple of weeks."

"We must get together. I'm going to be living here from now on; going in with the governor."

The passengers began to move out and they separated.

Mr. Applewhite descended to the wooden floor of the station amidst the excited chattering and laughing of the half dozen conspicuously clean non-travelers there to meet the train. He saw Abercorn in the embrace of a sun-burned older man in white, their four eyes with the uncanny homogeneity of father and son; then he caught sight of Pavinovsky pointing out his luggage to a grimy negro marked by those indefinable details of disrespect arising from having publicly served the lower classes. Apparently there was no one to meet Pavinovsky and in a minute he followed his porter down the platform alone,—one of The Metropolitan Ballet's first dancers. But maybe, thought

24

Mr. Applewhite, he was already becoming the shoemaker's boy again, Pavi the shoemaker's boy.

He turned away to the porter at his elbow and tapped his Gladstone bags with his walking stick. "I want a taxi," he said.

He was led through the waiting room and out into the sun to the side of an old Dodge labeled on the windshield, "Tom's Taxi."

"Do you know Mrs. Eubanks's boarding house on Davis Road?" said Mr. Applewhite to the hollow-eyed driver without hat or coat lending a hand at loading his luggage into the weather-stained body.

"Yes, sir, cap'n."

"Well, I see you haven't got a meter," said Mr. Applewhite in his best European manner, "so maybe you'd better tell me now what you plan to charge me."

"We get fifty cents, cap'n, to Summerville."

Mr. Applewhite crawled into the back and sank into a depression in one side of the cloth-covered seat and put his hat beside him.

"How come you don't take off your coat?" said the driver, smiling back at him solicitously.

"Maybe that's a good idea." Mr. Applewhite struggled out of his coat.

In a minute the driver said out of the side of his mouth, keeping his eyes on the road, "I hope it won't put you out none if I stop by here and get Mr. Lee Hill to put a couple of gallons of gas in my tank. It won't take long. I'd have some now but I don't like to tie up capital in gasoline any longer than I have to. I never get but two gallons at a time. It worries me to see capital lying idle—"

4. What of the Young Men?

LUCIAN striaghtened his straw hat with the colored band and hopped down the steps of the Pullman. Georgetown. Home. Small cities, where desirable young women watched their steps. Where young doctors, if they were wise, watched theirs. What did the young men do about it? What did the young men do about it? . . . There came his father, a year and a half older. He wondered if the old man would feel bad if he did not kiss him; they had always kissed each other. It would have to stop sometime. Not at all that he was not extremely fond of him. Admired him too. Genuinely. But kissing, that was for something else.

He put his arms about his father's shoulders and patted him on the back. "You're looking fine," said Lucian.

"Where'd you pick up the mustache?"

"How do you like it?"

They walked out through the shade of the building into the white sunlight.

"How's the old car?"

"Never fails me."

"Guess she could stand a coat of paint, couldn't she?"

"I reckon so. I never noticed it."

Only the surface of their words was strained; below them was a genuine friendliness, stammering a little in the uncertainty of just how to communicate itself after so long a silence.

The doctor backed carefully out into the street.

"Well, how's business?"

"About the same. I took a man's appendix out last month and he paid me yesterday with a bale of good middling cotton."

"Good Lord!"

"Say, rather, 'Hallelujah!'"

"What are you going to do with a bale of cotton?"

26

"I told Telfair & Company to sell it."

"What'll you get?"

"About fifty dollars. . . . Miss Cope's gone away, you know."

"Quit?"

"No. Gone on her vacation. Gone to Europe. I gave her six weeks. I thought when you came we could manage to get along without a nurse until she got back."

"You haven't got anybody now?"

"I hired a colored girl temporarily. I was thinking I'd let her go when you got here. There isn't much for her to do."

"You'll probably need somebody, won't you?"

"I don't know. We can see. We'll keep her if you want to. . . . Tell me about your trip."

Wide hot streets. Long verdant tunnels, still, shady. At the intersections, brilliant pools of swimming sunlight. High-porched houses, the dull paint blistered and peeling. A feeling of home, of calm, of security, a feeling of close-confining walls. A feeling of *table d'hôte* contrasted with *à la carte*.

"Well, I see it's the same old cat," said Lucian.

"What do you say?"

"I just mean—"

Who would be in town that he knew? Maybelle Telfair, perhaps. But she was married now, anyway. Mrs. Branch Wheaton now. Probably had three children and a pine house at the seashore. Never interested him anyhow. The South was very weak on women; beautiful sun-ripened women, about as interesting as a cotton blossom! Nora. Nora was different, but she was only half southern. Worse than the real article, as a matter of fact. Too complex; echoes in her of the North. Music. She had an aim. God deliver him from girls with aims! Good to look at, though, in her way. Aims were sublimations. It was an armor almost as good as religion. Better, maybe. New channels for the river.

"Who's in town?"

"Austin Toombs was asking about you."

27

"Good Lord, hasn't he gone yet? I thought he'd be in Singapore by this time."

"It's a shame about that boy. Throwing away his life."

"It'd be something if he'd throw it."

"He ought to do something."

"Are the Fenwicks in town?"

"I think so."

"There was an old fellow on the train that somehow reminded me of that girl, what's her name?"

"Who? Nora?"

"Yes. No resemblance, you know, but somehow suggesting—funny."

An old patch of cracks in the cement sidewalk in front of the house; he could still feel the quick racking jolts shooting through his small body as the rollers of his skates crossed it. Home. The old familiar drop in temperature as you entered the dim hall of the basement. Home. But it was a shock to see the colored nurse standing in the waiting room.

He glanced in her direction, nodded, looked away. He was sorry she was there; they made him uncomfortable; he could never look at them.

5. Like a Downward Smoke

Wednesday, June 17

AUSTIN sat on the high screened porch at the side of his house in a straw-bottomed rocking chair. Beyond a wicker table of ginger ale and half-melted ice and clear brown corn whiskey, sat Dr. Abercorn, an elbow on the arm of the chair, a white shoe against the banisters, his chemicals apparently once more in adjustment; he lighted a fresh cigarette from the end of an old one:

"He's been away a long time. He's sort of forgotten some of our ways of doing things. He was surprised when I told him a patient of mine had paid my bill with a bale of good middling cotton. He said, 'Good Lord!' I said, 'Say, rather, "Hallelujah!", son.'" He turned his glass up with a certain ardor and emptied it. . . . "How you feeling?"

Austin looked away through the screen for a moment; "Something's the matter with me."

"What the hell do you *think's* the matter with you?"

Austin shook his head.

"Have you lost your appetite?"

"No—"

"Do you sleep all right?"

"Yes, but—"

"What you need is a job."

"Oh, God deliver me!"

"Something definite on your mind, a must."

"If you think I haven't anything on my mind you're just crazy," said Austin, relapsing into mystery.

"I know you have," said Dr. Abercorn, "and I know what it is. It's your health."

"I don't mean that."

"Forget your health. I tell you as any watchmaker would tell you, leave the thing closed up. It keeps good time. Quit fiddling with it."

"Yes, I know. . . . Let's have a drink."

"Nothing would please me more."

The doctor put his glass on the table and Austin began fishing in the melted ice.

"Isn't liquor, after all, rather bad for you?"

"They tell me," said the doctor, "and for all I know with possibly some truth, that every kiss shortens your life by about three minutes. I figured it out once, many years ago when the subject really interested me, that in exchange for a paltry day of

29

my life I could get some five hundred kisses. Think of it! And in return for allowing Fate the petty privilege of killing me in January instead of the following July—why, a man could live in luxury all his life—"

"I can't offer you anything but corn, you know."

"Let me caution you, Austin, against apologizing for the *vin du pays;* it's a way of apologizing for the *pays* and I'm touchy on that. This is my country. I was born here. I have fished in these swamps, I have followed a bird-dog all over these sandhills and all through these scrub-oak barrens; I was bred in this brier patch and I don't like for anybody to apologize for it. I do feel, of course, that taken all in all it is one of the ugliest countries I have ever seen, but I don't care. It don't matter. It's run down, but—I like it run down. . . . I blame the nigger for it, Austin. He is predatory. He is picturesque but predatory. He never improves anything. He always leaves a place a little worse than he found it. He is doing to the South exactly what he does to the little one-horse farm he rents; he deteriorates it, he uses it up. The South to him is just a tenant farm; it ain't his, it belongs to Mr. White Man. Everything belongs to Mr. White Man. So he uses up. In a way, I think he's a charming fellow. He is so affectedly natural, so complexly simple. They put up such a convincing front that you are amazed when you catch a glimpse of the rest of their life, out in The Terry. If you could see your cook, Oregon, on his night off— You don't know Oregon; he has been with you for twenty years, but you don't know anything about him. You don't hear any talk about him; you only have him from one angle; you only know what he wants you to know. But he knows all about you. My old friend Mrs. Duncan used to say, when somebody asked her if she had any gossip, 'My dear, I have reasonably well-informed servants.' . . . Oh, the influence they have had on the white people is incalculable. Leaving out the matter of language, in which their influence is obvious, and manners and dress, they have had a tremendous effect on the at first glance apparently somewhat removed matter of architecture.—I think this is original, but it may very likely be that I have just forgotten where I read it.—They have made us develop the front of the house at the expense of the back; the front is European, the back is African. And the back is always mildly filthy. Doors are smudged, corners are broken off, pails are dented; it is a different world. It is soiled linen. It is a place of dogs and cats and old shoes, and broken things being saved up for some impossible emergency; it is the household's own little nigger-town. Nobody goes there but the mistress, who must needs be long-suffering. To get as far away from all that as possible, we have developed the front, the imposing columns, the great porch, beyond which, metaphorically, the visitor almost never gets. It has developed a psychology of concealment, and it is a rare day when you gain the confidence of a true Southerner. You are allowed into the dining room, but you will almost never get into the kitchen of his character with its old shoes and broken things. It is a pity in a way, and yet a man deserves some privacy. . . . With a white servant class, though, there wouldn't be this line; the backyard would be presentable and there would be no reason why you shouldn't walk all round the house. Young people, wanting something new, try an imported style of house with the kitchen somewhere else but in the farthest possible corner, but it doesn't work. It's just putting old shoes on the front doorstep. The only place for the kitchen in Southern architecture is where it used to be when our style was growing free, way out in a corner of the backyard— Am I talking a lot?"

"Not at all."

"I find them charming, Austin, but isn't indolence always charming. They are not indolent, you know; they are indolence. They are the thing itself. If you could ascertain the facts, Austin, I think you would find that God had made them in an idle moment. . . ."

When Austin was twenty-one he came into a portion of the money his grandfather had made by selling out his interest in a boatline that ran from Georgetown to the gulf. The old man hadn't made it by luck as much as by what is usually considered rare business acumen. He learned confidentially one day that plans were being debated in the North for laying a railroad from Georgetown to the coast that would parallel the river and probably carry freight to the port in one-fourth the time; while the business heads of Georgetown were still enumerating the reasons for such a thing's being impossible, Grandpa Toombs sold his control for the apparently sacrifice figure of three hundred thousand dollars and retired. The following season the boatline made the biggest profits of its existence and old Mr. Toombs's reputation for business sagacity sank to a low mark. But five years later it rose to its proper level and he used often to go down to the river bank on summer evenings and watch *King Cotton* go throbbing by, its stern wheel scarcely touching the yellow water from the lack of cargo, its superstructure faded and blistered and unkempt, and he would smile at the whole prospect as one of the great men of the cinquecento might have smiled at what he considered his supreme canvas.

His son, Austin's father, worked himself into an early grave by intensive worry over the agricultural situation in Alabama and Georgia, pondering for six months of the year on how many bales of cotton the weather was planning to permit to be raised in his section, and for the other six on how he could sell what passed through his hands at the peak price for the season. He wouldn't have had to work, but it was a tacitly-understood maxim of his generation that a man's not having to work all day for his living was no excuse for his not doing it; nobody refused to work but the riff-raff connected with the cotton mills and here and there a socially-prominent inebriate.

It was a mercy, therefore, that he died before his son finished college, for Austin, being provided for by his grandfather in a modest but secure way, turned his attention appreciatively and critically to the world about him and to the more impractical of life's details. At Princeton he wrote a good deal of verse, as most of his friends did, but when they took their A.B. degrees and settled down to some kind of work, he left a Paris address to which his $4,500 should be sent as the sundry branches of American government paid it to him and lived in Europe for three years with different friends. When times got hard and the business his principal friend was in closed its Paris office and called him home, Austin, never being, at heart, much of a one for solitude, crossed the ocean too and appeared one morning in Jackson Street as quiet and sad eyed as ever. He greeted the few people who remembered him as if he had seen them the day before and said, in answer to their polite question, that he would be in Georgetown a week or two; he was going back to Princeton to take a Ph.D.

But he didn't go. He said his health wasn't good. He looked perfectly well, but after eating he would put a little white pill into his palm and pop it into his mouth, stoically and with a certain sophisticated hopelessness. It was on his mind, though, as if a munificent Nature, lest he have nothing at all to worry him, was letting him make for himself his own synthetic cross. He played golf, thinking that the exercise might help him or at any rate enable him to hold his own. He was quite a nice-looking boy, slightly shorter than the average, and his face had a quiet sort of melodious expression that you see on poets and many blind men.

And he really had something of a poet's sensitiveness to colors and shapes and sounds, to words and feelings. He would stop in the middle of the fairway to listen to such things as the noise of an ax on a fallen tree in the hollow. He saw the summer golf course with "great jets from the sprinklers revolving about, blown out in a far smoke by the hot breezes, white veils with the sun on them, streaked in certain phases by a rainbow, revolving with a large jet and a small, weaving a harmonious symmetry like a vase, spinning slowly about on the Alabama hills, two to each purple and green hole,—our own Versailles, our Villa d'Este of the frontier. Your eyes, starved of beauty, look at it with a deep gratitude, as a man looks at a woman he loves." He wrote this in a little brown notebook which he carried round with him in the pocket of his linen coat. He wrote other things in it, such as, "Youth with its nostalgia for infinity!"

33

And "To the old men up front near the edge, we cry, 'What do you see, old men?' But they don't answer."—All in all, he made life for himself very poignant and rather difficult.

He looked forward to coming over the first hill and hearing the plea of the Sanctified Baptists for rain. He even saw with some regret the occasional gathering of the vast bruised clouds in the west, prophesying as it did the end of the drought and the inconsolable wailing. With disappointment he would feel the air quiet down with a still quality like a glassy pool. And when the clouds shifted to the north and caught the river valley, drifting down over the damper air and away to the southeast, leaving the burned hills behind lifeless under the moaning chant and the revolving plumes of water, he would feel almost joyous. . . .

In the halcyon days of Grandpa Toombs's *King Cotton* the élite of Georgetown had build their dwellings along the river bank below Center Street, tall brick houses behind iron fences and iron fountain pieces and now and then a pair of iron deer or iron grayhounds, shady under the heavy trees lofty and green in the fertile soil of the flood plain. It was a section of carriage-gates and liveries and short-checked horses.

But the automobile destroyed it, by motor, the village of Summerville, five miles out of town on the shoulder of a low hill, was hardly any farther from the Cotton Exchange than the river-bank section had been by foot and carriage. The arrival of the automobile was a signal for quitting the ship such as Grandpa Toombs might have recognized, but Austin's father, caring more for the old tradition than the old man had ever done, stuck by his sleek horses and his iron fences. When Austin was fifteen the Wheelis house, three doors down the street, changed hands and hung out a sign for boarders, and when his parents died the Toombs house was the only one left with the original owners. Austin tried to sell it, but the market had broken.

He lived in it alone with the help of a negro cook and yardman named Oregon, who swept spasmodically over the exposed centers of the polished oak floors and now and then sharpened a scythe melodiously in the brick basement and attacked the weeds that grew up so bounteously under the bellies of the iron deer. As time went on and Oregon worked sedulously toward the goal of making no exertion whatever, he persuaded Austin to sow the yard in peas; having already heartily endorsed Austin's idea of shutting all the windows and blinds and covering all the furniture in the house, except two rooms at the back, with dust-covers, he had practically nothing to do and stood in the old carriage gate in the side wall most of the day, gazing down the green vista toward the river or down the opposite toward the distant smudge of red of the factory of the Georgetown Chemical Company, wondering if he could persuade Austin to give up hot supper until the weather got cool.

The next afternoon about four o'clock Austin was in his straw-bottomed rocking chair on the screened porch reading a new batch of travel folders. He was tired of Georgetown. Two or three times a year he would study steamship booklets and touring pamphlets; but he hadn't been anywhere in three years. He was not feeling well enough; he would pause now and then in his reading to hold up his wrist and count his pulse expertly by sight.

He was on the point of putting the folders away and going back to the second volume of Gibbon, which he had set himself to finish by September, when he heard the scrape of a shoe on the sidewalk below and looked down to see a Western Union boy dismounting adroitly from his bicycle.

He waited for the boy at the top of the cast-iron banisters.

"Are you Austin Toombs?"

"I am," said Austin, always slightly resentful at evidences of the rise of modern insolence.

He signed for the telegram and returned to his chair.

When he opened it he read it three times without moving. Then he stared off into the trees in complete speechlessness. It said:

GWENDOLYN AND I ARRIVING AIRPORT ABOUT FOUR THIRTY. ELIOT.

35

"For God's sake!" cried Austin, almost tearfully. He shuffled his feet and glanced about him. He looked at his wrist watch. It was four fifteen. He stood up and took two uncertain strides toward the French window. Then he stopped and turned his head and called helplessly for Oregon.

There was no answer.

He looked at the paper again.

"Eliot?" he said with a frown, becoming really conscious for the first time of the signature. "I don't know anybody named Eliot!"

He read the message again, thinking there might have been a mistake; it was dated Atlanta, 2:45 P.M., and was addressed to Austin Toombs, Georgetown. The only Eliot he could think of was a boy he had hardly known in the club at Princeton.

But as he studied the message the signature seemed to lose all importance. Somebody and his wife were evidently coming to visit him; who it was didn't matter much. In any case the household would be disrupted: newspapers torn off the rolled-up mattresses, chairs and tables suddenly stripped of their covers, blinds thrown open, spider webs brushed down, Oregon in a ferment. His health wasn't equal to it; he didn't feel like having visitors, showing them the town, giving them a party, playing bridge with them all day; he thought it would probably put him in the hospital. Besides, he had hoped to go over a sheaf of poems that week; he had a novel he wanted to write; it was time he started research for his biography of General Oglethorpe. He thought if he could only pinch himself and find all this just some horrible dream, he would be able to start to work in earnest that very afternoon.

Half an hour later he was standing on the sand-blown apron in front of the hangar, lighting cigarette after cigarette, squinting at the hot blue sky to the northeast, as miserable as any of his countrymen waiting to open their arms in fabulous hospitality. He moved about restlessly in the black shade cast by the shelter, stopping as he neared the sharp edges of the brilliant masses of light as if he were in a box; he cursed all visitors and

36

all means of transporting visitors, particularly the aeroplane. He responded unenthusiastically to the somewhat eager smile of Dr. Troupe, the dentist, who had been inspecting the ships in the hangar with a curly-haired little boy.

It was into the middle distance before he saw it, a small biplane, its motor firing in a deep whine. It shot across the hangar on the wind, its wings bright yellow and a red and yellow fuselage; then it banked in a wide arc over the valley and returned. The motor was suddenly cut off like the blowing out of a match. It slipped down, began to fall off, straightened up with a roar and landed in a spurt of orange dust. He watched it come bobbing in starts over the rough grass straight at him, as depressed as if it were Fate implacable and were running him down. He tried to summon a brighter expression to his face.

A gangly youth in oily khaki walked out of the hangar and stopped in the shade. Austin stared in weak enthusiasm at the two smooth balls with human mouths now visible behind the windshields. As the plane halted, the ball in the rear, looking at him as if through binoculars, suddenly lifted a hand and shook it violently. Austin clasped his hands out in front of him and wiggled them in welcome. He hurried over.

The lips went into a grin and the glasses were lifted; the flesh-colored oval still seemed strange to Austin, almost sinister.

"Glad to see you, old boy," cried Austin, stretching out his hand, fingers apart, palm down. "This is swell."

In the meantime a lithe figure in the forward cockpit climbed with complete self-possession over the fuselage and, disdaining Austin's proffered arm, hopped easily to the ground and felt for a cigarette.

"That's Gwendolyn, Austin."

Austin put his heels together in half-mocking punctiliousness. She gave him a solemn scrutiny for a second after he held a match for her, then unfastened her linen helmet and surveyed the surroundings.

"Where's all the cotton?" she said, giving a slight laugh.

Her face was of a flat sheenless pastel tan that made him as

37

conscious of the sky blue of her eyes as if they had spoken. He followed their glance and found them resting upon Dr. Troupe's oblivious countenance.

6. Off Season

Wednesday, June 17

THERE was hardly anybody at Mrs. Eubanks's. Summer, she explained to Mr. Applewhite with a trace of apology in her voice, was the off season; in winter Northerners came down to get away from the cold and she also had several out-of-town teachers in the girls' high school. She showed him the tops of some of the tables she had to put in the dining room, now leaning against the banisters on the back porch, markedly unpainted. "The fewer the better in summer, though; it gives you more room to breathe."

At two-thirty when he went in to lunch there was nobody with Mrs. Eubanks except her mother, a frail little old woman in white lace, and a middle-aged woman with short grayish hair named Tannahill; Miss Tannahill wore nose glasses, and gave Mr. Applewhite a nod and a smile while jabbing at the sugar in the bottom of her iced tea.

Mr. Applewhite replied with his best smile, anxious to like and be liked. Mrs. Eubanks got up from her table near the screen beside the door into the pantry, introduced him, and led him to his table by the open window. He stood in some embarrassment until she moved away, then sat down and cast a tourist's eye up at the wooden fan slowly revolving in the ceiling and creating a languid stir in the warm air. A very black waitress, with manner neither private nor professional, brought him a long glass of tea.

He was fishing with his spoon for the lemon segment in the bottom when Mr. and Mrs. Wheaton came in; he remembered the moment, having a mind that fastened to such things. The boy had thick black hair and the kind of good features which Mr. Applewhite thought he had often observed in Southern men, more symmetrical and appealing than strong. His first glance at the girl seemed to net him nothing; she was really arrestingly pretty, but he thought about her later and he wondered if she perceived quite clearly enough that her beauty was only a very small unit in Nature's great pageant; he was afraid she might be taking it too personally; then he thought about her some more and he decided that wasn't true; he wondered if she hadn't really decided yet, herself. She was bareheaded and her hair rippled away from a middle part in neat waves. She shook hands with him at Mrs. Eubanks's introduction, a firm, strong hand with pink nails. He thought at first that she seemed a little like a glass flower and he was relieved when he saw a faint gleam of perspiration on her upper lip; that somehow reassured him.

"I'd like for you to meet my husband," she said, reaching behind her for his hand. "Honey, this is Mr. Applewhite from New York. You brought us some mighty hot weather with you, Mr. Applewhite."

"It was pretty hot in New York," said Mr. Applewhite.

"I declare! But don't you think it's the humidity in New York?"

"The humidity *is* bad," said Mr. Applewhite; as he had grown older clichés had lost more and more of their poignancy for him. "Then we don't have anything like this either," he added, glancing at the ceiling fan.

"Isn't that a wonderful thing! I declare, I tell Mrs. Eubanks sometimes I'm right glad when my cook does get sick and I can make Branch bring me over here under this grand fan."

He stole glances at them during his rice and gravy and chicken. He had seen many young married people and he thought he had noticed this about them: sometimes they gave him a sense of wholeness and sometimes of parts. He had often

39

wondered about it, but he had no suggestion as to the cause. He had even denied the feeling, but it kept recurring, until now it was one of the first things he felt. He had tried to put his finger on why; it was not a congeniality in the usual sense, for he had felt wholeness with some who said very little to each other, and sometimes it existed even in the face of quarreling; he had been with one pair with whom he had felt it strongly during two days when they were not speaking. And conversely, he had noticed the opposite through layers of real pleasantness. He didn't know what it was, but he wondered if he were sensing the fact that the wound in each, where they had been grafted, had in one case healed sound and tight and in the other had, for some reason, failed up to that moment to get well; that was as much as he could say. But during the meal he stole glances at the two at the corner table and as he ate the dessert he said to himself subconsciously, while con,ciously perceiving the cool taste of the cream on his peaches, that Mr. and Mrs. Branch Wheaton, whatever the future might bring them, had up to then failed to heal.

He turned away and looked out beneath the awning at Mrs. Eubanks's scraggly ant-infested grass and the tall magnolia tree in the center, its blossoms running the gamut of life from tight balls of ivory yellow to open flowers flat like a clover.

"My grandfather planted that tree, Mr. Applewhite, when he was married."

But it reminded him of Nora. He had telephoned her as soon as he landed, but she hadn't been home. He thought he would call her again; then he changed his mind and decided he would just walk in. . . .

He swung slowly up the hill. Everything was very quiet. A negro in a wet shirt swept magnolia leaves into a pile in the gutter. The delivery boy from the drug store in the basement of the closed hotel pushed his bicycle up the road. A street car with two passengers ground its way wearily past. On a shady piece of wall a negro lay on his back, knees up, asleep. He wondered how Nora would be, amidst all this drowsiness.

She came into the hall as he was handing his hat to a negro butler in a white coat.

"Uncle John!"

He chuckled a little.

"What in the world, what in the world are you doing in Georgetown!"

"Oh, I don't know," he said. "What are *you* doing in Georgetown?"

She gave him a kiss on the cheek. "Let me go see if mother has waked up yet. . . . Where are your suitcases?"

"I hope you are going to understand about the suitcases," said Mr. Applewhite. "I'm staying down at Mrs. Eubanks's—"

"Oh, but—"

"I'm an old bachelor, my dear, and I'm used to the freedom of solitude. And what's more, I'm an *old* bachelor and I'm too set in my ways to be good company for very long at a stretch."

"Oh—"

"I know you will understand, though I confess I'm less certain about your mamma."

She gave him a chiding smile. "Come back in the library," she said. "It's cooler."

They went back into a shady room with leaded glass book cases. A cool light, reflected from the green garden, drifted through a north window, falling upon the music rack of an open piano. She moved a mahogany rocking-chair into the draft between the doors and told him to sit down.

He thought she guessed in a general way why he had come, though for a quarter of an hour she led him to talk about other things. She seemed to avoid looking at him.

At last he said to her with some misgiving, "I expected you to be half way to Vienna by now."

She did not say anything for a minute, looking at her hands, then she smiled at him.

"Well?" he said.

"I still want to go."

"As much as ever?"

"Oh, yes."

He was a good deal relieved at her reply, having begun to wonder if the protection of home hadn't weakened her independence.

"It's just—it's just, Uncle John, that I don't feel like leaving mother and father,—now."

"But now's the time."

"And I want you to promise me one thing, Uncle John."

He looked at her.

"You must promise first."

"Oh, no!"

"You mustn't say anything to mother and father about it."

"Why not?"

"They wouldn't want to stand in my way."

"So much the better."

"No."

"My dear, the important thing is that you go to Vienna. How you get there, over whose dead body,—just doesn't matter."

She shook her head. "We look at it differently."

"We look at it from different ends. You would bet on lots of things from your end, but looking back I think I can safely tell you that going to Vienna is your best bet."

"Surely that depends on your temperament."

"But you are interested in going."

"Oh, yes, I—I think in a way it would be fun."

"That's the temperament that needs to go. . . . Oh, I don't mean Vienna necessarily. I just call it Vienna; get out on your own. I'm—I'm just afraid of Georgetown for you."

"Georgetown's not so bad."

"My dear, Georgetown *is* bad, and in this way. You will get a feeling here that you are 'different,' and that's a feeling that will motivate you in directions that aren't true to yourself. Either you will force yourself, maybe through a kind of loneliness, to conform, or you will find you can't conform and will give up hope and take your refuge in eccentricity. . . . I'd rather the question of being different simply didn't come up. But we'll talk it over from time to time; I'll be around for a while."

"I haven't thought about going much for a month."

"You keep up your practice?"

She hesitated. "Yes. Of course I don't keep the long hours."

He looked at her as if this confirmed him in an idea.

"I'm not at all sure I want to be a musician."

"I don't care whether you become a musician or not. You can decide that later. The important thing is that your mind is young, and that it ought to be fed its rightful trip to Vienna."

She laughed at him in a kindly way. "I'm afraid my reasons for wanting to go were a good deal simpler. I just wanted to go for fun."

"Don't put it in the past tense."

"Well, I just *want* to oo for fun."

They laughed.

"I'm very hard headed on the subject," he said. . . .

A gray cat used to come into the Fenwicks' garden, walking through with measured tread, its noncommittal tail swinging slowly right and left, its cool eyes leveling a composed scrutiny at the privet hedges and the black-green ivy and the azalea shrubs with their canopies of scarlet flowers. It would appear sometimes audaciously in the center of the porch or in the walk surrounding the soft lawn inside the hedge-wall and look at you if you happened to be sitting there with a cold stare as if it were on the point of saying, "Scat!"

Sometimes you wouldn't see it at all at first. You would be sitting there in the late afternoon after the hoses had been turned off, the grass bristling with cool and damp, the sun beyond the top of the opaque water-oak, and all at once a mocking bird would swing down in a sharp arc beyond the hedge and up again and a squeaking and twittering would begin from all sides. It would continue without pause for perhaps a minute, a discordant unhappy noise, with now and then a bird shooting up and about in an awkward turn.

43

You could then cross over to the walk and see the gray cat sitting in the gate to the rose garden, watching the worried flight of the birds as nonchalantly as you might glance at the clouds or watch the Birmingham-Augusta mail plane go by. Sometimes, with a fluttering of wings, a bird would make a vertical drop at the cool disjointed little bag of bones and it would recoil slightly, pulling its head in.

After a time, when it was at length ready, it would take a dozen strides out of the open to the tunnel between the hedge and the azalea bushes and stretch out on its belly; the squawking of the birds would die away, though now and then one would make a quick circuit of the garden and hedges, not quite reassured. But slowly the commotion would subside,—the gray cat on its belly under the hedge, flexing the end of its tail.

Then half an hour later, suddenly, tumult and pandemonium!

But the gray cat sitting in the rose-garden gate was a picture you wouldn't forget. Nora remembered it when Gwendolyn appeared.

The first time she saw her, Gwendolyn was walking across the porch to the lawn, a slow lithe walk. She was slightly stooped, probably not wishing to seem as tall as she was, but the effect was better than if she had put her shoulders back and stood up straight. Her husband, who followed her through the screen door from the house, which Austin was holding open, was of about the same height, though he was erect and moved quickly. She walked out among them with perfect self-possession, her face interested but serious.

With some of the trepidation of the mocking bird, Nora rose and went to meet her.

"Nora," said Austin, "may I present Mr. and Mrs. Owens?"

Nora smiled and gave them a firm hand and led them out to the metal chairs and the table.

"This is Miss Tannahill, Mr. and Mrs. Owens. And this is my uncle, Mr. Applewhite. And this is Mr. Elbert Meigs. . . . Austin tells me you flew down."—

7. Bulloch County Farmer

THE June sun burned on the purple pyrites cinders. There was a certain harmony between the red boards of the factory and the cinders that surfaced the yard, broken and crushed by the trucks from the country as they backed and wheeled getting their mud-yellow tails up to the delivery platform. It was unintentional; the idea about it was that the ore, after the sulphur had been burned out in the making of sulphuric acid for the fertilizer, had to be disposed of and that in January, February, and March the winter rains and the trucks tended to churn the yard into a black bog; so they surfaced it over with the cinders. In summer with the bright sun on it, it looked a good deal like a bed of live coals. But nobody minded that; they claimed at the factory that there was always some air stirring from the city taxes dashing and pounding against the barbed-wire fence, which was the city line, trying to get across and wash away the building; Jesse Ferkler, the assistant superintendent, claimed that he could stand on the delivery platform and feel the walls quiver like when he went fishing on the jetty down at the Isle of Palms with the tide coming in.

He was up on the flat roof with three of his hands (June was the slack season) putting on a coat of black waterproof paint with a whitewash brush when old man Ben Gray's truck lurched slowly over the drain at the gate and came on across the cinders in second. He lowered himself down the ladder.

"Hoddy, Mr. Ben Gray? How you do, sir?"

"Hoddy, boy." Mr. Ben Gray lifted his hand in greeting and got down on the cinders, his boots with the cowhide laces crunching heavily about as he shook hands with Jesse Ferkler and directed his grandson, who was driving, in backing the truck against the platform. Jesse saw the usual 'thirty-eight' strapped to the steering wheel.

45

"How's everything up round Due West?"

"Need rain."

"Need rain around here too."

"It ain't rained up in Bulloch County to amount to nothin' in goin' on three weeks. Everything's burnin' up. Had a little sprinkle last week, but didn't even wet the ground."

"We never got any of it down here."

"Well, you never missed much."

"How's your cotton?"

"Cotton's lookin' pretty good. Needs rain though. But that boy's got a hundred acres of the prettiest-looking young cotton you ever saw in your life."

"That's what you get for buyin' good fertilizer."

Mr. Ben Gray smiled a little behind his stained mustaches, pleased at even this prejudiced hint that he had bought well.

"I tell the boy I don't know what in God's name he gonna do with it. It ain't worth nothin'. Yesterday cotton closed at eleven and five-eighths."

"I heard so."

"Cost him thirteen cents to raise it."

"That ain't the way to make money, Mr. Ben Gray." They laughed.

"How's the market today?"

"Haven't heard. Y'all come on in here to the phone and I'll call up the main office; they'll know."

"Come on in to the phone, Hardee; we gonna find out what the market's doin'."

As they walked down the platform to the mill office Jesse looked back with a grin, "You still holdin' your cotton, Mr. Ben Gray?"

"I still got it. Yes, sir, two hundred and twenty-six bales! It's been sittin' in Telfair & Company's warehouse since October, 1930, near to two years."

"What you gonna do with it?"

"What you reckon I'm gonna do with it? I refused twenty cents for it in 1930. I ain't gonna turn round now and let it go

46

for eleven. And there's carryin' charges to come off of that. On today's market it wouldn't net me nine cents."

"Storage and insurance eat it up."

"Eleven cents ain't enough for cotton. Cotton's going up."

"You gonna hold it for twenty cents?"

"I think I'd let it go for fifteen."

Jesse Ferkler leaned his elbow on the high desk and called the up-town office.

"Georgetown Chemical."

"That you, Branch?"

"Hello, Jesse."

"Branch, Mr. Ben Gray's out here. Y'all heard anything from the market?"

"Tell him it's just about like yesterday's close. Not much trading."

Jesse Ferkler turned his head and passed the information on to Mr. Ben Gray.

"All right, sir," said Mr. Gray. "I'm much obliged to you. . . . Oh, you might tell him I want to get three tons of eight-four-four and two tons of soda,—the old-style Chilean."

Jesse turned back to the telephone. In a minute he lifted his chin; "He says that'll be all right, Mr. Ben, but to ask you if you don't want to try some of this new Arcadian soda."

"No, sir, tell him, I'll stick to the old-style Chilean, tell him."

"Mr. Wheaton says to tell you it's the same price and it contains almost a whole unit more of nitrogen."

"No, sir, I'll just stick—"

"The old-style Chilean tests about eighteen, but this other runs about eighteen and three-quarters. If you'd like to see some I've got it right out there in the shed."

"No, sir, I don't feel just right about that. I b'lieve in stickin' to the old-style way of doin' things."

"All right, sir. . . . Hello, Branch. No, Mr. Ben don't want that. He wants the old-style Chilean."

8. Of the Genus *Lotus*

MRS. PICKENS didn't know what she was going to do without Bessie Charlton. When, usually about the first of June, she closed the Villa Felice, put her Italian chauffeur, Giulio, who was also her butler, and his wife, Rosa, who was her personal maid and emergency cook, into the front seat of the Lincoln limousine and drove to Southampton, she could stand the initial solitude of the cottage on The Beach Road knowing that in a week or ten days Bessie would be coming up to spend the summer. The cottage wasn't large but it assumed a very distressing quiet and futility when she tried to occupy it alone. She had tried once, the summer after her husband died; after that she regularly sent Bessie a railroad ticket to Southampton and met her with an irrepressible trace of condescension at the station. Bessie irritated her with her meekness and gratitude and adulation, but she was somebody in the house, somebody to talk to, to go out with. She would have asked somebody else, she had often searched her address book for somebody else, but there wasn't anybody else. And now poor Bessie was dead, and June was settling over Georgetown, summer was being pressed into every crack and cranny; she didn't know what she was going to do.

The only possibility she could think of was Saint Julian. She didn't know Saint Julian very well. She had known his mother long ago, but Saint Julian, up until five years before, had spent most of his life in Europe studying the violin. Word drifted back from time to time of his success; the *Daily News* once printed half a column quoted from the *Times* in London, where he had appeared as soloist with the London Symphony Orchestra at the Albert Hall. Then one day he showed up in Georgetown; she never heard exactly why, some people said a law suit connected with some real estate his parents had left, some said he was ill, some said he was penniless. She didn't know; the few times she had seen him she had had to do all the talking herself; he seemed to have nothing at all that he wanted to say. She had asked him once if he would play at her spring *soirée musicale*.

"I'd be very glad to," he said, clipping the 'r.' He answered so promptly that she waited a second for a 'but.' That was all he said though. He played, played beautifully.

She knew the gossip about him; they said he 'took something.' She didn't believe it; he had always been the perfect gentleman with her, always bent with easy elegance over her hand and touched her knuckles with his lips. She was sorry for him; if he 'took' anything, he was driven to it by an uncongenial environment. Anybody might be driven to that, used to what he was and living now in a wretched room by the railroad station. In a different setting he would probably get hold of himself. If he spent the summer with her he would get away from all this; it would give him a new point of view, start him off again. He was a genius. He had it in him to be a great artist. Of course forty was a little late,—but not too late. And she could sit in her garden with the long tumble of the waves just audible and hear him practicing in the conservatory; people would ask her to invite them to hear him play. They might say things about them, but she didn't care; it might add a little poignancy to their thoughts of her anyway. America was getting quite European in that respect.—And if she did not invite him, whom should she invite? There was nobody else.

But she postponed doing anything; it was a big decision. June came and wore on. On the eighteenth Giulio and Rosa came to her and complained politely of the heat; the kitchen was getting to be unbearable. She knew then that the time had come either to go to Southampton alone or invite Saint Julian.

She decided to do it. She sent Giulio to him with a note asking him to luncheon on Sunday; she would invite him then.

He replied next day in quite a beautiful and touching letter:

Dear Mrs. Pickens,

You do not know what a deep pleasure it will be to come to luncheon with you on Sunday. Life for me is very drab and empty.

49

I sometimes run away from it for a little while and wander about in the yard of the old house among the magnolia trees; the air is honey sweet, heavy like a cloud. What is so exquisite as these creamy petals, flannel thick, smooth as skin yet no smoother, the middle of a great ball of melancholy fragrance, the very shape of repose, of sleep. They lie open like a hand flung out on a pillow, the fingers curled in languor. They belong to the lotus family, you know,—lente, lente. My pleasures are so rare—

She locked the letter away in her desk. He was a genius. This summer might be the turning point in his life. Whatever people said about him, it was evident from the letter that he had himself in hand. The prospect of the summer began to reverse itself from something almost terrifying to something almost intoxicating.

She sent Giulio for him at half-past twelve. Luncheon was at one; she hated the Southern custom of dinner at two-thirty and quarter to three.

"You are having cold consommé, aren't you, Rosa? I forgot to tell you."

"Yes, madam."

"That's nice. It's so terribly warm."

Rosa wiped the back of her hand across her forehead.

"Never mind. We'll be going day after tomorrow. . . . I am inviting Mr. Saint Julian to spend the summer with me."

She looked over the table. She was using her black monogrammed service plates; they went so beautifully with the mirror top of the dining-room table, the jet reflections in the silver sea, the silver gleam of light on the velvet black. She thought of putting a magnolia blossom in the center, but decided against it; some color was better. She left the bowl of roses.

She took a silver shell of green mints into the living room, put it on a wall table to be served with the coffee, and changed the pitch of the Venetian blinds, blocking out the June glare that surged across her lawn like an advancing wave. What a relief to leave all that behind her! She would bring up the matter of the summer as soon as possible; he might be a little diffident

50

about talking, having been so much alone, and this would put him at his ease and interest him. And, too, having it definitely settled would lift a tremendous dark weight off her mind; that specter of solitude! She shuddered involuntarily and turned away, as if from the thought. Should she have cocktails? Perhaps she shouldn't. She didn't know what it was he was supposed to 'take,' but it might be that a cocktail would start him on the down path again. She rang for Rosa and told her not to serve cocktails; serve some very cold tomato juice with the appetizers. She lighted a cigarette and went upstairs.

She was sitting at her Louis XIV *poudreuse* when she heard the car return, stop under the porte cochère, drive on to the garage. She listened for the doorbell, gazing obliquely through her window at the down-pouring sunlight muffling the lawn and the shrubbery with a still woolen heat. Already the green of the spring grass was old, patched with ragged spots of oak brown that gave it a color at a distance like the uniforms the boys wore just a few years ago when she had put on the white dress and the cap with the red cross in it and shown the season's débutantes how to roll bandages,—khaki, no, olive drab. . . . She thought he must have rung and she had failed to hear it. She went down.

He wasn't in the living room, though, and she walked to the door to the veranda. The yellow wicker chairs were empty, giving off a sort of phosphorescent glow under the green and orange awnings. She turned back with a slight frown between her eyes and lifted the hanging band of tapestry by the fireplace to ring for Rosa and ask where he was. Then she heard the latch on the front door move with a subdued click and saw the dark hall fill with a growing daylight and the door opening slowly. A cluster of thoughts appeared in her mind then sank away: the bell must be out of order, get Rosa to go to the door, go herself, the informality might appeal to the artist.

"Come in, Saint Julian. I am *so* glad to see you. The bell is out of order. Rosa didn't hear you ring—"

He looked solemnly at the V of her neck as she smiled and

51

held out her hand, a gray-streaked twist of black hair out of line on his temple as if he had run his fingers through it; then his face lighted up and he handed her his walking stick.

She flushed slightly, taking it, but went on, smiling, "I hope you didn't have to wait in the sun. But there is usually a little shade out there—"

He left her to put the walking stick away and strolled into the living room. She hung the stick on a chair and followed him; the air seemed to be filled with the warm scent of magnolia blossoms.

"It is terribly warm, isn't it?" she said; evidently it was going to be a little difficult. There was something almost childlike about genius.

He rested his relaxed eyes blankly on her smile for a moment, then said with his marked English accent, "I beg your pardon."

"Summer's beginning early this year," she said, thinking of his accent and his calm austerity and the weary ennui of his manner; all that could be very attractive against the right background.

He lifted his shoulders slightly and picked a green mint out of the dish. "It's always summer."

"How true that is! Yes, that's so true. I wonder sometimes if it is really very good for us down here in Dixie to have no cold weather."

He bit the mint, looked at the half in his fingers, then put that in his mouth too. She watched him for a silent second, surprised, then glanced at her Venetian blinds drawing the sharp black lines across the bright window; peculiarly full of summer, those dark bands across the sunlight,—and that sweet odor of magnolia, heavy like poured honey.

"Sit down, Saint Julian. Tell me about your plans for the summer. . . . What kind of cigarettes do you smoke?" She offered him a long silver box containing four kinds, then sat down opposite him on the linen-covered divan as Giulio in a black coat brought the tomato-juice cocktails.

Saint Julian declined the cocktail but took another mint.

She felt that she ought to speak to him, as a child might need to be spoken to. "Don't you think, Saint Julian, you'd rather have the mints *after* luncheon? They may spoil your appetite if you eat them before."

"If Beethoven, madam, came to your house and ate mints before luncheon you would be proud you had seen him do it."

She gasped slightly. "I—I don't mind at all, Saint Julian—"

"By the way, madam," he said, glancing round the room, "is your husband here?"

"My husband?" she said, startled, her voice choking a little. "My husband is dead."

"Ah!" He reached for another mint, bit it, then turned toward her sincerely. "Did *you* kill him?—Or did I kill him?"

She tried to set the cocktail deliberately on the table beside her but some of it shook over the rim; she somehow wanted her hands free, she didn't know why.

He glanced at his cuffs in the silence, then pulled a magnolia petal out of his sleeve. "I'm lined with magnolia blossoms," he said seriously.

Her forehead went cold and she stared at the petal almost tearfully.

He bent his other arm and looked up the sleeve, then carefully slipped out a crumpled bloom, brown-streaked where his fingers had rubbed it. He stood up and bowed before her, handing her the flower.

She accepted it with a wan smile, dabbing at her lips with the cocktail napkin. She tried to speak but nothing came.

"I am stuffed with magnolia blossoms. I am replete with lotus flowers." He opened his coat and showed her the waxen leaves and flowers protruding from the inside of his frayed sleeves.

She drew herself up and inhaled deeply through her taut nostrils; the fragrance of the blooms almost stifled her.

"Daphne, fleeing from the sun god, my lady, became a laurel tree. But I am a Southerner. I am becoming a magnolia flower. . . . There are some more growing behind my neck."

She thought she was going to faint. She didn't know whether

53

she could lift her hand to pull the bell or not. Then she saw that he was going and she felt like weeping with relief.

"Good-by, madam." He bent over her shaking hand and touched it with his lips. "I wish I could stay longer, but I am having luncheon at one with Mrs. Winthrop Pickens."

She pulled the bell and Giulio came and showed him out.

When Giulio returned she said to him, staring straight in front of her, "Tell Rosa to bring me a cup of tea upstairs. I won't be down to luncheon."

Giulio glanced at her with quick solicitude.

"That's all, Giulio."

"Yes, madam."

9. Local Page

Wednesday, June 24

MR. JAMES McFARLANE snatched the first paper that fanned out of the *Daily News* press, retreated to his cane-bottomed chair, tilted it adoitly back under the green drop-light, whipped the edition open to the page of local and sectional news, and settled himself to a critical examination of his handiwork:

HOG BUSINESS IN
GEORGIA LOOKING UP—

S. C. DRY LEADER
DECRIES DERN'S
VIEW ON REPEAL

In a sweeping reply to issues raised by repeal-
ists, Dr. J. C. Roper, chairman of the federation
of organizations for prohibition in South Caro-

54

lina, said today that prohibition had decreased drunkenness, reduced—

COTTON CHOPPING
JOBS OPEN HERE—

UNSUCCESSFUL ATTEMPT OF UNION SOLDIERS TO HOIST THE SOUTHERN FLAG RECOUNTED

DETAILS OF FORT SUMTER INCIDENT COME TO LIGHT FROM LONG LOST EPISTLE

Mrs. W. Winthrop Pickens left on Monday for her cottage in Southampton, Long Island, after spending the winter in Georgetown at her home, the beautiful Villa Felice—

JENKINS CO. POSSE USES BLOODHOUNDS IN TRACKING NEGRO

ALLEGED SLAYER SOUGHT AFTER SHOOTING AT AN ALL-NIGHT JAMBOREE

Sheriff G. M. Fennells of Jenkins County and a posse of men gathered for the purpose, spent Sunday tracking with bloodhounds Charlie Knight colored, alleged to have shot and killed another negro named Farlow about Sunup Sunday morning at a frolic near Herndon. There was not a mark on the negro's body; one shot through the open mouth, direct to the vital spot, ended the life and broke up the party—

BAPTISTS GATHER AT MILLEN SOON FOR ANNUAL MEET

TRI-COUNTY SESSION—

The many friends of young Dr. Lucian Abercorn are delighted to learn of his return home

55

to Georgetown after an extensive sojourn in
European capitals—

LOCAL COTTON
DECLINES AFTER
EARLY RESPONSE

Middling cotton declined eight points yesterday to close at 11.65 as compared with the
previous close of 11.73—

CHAPTER TWO

1. Patrimony

WHEN Louis XIV revoked the Edict of Nantes, young Henri d'Aragné (his family, according to the records, was of apparently some consequence in Bordeaux), joined the host of some 500,000 Protestants who were fleeing the country and took ship to England. The next thing we hear of him was in 1689, when he was put in charge of a shipload of Huguenots sailing for the English colonies in America. "After a weary voyage and many trials and losses," says his journal, now in the possession of the South Carolina Historical Society (his wife died at sea and he speaks of himself elsewhere as one *'usé de chagrin'*), "but with undying faith, we landed first at Port Royal, South Carolina, and subsequently at Charles Town, where we were kindly received and succored by the City Council." He seems to have been a person of some education and was a tutor in the family of a Mrs. Boyle of Charleston until his second marriage, to Mrs. Boyle's eldest daughter. There is a letter in the collection of the historical society to his father in Bordeaux, dated 1695, in which he says, "We enjoy perfect health here and an abundance of all that is necessary for me and mine. God gave me a son on the 17th of July."

Either this son, or possibly a younger son (the record is not very clear), was evidently named Pierre after the old man in France, for in 1739 a regiment of volunteers took ship from

57

Charleston for Savannah to join Oglethorpe in an expedition against the Spanish possessions in Florida, and the Charleston regiment was in command of Pierre d'Aragné. He married the daughter of a well-to-do Englishman who owned a large plantation on the Savannah River. He seems to have lived for a while in Charleston, where his wife bore him three sons and a daughter, but his death is recorded in the Horse Creek Methodist Church a few miles above Savannah, so it would seem that he returned with his family to the plantation.

Two of the boys died when they were children, in an epidemic of malaria, but the eldest, Henri, lived to be appointed Lieutenant Governor of the colony under the Crown. He was evidently quite an eminent man and J. T. W. Bulloch in his *History of Colonial Georgia* devotes a whole chapter to him and his works. For our purpose, though, it is enough to note that at his death he was survived by four daughters and three sons.

In the third year of the war, before his death, Henri's son, Jules d'Aragné (though they seem to have begun to spell it at about this time as one word, Daragné), quarreled with his father, ran away from home, and joined General Marion. After the war Jules found himself in Georgetown. The quarrel with his father may have contributed to his not returning to Savannah; at any rate, the next thing we hear of him is in Georgetown in 1807, when Colonel Jules Daragné is mentioned in the court house records as defense counsel in a case involving a land dispute.

William N. Daragne, apparently his grandson (the accent seems to have been dropped, and the probable pronunciation of the name was the same as today: Daranny), "attended the then famous school of Professor Waddell at Willington"—the quotation is from some private papers belonging to the family—"graduated at the Alabama College and afterwards continued his studies at Berlin and Heidelberg. He practiced his profession of law in Wedgefield District, Alabama, served in the Mexican War under General Scott as Captain of D Company Palmetto Regiment and was killed at the gates of Mexico City, September 13, 1847."

One of his sons, Nathaniel, rose to be a colonel in the Army of Northern Virginia and was wounded in a battle on the outskirts of Richmond; he returned to Georgetown with the bones of his left wrist shattered and an arm that he wore in a soft leather sling until his death in 1908. He had two daughters and a son (who died as a child), whom he had named Lee.

The eldest of these daughters married Thomas Hill, a lawyer. They had two daughters and a son before Thomas Hill's death from pneumonia in 1918.

This son, Lee Hill, equipped with the ingredients that have been described to you, returned home after the Armistice, tried first this job then that, sold securities, was a salesman in the Dodge agency, then a clerk in a cotton office, and finally after ten years, in 1928, seemed to hit at last upon the one thing that he was best qualified to do, for he had held the job for four years and gave every outward sign of having caught his stride. He was the assistant manager of the Sinclair filling station on the corner of Green and Marbury Streets at which Mr. Applewhite's taxi driver paused to have him put in two gallons of gasoline.

2. Company

Friday, June 26

IN not going into the state of their finances with Austin, neither Eliot nor Gwendolyn had any desire to mislead him. They weren't trying to stand before him in a false light of wealth; it was just that they wanted to avoid the serious misconstruction he might put on their arrival if they laid all their cards on the table and told him they had between them just about eighty dollars with nothing else in sight until the first of September. He might have thought they had come down because their money was running low; he might even have thought they were going to ask him for a loan. This would really have put them in an unfair light. Eliot hated to borrow money from his friends, and on the one or two occasions when he had been forced to, he had paid it back immediately upon receipt of his quarterly check; he owed a Philadelphia tailor and three of the best women's shops in Fifty-seventh Street, but he didn't owe any of his friends. He wasn't embarrassed at all by having about seven dollars a week until September and he would gladly have discussed it with Austin from all possible angles except that he didn't want their visit to be clouded by Austin's fear that he might have to refinance them.

He was fond of Austin. He remembered him well. Austin had been two classes ahead of him, and though Austin had seen him round the club for only one year and never heard of him since, he had seen Austin for a year and heard stories about him and his Southern accent until he graduated. He remembered particularly well the June dinner at the club the year Austin graduated when Austin stood up in his chair after declining the dessert and said that he came from a place where the hospitality grew on trees. "There's *plenty* of hospitality," Austin said, "and I want you all to come to see me. I don't want you to wait for any more invitation; I'm inviting you now. And if any of you get within a hundred miles of my front door and don't come in to see me I'm going to feel mighty, mighty bad."

This made a tremendous impression on young Owens. He would never have considered issuing such an invitation himself and the picture of that broad and generous land where the son of the house invites a hundred of his college friends to see him without even naming a date brought him to his feet with loud and sincere applause. He wondered what his own mother and father would say if he told them that even ten of his classmates were coming home with him tomorrow; he knew that though his indulgent mother might send their Swedes off immediately for sheets and towels, his more business-like father was likely to tell him to go at once to the telephone and wire at least nine of them to stay where they were. He had never been south of Pinehurst but he thought Alabama must be a wonderfully fertile place to breed hospitality so colossal. Being then at the end of his Sophomore year, the amount of real disillusionment he had covered was practically negligible, and it didn't occur to him that the telling difference between his invitation of ten for tomorrow and Austin's of a hundred for anytime was not so much a matter of number as of definiteness; he hadn't yet been far enough South to realize that in a pause of the conversation where someone else might light a cigarette or cross his legs, a true Southerner is more than likely to invite everybody present to come spend some winter with him.

He never forgot that dinner and as the years rolled round to his graduation, then to his entrance into the Harvard Law School and his exit some three months later, then to his connection with the law firm of Owens, Scott, Wharton and (as he put it) 'his redemption thence' the following year, and finally to that Yale-Princeton football game with a friend of his and two blind dates and his marriage later on that evening to one of them, he always had it in the back of his mind that some day he would drop in on Austin Toombs.

The marriage was another turn of the screw on Mr. Owens's already rich cynicism and he told his secretary to mail no more allowance checks to Mr. Eliot until further notice. His mother, however, after a good deal more ado, transferred to him a certain block of oil stock that had been paying her a thousand dollars every quarter; she knew this would be quite a come-down for him, but she thought it might keep them from having to sleep on park benches or starving to death.

His wife, whose name he discovered was Gwendolyn, turned out to be the daughter of one of the original pilots on the Newark-Washington run. She had lost count of the number of hours she had spent in the air; she was twenty-two and she had made her first flight when she was ten. She had a private license and when he asked her at their first breakfast what she would like for a wedding present she gave him a really beautiful smile through a smear of butter and crumbs and said, "How about one of those Waco Wright 300s?"

He didn't know what she was talking about but he found out soon enough; it cleaned out his safe deposit box at the Philadelphia Trust Company, but he was glad to do it; he would have been glad to give her the Philadelphia Trust Company. He thought she was the most seductive thing he had ever seen and he was as proud of her as if she had been a shining new Rolls-Royce. Indeed, he liked to go about with her where people could see them and if casual males seemed habitually unable to hide the covetousness in their eyes, it did not cause him to feel resentment, but rather somewhat the same sort of satisfaction as having them envy him his Rolls; indeed, being a thoroughly good-natured boy, it would have taken very little more to make him stop and (to follow out our metaphor) offer them a ride. He did not analyze it so far, but she had, indeed, an extraordinarily cosmic attitude toward her beauty, being interested in it not so much for its own sake as for its exchange value.

They spent the first winter on the Pacific Coast, and had already used a good half of their check before it arrived on the fourth of March. Not having heard any further from Mr. Owens, senior, on the subject of coming back to his arms, they stayed awhile longer, then began a slow journey eastward through the South, using all but about a hundred and fifty dollars of their June check before it arrived. The middle of June found them in Atlanta with about a hundred dollars, and the opportunity seemed golden to Eliot to pay that long-deferred visit to his old brother in Georgetown.

He was a good deal impressed with Austin's hospitality; it began casually enough, but it seemed to have a cumulative quality that he thought was distinctly creditable to the South. New Englanders, taking you in, seem to think first of relieving you of any possible embarrassment you might feel if they appeared glad you came, and, anxious to have you sense their real emotions in the matter and not give them credit for more welcome than they may feel, receive you with a severity approaching a positive antagonism and, instead of contenting themselves with the Southerner's favorite phrase of 'make yourself at home,' are more than likely to proceed at once to make you at home themselves by subjecting you to various subtle annoyances that in all probability you left home in the hope of escaping. In the South, on the other hand, they appreciate unconsciously that you didn't come to see them in order to feel at home; they assume that you came to get away from home and that you want to be treated as much like a guest as the facilities of the place will allow. So, with a good deal of innate understanding, they tell you to make yourself at home, that they won't treat you like company, and concentrate all the energies of the more or less enervated Summervilles and Terrys into forcing you into the rôle of company and making you forget some of the more tantalizing discomforts of home.

The result of all this has been the development of a hospitality that has become axiomatic in most of the Western hemisphere as the quintessence of open handedness; it has nothing to do with the relatively sentimental detail of being glad to see you. There is nothing personal about it, as this would imply; it is more of a natural phenomenon, like the rain, and is completely indifferent as to whom it falls on. You are "the company" as you might be "the plumber" or "the gas man," and your further qualities are almost always irrelevant and often a bore. Though Eliot and Gwendolyn were perhaps somewhat deficient in the first requirement of company, effervescence, they more than compensated for it by Gwendolyn's face and figure, and it isn't at all surprising that Austin for the first day lived up to their expectations as a Southern host; the red brick house was not quite the old white-columned plantation mansion they had had in mind, but Oregon, sweating in a stiff white coat taking their luggage upstairs to Austin's vacated bedroom on the southwest corner facing the prevailing summer wind, became at once the

63

old family retainer and all was well. The curious thing about it all was the cumulative quality that impressed Eliot; this was what had worried Austin more than anything. The wearing grind of being pleasant he felt sure would break him down; it was not the first day or two that told on you but keeping it up. But on the second day at about one o'clock Gwendolyn's eyes began to penetrate, and something happened in him comparable to the change occurring in those old automobiles when, having started them sputtering on the battery, you reached over to the dashboard and switched them on to the magneto, and he looked up to see the clouds breaking. Was it possible that this wasn't going to be so painful after all? It was somewhat analogous to the moment at which you are having a run on your bank and have got down to within sight of the bottom of your till and a messenger rushes in to say there is an armored truck backing up to the rear door with Federal Reserve gold in it. The as yet almost indiscernible question in his subconscious mind changed from 'How long do you reckon they're going to stay?' to 'How long do you reckon you can keep them?'

"Well," said Austin, "I can offer you golf, pretty good golf, though it's fairly well baked out. And I can offer you a swim in John Fenwick's mill pond. Or if you like we can run down to the beach at Saint Simon's; it's only a hundred and twenty-five miles. Or I can show you the town—"

"How about a rubber of bridge?" said Gwendolyn.

This was completely satisfactory to Austin; it required an attractive modicum of exertion and, he felt, presented a good deal more variety than beaches and sights and millponds. He telephoned Nora for a fourth.

When Austin saw Eliot gather up the cards from the table and with almost one movement divide them, fan the halves together, and flutter them back with a whispering sound, whatever further qualms may have been lurking at the back of his head about his guests gathered themselves together and hurried away; if that agility meant what he thought it did, Eliot had not spent his four years at Princeton in vain and could probably

64

not only play creditable bridge but could play it indefinitely. This was as convenient as an invading army's bringing its own provisions; a person with bridge is somewhat like a caterpillar tractor and can get through practically anything because he takes his own road along with him.

When Nora and Gwendolyn came down from upstairs in silence, Austin paid no attention to the phenomenon; he had been subjected enough to the winds of the world to know that though it isn't at all indicative of friendship if two women return from the powder-room in frenzied talk, it is usually a serious matter if they don't, but it didn't make any impression on him. He went on with his job of adjusting the electric fan on the floor where it would blow upward under the table and not scatter the cards.

When the final figures showed Austin the loser by four dollars and sixty cents he was really quite pleased; he was perhaps not quite as pleased as if it had been two dollars and sixty cents, but it was only proper that the Southern host should be the one to lose. Eliot's appreciation of the outcome was enhanced by more material considerations, but he did what he could to pocket the bills with nonchalance. . . .

Coming on top of this, Gwendolyn's announcement from in front of the bathroom mirror that night, her head back and her mouth open and her tongue against a crevice between her upper left molars, that she had lost a cockeyed filling did not strike him as serious a blow as it otherwise would have.

"God!" he said, "you would!"

"But, Elly, I didn't do it on purpose."

"Let's see. You'll just have to do without it, that's all."

"I'm not going to do without it."

"Are you sure it's really gone?"

"Look right there where my tongue is."

"Hell, I can't see anything."

"Right there!"

"Never mind. The thing is how much is it going to cost?— You know how things are as well as I do."

65

"Good night, Elly! You just won five dollars."
"You can't get it fixed for five dollars."
She laughed. "I can do anything."
He gave her the four dollars and sixty cents.

3. Gayly the Troubadour!

Saturday, June 27

MISS SUSAN TANNAHILL rented rooms on the porch floor of an old house in Summerville owned by Mrs. Eubanks. It was convenient both to Mrs. Eubanks's main house, where she took her meals, and to the street car line, by which she could go into town; she could look out of her side window and see the cars, at long intervals, go up and down the hill; she had even figured their schedules out to a point where she knew that if she began putting on her hat just as the outward-bound car toiled past her window, she had exactly time enough to walk leisurely down the porch steps and to the corner and catch the inward-bound car rolling down the hill to town. This saved her from having to stand on the corner in the sun.

She was sitting in a green smock in the midst of canvases, easels, brush-pots, and all the paraphernalia of painting, writing a very positive letter to Franklin Simon about a credit of one pair glove-silk pants which they had failed to allow her on a return, when she heard an automobile stop at an unfamiliar place in the drive and a measured mounting of the steps. She kept the blinds on the tall porch-windows closed on account of the afternoon glare, but there was a crack in one of them through which she could see the front steps and the driveway. She put down her pen and tiptoed to the window; through the crack now appeared a tiny image of the Reverend Riley All, clad in white with a

66

stiff straw hat and a black bow tie. She laid the tips of her fingers on her lower lip as he pushed the bell and cast his pale eyes patiently at the ceiling.

Miss Tannahill was an expatriate of what Greenwich Village is said once to have been. She had spent a year there before America entered the war and been very homesick and very virtuous, but had managed to whip up her courage to a point of cutting her hair; she left Cherry Lane for home in 1917 at the age of twenty-eight, a model of almost wistful decorum, absolutely intact mentally, spiritually, physically, and morally, a large hat at not quite the right angle on the back of her head.

But as Car K-33 rolled persistently down the Atlantic seacoast, carrying her farther and farther from Sheridan Square, a metamorphosis began to take place in her comparable to that which occurs in a man who has refused to fight and begins to rage as his friends haul him away. Finally, as her train neared the Congaree River, she broke a lifelong precedent in the privacy of the 'Ladies' by unhooking the clips that attached her stockings to her corset and peeling them off. Having mashed her hat into a suitcase, she landed bareheaded and barelegged, and there in the Union Depot of her home town at last became Bohemian.

During the next few years she gradually came to understand the part that Georgetown was expecting her to play; with the bare legs and bare head as a basis and the reputation of Greenwich Village as a proof, she slowly learned that she had sown her wild oats in her time and was in all probability not through sowing yet. As the years clouded her New York days, she began to remember more and more the one or two occasions when she might have strayed and to neglect more and more the fact that she had not, and by 1922 she was having no difficulty in honestly seeing herself in the somewhat attractively checkered light in which the town saw her.

Fifteen years after she got home, her exoticisms, assisted by the influence of several trips to Europe, had grown into more maturity and she played upon them with a good deal more taste and cleverness; she wore stockings, and her variations from the

usual were confined to such things as wearing her smartly gray-
ing hair neatly clipped at the back of her head and carrying in
her wanderings about Summerville a slender black walking
stick. She had developed, too, a kind of noncommittal half smile.

She had become, by virtue of all this, really the most coveted
catch of Georgetown's clergy and all of them, young and old,
had, so to speak, shot at her at one time or another; hardly a
revival went by that some minister did not cast acquisitive eyes
upon her in the name of Holy Church. She held a position in
some ways comparable to that of Moby Dick and there was
scarcely a pastor in Georgetown who would not rather have
brought her to port safely lashed alongside than any number of
other fishes of greater sperm value and probably of greater mis-
chievousness; gentlemen of the cloth, meeting before the Receiv-
ing Teller of the bank on Monday morning with the Sabbath's
collections, or passing one another in their Fords and Chevrolets,
would sometimes haul up before the wind for a moment like the
masters of the old whaling ships, and say if they had any news
of the elusive mammal.

Why they did not abandon hope after approximately fifteen
years of failure was owing largely to Miss Tannahill herself,
whose list of male acquaintances was so meager, not to say wan,
that she could not bring herself to dismiss anyone. She received
their offers of the Father's love very much as if they had been
offering her their own and treated the whole affair as any adult
female would have treated so many proposals of marriage, having
no intention of accepting any one of them until she was reasonably sure that nothing better was going to turn up. She put
them off year after year with sundry purposely unconvincing
excuses, as if buoyed up by an abiding faith that something better in the way of salvation was going to reveal itself. She was unworthy, she would tell them. To which they would answer that
no one was unworthy in His sight. She would lower her eyes
and with a faint blush mounting her cheeks declare that she
had perhaps not been all she should have been. To which they

68

would reply in substance that He would have forgiven Cleopatra if He could have got her attention.

That summer Dr. All was the most persistent. He had not been in Georgetown long and he was as zealous in obtaining her for his flock as a new and untried salesman in landing his first big account. He was a frail little man with kind gray eyes that seemed futile enough behind their glasses, but seeing them without them, blinking at the world in astonished discomfort, you felt that here if ever there lived one was a righteous man; he stirred in you a kind of pity, as righteousness, peculiarly enough, so often does, and you tended to like him, wanting something good to happen to him and being somehow pretty sure that it never would.

She put her correspondence hastily into a drawer and picked up a palette and a handful of brushes as Nancy's disheveled black head appeared in the door and announced that there was a gentleman to see her.

He came in comfortably, used to visiting, and sat down. They talked for a few minutes about the hot weather. When there was a pause he cleared his throat and said, "I had a letter this morning from an old friend of mine that I thought might interest you. You probably know him. Dr. Dice Alexander?"

"I think I've met him."

"He's the pastor of the Broad Street Baptist Church."

"Oh, yes."

"We were boys together up in Colleton County. It was largely on account of Dr. Alexander that I got this call to Georgetown. He's a fine man, and one of the most eloquent preachers I've ever listened to. The town misses him."

"Has he gone?"

He looked at her in surprise. "Dr. Alexander's traveling in the Holy Land."

"I didn't know that."

"Oh, yes. He's been away from us now, going on a year. Mrs. Winthrop Pickens, you know, gave him the trip."

"I didn't know she ever went near a church."

"Well, she doesn't go to church herself very much, but she does a lot of good works with her money. A lot of good works. Dr. Alexander was very close to *Mr.* Pickens during *his* lifetime. He's having a wonderful trip."

"You mean Dr. Alexander," she said, a sparkle in her eyes.

"Yes," he said. "He won't be back until September."

"I was in Jerusalem in 1928."

"I recollected your saying so. That's why I thought you'd be interested." He smiled.

"Of course I am, Dr. All."

He unfolded the letter and read her a detailed account of the Reverend Dice Alexander's travels through the countries on the Mediterranean, ending with his arrival the night before in Jerusalem; the last sentence was, "I have seen a great deal of the unbaptized, Brother Riley, and I don't quite know what to make of them. Remember me in your prayers."

"What does he mean by that?" said Miss Tannahill.

"By what?"

"I thought maybe—maybe he might, I don't know, maybe be losing faith a little—"

"Oh, Miss Tannahill!"

"Maybe not."

"You don't know Dr. Alexander, Miss Tannahill. I have faith, Miss Tannahill, an absolute faith; but the man who wrote that letter has more faith in his little finger—"

"I guess I was wrong."

"You were wrong, Miss Tannahill. *You* must have faith." He smiled at her again.

"I'm afraid I'm a pagan, doctor—"

"Miss Tannahill—"

"I'm afraid I haven't been—er—all I should have."

"Miss Tannahill, all He asks of you, in His infinite love and mercy, is that you repent. As a father pitieth his children—"

"I can't repent yet, doctor," she said with an almost charming smile, "but there will come a day."

"Think, Miss Tannahill—"

70

"Someday, I know, temptation will cease to tempt me. Then, Dr. All—"

"Will you kneel with me for a moment, Miss Tannahill?"

They knelt and he prayed first for her, then for Dr. Alexander in a far country.

He took his discouraged leave and in the privacy of his bed assembled new prayers and arguments, as an explorer who has failed to reach the Pole, will patiently get together all the latest equipment in preparation for some future dash.

4. Paid in Full

Friday, July 3

THE southwest wind, caroming languidly from hill to hill across the Alabama uplands, banked against the pallid back of the twelve-story Cotton States Building and skidded straight into the ingenuous face of Dr. Christian Troupe, standing idly in the shade of his lowered awning. He enjoyed the hot dryness on his cheeks, deflected out of his eyes by his glasses. They were large black-rimmed glasses, sitting on his nose the least bit askew to the left since his sister Carrie's little boy had stepped on them. He had laughed and had had to stammer in the rush of words assuring her that he didn't mind. He really didn't. He was very grateful to his sister for renting him his room and he was extremely fond of both the children and he wouldn't have minded if they had broken the glasses to bits. He straightened them and put them on and they seemed all right. They were slightly askew but he didn't notice it; he could see perfectly with them and could look cheerfully and sympathetically at the reverse image of the most demoralized molar.

He hadn't a great many molars to look at and practically none of them had grown their cavities in the best part of Georgetown; most of them came from bungalows along the lower river bank or from towns outside like Due West and Hector and Societyhill and had deteriorated upon modest fare. But he was young and his framed certificate from the Southern Protestant Dental College at Birmingham was not yet ten years old, and he felt that it was only a matter of time and perseverance until his instruments would search out the most prominent cavities in Georgetown. Already Dr. Abercorn was a patient of his and he never answered the telephone without thinking that this might be the ring that would establish him safely in Summerville.

When the telephone rang on this particular morning he answered it with his usual optimism.

"I want to make an appointment with Dr. Troupe."

"All right, sir. This is Dr. Troupe speaking."

"Are you free any time this morning?"

"Just a minute, sir, let me be sure." He ran his finger conscientiously down the blank page labeled Friday, July 3. "Would eleven o'clock suit you?"

"Wait a minute."

There was a moment's quiet, while Dr. Troupe turned his pencil round in his fingers suspended over the line marked 'II.' If eleven wouldn't do he would try eleven-thirty, then twelve; the voice sounded promising.

"Hello?"

"Yes, sir."

"Eleven o'clock's all right."

"All right, sir. What is the name, please?"

"Owens."

"Mr. Owens. All right, sir, Mr. Owens. I'll look for you at eleven."

He returned with some buoyancy to the office and sat down in the chair. He contentedly took out a package of cigarettes, lighted one, and gazed peacefully out beyond his porcelain tray and beneath the arm and ball of his idle drill at the green Alabama forests across a bend of the Congaree. When the ash

72

grew to half an inch he tapped it off into the fountain at his left elbow and watched the jade water sweep it spirally round and down.

He was in his shirt sleeves running a broom over the linoleum of his office floor when the telephone rang again. It was Dr. Abercorn.

"Chris," he said, "these damned teeth are worrying the hell out of me."

"I'm mighty sorry to hear that, Dr. Abercorn—"

"I'm sick of 'em, Chris. I want 'em out. I want 'em out this morning. What are you doing right now?"

"I'm waiting for a patient right now, sir. Could you make it twelve o'clock?"

Dr. Abercorn said all right and hung up. . . .

At quarter to eleven Dr. Troupe took a fresh white tunic out of the bottom drawer of his cabinet and laid it on the arm of the chair. At five minutes to eleven he put his arms into the short sleeves and buttoned the collar behind his neck; he started his fan going to supplement the southwest wind. At five minutes after eleven he went to the window and gazed out at the summer clouds sitting on the horizon like cotton samples. At twenty minutes after eleven the doorbell rang.

He gave a last glance over the office and went out.

"Mr. Owens?" he said, bowing hesitantly. "But this is Mr. Toombs, isn't it?"

"Yes, it is," said Austin. "This is Mr. Owens."

"I'm very pleased to meet you, Mr. Owens," he said.

"My wife says she's got something the matter with her teeth," said Mr. Owens abruptly. "We'll just wait, if it won't take too long."

Dr. Troupe glanced at Mrs. Owens looking casually through the April *Screenland* on the table. She closed the magazine, flung him a slow serious scrutiny, and began languidly pulling off a pale Leghorn hat.

"Will you just step inside, ma'am?"

73

He held the door open while she gave Austin a glance to think about and handed her husband her hat.

"Just take a seat, please," said Dr. Troupe, and turned to the basin and nail brush. As he dried his hands he came round the chair and said, "Is there anything in particular troubling you or do you—"

She looked up out of the tops of her eyes supplicatingly; "I think a filling has dropped out."

He nodded, returning behind the chair. He hung the hand towel on a rack and glanced surreptitiously in the mirror; he caught his own eye and looked away.

"This is a mighty hot spell we are having," he said, taking a clean napkin out of a drawer.

As he hung it round her neck she lowered her eyes. He usually associated this with tying the bibs round the necks of his niece and nephew, but this trivial gesture of hers made them seem now somehow not quite comparable. He turned away quickly to his porcelain tray.

"Well, let's have a look," he said with professional cheer, picking up his mouth mirror and rubbing his thumb over the disc.

"Don't make me look any uglier than necessary, will you?"

He gave a minute start.

Then he recovered himself and managed to smile. "You have a very fine set of teeth. You have practically perfect articulation."

She laughed a little; "Oh, doctor!"

He thought his face was becoming slightly warm; he had never had an appointment quite like this before. He was going to get lipstick on his fingers too, which was unusual; as a rule his women patients didn't wear rouge,—at any rate, he had never noticed it before. She seemed somehow to make him notice a good many things about her; the temperature of a patient's skin was something he had never thought of before, either. . . . He thought he had better get to work. Good molars, remarkably few fillings.

"I don't find any cavity," he said after a few minutes.

74

She blinked up at him, puzzled.

"Sometimes a tooth will get a little rough spot. A tiny piece of the enamel may get chipped off. But it isn't a cavity. Where did you think it was lost from?"

"Back here somewhere," she said, putting her forefinger in her mouth.

He looked again.

"That's what it is. It's a *tiny* little piece of the enamel chipped off."

"God, what a relief!"

"I'll just polish it down for you and it'll be all right."

"Will you just clean them for me, too, as long as I am here?"

He rigged up his drill and smoothed out the rough spot. Then he filled a little glass cup with Clay and Goodwin's No. 1 Polishing Powder and carefully cleaned them.

When he straightened the chair and unclipped the chain round her brown neck, she broke the silence by asking softly for a hand mirror and relined her lips.

"You—er—don't live in Georgetown, do you?" he said.

She shook her head. "How could you tell?"

"Oh, I don't know."

"We're visiting Mr. Toombs," she said, turning back to the mirror and stretching her lips apart over her teeth. "You did a good job."

He smiled. "It—it wasn't very difficult."

She put the mirror on the tray, stood up, and gave him her hand. "Thanks," she said. "I think you're a first-rate dentist. First rate."

His face turned red again and he glanced at his working glasses in his hand with a smile. "You—you're a first-rate patient," he said.

"That's sweet of you." She patted him on the back of his hand. "I'm usually lousy."

"I—I don't believe that."

She took a step toward the window, gazing out. "You have quite a nice view, haven't you?"

"It is nice," he said, his heart pounding with the thought that she wasn't hurrying away.

Then she turned toward him, smiling; "You don't remember me, do you?"

He jumped.

"I saw you out at the airport the day we landed."

"Oh! Was that your—"

She laughed, moving away from the window. "Well, good-by." She looked at his eyes and held out her hand.

Before he knew what had happened he was holding her unfamiliarly about the shoulders, pressing his lips to an unfamiliar mouth that tasted faintly of Clay and Goodwin's No. 1 Polishing Powder.

"I've got to go!" she gasped suddenly, freeing herself.

He watched her, stunned, while she rouged her lips in his mirror, then, in a minute, went to the door.

On the threshold she turned abruptly. "Oh, dear me!" she said with a smile that pleaded indulgence, "I was forgetting about the bill—"

"Please!" he said. "Please—"

He was scarcely conscious of anything further until he was alone again, leaning his bare forearm weakly on the headrest of his chair, gazing out into the view that she had admired, a creamy sweetness on his lips. . . .

It was from a long distance that he saw Dr. Abercorn enter in his loose white clothes and heard him say,

"I'm sick of 'em, Chris! Kindly pull the God-damned things out."

He could never remember how he had got those teeth out. He hadn't seemed to be thoroughly conscious; the thing that finally seemed to arouse him was the sudden picture of Dr. Abercorn standing pale in the door, his cheeks sagging, shadows under his eyes, his collar wilted, his nerves badly shocked, and he remembered later suddenly wondering if perhaps he hadn't pulled too many at one sitting.

"You go home now, Dr. Abercorn," he said, "and go to bed.

You keep a glass of warm salt water by your bed and rinse your mouth out with it now and then." He wiped the perspiration off first one cheek, then the other. "You'll probably get a little pain this afternoon when the novocaine wears off. I'll come by on my way home and see how you're getting on."

5. What of the Young Men?

Friday, July 3

THOSE fans, with their ceaseless drone, gave Lucian a strange feeling of remoteness. They seemed to draw something between you and the world, something, in a way, like the thing between you and the world, at first, in a foreign country. They seemed to change values a little. They wove a veil of soft sound about you. You felt, somehow, you might do things you wouldn't have done.

Perhaps, though, it was not the fans so much as the dry clear heat which the fans epitomized. They were the voice of the heat; they made the summer audible. Scarcely audible, for after the first moment you hardly noticed them at all and if you weren't careful you would go out of the the room and leave them running, but still probably palpable to your ear whether you noticed them or not, slightly hypnotizing to you whether consciously or not. Or possibly it was the dull lucid heat that was slightly hypnotizing. The afternoon-ness of everything.

How was all this going to work out, anyway, this coming home business? You came home loaded for bear; all right, bring on the bears. He hadn't even heard a growl. It seemed like months since he had got off the train; it was really only about two weeks. Things had been very quiet. It might be a little different now with the governor knocked out; he would probably have to take over a few calls for the next day or two. Even with that, though, there would be plenty of time on his hands. What did the young men do about it? This would be a fine time to get some reading done, to get some leisurely cogitation done, to take a long inventory of what he had collected during the last ten years. He had really been looking forward to coming home; to sitting down in peace and doing a little sorting. He had something in his mind he wanted to organize about By-Products, about the importance of the by-product over the main product, about life itself being a by-product of pleasure; even food was, in a sense, a by-product, consisting either of the seed itself or of a substance created and stored up by the plants and animals primarily to nourish the seed;—something he wanted to organize about Nature the prodigal, fertilizing maybe one in three million, a few great people in the world—but hell! He didn't feel like thinking! Something was in the way. What did the young men do about it? Southern womanhood! Nurtured with such infinite care to fill a need that existed only in theory, trained to be neither intelligent nor exciting and to make a pretense of being both!

He heard their neighbor's butler on the lawn beyond the wall turn on the hose with a barrage of quick spurts followed by a quiet raining hiss. He heard the nurse in the front room swish over the page of a magazine; he shut off the fan and went up-stairs. He thought he would go out. He was restless.

He looked in at the open door of his father's bedroom and saw the old man lying on the bed with his face turned away. He watched him stir uneasily, then tiptoed down the hall; quite a shock at that age to have six teeth pulled.

It was four by the hall clock clicking emptily beside the front door. Maybe there was something going on out at the Country Club. He got his father's car and drove out. . . .

There was nobody in the locker room but a black boy in his shirt sleeves.

"Nobody round?"

"Naw, sir; hit's mighty quiet. They gonna have little tournament out here tomorrow, but look like nobody don't care much."

"It's too hot," said Lucian, reaching for his handkerchief.

"Yessir. . . . Mr. 'Dub's' out, sir; him and a foursome."

"Who?" said Lucian, not caring.

"Mr. 'Dub' Meigs."

"Oh, I guess I've heard about him. He's pretty good."

"If he take seventy-five he mighty put out."

Lucian wandered up the inside stairs and across the ballroom floor, strange with its straw rug and the light coming from outside. He walked out on the porch, squinting into the glare that filled the afternoon hanging somnolently over the woods and clearings, over the smooth fields brown and green and plumed with the spouts of the sprinklers. He was standing by the white banisters when a roadster shot round the curve beneath, hissing over the gravel, and swung into the parking space. His attention fixed itself vividly on the two girls who got out of the car and crossed the road.

They disappeared for a moment under the porch, but he could hear them chattering and mounting the stairs. As their heads appeared above the floor he received an indefinite shock of alert beauty, though his eyes saw nothing more specific than brown skin and blue broadcloth pointed up to a peculiarly provocative pitch with a bright lipstick; it was that confident implacable crimson that so startled him.

They came loose-jointedly up the steps, chewing gum with a white smile between phrases, flung him a quick glance that said to him somehow that they consciously made it short but were as aware of him as the longest stare would have made them. He watched their figures as they moved about in opening the screen door, passing through it, and fading out; then he looked back at the pattern of green and burned grass and the brown-splotched pine trees. He reached for his cigarette case, though he didn't particularly want to smoke; he felt different from sixty seconds before; he knew what it was.

He lighted the cigarette. He ought to go home; there would be nobody with his father after the nurse left. He moved away

79

from the banisters and strolled up to the corner of the porch and back. He ought to go; it was probably after five. But he felt that he couldn't go, that he hadn't the power to leave the porch. He wondered how long they would be inside. Perhaps they had gone down by the inner stairs. Then he heard a careless bang on the piano in the ballroom and a laugh; it somehow struck the same response in him as the color of their lips, he didn't know why. He walked along the banisters to a point opposite the door.

He was standing there, looking out over the empty course with assumed indifference, when the door opened. He turned and saw one of the girls moving toward the steps, slowly as if waiting for the other, a bathing suit swinging from her fingers by the shoulder straps. She looked past him up the porch for a brief second, then moved the chewing gum in her mouth and glanced at her waist.

"Excuse me," said Lucian, "but have you got a match?"

She looked at him in surprise. "What did you say?"

He laughed pleasantly. "I said, Have you got a match? or What time is it? or simply, Hello."

She turned away and swung her weight with leisurely grace from one foot to the other in a kind of dance.

"Going swimming?"

"Maybe."

"I can swim."

"Well! Isn't that nice!"

"If you don't believe it I'll come along and show you."

"Well, for Goodness' sake!"

She gave him a cold stare that seemed on the verge of going into anger and started to turn away; the instant before her face was hidden a corner of her mouth broke into a smile.

"Wait a minute," said Lucian.

She leaned against the post at the head of the steps and flung him an oblique look, chewing the gum with the left side of her mouth, slowly, with an amateur toughness.

"Don't you think you need somebody along," said Lucian,

80

trying to disguise his eagerness, "to—to buy you chewing gum and things—"

She tossed her head away from him, apparently really offended now, and went deliberately down the stairs. The other girl ran out with an inquisitive glance at Lucian and overtook her; they linked arms and walked carelessly to the car.

He watched them with some anger, saw them plop down in the seat of the roadster, and went inside.

He paused a minute on the dance floor, then went back to a window; as he watched them, he saw them pass beyond the porch and fling a laugh up at the spot where he had stood.

He got in the car and returned down the hill to the city. As he coasted down the trolley line, his stimulated eye fell upon three girls in summer clothes waiting on a corner for an up-town street car; two of them were standing facing the road, the third, her back to him and hatless, was sitting on the conical top of a fire plug, the point of it between her legs.

When he stopped in front of the house the street was quiet. Up the sidewalk a negro yardman with a long black hose was watering the warm brick of the pavement. A street car bumped leisurely over the switch at the corner. The bright sun was already behind the top of the magnolia tree.

It was dark in the empty waiting room. A dry tepid air filled the twilight. He glanced toward the window where the desk was. The typewriter was covered, the drawers closed. A wave of blinding disappointment rose over him; she had gone.

Then he became conscious of the fan on the marble-topped table, droning its hot summer song, swinging its beacon slowly over the empty chairs. He stared at it; she always turned it off before she went home.

He went to the door into the office.

Here he stopped for an instant and swept his eyes quickly over the room; it was empty too. Then he saw something move beyond the half-closed door into the examining room.

He walked deliberately across the floor and paused in the opening. She was standing on one foot in her underclothes,

81

pulling off a white stocking, steadying herself on a corner of the operating table. She gasped when she saw him and stood there a second or two too startled to move, her foot raised, the stocking half off. Behind him the humming of the fan came to him from the outer room, loud and soft as it looked to the right and to the left. He waited there for a minute, uncertainly, then he saw the expression in her eyes begin to change.

6. Local Page

Sunday, July 5

MR. JAMES McFARLANE hooked his eyeshade over his forehead and flung open his new paper to the local page:

YOUNGSTER CARDS
LOW MEDAL SCORE
IN JULY TOURNEY
ELBERT ("DUB") MEIGS
NETS SNAPPY 71 IN 4TH
JULY MEDAL PLAY CLASH—

*1,600 REGISTERED
AT LOCAL OFFICES
FOR EMPLOYMENT—*

CURTIS BAPTISTS
HAVE GREAT FALL,
WINTER PROGRAM—

"What the hell kind of a headline do you call— Dewey!"
"Dewey gone."
"For Christ's sake—"
82

SOCIETYHILL POET WINS HIGH
PRAISE FROM DR. W. L. PHELPS—

The Female Secret Saving Club will meet
this afternoon at 4 o'clock at the home of Miss
Navey Green, 1229—

*ONE BOUND OVER
ON PROHI CHARGE—*

OVER 200 ENROLL
IN BIBLE SCHOOL—

"HUMAN CORK" BEGINS
ENDURANCE SWIM HERE
SUNDAY AT MUNICIPAL
Norris Kellam, the "Human Cork," present
holder of the world's endurance record in fresh
water, will throw his 307-pound floating bulk—

*BAMBERG'S MELON
SEASON IS OPEN—*

FINISH PLANS FOR
STATE GOLF EVENT
ALABAMA AMATEUR TO
BEGIN SEPT. 2 WITH
18-HOLE QUALIFYING

*OVER 500 ATTEND
TYPHOID CLINIC—*

ROTARY CLUB WILL
DOUBLE CAPACITY
OF SUNSHINE CAMP
EXTRA PERIODS PLANNED
FOR 100 KIDDIES—

PEACEFUL LITTLE ICEPICK
POPULAR AS DEADLY WEAPON—

83

GRIM REAPER PACES
STORK IN RACE FOR
SUPREMACY IN 1932—

COLORED EVANGELIST
SCORES TRIUMPH AT
WAYCROSS GA RALLY

NEGRO PREACHER PROMISES

OLD-TIME MIRACLES AT HIS

SOUTH GEORGIA REVIVAL

"Bishop" Divine, itinerant negro Evangelist,
who has been conducting an old-fashioned revival meeting—

CHAPTER THREE

1. Beauty is a Beast

Thursday, July 2

"LISTEN to me a minute," said Austin; "I think I've got something."

"Great God!" said Dr. Abercorn. "How many times do I have to tell you you haven't got anything. You don't recognize perfect health when you—"

"No, I don't mean that. As a matter of fact, I never felt better. I don't know what has happened but I'm feeling fine."

"I'm glad to hear it."

"What I mean is, I think I've discovered something. I think I've hit on a big truth."

"Well, some kind and Christian executioner ought to do away with you right now while you still think so, right now in your bliss—"

"Wait a minute now. I think this means something. . . . Have another drink."

"I follow you so far," said Dr. Abercorn. He reached for the decanter and held his glass up in front of his eye.

"Don't you think you're over-skeptical about the discovery of a big truth?"

"Do you call it skepticism, Austin, to doubt if acid will turn pink litmus paper blue?"

"But truth isn't a matter of pink or blue," said Austin, somewhat nettled. "You can't put your finger on it as easily as that.

85

It seems like the kind of reasoning that used to say if a person isn't guilty he won't burn. It's a sort of Yes or No attitude."

"Go ahead, I'm listening. I think you're wrong about everything in the world, but I'm listening. What is the big truth you've discovered?"

"It's about beauty."

"All right."

"I saw Branch Wheaton the other day. He's in the fertilizer business, you know. I didn't have anything to do; Gwen had gone out to the air field—"

"Who's that?"

"Mrs. Owens. She and her husband are staying with me."

Dr. Abercorn gave Austin a penetrating look but made no comment.

"Branch was going out to the factory. I went along with him and he showed me round. He told me a few very interesting things about the fertilizer industry—"

"Are you talking about fertilizer now, or beauty?"

"Both,—if you won't think I'm crazy—"

"Insanity, Austin, is purely a police-court term. It is merely a convenient way of describing a person who is no longer capable of living on quite the same basis as the majority of us."

"All right then. I'm sane—"

"Why not just say 'reasonable'?"

"Well, anyway—"

"All right, Austin, 'anyway.'"

"Branch Wheaton took me to the fertilizer factory and told me a few very interesting things. He told me that in the thirteen Southern States there were about four hundred and fifty fertilizer factories. Of that number, two hundred and twenty are located in South Carolina, Georgia, and Alabama. Half, you see, of the fertilizer factories in the Southern States are right down here in our corner. In the whole country there are about six hundred and twenty-five factories. One-third of all the fertilizer factories in the country are right here in three states. And these three states are really the South, mind you. Texas is West, Mississippi and

86

Louisiana are French and Creole, North Carolina and Tennessee are influenced by the mountains, Florida—well, Florida is Florida. This is the heart of the South; you can't get any farther into the South than this. This is Anglo Saxon and African, this is the original cotton country. These three states are the South; and these three states have one-third of all the fertilizer factories in the United States. The fertilizer factory isn't on any of their state seals, but it ought to be. It is the real symbol of the South. . . . Are you listening?"

"I'm listening."

"In other words, the unfertility of the soil must be something special."

"It's exhausted, not unfertile."

"It's the same thing today; it makes a hard living. You have to put almost as much money into the ground as you get out. So you miss, right off the bat, one of the most important ingredients of art and beauty: an excess, a superabundance. Before you get art and beauty you get an excess. That's true with a nation or with a city or with an individual; no artist does his best work when his feet are cold. But I am thinking, not so much of a conscious art, as of an unconscious beauty, and I am wondering if it isn't a good deal more than a mere coincidence that these three states which are so strikingly unfertile are at the same time so strikingly ugly. You do recognize that this is an ugly country, don't you?"

"In a way, Austin, but—"

"No, it's undoubtedly ugly. You feel attached to it because you have associations with these red rivers and these sandhills and these pine barrens; you may even prefer rusty galvanized iron to weathered stone, but you wouldn't anywhere except in your home country. . . . What I'm getting at is that I think there's some connection between the beauty of a country and its fertility. In fact, what I'm getting at, doc, is that they're the same thing. It's the same thing interpreted by two different parts of a man's make-up. Beauty is the soul's word for fertility."

"Well—"

"Now that must be qualified to this extent. I am speaking in reference to an average man, one whose natural instincts are free and unconscious. Many people will find beauty for them in a barren landscape, in rocky mountains; but that's a cultivated taste; it isn't simple and spontaneous. Spontaneously beautiful countries are places like Ireland and southern England, Kentucky, all strikingly fertile. It's a conditioned reflex—"

"Ah!—"

"The farmer doesn't think of a sunset as beautiful; it just means clear weather or rain. . . . Man's soul has followed along after his body. For thousands of years his body has rejoiced at the sight of fertile ground. It means ease and plenty. It's a land of Canaan. Milk and honey and all that. And after a while a land with that appearance became the symbol of beauty. He saw beauty in a land that was full of the characteristics which generations of his ancestors had found to be indicative of fertility. . . . I have often wondered why I could never see anything really beautiful in one of our fields of cotton, for example, or fine corn. And I think it is because the rest of the landscape doesn't fit in with it. You can get a field of fine cotton with artificial fertilizer in an unfertile land. But that's all you can get; you can't get the real things that make it beautiful. In a country naturally fertile you get a lot more than rich soil; you get order, you get a sense of excess, of surplus; you get good houses, good barns, good fences, you get a little paint; you get self-confidence and pride, the pride of an engineer in his locomotive. All that has an effect on the visible country. . . . Now you may be going to object that the beauty of a country depends a lot on the contour, which these things can't change. I grant you, of course, that the contour is a tremendous factor, but the curious thing about that is this: broadly speaking, you will find all fertile country of the same general contour."

Dr. Abercorn frowned, but Austin went on.

"The case of a fertile river valley is exceptional; the fertility there has been built up by deposits from floods. I am speaking of naturally fertile land. You can almost look at a topographical map and pick out a fertile country. And for this reason. The fertility of a country, aside from its natural ingredients, the ingredients it had in the beginning, depends on erosion. On steep hillsides the rain has tended to wash the soil into the valley. In general, a fertile land will be an easily-rolling land, the slopes gentle enough to hold the soil. So I claim that the contour we think of as most beautiful is the contour most effective in preserving the plant food from erosion. . . . I really think there's something in it."

"Maybe there is—"

"Now the interesting thing about it all is that you find a corresponding attitude when you consider human beings. It is complicated there by the various inhibitory influences of civilization and government and Christianity, so that the externals are sometimes deceptive as to the form beneath. But I believe when we say that a woman is beautiful we mean exactly what we mean when we say that a land is beautiful. We mean that she has a great many of the attributes which, over thousands of years, the males of the race have come to find indicated fertility. The more-or-less unconscious desire to preserve our kind has conditioned our idea of beauty. You go to the Orient and you are a little bit befuddled. You think the women are terrible; at first you think they are all ugly. That's because you don't know the clews, they have a slightly different set of attributes to indicate fertility. But after a while you begin to catch on and the women begin to get beautiful. . . . Look at the characteristics which the average uncomplicated male thinks of as beautiful; one of the first is the eyes, large, deep-colored eyes. Hair is another, gleaming hair, long eyelashes. The voice, the pitch and the resonance of the voice. All of these things are connected more or less directly (I think I'm right in saying so) with the endocrine glands. They are indicative of the state of the glands, which is to say they are indicative of fertility—"

"Wait a minute. That's saying a good deal. We don't know—"

"We have had plenty of hints. We know that the thyroid gland affects the eye in some way; some other one seems to

89

affect the growth of the hair. For thousands of years hair has not only been a symbol of beauty in a woman but of strength and power, and, probably unconsciously, of fertility, in a man. Has there ever been a popular conception of a 'he man' without hair on his chest? I can't imagine it. And look at the change in the growth of hair at puberty. Look at the change in the voice. They go together. They are all connected in some way. They are all lures to supply the individual's demand for procreation. And they change as the demand changes, become more alluring as the demand grows, less alluring as it declines. They are the scent of flowers, the color. As the demand becomes greater these indices become more, what we call, beautiful. You can almost tell if a woman is in love by looking at her. . . . What I say, in other words, is this: no woman can possibly be emotionally cold if she is beautiful,—except through environment and training. Of course that's quite an exception, but I think you've clarified a lot if you know that left to itself, left to itself, I say, ardor coincides with beauty."

Dr. Abercorn gave Austin the half-amused penetrating glance he had given him before; "You speak as one having authority, Austin, have you checked these things, so to speak, in the laboratory?"

Austin flushed slightly. "No, I haven't," he said parenthetically. Then he went on again, trying to maintain the scientific note in his voice but having some difficulty in ignoring the specific application to Gwendolyn, "But the unknown quantity is reduced by my theory from the woman herself to her training and environment. If you can ascertain these and find they have been relatively unimportant, have not interfered particularly with her natural development, I believe you will find her true to her appearance. I don't mean, of course, that in any individual instance a man is primarily interested in fertility, but that what he's interested in goes hand in hand with fertility—"

"In the cause of furthering scientific knowledge, I think you ought to be encouraged to go into the field and conduct whatever experiments you feel are necessary to establish—"

90

"Now just how this theory of beauty can be applied to works of art, I am not quite prepared to say. The problem is made a good deal more difficult by our art's being built today on so many layers of self-consciousness. We try to be natural, but we only become more artificial by trying; it is like asking a man of sixty to forget all the things he has seen and heard and felt during his life. It isn't possible. But in the old days, when art was natural, I think my idea of beauty could be applied quite readily."

"In China you can hire a man for thirty cents who will come to your house and stay all day painting beautiful things on the wall—"

2. Pity the Blind Man

Thursday, July 2

THE Georgetown & Southwestern Alabama ran a freight that summer that got into the yards about three in the morning. You could hear it for a quarter of an hour before it got in, rolling down the ridge between Brier Creek and Upper Three Runs, blowing its long whistle with a sort of contented melancholy like a negro walking along a country road singing to himself. If it happened to be a damp night you could hear it from Summerville as it stopped for a minute in silence at the yardmaster's office, then went on in, ringing its bell.

Beaver dropped off as it slowed down and lay on his belly against the embankment until the caboose had passed. Then he lifted his head and looked round him. It was a dark night. There was a yellow lamp in the window of the office, but no other light except the two lanterns on the tail of the caboose drawing in together down the track amidst the diminishing chuckling of the trucks over the joints, and a rosy glow in the sky farther up over the engine from the open door of the firebox. Off somewhere in the dark the frogs began to take up their call again. He sat up in the short weeds and began groping through the ragged pockets of his trousers; mentally he checked each item as his fingers touched it: cup, spectacles, sign, pencils, three dimes, two nickels, three cents. The Bishop had given him half a dollar to get started on. Sometimes the Bishop didn't give him anything; it depended on the collection. They were doing a pretty good week in Waycross, considering the price of cotton; the Bishop was getting about all the free money those Waycross niggers had.

"You go on up to Georgetown, Beaver. I ain't goin' to cure you this time. And here, here's half a dollar for you."

The Bishop always looked after him. That was why he hadn't given him any more than half a dollar; he didn't want him to enjoy himself right yet. When they finished with Georgetown he was going to give him something good; Georgetown was the last stand. The Bishop was getting tired. He was planning on going back to Jamaica after Georgetown. He told him he was going to give him two hundred dollars if everything went well.

"You conduct yourself until then in Christian purity, Beaver," he said with his wide white grin, "and I'll give you enough money to buy yourself all the black girls in the state of Alabama!"

"Yassa," said Beaver, laughing, hitching up his shapeless trousers.

"You rascal!"

He was grand, grand. Class; all the class in the world. Maybe he didn't ride that Lincoln limousine!

"You go on up to Georgetown, Beaver; I'll be along in a few weeks. You just 'tarry till I come.'"

He felt round in the weeds for his stick, got up and set off down the track.

He had never hit Georgetown on the G. & S. A. before. But the Bishop had given him directions: drop off the train when it stopped at the despatcher's office on the edge of the yards, then walk on in, keeping on the left side of the bank.

In about a mile he would come to a canal; walk on across the trestle. Leave the track beyond the canal and he would be in The Terry. The Bishop always told you just how he wanted something done. You did things just so for the Bishop. You didn't usually fail him but once; he could smile at you in a way that made something at the back of your neck get cold. He had never failed the Bishop but that once and he wouldn't have failed him then but for that yellow gal. Yellow gals! Make a preacher lay his Good Book down! . . . Listen to that old dog gone rooster! Must be getting on to day.

3. Rain Cloud

Friday, July 3

IT was about six o'clock when Dr. Troupe closed his office door and set out to see his patient. The high sun glared down Broad Street like the blast from a furnace, but he didn't notice it; he was digging in his memory for perhaps one more detail of her stay in the office that he might not yet have relived. He was still somewhat dazzled by all of it; during the afternoon he would have decided that the whole thing had been a dream, but there on the rack was the towel with the pink smear on it where he had wiped his lips after she had gone. There was no denying that. And he hadn't seen her at the airport; he remembered an open plane with a red and yellow fuselage and a metal propeller, but he hadn't seen any women at the field at all. . . . He crossed over to the shady side of the street.

The traffic was mostly outbound. All along the row of parked cars he could hear the grinding of starters; there were spaces in the line; people were going home.

As he crossed the baked convexity of Broad Street the sun's

93

light changed to a reflected lividness; the air seemed to settle into a still sheen like a pool as the pebble sinks. He looked about him for the cause; up the street to the west beyond the dome of the water oaks, he saw a great bruised canopy of clouds, heavy with rain. He paused a moment on the corner to watch it.

"Looks like we're going to get it this time," a stranger said to him, stopping too.

"We certainly need it."

"It'll break up this heat."

A line of lightning split the curtain without a sound, the sun faded out, and a soft noise drifted in as of a chest pushed across the bare floor of the room above.

He left the corner as fast as he could walk; if he hurried he might be able to get to Dr. Abercorn's before it broke. A spiral of wind on the sidewalk ahead of him twirled some pieces of paper into the air. He started running.

He stopped in the areaway under Dr. Abercorn's steps and looked back, the perspiration pouring down his cheeks. The clouds had already shifted to the north; almost as he watched, they moved into the northeast and the sun appeared again, as if the town had been a dirigible that had changed its course to go round the storm. He took off his hat and wiped his wet forehead while the purple diminished perceptibly into the northeast. A pedestrian across the street slowed down to a walk. A blind man tapped his way out of the shelter of an old livery stable door. With a disappointment almost personal, Dr. Troupe turned about and went into the waiting room.

There was no one there, but a fan on a marble-topped table swung its beacon slowly over the empty chairs. Then he remembered that in his haste he had come in the wrong door; the doctor was upstairs. He took a step toward the hall, then paused; they had evidently forgotten to shut off the fan. For a moment he considered going on, then he went back into the room and cut it off; the humming died away into silence while the blades were still whirling.

He went upstairs.

94

4. Telfair & Co.

DOWN in that part of Georgetown where B.C. means, not Before Christ, but Bales of Cotton, there was not as much activity as there used to be. A good deal of cotton still passed through the town, but there were not quite as many mule-drawn vans clattering up and down Cotton Row and not quite as many cotton factors tilted back in front of the board in the Exchange. Cotton was still, however, the principal crop of the countryside and trading in it still the principal business of the city. The old warehouses still lined the river bank and their worn red walls, pierced here and there by the great square portals into the yards, still rose up with some dignity behind the water oaks along the Row. The gravel yards were comparatively little used, but the ponderous barrels of black water, "For Fire Only," still sat ready on bricks round the court and the red round-bottomed buckets still hung above them on their old wire hooks. Telfair & Company's warehouses ran all the way through the block to the spur track on the river bank.

At nine-fifteen, when Showers took off his hat and walked through the office, Mr. Telfair hadn't come in. This meant that Mr. Telfair had taken himself out to the clay mine; he drove out every now and then to make sure things were getting along all right. Mining clay wasn't Mr. Telfair's business; he had cussed all day when old man Baker sent word he couldn't pay him and he would have to take the clay mine or nothing; he took it, though, and he was making money out of it; Mr. Telfair knew how to make money. When he went out to the mine it also meant that at about ten-thirty he would drive his car up on the sidewalk in front of the warehouse and call for Showers to come wash all that country dust off it.

But that gave him over an hour. He went back to the shady platform on the river side, propped himself in the angle between

95

a barrel of water and the brick wall, and let his heavy eyelids drop. He was badly in need of a little sleep; the night had been exciting but wearifying. . . .

He was awakened by somebody up front bellowing, "Showers!"

"Comin' up!" he shouted and glided into the black warehouse. Across the building at the other end of the aisle between the walls of cotton bales lying on skids and stepped up in tiers to the high roof, was a bright line of sun beyond a partly-opened tin-covered door. In the light of it he found a bucket and threw out the water in it with one big hand; he picked up a stiff chamois skin from the end of a bale of cotton where it had been left to dry, then, with the straw hat that had belonged to Mr. Telfair in 1922 slanted forward over his eyes, he crossed the court to the broad gate and went out on the sidewalk to Mr. Telfair's car. He put the bucket down and stood with his fists on his hip bones while a short negro, his bow legs accentuated by his trousers being clipped at the ankles for riding a bicycle, pushed his machine by close in the shade of the high russet wall.

"Wal, Pig Meat!" he said. "What you say?"

"Just tol'able, Mr. Showers," said Pig Meat. "How's yourse'f?"

"Oh, I'm rackin' along."

"Kinda hot today, Mr. Showers."

"It's been hot since four o'clock. The sun rose hot." He looked off down the street after the two-wheeled cart and the tinkling bell of an ice-cream peddler. Then his manner changed: "Aw aw, boy!"

Pig Meat turned round. "Aw aw, Mr. Showers!"

"Here come sump'n, Pig Meat!"

A negro girl in a red béret and beach pyjamas, carrying a purple umbrella, had come round the corner and was walking toward them, chin up, eyes sightless.

Showers ran his fingers up the back of his head and tapped his hat forward.

"Hot dog!" said Pig Meat, as she passed between them.

"Great God, Miss Agnes!"

She walked with elaborate deafness two strides beyond them,

96

then, on the third, managed to give her seat an almost imperceptible twitch.

Showers flopped over with a long-armed crack of his palms, a scraping of ecstatic shoes, and a ringing shout of explosive laughter. Pig Meat let the bicycle drop and butted his shoulder against the wall.

The girl looked back and flung them a wide grin, walking on and with innate artistry refraining from repeating the gesture.

"Lord, Mr. Showers, you're a sight!"

"Mind out there, Pig Meat, for the blind man."

"Aw aw, brother! 'Scuse me."

"What's the matter, brethren?" said the blind man. " 'Pears like y'all enjoyin' sump'n."

"Dog gone, brother, I sho is sorry for you! Yo' eyes is sho a calamity to you!"

"Go your route, Pig Meat, go your route!" Showers hitched up the crotch of his cotton-flecked trousers and went under the gate.

He came back presently dragging a leaky garden hose and sent a languid squirt at Mr. Telfair's pink front wheels. . . .

Mr. Telfair paused in his sky-blue sample room, pushing his hat back on his round bald head and looking over the sky-blue slat-bottomed tables. Most of them were empty; the market, that July, had dropped to about ten cents and there wasn't much cotton moving. On one table, though, he saw a new lot of samples.

"Whose cotton is that, Tucker?"

"Old man Ben Gray, sir."

"He tell you to sell it?"

"Yessir. We had a letter from him this morning. Miss Judy, have you got that letter there from old man—that's it. Thank you, ma'am."

"He's got a good margin, hasn't he, Tucker?" said Mr. Telfair, pulling his starched sleeves out of his linen coat. Miss Judy reached for it; "I can hang it up, thank you, ma'am, Miss Judy.

I'm not altogether ready to drop dead yet; I can still stagger to the hatrack."

"He's got about two cents, Mr. Telfair."

"How did the market open?"

"October's up about eight points."

"I don't see what he wants to sell it for now, he's held it this long. That cotton's been here two years, hasn't it?"

"Mighty near."

A messenger leaned his bicycle against the door post and handed Tucker a telegram.

"Well, go on sell it, Tucker, if that's what he wants—"

"Here's a wire from old man Gray now. He wants to know what you think about selling."

Mr. Telfair read the message and walked on into his office. In a few minutes he turned to Miss Judy, "Take a telegram to Mr. Ben Gray at Due West, Georgia. October stronger this morning don't want to advise you because I may be wrong but feel generally more optimistic about price outlook. Get that off right now—"

He was interrupted by Miss Judy's releasing the buzzer that in fifty seconds would bring the messenger. She flung back the typewriter carriage with a slight cocking of the head and finished the line in a dry flurried clatter.

Mr. Telfair took a cigar out of a drawer.

"Write a letter, Miss Judy, to Mr. Charles R. Snelling, President. The Great Lakes Paper Company, 205-9 Woodward Avenue, Detroit, Michigan. Dear sir. Make that Dear Mr. Snelling. In reply to your favor of the eleventh regarding the four notes of your company to The Alabama Clay Company, due July fifteenth, two of which you are paying and two which you would like to carry over unrenewed to be met by you October first or prior, would say this will be quite satisfactory to us. The mortgage we hold we consider adequate security, and any little thing like this we can do to help a good customer weather these hard times we are glad to do. We are pleased to learn that prospects look brighter for you and that you expect to clean the notes up

98

in the early fall. Paragraph. We enclose two of the notes stamped paid. With kind personal regards, we remain, yours very truly. Just run that off on The Alabama Clay Company stationery—"

"I understand perfectly, Mr. Telfair."

She was the only woman stenographer on Cotton Row. It was a tradition in Georgetown that the cotton business was for men; there were women in the real estate offices and in the brokers' offices, but until he hired her there had never been a woman in a Georgetown cotton office. She herself was proud of the distinction, but there were times nowadays when he was not so satisfied; he thought she was one of the best stenographers that had ever hung up hat and pocketbook but she somehow bothered him. Now and then she would catch his eye and hold it a split second longer than necessary, and he would begin to wonder all over again what in the world was he going to do with this woman; in one split second the past fifteen years were summed up and tossed back in front of him with a sly laugh. She had proficient eyes, dark with a richness suggestive of her Jewish father, and her hair, now going gray at the sides, had once undulated beyond the sensitive corners of Mr. Telfair's eyes in raven-black waves.

He had seen her first behind the counter in Pavinovsky's Shoe Hospital on Marbury Street. It was his habit to let his chauffeur Sam take care of his shoes, and he might never have seen her had not Sam carried the shoes one day and early the next asked permission to go down to Meyer's Mill to his brother-in-law's funeral; so on the way out to dinner he stopped for the shoes himself. She called him by name, which pleased him, and gave him the package with a smile. Having an eye for such things, he thought that the upper part of her figure, all that was visible above the counter, was really of exceptional charm, and its gracious and living curves remained with him half way home. He felt that he would like to do something for her and a few days later he sent Sam out to ascertain however he could where she lived, if she were married, and things like that, having in mind the possibility of eventually offering her an apartment on lower

Walton Way or perhaps even a bungalow in Highland Court. Sam brought him the news that she was Miss Judith Pavinovsky and that she was usually met at the door, both at noon and at five-thirty, by a Mr. Jebby in an old Ford. So Mr. Telfair desisted.

But he didn't forget her and when, one afternoon about a quarter to six, he saw a pliant figure waiting for a street car near Marbury Street, he scrutinized the curve of her bust accentuated by the flatness of her abdomen and, hoping it might be she, he offered her a ride home.

He thought she was about twenty-two, but she was nearer thirty, and she was positive in her outlook. She said she had been a stenographer in Atlanta, but when her father died the year before she had come back to work in the business and be near her mother.

"Stenographer?" said Mr. Telfair. "Are you good?"

"Pretty fair," she said, giving him the look.

"How would you like to go in the cotton business?"

She laughed an honest knowing laugh.

"I'm in the shoe repair business."

"There's a better future in the cotton business."

"And besides, my boy friend wouldn't like for me to be in the cotton business, and besides—"

But she came and she stayed.

She liked the way he addressed her, the way he smoked his cigar, the monograms on his shirt sleeves, the whiteness of his canvas shoes in the summer. He never rolled up his sleeves and only on the hottest days would he take off his coat. He wore a clean shirt every morning. Her father had never done that; Jebby didn't do that. She realized with a quiver that she was associating with something better than she was used to; she was shocked at herself to remember that she had once been considering marrying Jebby. That winter when she moved into the apartment at the Oglethorpe Arms, Jebby threatened to shoot himself and her and Mr. Telfair; but at just that moment he was offered a job as linesman by a friend of Mr. Telfair's in the

Atlanta office of The Southern Bell Telephone and Telegraph Company, and he was persuaded to accept that alternative.

She lived contentedly in the apartment for nearly twelve years and she knew good things to eat and good manners and good clothes. She was philosophic about Mr. Telfair; he treated her like a lady and she loved him for it; she thought he showed her far more respect than her father had shown her mother. She knew him through and through and her eyes sometimes filled with that removed expression of tenderness that a mother has for her one boy. Whatever he said was compact with truth and wisdom, and anything he recommended her doing was as good as done. The prime quality of his linen vouched for his opinions. She had even on one occasion made $40,000 for him by extending her hospitality at his bidding to a gentleman from Liverpool who represented the English firm with which Mr. Telfair traded the next day when he bought 10,000 bales of cotton in Liverpool on the very friendly and confidential assurance of this Englishman that his country was going off the gold-standard; when that happened forty-eight hours later, Liverpool cotton jumped $4.00 a bale and Mr. Telfair sold. In return for this he built a neat bungalow of what he thought was Spanish design in the lower part of town and gave it to her and her mother. He kept the apartment, but they used it only spasmodically. She made no attempt to deny to herself that now, after fifteen years, she was something of a nuisance to Mr. Telfair.

He said to her on one of these occasions, standing in front of the fire, his *Commerce and Finance* on the mantelpiece behind him, speaking in his manner of mock brusqueness that she liked so much,

"Woman, I want you to get married."

"Who am I going to marry?" she said; she had learned the solecisms permitted a lady.

"Who! My God, there are plenty of people. You are good-looking, you've still got one of the best figures in Davis County."

She shook her head with a little smile and went on with the monogram on one of his shirt sleeves.

"I can't marry you, you know," said Mr. Telfair.

"I don't want you to marry me."

"But suppose I want to marry somebody else."

"That's a widower's privilege."

"I'd feel better about it, though, if you got married."

"You don't have to worry about me."

"But you think it over, will you?"

She laughed a little and shook her head again. . . .

Mr. Telfair lighted the cigar and turned to his morning mail. She reached for a fly-killer and smacked one on a corner of his desk. He frowned but read on: "Dear Sir, In reply to yours—"; "Dear Mr. Telfair, My Cotton—"; "Gentlemen, Answering your favor—"; "My dear Mr. Telfair—"; "Dear Sir—"; "Gentlemen—"; "Darling—"!

He jumped back as if someone had just told him the Cotton Exchange had closed.

DARLING,

I love you. I have always loved you. I will forgive everything if only you will marry me—

Mr. Telfair looked at the signature but "Jeb" meant nothing to him; he bit down on his cigar and reached toward the waste basket to see the address on the envelope.

"I'll get it for you, Mr. Telfair."

"Get an envelope from the—The Southern Bell Telephone and Telegraph Company, Atlanta. This ain't for me."

She leaned quickly over his shoulder. "May I see it, Mr. Telfair?"

Mr. Telfair shoved it at her and went on with his mail.

When he had finished he picked up the morning copy of the *Daily News,* announced that he was going to step up to the exchange a minute, took a key with a Dennison tag on it out of a drawer and retired, via the exchange, to a private cabinet in a corner of the warehouse adjoining his office.

It was here that the name, Jeb, began to take shape before him and he remembered at last his secretary's old suitor. He exhaled a cloud of cigar smoke and turned this cogent fact over in his mind. Devoted for fifteen years. Willing to forgive everything if she would marry him— If! Why, certainly she would marry him. Here was the chance he had been waiting for. Give them a present; give them a trip to Niagara Falls, to Europe, round the world! It was the chance of a lifetime! He would have to get a new stenographer, they would have a baby in nine months. He would have to get a new stenographer. Have to? Good Lord, what a privilege!

It was about noon when he looked round and saw that the outer office was empty.

"Well, I reckon you're due for congratulations," he said, grinning.

"Why?" said Miss Judy innocently.

"Atlanta's a fine town."

Miss Judy sniffed.

"Look here, girl, you're not by any chance considering the possibility of turning this fine boy down again, are you?"

She hit at a lone and cheerless fly on her shorthand book; "You don't think I'd marry Jeb—er—now, do you?"

"Why not!"

"Oh, I don't know."

"Listen! You'll make him a fine little wife, better than he deserves, I reckon—"

"No," she said, patting with the fly-killer on her typewriter. "I'm spoiled, Mr. Telfair." She laughed.

"Spoiled, hell! Do—do you mean to say I've—I've spoiled you!"

"Yes, sir."

"What the—"

"You have, Mr. Telfair; there's no use—"

"But, God almighty, girl—"

"You don't really think I could put up with Jeb now, do you?"

"But—"

"I'm used to gentlemen now, Mr. Telfair. I just couldn't possibly. I've been with you too long now—"

The telegraph boy came in through the blue room and handed a message into Miss Judy's outstretched hand. She opened the envelope neatly with a paper knife and gave it to Mr. Telfair. It said:

THANKS FOR YOUR TELEGRAM HOLD MY COTTON
BEN GRAY

Mr. Telfair looked up as Tucker came through the warehouse door with his weight book and a handful of stencils.

"Tucker," he said, "here's a telegram from old man Ben Gray. He wants us to hold his cotton. Just take it off the tables."

"Yes, sir."

"And, oh, Tucker."

"Yes, sir."

"Just step out and see what the market is."

Tucker shifted his yellow straw hat from the very back to the very front of his head and strode out into the brilliant sun.

"Miss Judy, take a letter to Mr. Ben Gray at Due West, Georgia. Dear Mr. Gray. Your wire received. We are holding your cotton. There is, I think, every reason to believe the market is going to improve. In spite of the fairly favorable weather, the crop through all this section from what I hear is short, and recent reports of heavy rains in Texas point to the possibility of a million bales shortage. As I wired you, I don't want to advise you one way or another; I've been in this business too long to think I can tell what the market's going to do. And it's too early in the season yet to make any responsible guess about the crop. I can't see much reason for the market to decline appreciably, though, and there is a good possibility for an advance. Anyhow, this is my candid opinion. Paragraph."

"I understand, Mr. Telfair."

"The latest quotation is— What's the market, Tucker?"

"October eased off a little bit, Mr. Telfair. It's ten and an eighth."

104

"Suppose you just leave out that last sentence, Miss Judy."

"Ending, 'Anyhow, this is my candid opinion.'"

"Yes. Oh, say, 'Drop in to see me when you come to town.'"

5. And Thou—

WHEN Nora's mother and father shut the front door behind them the clock at the Arsenal was striking five. It was really not only striking five, she thought, but five o'clock on a Sunday afternoon in midsummer; she thought she could have heard it and known by the sound it was Sunday and midsummer,—Sunday and summer and the servants gone and the clocks ticking and a vacuous melancholy floating in the air on the solemn green perfume of the tea-olive by the garden window. She sat down at the piano and laid her fingers desultorily on the keys; she knew the paragraph by heart:

> The many friends of young Dr. Lucian Abercorn are delighted to learn of his return to Georgetown after an extensive sojourn in European capitals. He is staying with his father, Dr. Henry Abercorn, in the Abercorn home on—

The paper was old; he had probably been in Georgetown for two weeks. Maybe he wasn't going to telephone her at all. The clear notes of the treble, venturing timidly off the strings, masking themselves with a sort of rigid matter-of-factness, fell off suddenly into the futility of a minor chord. Her left hand traced three notes of the *allegretto* of Brahms's Symphony in C-minor. Her eyes changed. She lifted her head. She began the first movement of Beethoven's Third Concerto.

105

She remembered music downstairs when she was a child in the nursery. She knew that now, through all the empty rooms of the old house music was beginning to flow,—space, filled with the poetry of time passing; time, flowing silently by, now beginning to sing; mute seconds, now embroidered with patterns of sound, flowing out from no origin into no fate. Or was there an origin? Time, coming from somewhere, going somewhere else; growing out of some embryo time, flooding past, dying and changing into something else; growing like a river out of cold springs on the slopes of far mountains, flooding past and down into an infinite sea. Or, time the recorder, the inanimate static recorder of change in everything else, non-changing, non-existent except through the changes of changing things, measurable only by change, the less change the less time. You might live a hundred years while someone beside you was living ten! Time, for one a thread of water, for another a streaming river; for one a chord, for another a symphony! . . . She stood up and walked away. Where was the crowded hour?

Certainly not here. This was home. Where people knew you,—knew you to just the wrong degree. It was just that kinship that threw things off, just that speaking what seemed to be the same language but wasn't. It was trying to teach somebody the proper way to play the piano after he has already learned an improper way; easier to teach somebody who has never seen a piano before. Easier to teach somebody to know you, easier to learn to know them, if you all begin as strangers. If you wanted to stand for what you were, for your own special uniqueness, go any place but home. You were just a certain generation at home,—just one of the fourth or fifth generation, as you might be a chicken out of the batch of eggs in the fourth or fifth incubator. You were not a person, you were an incubation. You settled into your parents' groove, you saw one small class of people. Imagine being where Pavinovsky was out of the question! Think of Pavinovsky's being out of the question! Her uncle had come down on the train with him, suggested innocently to her mother having him out to supper. And it was unthinkable. It really was.

You didn't see even somebody like Lucian. Just a slightly different groove. Still that was not impossible; she might see him,—if she stayed. She certainly wouldn't see him if she went away. What should she do? Stay as one of that generation and see him again, talk to him again, or go away as Nora and close that little page of her life. And then she might stay and still not see him.

She turned petulantly away from the window, then came back. He wasn't going to call her. That was two years ago, beyond the memory of man. And nothing to remember, even then. What difference did it make whether she saw him or not; better, maybe, if she didn't. Her mother hadn't liked him. People didn't understand him. He had his faults; perhaps he wasn't very kind; perhaps there were other things. But he had his feet on the ground; he didn't go mooning round, like Austin. He had more drive and push to him than anybody in Georgetown; he was going somewhere. If she had a little more of that—that fervor,—things might be different.

She watched a long-billed humming bird standing in the air in the midst of a sort of blur to snatch a glance into the bell of a flower on the trumpet vine. . . . The hard, flat beach of the Isle of Palms, the glare of the sun pressing down upon her, the dry wind hot against her face and legs. He came out of the chilly wet shade under the pavilion and spoke to her as he passed. She went on into the shadow and sat down, looking out over the shelving sand through the forest of dark barnacled posts at the lazy surf; then she turned away and watched him, small and vivid against the brilliance.

They walked up the beach to Fort Burke the day before he was coming back to Georgetown. At first he talked about the South; she remembered what he had said, remembered the half-jesting way in which he lifted his finger and said, "Listen, girl."

"Listen, girl," he said, "this is just a geographical human experiment. For the first time in history Nordics have lived below the 39th Parallel for as long as three generations. In India they are reënforced continually from England. We have been down here two hundred and fifty years, long enough to really contribute something. All right, what have we contributed? I say, 'All right, old South, let's see what you've got; just empty your bag out here for us and let's have a look.' What do we find? Lawyers? Oh, yes, plenty of lawyers. Doctors? Yes. But how about scientists and engineers and musicians and painters and poets? I want to lean backward on this, so suppose for the sake of argument we call Sidney Lanier a poet—. But our contributions, to say the least, have been very limited. Where are our Henry Adamses, our Copleys, our Holmeses and Lowells and Jameses—. Did it ever occur to you that the experiment might not be going so well?"

"That's silly."

"You have put Nordics on the 32nd Parallel and maybe it's not going to work—"

Under the palmetto trees, past the yellow and white barracks with the screened verandas, down along the sea wall molded of shells and pebbles, the slow somnolent surf tumbling in the heat.

"You aren't going to live here?"

"Oh, yes, I am. I'm interested in it,—more interested now than I ever was before."

"What do you mean?"

"I love you."

She laughed. "Impossible!" Then she was sorry. "At least it's very unlikely."

He wanted to kiss her, but she didn't want to.

The next afternoon he went away, and the beach seemed very broad and flat and finite. Four days later she found some pretext to drive up to Georgetown; she wanted to see him. The nurse answered the telephone.

"Mr. Abercorn's gone away."

"Gone? I didn't think he was going until next week."

"He changed his plans."

"Will—will he be back before he sails?"

"No, he won't."

"Thank you." She pulled the receiver fork down with her finger coldly and broke the connection; then she slowly took the receiver from her ear and slowly hung it up. She had a feeling that this was a portentous moment. . . .

Now, after two years, he had returned. And *she* was going away. He wasn't going to call her. Even if she should meet him accidentally, it wouldn't mean anything. It hadn't mattered to him. Or if it had, he had forgotten—

And there was the telephone ringing—

She was on her feet with a spring. . . . But, no. That was somebody else. Of course it was.

"Hello," she said.

"May I speak to Miss Fenwick, please?"

A flush surged up into her cheeks. She didn't know that voice! She tried to disguise her rapid breathing as she said, "This is she."

"Oh, Nora; I didn't recognize you. This is your old Uncle John."

"Hello, Uncle John," she said, suddenly empty. "I didn't recognize you either."

"I thought I might drop by if you weren't doing anything."

"I'm not doing anything."

"Are you all right? Your voice—"

"Yes, I'm fine. I've got some news for you."

"News?"

"I'm not going on our little trip."

6. Opaque

Sunday, July 5

IN 1841 old Hy V. Toombs, Austin's great-grandfather, head of the firm of Toombs & Daragne, Bankers, acquired, through the failure of one Jules Hardee to meet a note of $6,000, a tract of some ten thousand acres along the upper Congaree River fifteen miles above Georgetown on the Georgia side; a northern corner of it came within a few miles of the cross-roads called Due West. It was mostly pebble land and fairly fertile, but owing to the fact that between it and the Georgetown market lay Seven-Mile Shoals, making it inaccessible by water, and the impracticability of the winding Georgia roads, making it almost as inaccessible by land, the ownership of it descended upon him a good deal more like a debit than a credit. For a while it looked as if the only thing he could do to improve its value was either to rebuild the Georgia roads leading to it or to dynamite Seven-Mile Shoals. Neither of these methods, in the character of one of Alabama's more astute financiers, appealed to him in the least, and for several years he annually paid the taxes on the Hardee Place with considerable pain, not to say humiliation.

In studying one day, however, a large map of that part of the world hanging on his office wall, another scheme began to dawn upon him and he took his cheroot out of his brown teeth and stood before the map stroking his imperial for a quarter of an hour. The result of this was the formation of the Georgetown Canal Board, an organization of half a dozen leading citizens (Mr. Toombs declined to serve on the board) whose worthy purpose was to promote the civic importance of their town by digging a canal from a point on the river above Seven-Mile Shoals straight into the heart of Georgetown. The *Daily News,* privately owned in those days, having allowed some twelve thousand dollars of Mr. Toombs's gold to disappear apparently irretrievably over its dam, permitted hardly a morning to pass for half a year without in some way emphasizing the fact that with the opening of such a canal Georgetown would become one of the world's most thriving markets; lines of tight barges towed by fat mules would ply the stream from dawn until dark, hundreds of tons of farm equipment and manufactured goods would be carried regularly upcountry to the impatient plowmen, thousands of square miles of the fairest cotton land in Dixie would burst into blossom over night. When at length the brass tacks of a bond issue were got down to, it was voted with an enthusiasm that might have brought a blush to the cheeks of a lesser financier.

But five years later, though occasional barges were in truth hauled up the torpid stream and through the locks with a few plows aboard for the upcountry, and a few bales of cotton and tobacco were landed in the heart of the city, Georgetown's prosperity still lay shrouded in its perdurable obscurity, and Mr. Toombs still paid the annual taxes on the Hardee Place.

One day, however, Mr. Toombs's surveyor and a lean man of indeterminate age with flame-colored hair and freckles over the narrow bridge of his nose who gave his name as Robie Gray, went up the canal on one of the barges, were poled across the shallow river to the Georgia side, and landed at length on the old wharf that had belonged to Jules Hardee. He bought the place from Mr. Toombs for ten thousand dollars; he paid him two thousand down and a thousand a year for eight years and interest. Mr. Toombs heaved a great sigh and turned his mind to other projects.

He put half the money into Canal Bonds, which could be bought by then for about eighty dollars, and took up the matter of developing the canal into a power plant, his engineer having informed him that with the drop of fifty feet at the Georgetown end between the canal and the river there was room for several mills of one kind and another to be built on its inner bank. Before he died The Georgetown Manufacturing Company had dug a spillway connecting the upper level of the canal with a lower loop and erected a cotton mill of 14,000 spindles and 325 looms. By 1890 there were six cotton mills lining its bank.

As you go about the Georgetown streets today you cross one or another level of it innumerable times, one level wider than you could throw a rock, lined with a tow path of Chinese-red and stretching away more or less due north, through the tall water-grass and under the rows of willow trees planted to hold the bank, straight in the accusing direction of Mr. Toombs's old farm; another level is merely a narrow shallow ditch of orange

III

water, hardly moving, almost brushing the under sides of the flat bridges; another is a deep muddy cut with sycamore trees growing obliquely out of the inner bank and meeting over the water where you see an occasional negro fisherman baiting his hook out of an old tomato can. It finally wakes from its lethargy and leaps out from beneath the bridge on Broad Street in a tawny flood, plunging heavily downward with a smooth pink sheen and a savage tumult of sound into the caldron below and racing back into the river. Everywhere it is opaque.

Even when, now and then, an emergency arises and the gates at the locks up the river are closed and the water drains out to a depth of two or three feet, it is visually impenetrable and it hides to the last what has been entrusted to it. It keeps its counsel, as they say.

It cuts through a section of town that keeps its counsel too; a section of wooden weather-blackened houses, of dirt sidewalks, rain-washed, broken by the protruding roots of the oak trees that separate them from the unpaved streets; a section that glories in Sunday, teeming all day with sensuous life, ringing with whole-hearted wide-mouthed laughs, very striking to you if you happen to pass through fresh from the bare streets elsewhere, oppressive with a sabbath silence. They call it The Territory, or usually The Terry, and it hides its private business under an opacity like the canal's.

Mrs. Mattie Small lived on Kollock Street about two hundred yards before it crossed the second level. She had been there only about a year, but she was already considering moving. She didn't stay in one neighborhood very long. After a year or two she hired a dray from somebody not near by, loaded it with her iron kettle and washtubs and two trunks, and gave the man the new address, following along behind the cart as casually as if she had been going up to Lim Tom's Grocery or to Glover's Drug Store on the corner where the street car stopped.

Sometimes she moved only a few blocks, sometimes she moved quite a distance into an entirely different part of The Terry. But if you had had a map of the town and drawn a line between her successive houses, you might have noticed that they all had one thing in common, the canal. She never moved very far away from the canal. Once or twice she had lived just under the weed-grown bank, the clay-streaked mound running across her backyard like a wall.

It was very handy; you could drive a stob up to its hilt in the clay, fasten your clothesline to it, and lead it off at the height of your head. It sheltered your kettle too, sitting on its broken bricks with its Monday-morning fire smoking blue up through the little khaki balls on the sycamore trees, a soggy mass of boiling water and clothes which you stirred from time to time with a bleached paddle. When the wash was on the line and the moon was in the right quarter, you could fish practically in your own backyard; there were plenty of earthworms in the corner near the hydrant and it didn't take long to dig up a handful, pull your pole out from under the house and climb up the bank, over the path, and down among the tree trunks on the inside to the worn root by the slow stream. The normal height of the water was just below the root; when the gates up the river were closed it fell a foot or two on this level, but no more on account of the other gates at Hawk's Gully. After a long period of rain, though, when the river was high, the water would back up and cover ten feet or more of the sycamore trunks; there was no fishing then, and even when it subsided it took three or four days of hot sun for the cracked mud to dry out and give you a foothold. But it would dry at last into a sort of flesh-colored powder and you could go down and sit on the root for a while in the afternoon, your line cutting the little floating islands of yellow foam that drifted by on the current, and if the moon was right, you might pull up a sluggish catfish, hanging sullenly on your hook like a wet rag. You could skin him with a pair of pliers and make a chowder; anybody in The Terry would eat a chowder, though there were some yellow niggers over on Gwinnett Street who were too high and mighty to eat Mr. Catfish himself.

The present house on Kollock Street was as far away from the canal as she had ever lived. She didn't fish so often nowadays.

113

The only way to reach the canal was along Kollock Street with everybody sitting on the front porch watching her; go to the canal now and in five minutes the whole neighborhood was saying, "Well, Sister Mattie's gone a-fishin'." Nobody wanted all the town nosing into his business.

But it had been the only house she could find at the time and the damned real-estate man probably wouldn't have let her have that except that it had been empty for so long and business was so bad. The first chance she got she was going to move again; she didn't quite like the cop on the beat. And she didn't like the neighborhood much, either. She enjoyed a little sociability and she thought they seemed to avoid her; they didn't seem quite to want to take her in. When she went visiting and laughed, everybody laughed, and when she said something everybody stopped to listen, but she thought the sociables broke up early when she was there and when they came gingerly to her house she thought she noticed they began to get restless almost before it was dark. She didn't like it.

There were more vacant houses now, with people going back to the farm on account of hard times. She had already looked at one on the other side of the canal near the fertilizer factories and she thought if she could scrap together a little money she would just go on and move. Scrapping together a little money, though, wasn't so simple.

7. *Air de Ballet*

PAVINOVSKY lay in the canvas swing on the side porch in his pyjamas. He was listening to the church bells, almost feeling the waves of ringing puff against his ears. It was the middle of the morning, but they gave him a sense of twilight, of night falling, deep empty endless night. They weren't discordant; there was nothing intrinsically sad about them; the tone of them was quite lovely in fact. The same note on a horn would not be sad at all. Maybe it was bells; bells were sober-minded. Or maybe it was the tempo of these bells; maybe it was the pause between. Maybe it was the footsteps of the Sunday shoes on the pavement in the pause, newish shoes without rubber heels. Whatever it was, they were melancholy, as melancholy as twilight. He had forgotten church bells. He never heard them in New York. They were something for the country, slow, clerical, sepulchral,— tainting the sunshine. He thought the same sunshine, after the bells had rung through it, poured out over the tops of the para- sol trees slightly chagrined, reprimanded. They withered the sun- light. They withered Georgetown for him. Among the ways in which he remembered Georgetown was a very strong one of dying light and a sense of joylessness; his frame did not include the bells, but the color of it was like a Sunday, as if the bells had not been long still. And there in the evening light, in his black-ribbed stockings and his tight pants that were straight at the knee and didn't buckle, stood the shoemaker's boy, not know- ing what was the matter.

"Never mind," she used to say (she was eight years older), "everything will be all right tomorrow." Sometimes, as he grew up, she would say, "You mustn't be so sensitive." She still said that to him, though now it was only a glance, sometimes at him, sometimes away at the sky.

He took his watch and chain out of his pyjamas pocket and looked at it. Then he forgot the watch in looking at the little white-gold moon on the chain; it was carved with the craters and mountains in fine relief on it, like the photographs in the Natural History Museum. If you held it away from you with the light on it in a certain way and squinted, you could see the Man in the Moon. A Vanishing Cloak. "A turning over on the other side when the dream gets too bad"; that was what he had said, opening it with one of his thin fingernails that he took so much care of, and showing him the little paper-white pill, smiling slightly. "Don't you mean *if,* my dear?" he had said to him. But he had shaken his head, still smiling: "When." There had been tears in his eyes, pathetically beautiful. He thought if he could see him again, now, the pale parchment of his forehead, the pale carving of his ears,—how the world, how the stars would leap to life!

He was gazing out through the pink plaster arch of the bungalow across the tops of the two rose bushes she had planted against the porch, when she came out of the house.

She was dressed in something clean he had seen her expertly washing. She looked like a different person on Sunday, with Telfair & Company so far away.

"It's right hot, isn't it?" she said.

"God, it's awful." Then he smiled.

"Sunday's always the hottest day of the week." She wiped a fresh handkerchief across her lips and picked up a section of the Sunday *Daily News* lying under his blue slippers. "You'd better go put on some clothes; it's almost time for Dr. Abercorn to come by."

"How's mamma?"

"Her temperature was normal again this morning. She's really going to be a lot better. It's meant so much to her your being here. I don't believe she would ever have had the operation without you."

"It's been pretty hard on you, the uncertainty and all that."

"It's probably been worse on you; it's been such a change for you."

"I'm glad I could come."

"You get way off up there and forget all about us."

"Oh, no, I don't. You know that isn't so."

"I know it isn't. We're all so proud of you."

There was a minute's silence, then he said, "You know, I've got to be going back before long."

"Go put on your clothes. I won't talk about it."

"The worst is over now; she'll be improving steadily."

116

"You can't go now."

"Oh, I don't mean right now. I mean in a couple of weeks—or something like that."

"You're ruining my Sunday!"

He got up and patted her on the cheek. "Isn't that the doctor's car?"

She glanced round at the car stopping at the curb. "Yes, it is. And you're not dressed."

"I'll get into something."

"Answer the door while I straighten up the room."

He went into his sister's room where he kept his clothes (there were only two bedrooms and he slept on the sofa in the living room), and put on his silk kimono with the yellow lining.

When the bell rang he stepped into the hall and saw at the other end beyond the open door a bareheaded young man with a clipped black mustache whose appearance seemed familiar; he carried a black doctor's bag in one hand, which reminded him that Dr. Abercorn never seemed to bring anything.

"Good morning," he said briskly through the screen door. "Oh, hello, Pavy."

"Hello, Lucian."

He gave Sergey and the kimono a swift probing look, then he said, "Father asked me to drop in on your mother for him; he's a little under the weather himself this morning."

"Is Dr. Abercorn sick?" said Judy.

"Nothing serious. He'll be up and about in a few days. I'm Dr. Lucian Abercorn, Dr. Abercorn's son. He asked me to call on Mrs. Pavinovsky for him—"

"Won't you just come in, sir. Mamma's in this way."

Sergey, turning away from the bright sunlight, watched them fade out into the black hall. His hand touched a pack of cigarettes in the pocket of the kimono. He shook one out going through the living room to the porch, stood at the edge and struck a match on the bottom of his slipper, looking into the untrimmed privet between their house and the one next door. The fellow made you feel uncomfortable.

He wondered if he really ought not to be getting back to New York; something told him he had stayed almost long enough. He hadn't thought of that danger at all; it had seemed so remote he hadn't considered it. If it hadn't been for that fellow in there—and maybe he was mistaken about that too; maybe it was all his imagination that Lucian had seen something; the old doctor hadn't seen anything, never a word or look or gesture. He wondered if he might not be reading too much into that little glance. It often happened; you were aware of something about yourself and you thought everybody you saw was aware of it too. But then it often happened also, didn't it, that people knew a lot more about you than you thought they did?—which left you just where you were before.

He stayed out on the porch until the doctor left; he didn't want to see him again. Aside from everything else Lucian represented "Pavy." He hated that name; it was so wrapped in old pictures of petty persecutions, ostracism, aloneness, condescension; not so much pictures of specific times as of the moods they brought up, black wet-faced moods whose existence he thought he had completely forgotten; other people seemed to remember the shoemaker's boy more clearly than he did. It was coming back though.

He went to the bathroom off the hall and drew a tub of water from the cold faucet; it was so warm that if he closed his eyes he could hardly tell when his foot touched it; he sat down in it without even having to catch his breath. It didn't help him much; perspiration was rolling down his neck before he finished drying himself. He remembered how his father used to say that a house was hotter with screens in the windows; he used to laugh but there might be something in it. It would certainly be hotter with cloth stretched over the windows and screens were the same idea with slightly larger—that fellow made him uncomfortable. Just how far into him did that did look go, anyway?

He thought he would like to be by himself for a while. He thought he would go for a walk, anywhere, it didn't matter,

118

change the direction of the day a little, straighten things up, pick up his room a little.

He laid his coat on a living-room chair while he stood in the door to the porch tying his tie. "I'm going for a walk."

"Walk!" she exclaimed.

"Yes. I've hardly taken a step since I've been here."

"Don't be foolish. You'll get a sunstroke."

"Oh, no, I won't."

"But whoever heard of walking in weather like this."

"I need some exercise."

"Take the Ford."

"See you later." He put on his coat and went out, waving at her in the shade as he passed on the sidewalk.

When he came to a bridge over the canal he stopped under a willow tree and took off his hat. The flat pink lane of water stretched out eastward in a long bend, the heavy canopy of foliage drooping over the path with a dark shade hardly pierced at all by the sun. It looked cooler there than on the street. He didn't know where it led, but the bend seemed to be circling round in the direction of home. He thought it might take him through the Negro section of town, he didn't remember; he couldn't recall ever thinking about the canal when he was a boy. He strolled off down the path. But the still shade was not cool; it was merely somewhat less boldly hot.

These people were right not to walk; it was no climate for walking. He had worn the lightest clothes he had, but they were flannel. He had no cotton or linen, it had been so long since he had spent a summer in the South. He could feel the perspiration trickling down his arms and down his legs into his socks. He was sorry he had come.

He hadn't wanted to take off his coat on the street with people driving by, but there was nobody at all on the canal; he took it off. He noticed, taking it off, as he always did, the green top of the fountain pen in the inside pocket that he had given him. It was somehow quite a shock to discover it there as he walked on the bank of the Georgetown Canal; but there was some-

119

thing reassuring about it. It was a little like seeing the unused half of the return tickets he had always bought when he came to Georgetown; it seemed to point away in the same manner. (Funny he hadn't bought a return ticket this time; no, he had thought he might be staying too long.) There was a sense of security in the world it brought up, of understanding, sympathy; it brought up the same sense of security that he had felt when he first went away and they sent him a postcard of the Confederate Monument up the street. And now that security had completely changed places. He would be going back soon, though. . . . He hung the coat over his arm and walked on.

He wondered just how soon. It seemed ungrateful of him not to stay as long as he could, with his mother ill and his coming so rarely. He was very fond of both of them; he enjoyed hearing the old phrases that his ear had become such a stranger to, phrases his father had used and left behind him saturated with himself like a watch or a knife. He enjoyed the forgotten unobtrusiveness of time,—enjoyed it in a way, though in another way it was maybe a little sinister with its feline tread.

But beyond the walls of the house! He couldn't understand these people. Lee Hill, when he stopped one day for gas in his sister's car.

"Are you down for good?"

Think of it! Down for good! Had they never heard of The Metropolitan Ballet? Did they think he was coming down for good with all that ahead of him? With Nikelief and his *pas seul*? It was amazing.

They made him unhappy. It was always difficult to adjust himself to their opinion of him; if he didn't mean to them the shoemaker's boy, he meant nothing. Several people had said to him, "What are you doing now?" And to save his life he couldn't say dancing without becoming self-conscious. At first he had been very impatient of this; but sometimes now it made him wonder just a little. Could there be some strange little hidden pearl of beauty in selling bonds or cotton or gasoline that he was blind to? They seemed so sure.

120

Judy laughed when he asked her that. "They're lonely," she said, "just plain lonely. Business, you see, is—what is the word?—gregarious? They keep each other company. They reassure each other. But the funny thing about it is that you are the thing they are all unconsciously working toward. You're an artist. After they have made money the next generation evolves toward art."

"That doesn't quite explain me, though," he had said. "We never had much."

"Now and then an exceptional person will skip a jump." She laughed. "Don't pin me down too close; my theories may not be *too* well founded. . . . But it has seemed to me that the more a person evolves, the more capable he is of withstanding loneliness."

Usually she was much less articulate, though; much more simple. She begged him for his New York adventures; she had clapped her hands like a child when he told her about Paris and the *pas seul*. She seemed happy. Sometimes he went by Telfair & Company at five-thirty and walked home with her down the bright streets. "Dope?" she would say, as they passed Dunovant's; and they would go inside in the shade and drink Coca-Colas at a table with a warm white top.

He enjoyed being with her. She was real and good. (He had met Telfair; he had rather liked him, as a matter of fact. He had been kind about the thing in many ways; he had been the one to call in Dr. Abercorn.) She was the only real person he knew in Georgetown; it was so difficult to be real in a small town with everybody's false opinion of you blowing you off your course; she didn't seem to be blown about much. But then she was independent; she wasn't trying to please anybody, wasn't trying to accomplish anything. It was pleasant to be with somebody who was happy. In a way, he would have liked to stay with her all summer.—That fellow, though, made him uncomfortable.

He walked on along the path, noticing only half-consciously the change in surroundings; he thought once or twice that he must be getting into The Terry. But it didn't matter; it was hot anywhere. He decided if he came to a street car line he would go on home by trolley.

He crossed Kollock Street and continued on down the path, the tall weeds growing rank beside it, the pink water now low inside the banks almost stagnant beneath the drooping branches of the trees jutting out of the dried mud. The water slipped by with slow flecks of foam from the fall at The Georgetown Manufacturing Company. He stopped once to watch a jet-black negro woman in a man's straw hat drop her line into the pigment-like water, fasten the butt of her cane pole under a root, and deliberately fill a clay pipe. He thought there was something almost rotten about the luxuriance of the plant-life.

A hundred yards farther on he shifted the coat from his damp forearm. Then he halted with almost a cry. The pen was gone.

The visual world seemed suddenly to fade into gray. Time ceased. Utter despondency seemed suddenly to be closing heavily over his head as if he were drowning in thick water, drowning in the canal. He gazed at his hand thrust into the empty pocket, not moving, hardly breathing. . . .

He walked back along the path to the Kollock Street bridge, crossed the street, and continued on to the place where he took off his coat. He stopped and returned once more, stirring the weeds with his foot. He covered the distance four times, then he stood still at the Kollock Street bridge and gazed up the path, his shirt sleeves wet where he had wiped them across his face. He felt like sitting down on the red clay and weeping, almost like opening the little white-gold moon.

What could he do? He looked round for the negro woman he had seen fishing in the canal, thinking of giving her his address and offering her a reward if she found it; but she had gone.

Then the thought of offering a reward suggested the newspaper. He could advertise for it. That might be better than giving his address to some stranger, anyway.

He saw a Chinaman standing in front of a grocery store on Kollock Street smoking a corncob pipe.

"Pardon me," he said to him. "Can you tell me the shortest way to the *Daily News* office?"

8. Lost and Found

Monday, July 6

THE Georgetown *Daily News* had some characteristics in common with the dredge-boat that the congressman from that district had once wheedled a long-suffering and munificent Federal Government into placing on the Congaree River; with its three reporters buzzing about like the blades of a suction propeller, it drew up a good deal of indiscriminate sediment, passed it through its numerous channels, and finally poured it out upon Georgetown and the vicinity in a murky flood,—the dredge-boat of some out-of-town contractor, for the *News* was now one of a chain, with headquarters in Woodward Avenue, Detroit. Its slogan was simply *"All the News,"* but it printed a good deal more.

The Board of Directors of The Great Lakes Paper Company, which owned the chain, had been, at their quarterly meeting in October of the year before, in something of a quandary about the Georgetown *Daily News;* should they, so to speak, fold now, while the folding was still relatively good, or should they throw in some fifty thousand more and see the next card. They might even raise by transferring one of their more vivid men to Georgetown with instructions to bring the *Daily News* to life or take the consequences.

They had discovered that what many of their Southern papers needed to put them on their feet was simply a high-percent injection of sex hormones. These papers tended to run on the

123

principle that sex was something whose secondary manifestations needed to be relegated to such stag gatherings as barbecues and Saturday-afternoon card games; and though as far as it went the principle was sound, for the usual manner of approaching and dealing with the subject was bare-fisted and would have turned the hair white on the good Queen of Navarre, it apparently took no account of the existence of a subtler and good deal more insidious form of sex,—a form so subtle, indeed, that a newspaper reader scarcely noticed its presence except when he was faced at a newsstand with the choice of several papers and might have observed his hand moving irresistibly in the direction of the unclad. This kind of sex, consisting simply in the mute display in every issue of one or two semi-nude females with the high-powered look, bringing life to all concerned as an aviator might fly a thousand miles with the precious virus to save the lives of a doomed community, could very easily be infused into a paper, and the gentlemen of the Board had found in many cases that it had a potency scarcely less miraculous than that which awoke the young man Lazarus in Galilee. Their latent sense of philanthropy led them straight to the conclusion that it was absurd to print a newspaper for the five percent of the population who asked for news, while the other ninety-five percent, asking for nothing but a few unvarnished suggestions as to what an outlandish fortune might yet give them to sleep with, went starved and morose and hopeless down their piney hills, eking what solace they could out of corn whiskey and an intumescent religion.

While the gentlemen in Detroit were considering these matters, Major Bain, the former owner and present more-or-less powerless occupant of the editor's chair, a lean and cavernous Mississippian with a short white mustache and a close-clipped gray stubble on his chin, was considering in what way he could coerce The Great Lakes Paper Company into removing from his once-respected paper the cheap scourge of the seven so-called comic strips. He had written them on the subject before, when there had been only six, asking them in high sarcasm if they

124

were trying to conduct a paper for decent God-fearing citizens or for the dregs and scum that infested the back alleys and street corners. "Of course," he wrote, "if the latter is your prospective clientele you can hardly supply me with too many." They answered very politely the following week, thanking him for his letter and saying that in accordance with his suggestion they were forwarding him that day by separate post a new comic called "Hollywood Helen." The major read the letter as he might have read the notice of his daughter's seventh illegitimate child; he laid his two thin hands on the blotter of his roll-top desk and remarked to himself in a slow and emphatic undertone that he was a son of a bitch.

The incident was still on his mind when the Board of Directors made their decision and Mr. James McFarlane (early in November) walked in the open door.

"Mr. Bain?"

"Yes, sir," said the major, sliding his long narrow shoes under him preparatory to rising.

"Keep your seat, Mr. Bain. McFarlane's the name."

"How you do, Mr. McFarlane? This is beautiful weather we're having, sir."

"Mr. Bain, I'm your new managing editor."

Major Bain looked at him trying to hope it might be a hoax. But Mr. McFarlane began feeling among some papers in his coat pocket and he decided that it was all true and that his good man Lombard, a deacon in the church, a father of four children, an officer of the Y.M.C.A. and secretary of the Kiwanis Club, a righteous and an upright man, was through.

"I—I have a managing editor," ventured the major, hopeless but with a reflex resistance. "Charlie Lombard has run this paper for me for twelve years."

"You'll probably have to let him go."

"But we don't do that kind of thing down here, sir!"

"Don't do what?"

"I have never discharged but two men since I have been in this office. One of them was hopelessly addicted to strong drink and could never do any work on Mondays; the other one repeatedly took money out of my private lock-box. In a case like that there's nothing to do but turn the man off. But Charlie Lombard, sir, is the soul of honor. Never touched a drop of liquor in his life—"

Mr. McFarlane handed him the letter from the paper company. He read it in silence, moving his fingers on the desk. It directed Mr. James McFarlane to proceed from his desk on the Cleveland *Mirror* to the city desk of the Georgetown *Daily News* and outlined to him with cool terseness the matter-of-fact proposition that if he had failed to get the latter out of the red by one year from date he might consider himself, as far as they were concerned, among the unemployed; the words were, they "would then be compelled to take further precautions to safeguard" their investment, but from the context it was perfectly clear. . . .

Georgetown responded to the new policy as if for the first time it began to understand what journalism was all about. The circulation, during the first month, rose from eleven thousand to eleven thousand eight hundred and something. Nine old subscribers in Summerville canceled their subscriptions but eight hundred odd from Harrisburg and Pinchgut and The Terry rushed in to take their places. Major Bain took counsel with himself and decided that he had lived beyond his time; prominent citizens die in waves, as every journalist knows, and though at present there seemed to be a hiatus, when next they began to fall the major felt sure he would be among them, and he thought he wouldn't mind very much.

One hot July afternoon about four o'clock Mr. McFarlane, on his way to his desk upstairs (he had been there now some eight months), stopped in the advertising office to pass the time of day with Miss Idis Jesup. It was a Monday, and the rotogravure section of the Sunday *Times* lay on Miss Jesup's wire basket; the major, who subscribed to the paper but disdained the photographs with as much state as any sound Southern lawyer disdains fiction, had laid the pictures on her desk, as he usually did, on his way out to two-thirty dinner in Summerville. She had rather a pretty face and wore at this season of the year (quite by chance, for she bore her charms somewhat in the nature of a cross and resented any chemical activity they might cause in the male laboratory) light and summery clothes that enveloped her in such a manner as to emphasize what Mr. McFarlane had long since appraised as a seat of rare and celestial symmetry, compelling him to pause daily in the advertising office on his way to work and refresh himself for a few minutes with its cogent proximity.

He spread out the rotogravure desultorily over the high counter between his elbows while she scornfully finished typing a letter. Destroyer launched, passenger plane down, President off on a cruise, Metropolitan Ballet dancer off on a vacation, Miss Atlantic City, aeroplane view of Manhattan—. He turned over the page as somebody walked in from the street.

"Can I get an advertisement in tomorrow's paper?"

"Lost or found?" said Mr. McFarlane intuitively.

"I've lost my fountain pen."

"Give us a pad there, will you, baby?"

"Here's what I want to say: Lost, green fountain pen on canal bank in vicinity of Kollock Street Bridge. Initials S. P. on cap. Generous reward offered."

"All right. You want a number here, or you want to give your address?"

"A number, I suppose. You can notify me—"

"What's the name, please?"

"Sergey Pavinovsky. S-e-r-g-e-y P-a-v-i-n-o-v-s-k-y."

"Address?"

"117 Green Street."

"Do you want to pay for it, Mr. Pavinovsky, or charge it?"

Mr. Pavinovsky paid for it, took his receipt and went out into the shady five-o'clock street.

"Mamma's little boys ought to keep off of Kollock Street," said Mr. McFarlane, filing the ad on a spike. "Sister, would you

127

be interested in giving a fellow a break next Sunday night?
Have you ever been out to Buck Cannon's Rabbit Box?"
   "What do you think I am!"

9. Local Page

MINISTER WARNS
 AGAINST PRYING
  IN GOD'S SECRETS—

         THREE JAILED ON
           DRY LAW CHARGES
         After a short chase that led between a switch
         engine and the flagman, Wright Elzy, Alonzo
         Harris—

         HEAT IS KILLING
           MULES IN WILKES
           WORK ON FARMS IN HOT
            WEATHER TAKES HEAVY
              TOLL—

SOUTH GEORGIA MELON
 CROP MOVING THROUGH
  GEORGETOWN VIA G. & S. A.—

         CALLISON PLEASED
           WITH EFFORTS TO
            CURB MOSQUITOES
           HEALTH COMMISSIONER
          MAKES PERSONAL SURVEY—

128

COOLEST APPEARING WOMEN
IN TOWN FIND A REASON
Want to keep cool this hot weather? Here
are a few feminine reasons—

DETECTIVES SEIZE
SLOT MACHINES; 4
TO FACE CHARGES—

MERCURY SOARS TO
102 HERE; END OF
HEAT WAVE LOOMS—

GIBSON FARMER IS
SHOT AND KILLED
BY FATHER-IN-LAW—

The usual summer quiet seems to have settled over the social world of Georgetown, for
this is the season when everyone who can go,
takes their things to the mountains and seashore—

DR. HENRY ABERCORN SUGGESTS
CARE METHOD FOR HOT WEATHER—

MANY DIXIE GOLFERS WILL CLASH
SOON OVER ALABAMA STATE TITLE—

RED CROSS GIVES FLOUR TO
THRONG OF NEEDY NEGROES—

JUNIOR LEAGUE TO GIVE "RUMMAGE
DANCE" FOR "NELLIE NEW SHOP"
The Junior League, an organization noted for
their social affairs as well as their philanthropic
work—

*HE EXPLAINS THE
SECOND DEATH IN
IMPRESSIVE TALK*

GOD'S CAPITAL PUNISHMENT
TERMED THE SECOND DEATH
BY REVEREND RILEY ALL

"Prepare to meet thy God," was the substance of a strong sermon preached yesterday morning in The Saint John Baptist Church by the pastor, the Reverend All. He impressed upon his hearers that the universe is conducted along a divine plan laid down since the beginning of time, from which there can be no deviation, even though man, at times, strays far afield in sinning or uncertainty.

The sermon of the Rev. All follows:

"It is sometimes thought that those who go to heaven are those who stand at the great white throne of judgment, and escape the lake of fire, or the second death. It is thought that those who are mentioned in Revelation 20, as having their names written in the Book of Life, go to heaven. In other words, many believe that the opposite of going into the second death is going to heaven.

"Those who go to heaven will go there more than a thousand years before the white throne judgment. The elect body of Christ, chosen in Him before the disruption of the world, as we are told in Ephesians 1, shall be taken to heaven when the Lord comes in the air, as we find in 1 Thessalonians 4:13-18. This is before the millennium begins, and the white throne judgment will not take place until the millennium ends.

"Because the body of Christ, the Church, shall carry on a ministry in the heavens, among celestial beings, it is necessary that this group of which I am speaking be completely justified by faith while here on earth. This is the only group, so far as we know, that has complete justification in God's sight during the present administration. They have the full benefit of the blood of Christ, and shall be saved from wrath through Him. No amount of sins on their part can defeat this, for Christ has died for all, and God is free to make each one the righteousness of God in Him—"

MAN BOUND OVER
ON PROHI CHARGE—

CHAPTER FOUR

1. Isobaric

Thursday, July 9

THE summer weather that envelops Georgetown for five months of the year has a good deal of personality. Week after week the empty skies burn with a blinding light and week after week the vivid heat bakes the town; month after month the warm gusts of the southwest wind fan over the streets like the exhaust from the air dryer in Nanine's Beauty Shop. In June the white blossoms spot the conical magnolia trees; in July there are white busbys on the Spanish Bayonets and the great crape myrtle shrubs suddenly ripen one morning into pink, a bright watermelon pink, and line the streets with holiday colors like children with flags waiting for a Memorial Day parade; in August the green acres of cotton go pale. It is a season of awnings and dust and deep shadows under the trees, of late twilights and still evenings resting over the country like a glass dome magnifying the stars. Sometimes the temperature will reach a hundred every day for a fortnight.

Then one afternoon a cloud appears high over the hills in the west beyond the golf course, as welcome as daybreak after a night of fever. After a while it begins to descend and a deeper blue begins to gather behind the horizon. The dry breezes fall and a hush seems to come over the town like the quiet in a theater as the lights are lowered. The sun takes on a metallic glow. People pause in the streets and glance at the west. Then there comes a far melodious almost inaudible boom like a trumpet signaling a brigade of cavalry; the topmost leaves of the water oaks begin to stir and the thinner clouds advance over the sun.

It is sometimes half an hour from the first perceptible gathering of clouds to the arrival of the swift gray canopy of hissing rain; sometimes it is less. And sometimes it drives down the valley with a two-mile front, sweeping the plain from ridge to ridge; and sometimes it comes in narrow lines, as if tentatively, breaking upon part of the town in a breath-taking deluge and leaving the streets half a mile away with their coating of dry dust scarcely dampened. The copious gutters on Broad Street have been gorged with the flood, street cars stopped, pedestrians driven into whatever doorway they could find, while out on Kollock Street and the canal, not a mile away, the washerwomen stood in their gates and wondered if it was going to rain. Not until the last minute can you tell whether it is going to burst upon you or leave you untouched.

Then suddenly, sometimes after five minutes, sometimes after half an hour, it passes on; the steaming hiss subsides, a cool wet light gleams upward, the steeply-pitched sidewalks shed the remaining water, and pedestrians hold out their palms, looking at the blue in the west.

But while it lasts everything stops; people flee, the streets empty, the town holds its breath. As a rule not even an urgent errand makes anyone defy it; Austin Toombs was born before Dr. Abercorn arrived owing to the doctor's having to pull his horse under a tree on lower Broad while a midsummer storm emptied its low ashen clouds.

Such a rain was what the Sanctified Baptists were wailing for that summer and what an apparently wiser Providence was withholding. For five weeks now Mr. Estill, going daily to his rain gauge on top of the Post Office Building in the same state of mind as a disappointed farmer's wife visiting the nest of a non-coöperative hen, had found it empty and dry and warm to the touch; for five weeks he had watched the 'low' on his weather-maps move about over the New England States, shift round over the lakes, descend even down the Mississippi Valley, then shy away. "Georgia and eastern Alabama: Fair and Continued Warm."

The boys down at the *Daily News* pulled in their figurative belts another notch; they knew that four times out of five, after a spell like this, something broke loose. It wasn't superstition; it was one of the well-established tenets of Southern journalism.

2. Sabbatical

BY this time Dr. Riley All's good friend, the Reverend Dice Alexander, had got round to what we, occupying the center of the world, term The East. He was having, to put it mildly, a remarkable trip.

Its peculiarity was due almost entirely to young Mr. Wu Fu, whom he had met in Jerusalem and who firmly believed that Dr. Alexander had saved his life. It was an attitude involving considerable generosity inasmuch as the rescue in question had been far removed from Dr. Alexander's intentions.

The incident occurred on that miserable street, the Tarik Bab Sitti Maryam, better known perhaps as The Via Dolorosa, over which Dr. Alexander was plodding in the heat and dust of noon, following in his heavy-soled black shoes the legendary footsteps of his great leader toward Golgotha. He had come within sight of the chapels on the hill when a commotion down one of the twisted alleys off the street attracted his eye and he saw a little man in European clothes running toward him for dear life pursued at some distance by three or four of the scabby dogs that infest that part of the city.

Dr. Alexander took a closer grip on his gnarled umbrella

134

handle and accelerated his pace up the hill. When he looked back over his shoulder and saw Mr. Wu Fu turn up the hill after him, the leader of the pack now hardly thirty feet behind him, yelping with a most disconcerting monotony, he changed his pace again and started to run too.

The upshot of it all was that the dogs, being now offered a choice of victims, abandoned Mr. Wu Fu for the more promising bulk of Dr. Alexander and staged then and there a race with him for the door of the nearest chapel. Dr. Alexander beat one off the tail of his coat with his umbrella as he staggered over the threshold.

He was at luncheon in the hotel when a Chinese servant boy entered the dining room, got down on his knees in front of him and bumped his forehead two or three times against the floor; then, in very imperfect English, as if he were reciting something by heart, he begged to know if the honorable gentleman would condescend to be thanked in person by his master for a service of incalculable magnitude.

The interview took place with some formality under a date palm in the grounds of the hotel, Mr. Wu Fu, for all his youth and solecisms and smallness of stature, a figure of considerable dignity. He was tremendously grateful, not so much because Dr. Alexander had saved his life (a turn of affairs of apparently no great significance), but because he had been saved death by such a degrading means. Dr. Alexander's heroism was to him something magnificent and the fact of Dr. Alexander's mild protests only seemed to enhance what he had done.

He began by telling Dr. Alexander that his people were silk merchants of some wealth in Hang-Chow, City of the Morning Mist and Sunset Glow, dwelling not far from the Lake and the Island of the Three Pools and Moon's Reflection; that he had been educated in the University of Pekin; that he was returning now from his European tour; that he was a student in a modest way of religion and philosophy and was traveling home by way of one or two shrines in the Malay Peninsula and southern China which he had not yet visited. He begged Dr. Alexander to name something he could do for him in return for his great service.

Dr. Alexander was a little vague as to what he was referring to when he spoke of philosophy, but the word religion struck a responsive note in him and he confided to Mr. Wu Fu that he himself was a minister in the Baptist Sect of the Christian Religion. This seemed to raise him one more rung in Mr. Wu Fu's estimation and he began addressing him as 'Father,' though he pronounced it more or less 'feather.' To Dr. Alexander's ears this had a very odious connotation of Rome and he suggested that Mr. Wu Fu address him simply as 'Reverend,' which of course the little Chinaman was very pleased to do.

The result of all this was that Mr. Wu Fu invited Dr. Alexander to accompany him on his travels eastward and to come with him eventually to Hang-Chow, City of the Morning Mist and Sunset Glow, and there in The Hall of the Formerly Ardent Ones to be suitably thanked for what he had done by Mr. Wu Fu's grandfather.

Dr. Alexander, having already become lonely and quite homesick for Georgetown and friends, accepted gladly. They went down to Jaffa, Dr. Alexander, Mr. Wu Fu, and the boy, and took ship.

They proceeded, with one or two stops and side excursions, to Burma, where they visited the famous temple of Gautama Schwema-da. As guests of the high priest (to whom Mr. Wu Fu's grandfather had written a scented letter of introduction), they were present at the all-night vigil of the priestesses on the Holy Mountain and at the (to Dr. Alexander) decidedly strange rites in celebration of the rising sun on the day of the solstice. At Tsusha in the Malay Peninsula they attended the curious ceremonies of nature worship indulged in by the entire population of the village between sixteen and forty.

From Singapore they took ship north to Hongkong, where they changed to a smaller steamer and continued up the coast of China. At Fu-tsing they went ashore, hired some mules and traveled for half a day up into the mountains to visit the Monastery of the Resting Cloud, on the break of a dizzy precipice facing due east. They slept in one of the cells on straw pallets laid out on the floor. The next morning before daylight they were courteously awakened and Dr. Alexander carried his aching bones out into the courtyard; a bronze bell was just beginning to ring, clear, sweet, penetrating. Then another bell in a higher key began to fill in the intervals of the first. They went into the little temple just as the east was growing pale. The monks were gathered in prayer before the altar, the chilly gray air already growing heavy with incense. The bells began to quicken their strokes and a third in a different key began to ring, then a fourth. Then the monks lifted their black heads and began to chant and the sides of the temple toward the east were thrown back and there, just breaking over the rim of the far mountain, was the red line of the sun, sharp against an oyster-colored sky.

Dr. Alexander, in spite of his more mature outlook, was no little impressed and began, more or less in self-defense, to murmur, 'Our Father, Which art in Heaven, hallowed be Thy Name—.' After breakfast they left something in the little box at the gate and returned down the mountain. The captain was waiting for them, the oily smoke curling patiently out of his funnel into a southwest breeze.

As they sailed slowly up the rocky shore for Shanghai (where they would take train inland for Hang-Chow) it began to be clearly evident that a change had come over Dr. Alexander. It had been his habit during spare hours when he was not reading or listening to Mr. Wu Fu to write day by day on long letters to his good friend the Reverend Riley All, posting them from time to time when the ship docked; the night before they were to reach Shanghai he wrote late, describing some of the remarkable ceremonies he had seen and some of the conversations he had had with Mr. Wu Fu. He said that he was well physically, but that spiritually these things had upset him a little. "Some things have puzzled me, brother," he wrote; "I have looked upon things I don't understand. I have been thinking much. I have been wondering about our blessed doctrine of complete immersion. All these people I have been seeing, they have never been baptized. Remember me, brother, in your prayers."

3. Shadow of the Cross

Sunday, July 12

"I HAVE an idea," said Mr. Applewhite, "that though the Christian religion serves a good many practical purposes, it is a very bad influence on our moral and spiritual life."

"Hear, hear!" said Austin.

"It sterilizes the imagination. It's like checking a legitimate hunger with a piece of cake.—It seems to me; of course the Christian religion is not such an easy thing to put your finger on."

"Sir," said Austin, "you have tracked it to its lair."

"The South."

"The South, sir."

"That was one reason I wanted to come—"

"Christianity has entrenched itself behind the Mason-Dixon Line. Probably nowhere on the globe will you be able to find Christianity in such a perfect state of preservation,—absolutely uncontaminated by reason, absolutely untouched by civilization. You rub shoulders every day with people believing in Adam and Eve and Jonah and Noah."

"I should think such a unity of—of driving force might produce art. There was such a unity in the great days of Greece and Italy. Maybe, though, you call the negro spirituals art."

"No. The only artistic thing the South has ever done is decay."

"Well,—"

138

"It seems to me that a place, to be valid, has got to be shaped by some great force, some great natural force, must have a sort of umbilical cord to Mother Nature. A seaport becomes what it is because of the sea; a mountain town, because of the mountains; a tropical town, because of the heat. Even army-posts have a certain validity; they are thus and so because of Army Regulations. When you can't determine the shaping force behind a place, can't find that umbilical cord, you get a feeling of its being—well, still-born. I get that feeling about this country through here; I don't know what shapes it."

"The climate is very conducive—"

"I think, sir, if you will pardon me, the climate has been overestimated. It has some effect unquestionably, but I think the greatest element is the food. Who killed Cock Robin? I'll tell you. Hominy! Hominy killed Cock Robin. . . . I've noticed a strange thing in the South, at first glance strange. The great majority of people in the South die where they were born; that must necessarily be the case, I suppose, in an agrarian country where your subsistence comes out of the fields that belonged to your father. You don't find many people selling their farm in Statesboro and buying a farm in Millen; the farm is quite an anchor. There isn't much migration. What at first glance surprised me was that the people of one town have a subtle resemblance to each other and a subtle difference from the people of a town forty miles away. In their appearance, I mean, their build, physiognomy. Of course, it's natural enough in its broad aspects; Americans don't look like Frenchmen, and even New Englanders don't look like Westerners. But to see a difference in forty or fifty miles is extraordinary. They don't migrate, for one thing; they stay amidst one group of fields which are afflicted with their own special problems of fertility, drainage, arability, and so forth, and these special problems exert a shaping influence on all the facial muscles in that district and tend to set them in the same molds. But I think the biggest influence is the food they eat and the water they drink; the chemical ingredients of their food and water are slightly

139

different from those of another place, varying according to the variations of the soil they come out of, and the very finely equipped laboratory of the body perceives a difference probably imperceptible to the scientific eye."

"I agree with you, anyway, to the extent that Southerners have a racial resemblance. They respond to a given stimulus in a fairly homogeneous way. I am probably going to make myself ridiculous venturing an opinion on so short an acquaintance,— but I have been noticing what they laugh at, what they think is funny."

"They think sex is funny," said Austin with a trace of bitterness. "They laugh at sex and manifestations of it the way children laugh at a man with a beard or spectacles; they can't quite connect it up with the things they understand. Incongruity tends to be funny, and sex always seems incongruous to them."

"But what I've observed, Toombs,—you probably won't agree with me at all, and maybe I am speaking too quickly, but it seems to me that one of their important characteristics is melancholy. They seem a little sad to me—"

"Melancholy?"

"Yes. They don't seem to be light-hearted."

"Maybe it's the hominy."

Mr. Applewhite smiled. "It may be the food and the water, I don't know. It may be simply that I don't know what I'm talking about. But it remains to me an almost tragic country. They don't seem to be having a very good time of it, somehow. That sounds a little paradoxical, in view of their being so rarely serious, contemplative, in view of the general opinion about them that they are the ones who know how not to overwork, who enjoy life. But I don't think they do; they aren't gay. And I realize too that there is quite a marked humor in Southerners; they are often very funny. But it isn't a light-hearted humor, it isn't a contented gayety. It's the kind of thing, it seems to me, that would arise out of dispositions that were inherently melancholy and inherently anxious to escape it. It's a forced laugh.

But isn't that exactly what you would expect from crossing Anglo-Saxon blood with a Latin climate?"

"Are you sure you aren't arguing, though, from cause to effect? Saying that is their origin, therefore—"

"No, it was the melancholy I felt first. I felt it immediately. I came down on the train with a boy who had been away from the South for ten years, and he seemed light-hearted. He may have been at bottom melancholy, but his good spirits had a certain validity about them. I didn't think of it until later when I saw what I feel is a forced variety. . . . Then I set about wondering why."

"That's interesting."

"I thought it might be the negro; we seem to blame him for everything. But it seems to me he might be responsible for it on two counts. His is really a tragic race. His day won't break for a hundred years,—if ever. He may not be particularly sensitive to it; it may not depress him; but even so, his eyes are sad. He may sing and dance and get drunk and go to church, but I think he has the sad eyes of an old pointer, still. It may be the silent presence of this racial tragedy that—that sets the tone of life for the white Southerner. And it may be also that the servant class is so large and so defined that the employer class can never escape from them; can never be natural and spontaneous because of their so all-pervasive presence reminding them of their sense of responsibility as master. That is, maybe this attitude had been uppermost for so long (five or six generations, wasn't it?) that it became an almost inescapable part of their natures. . . . Perhaps the gayety I'm thinking of, though, is something urban. Because I think I notice a change in myself; life seems like a more serious proposition when you can more or less watch the progress of death among your friends. In a small place you know indirectly so many of the people that die; hardly a day passes that you don't hear directly or indirectly of death or disease. In New York you don't hear of it unless it comes near you; you don't hear the bells tolling; you hardly ever see a funeral. And even when it comes near you it is diluted by all the life and health and sin that throbs through the streets. It probably hits you harder in a big city when it strikes close, being something of a novelty, but the important thing is that it isn't enough before you to color your outlook. It may be a good thing to realize the transiency of life, but death is such a negative quantity that I think there is no great gain in putting much thought on it. I think it muddies the waters a little, though it may be superficial of me to think so. I believe it's just as well for it to surprise you. I feel very much older since I have been here and I confess I am a little depressed by it. Maybe this lack of light-heartedness is just a provincial quality that the South has in common with our other rural sections. Anyway, the young men seem to grow old early; they are mature at twenty. It may be that the Southern climate develops them quickly, but I think it is more that they have looked upon life and death and disease so early. Their range of primitive experience is so much wider than a boy's who lives in a city; it leaves its mark upon him. Maybe it's a good thing for him; if these boys developed into great artists I should be inclined to think so. . . . Of course that's only *my* criterion of worth. That's the end of all purposes, it seems to me. A great scientist has done nothing but smooth out some of the difficulties that might stifle a potential Beethoven. What is the use of stamping out typhoid fever except that in doing so you may preserve the progenitor of a Keats or a da Vinci? (I shan't live to see the revolution, so I speak freely.) . . . But, as you point out, these boys do not develop that way. And maybe that shadow isn't such a good thing. It's possible, you know, that it may be just the thing to break the force of their stroke. Certainly it is true that the sense of life is the important thing, not the sense of death. Great men seem all to have had a vivid sense of life; it has been so vivid that they have usually been pretty scandalous morally. They haven't had much time to give to thinking of death; they may even have felt a little annoyed at being distracted from their work by such a stupid detail. I wonder if it doesn't take a little of the edge off for these young men."

142

"If they're unhappy they don't know it,—which takes all the sting out of that."

"But that's not quite it. They may not realize they are unhappy, but it might still impair their effectiveness, relative to people elsewhere."

"It seems to me, sir, nobody's outlook is sound if he blinds himself to something as important as death."

"But it isn't important, Toombs. It's the most unimportant thing that happens to you. . . . If you take a map of the world and shade in the areas where Christianity is the religion, I think, as I say in my book, you will then have drawn the shadow of death,—and you will have drawn exactly the area that has been saved from death by Jesus Christ. . . . The heathen in his blindness, he doesn't think death matters very much. Maybe it's the Southerner's Christianity that helps to make him melancholy."

"I have thought that it was just that taking death into consideration which was the distinguishing trait of wisdom as compared to wit. Death, testicle of wisdom."

"No. I think the really wise man puts death as completely out of his consciousness as he can."

"You must think then the city is wiser than the country."

"I shouldn't be surprised."

"I wonder about that."

Mr. Applewhite laughed. "I wonder a little too. . . . I wouldn't have wondered once, and I'm not sure it's a good sign. Nora started me wondering."

"Nora?"

"She feels a little like you about it now. Two months ago the prospect of the provinces depressed her, now she likes it. And I don't know whether she is finding wisdom or just succumbing to the field of poppies. I still think it's the poppies. But I'm not as sure as I was. And that brings up the question of whether my new hesitancy may not mean that I am succumbing too! Why, damme, it gives you quite a turn!—"

4. And Thou—

WHEN Nora left them she shook hands with Gwendolyn, then with Austin. Then, looking Austin in the eye, and with a perfectly straight face, she gave him a scarcely perceptible but comprehensive wink. He turned a little red and tried to seem disapproving, but a grin broke through.

She drove away, mildly contemptuous. Poor old Austin! Behaving like a ten-year-old. Standing on his head, hanging by his knees from a limb, running along the top of a fence, anything to hold the eye of the little girl on the corner. Every move he made was different; he lighted their cigarettes, he popped up and down fetching this and that, he even had a different way of reaching for the bottle of corn whiskey. He chattered on interminably about the modern world, Palm Beach and Pinehurst and Placid, the gold standard, the stock market, the war cloud in Europe, the political situation in the Far East. And she knew very well that though he might have crammed on the last issue of *Time,* habitually he never read a newspaper of any kind and tagged along indifferently after the events of the day, his knowledge of current history deriving almost solely from an occasional newsreel and the radio; in reality, as she well knew, his reading was confined to the selections of the book clubs, though he also had a D.A. at Macy's and ordered a book down now and then that had had attractive ads in the literary section of the Sunday *Times.* He kept a volume of *The Decline and Fall* on the library table, but she doubted very much if he had ever read any of it or if he ever would; she didn't hold this literary hypocrisy against him particularly, though, for she felt that all she had to do was corner him and he would readily admit that he hadn't read it and didn't intend to.

His present antics, however, were more than slightly ridiculous. Imagine any man's thinking he must do thus and so to hold

Gwendolyn's eyes! There were mothers and there were mistresses; she and Maybelle on one side, this girl on the other. And no matter what she and Maybelle might do it wouldn't change the fact. She sometimes thought that if the circumstances were just right and she could discern in a man enough of his genuine insufficiency to touch her pity she would be very deeply and warmly pleased to live with him. Under very special circumstances, she thought she might even be willing to go to bed with him once and never see him again, but it was hard to imagine that. She thought she wouldn't be much tempted if it was going to die so quickly. And she was sure that, no matter what happened, it wouldn't change the fact that she was a mother. And nothing that Gwendolyn might ever do would make her a mother. She with her intrinsic understanding of children and Gwendolyn with her intrinsic understanding of men; she needing them to touch her pity, Gwendolyn her pride. So they all stood on their heads and hung by their knees, all of them innately wanting Gwendolyn, all of them with an inborn fear that their insufficiency, their futility, might still be apparent, born with the knowledge that this would spoil them for Gwendolyn,—the whole of their acquired selves acquired for Gwendolyn, of their natural selves, their sentimental boasting, blundering, inadequate selves, for her. All of which, for fear of Gwendolyn's scorn, they buried under as many layers of swagger as they could grow. . . . She wondered if women seemed as lucid to men as men seemed to women.

But that was a little silly; they were individuals. They were like the magnolia trees, the leaves of their individuality almost completely obscuring the trunk of their type. Why did she, as an individual, have a faint but still discernible trace of envy of Gwendolyn? She hadn't! Not the slightest.—Well, perhaps the least bit. But it hadn't anything at all to do with Austin; Austin meant nothing in the world to her. If it existed, it was only because, with a little more of Gwendolyn in her, Lucian—

She shook her head. She had seen him once or twice from a distance, but that was all. There was nothing she could do about it. She was a fool to let her plans be swayed by him. Her thoughts suddenly clouded and her mind became blankly melancholy.

Then as she waited on Broad Street for the traffic light at Jackson she saw him. He was looking at some bright-colored summer ties in the window of Tondee & Company's department store.

Something happened in her like the sudden spurt of a match in a dark room; she seemed suddenly illumined from within. The band of his hat had a colored stripe in it and the brim was cocked negligently to one side, exotic touches both of them, —bravely colored and bravely cocked, trying to hide from the world the softness she had seen once in his eyes. She started to blow her horn but didn't. Then the light changed and she saw him saunter into the store as she had to drive on.

She was halfway up the next block when she saw a parking space and without deciding anything turned into it. Standing on the dazzling white pavement, the heavy sun burning against her shoulders, she paused for the first time and considered what she was doing: going back to wander through the first floor of the store, even stopping perhaps at the men's department and buying a necktie, buying her father a necktie, throwing herself in front of him until he spoke! She turned toward the car again; she wouldn't do it! Not if they never spoke. If he had wanted to see her, he would have telephoned her, come to the house. That he hadn't, proved his indifference. Better to leave things as they were than have more conclusive proof.

But her father needed some washable ties. Hadn't she often thought she would surprise him with some? Now was a good time to do it. She wouldn't be going back just to see Lucian. It didn't matter whether she saw him or not; the real thing was the ties. He might have gone on by now, anyway.

She turned again and walked back, not looking at any of the passers-by for fear they would give her a knowing smile. There seemed to be at least two or three people who had been watching her all along, who had watched her waiting for the light, staring at his back, a flush beginning to burn through her cheeks, watched her park at the curb, hop out. She gazed straight ahead of her as if deep in innocent abstraction.

In front of the window she stopped again and all the reasons for her going inside suddenly turned tail and fled. The moment seemed to become all at once the last in which she could escape. She had nothing to say to him, nothing to ask him; he had nothing to say to her; he would have called her if he had had. There they would stand, fumbling with the cotton neckties, neither having the smallest thing to say. Then she would say, "It's terrible weather, isn't it?" She glanced at her reflection in the window.

She wasn't conscious of anything further until she stood in front of a glass case alone; there was another person at the next case, but she wouldn't look to see who it was. She took down some ties from a rotating rack on the counter, glanced at them, tossed them aside, hardly knowing what she did. Then she saw the figure moving toward her and turned one of the ties over. She read the neat label: *Guaranteed not to Shrink*. "Lord, I wish I were!" she thought, and felt better.

"Hello," he said.

She looked up with histrionic surprise. He must have forgotten her name. "Why, hello," she said. "How are you?"

"Did the window catch you too?"

"I thought I'd get some of these ties for father. They're very nice, don't you think?"

"I've been thinking of what old Mrs. Duncan used to say about Tondee's window."

"I don't remember."

"She saw her daughter one day looking at some things in the window out there, and she said, 'Sugar-lump, when you begin to admire the clothes in Tondee's window you know it's time for you to take a trip to New York.'"

She laughed, though she wasn't in the humor for something like that.

"Don't you think that's funny?" He laughed again. "That's

147

one of the funniest things I ever heard. So I said to myself a while ago, 'These ties don't look half bad; I wonder if I need a trip to New York.'"

"Oh, are you going away again so soon? You just got here, didn't you?"

"I've been here a long time. I've been here one of the longest times I've ever seen." He laughed. "But I'm living here now, you know."

"You are?"

"Yes. I think I'm one of the oldest inhabitants. . . . But I like it a lot, as a matter of fact. It was a little hard at first, but— well— Are you going to be here all summer?"

"Yes. I'm living here now, too."

"Are you? That's fine. How about going to the movies some-time?"

"All right."

"How about—how about Friday?"

"Let's see. Friday. All right."

"I'll come for you about eight-thirty."

"I'll be ready."

5. Discerptible

Saturday, July 18

BRANCH WHEATON and his wife, Maybelle, somehow in-terested Mr. Applewhite. He couldn't quite account for it. Their point of view, their experience, their intelligence seemed to him really wholly commonplace; but these things didn't mean as much to him now as when he was younger; they didn't mean as much to him as the relation of these two babes in the wood to their problem, and this to his eyes seemed rather apparent.

148

He spoke of them in his *Sentimental Journal* as "discerptible."
He thought perhaps that might have been what interested him,
—their having (if his old guess was right) failed to "heal."

He hadn't seen them for about ten days, since their cook
came back. He went to call on them one Saturday afternoon
after the sun had dropped down behind the high tile cornice of
the closed hotel. It was three hours until sunset, but the eastern
slant of the sandhills had already grown a little dark. He asked
a stout informal servant, whom he took to be the much-spoken-
of cook, if they were at home.

"They all down on the tennis cou't, sir. Just come right in."

He was led through a living room furnished in uncomfortable
family pieces of mahogany and shown on to a side porch. He
could hear their voices from below, beyond a screen of Carolina
Cherries.

"Just go right down, sir. They be pleased to see you."

She was playing badminton with the Owenses and the young
man who had sold his taxi-driver two gallons of gasoline the day
he arrived. She stopped and ran to meet him, interrupting the
game while she introduced him again to Austin Toombs and
her husband and some young people in white sitting under a
chinaberry tree, whose names he didn't catch. He sat down on
the stiff grass beside her husband and Toombs. Branch promptly
offered him a cigarette.

"Thank you," said Mr. Applewhite, taking one. "Aren't you
afraid of sunstroke, playing in such heat as this? Isn't anybody
afraid? 'Is there not one maiden here—'"

He laughed and accepted a light, as the cook appeared round
a camellia bush with a large tray of glasses and ice and small
black bottles.

"Let me get you a dope, sir," said Branch.

"Well," said Mr. Applewhite, "if the Romans drink dope I
suppose it's incumbent upon the stranger to—"

Branch Wheaton was working up in the Georgetown Chemical Company, of which his Uncle Jake was president. When he

graduated at the University of Alabama his uncle, having no boys of his own, called Branch's father in to see him one day and offered to take the young man into the fertilizer business. He offered it somewhat casually in a way he had, sniffing at the open top of a sample jar of muriate of potash.

But it wasn't a casual offer to Branch's father; he had long been wondering what work the boy could find to support himself, he having all he could do to scrape together money enough to maintain himself in suitable idleness, corn whiskey, of which he was a connoisseur, having gone in those days to five dollars a gallon.

Branch went down to the office on Cotton Row in July, his fraternity pin on his shirt front under his necktie. During the summer he worked with Jesse Ferkler out at the factory and he learned to distinguish between acid phosphate and kainit and tankage and Cyanamid. In the fall he was introduced to his 'territory' by Charlie Lack, the regular salesman, whom Uncle Jake was transferring to South Georgia; they drove over red-clay highways and sandy back roads, through pebbly uplands that with the help of a little G.C. Special 8-3-3 would produce four hundred pounds of cotton to an acre and through waste hillsides hardly able to support their stand of gnarled scrub oaks, he met his customers and his competitors, he learned what hotels were coolest in summer and what hotels had steam heat in winter. He learned the pros and cons of "whether bones other than human shall take the freight rates applicable to fertilizer materials," and he learned that it was not advisable to accept a bird dog in payment for a ton of 10-4-4 without consulting the home office.

In February Uncle Jake had him provided with a black brief case, an expense book, and a Ford coupé, and early one frosty morning he set out on his circuit, the orange road brittle at the edges where the ruts had frozen, the horizontal sun shining over the bare fields into his right-hand window. He was as excited as on the day he first took train for the university. He whistled and sang and leaned over the wheel and lifted his hand in professional response to the greetings of the other coupés he met; he felt as if he had been taken into another fraternity and as if that lifted finger were the countersign; he was "the G. C. man," and there went "the Reliance man," and there "the Southern States man." He called on Mr. Ben Gray at Due West, on Mr. Sancho Bell at Oliver, on Mr. Jo Guess at Harlem, on Mr. G. W. Thornley, dealer in fertilizers, drugs, coffins, and soda-water supplies, at Ninety Six.

He leaned against the stained posts of general stores and commissaries, of whitewashed fences, and talked of cane syrup and Nitrate of Soda; he stood among the high pines in sandy front yards and talked of hams and pecans and 8-3-3;—old Mr. Jo Guess, with his broad black hat, sweater, tall laced boots, gold-rimmed glasses and ruddy face;—somebody in the commissary at the fork, "Prised up the floor from underneath," gasoline pump, turpentine still, "Went down the road, got a shot-gun," big unpainted houses, cotton bales on skids under the shed, "Shot at him twice," turpentine, rosin, yellow barrels on the truck and trailer;—stoves hot and rusty, pecan hulls, raised office at the back commanding all entrances from the street;— nigger boy in the sand road, shaky bridges through the swamps, moss, pebbly roads between the fences, railroad tracks incongruously straight;—alligator coming down the middle of the road, bullets whining off into the trees from his hide, "Shot him in the throat";—shed with the pine fire roaring in the furnace under the kettle, black smoke blowing on the wind, three pink hogs hanging from the beams by their Achilles tendons;— morning breaking beyond the black rooftree, empty roads, niggers with their ears covered up, black hogs running in the furrows, hawks skimming over the roads and fields, a swank and gleaming hearse plowing through the mud-holes—

He had a very narrow and significant escape on that trip. It wouldn't have mattered to most boys of his age, but he was somewhat shy and had been brought up on the principle that, among the legions of good women that adorned the South,

151

there were a few bad ones, all of whom were coarse and, in the vast majority of cases, contaminated.

It had occurred to him after his second fraternity dance at Tuscaloosa that there must be a fallacy here somewhere inasmuch as there seemed to be an extraordinary number of very personable young women who didn't fall readily into either class. But he led a quiet life at the university, having taken his father very seriously when that experienced gentleman had warned him of whiskey and women and said to Branch that he would ask no promise of him in regard to these things but would leave it all to his discretion, having, he said, implicit faith in his son's judgment and taste. This putting it on a basis of good breeding rather than of religion bound the boy with really obdurate fetters, and only once during his four years at Tuscaloosa did he so much as dare to kiss a girl. And even in this case (it was at a dance in his Sophomore year) he would probably never have brought himself to the point had he not subconsciously convinced himself that, though he would not have voluntarily picked her out to marry, still if she or her father should turn out to be considering such a sequence as the rôle of a gentleman, it wouldn't be absolutely unbearable. He kissed her with a good deal of disappointment and was glad to return to the ball room.

During the other two years he considered himself in love with one of the professor's less popular daughters and had seriously every intention of marrying her when he graduated. After he left, however, he found that absence wasn't the specific it had been recommended to be, and learning in Georgetown four months later that she was going to be married to someone else, he was at heart very much relieved, never having felt completely satisfied with the shadow of not quite imperceptible hair at the base of her cheek and the fact that one of her fingernails had been so hammered at the age of ten as to have a thickness of perhaps a sixty-fourth of an inch more than normal. He wrote her a dramatic and tender farewell, wishing her all happiness, and believed himself quite miserable for several months.

152

He was sitting in the lobby of the steam-heated hotel at Chatham just after dark, reading the Saturday morning *Daily News;* it had come down the hundred and fifteen miles from Georgetown by bus at noon, but it was the latest paper he could find. He hadn't intended to spend Saturday night on the road, but G. W. Thornley, their dealer at Ninety Six, five miles north, had been away at a funeral that afternoon when he had gone to the store, and it seemed simpler to stay over Sunday at Chatham and see him than to drive home and make a special trip back on Monday. He was sorry there was no other way round it; the evening and the long Sunday stretched before him with almost terrifying emptiness. Monday morning when he could get back to business seemed hopelessly far away.

There was nobody at the hotel. All the salesmen had gone in for Sunday. It was a lonely sort of hiss the steam made running into the gaunt radiators; even the radio behind the desk which the stout manager, smoking a curved pipe, was tuning through his spectacles seemed lonely. His face still burned from the wind and the warmth. He thought of himself walking through the double doors into the dining room; he would probably be the only person at supper.

He turned back to the *Daily News* and read the sports page.

When he heard a noise he looked up and saw a girl sitting in a black rocking-chair across from him under a standing lamp with a bizarre shade in deep orange. He thought she wasn't so much slender as thin, but her face was attractive in a cool appraising way. It made him feel a good deal more miserable than before to glance at her and wonder whom she was meeting and where they were going together. He thought she had good legs, and instantly she lowered her eyes and pulled down the hem of her dress; he glanced away, a little embarrassed.

Through the great window with 'HOTEL' on it he looked for a moment at the dim street; a car with a deafening exhaust passed. He looked at her out of the corner of his eyes; she was holding a cigarette and turning her head inquisitively to the right and left.

He felt in his pocket, his face beginning to flush. His fingers touched the stems of two or three matches. He glanced at her again, then away, rubbing the matches between his moist fingers; he felt very helpless; he didn't know what move to make.

Then he caught her eye and before he knew it he was beside her chair. "Can I—can I give you a light?"

Without replying she put the cigarette to her lips and watched his hands. "Thank you very much," she said.

She picked up the pack in her lap and held it out to him.

"Got one right here," said Branch.

She offered him a light from her cigarette. He took it with a peculiar sense of intimacy.

"Are you waiting for somebody?" he said, sitting down with a certain self-satisfaction on the other side of the brass spittoon.

"I'm not going to wait much longer, I can tell you that."

"Why—why wait any longer?"

She lowered her eyes and tapped the ash off her cigarette.

"Have you had supper?" he said.

"Not yet."

"Let's—let's have supper together."

She let her eyes run round the lobby. "I reckon I better wait a minute longer. If he comes and I'm not here he'll be awful sore."

At the prospect of someone's walking in now and taking her away from him, Branch became insistent. "Let's go have supper. Then maybe we can stir up a dance somewhere."

"There's a dance out to 'Thirty-One.'"

The 'to' gave him a momentary feeling of distress, but he put it aside. "What's Thirty-One?"

"Haven't you ever been to Thirty-One?"

"I don't think I have."

"You're new down here, aren't you?"

"In this territory," he said, not wishing it to appear that he had never sold before. "I'm with The Georgetown Chemical. I'm taking Mr. Lack's place—"

"Charlie Lack?"

"Yes. You knew Charlie?"

154

"I'll say so. Charlie's a good sport. Did he ever tell you about the time we all went out to the bathing pond and they pushed Charlie and I in with all our clothes on?"

He laughed weakly, trying not to think of the pronoun.

"Maybe we can get supper out at Thirty-One."

"Sure we can. And that ain't all." She laughed and stood up. "I'll go comb my hair."

But before she had disappeared Branch's plans had already violently changed; her laugh had revealed to him a first molar of gold and he felt himself pulled up as short as if he had been on a leash.

He stared helplessly about the lobby for a minute, then went boldly to the desk and paid his bill.

"Anything wrong?" said the manager, taking the curved pipe out of his teeth.

"Just got word to push on to Metter."

He dashed her a note on a telegraph blank, got his suitcase and sneaked out of a side exit, leaving the note and a quarter with the waiter standing by the screen door into the dining room.

By such a margin did Branch's innocence escape.

It wasn't threatened again. On Monday he returned to Georgetown and, while he was waiting for the afternoon train of The Georgetown & Southwestern Alabama to creep ponderously across Broad Street, leaning on his wheel looking into the car windows, wondering if there were any possible way in which he could keep the trade from knowing what had happened at Chatham, an automobile stopped beside him and a girl he hadn't noticed since he went to college gave him a quick and guileless stare, then a friendly and casual wave of her fingers. She was, at first glance, hardly distinguishable from the girl at Chatham, wearing the same sort of clothes, the same coloring, but there was something about her that seemed an absolute guarantee that none of her teeth was or ever would be gold. Branch responded to this subconscious reassurance with an appreciation

155

that would have been a good deal less intense without the incident at Chatham.

"Hello, Maybelle," he said. "Where have you been?"

"Not a place."

"I hardly knew you."

"Sure enough? I knew you."

"Did you really?"

There was a sudden squawking of horns behind them and they looked ahead to find the train gone and the street clear; they laughed at each other, partners in confusion.

"Call me up sometime," she said, shooting ahead of him.

"You know it," said Branch. . . .

Maybelle's father was Lamar Telfair, of Telfair & Company. A few years after the death of his wife some rumors began to be circulated about Georgetown concerning his private life and he sent Maybelle away to the very best conservative school he could find in the South.

He had never been, himself, a very good churchman, but he had encouraged that interest in his daughter and, contrary to what might have been expected, she accepted the training, went to church in all honesty and sincerity, and when she went away to school, wrote home from Richmond every Wednesday and Sunday nights. She was genuinely fond of her father and obeyed him to the letter in many things, including his injunction not to touch a drop of liquor until she was twenty-one. This would, of course, have been hard on her career in what the *Daily News* was pleased to call Local Society, but she was saved by having an undeniably fair face, a complexion like milk, and a disposition as light-hearted as strong muscles and an easy conscience could make. During her holidays she was very much in demand among the more steady of Georgetown's young men, which was exactly what Mr. Telfair most desired; he felt that she couldn't go wrong on them, that no matter which one of them she subsequently married, the result would be to all practical purposes the same. When young Branch Wheaton appeared one evening,

156

hatless, beyond the screen door, Mr. Telfair shook his hand with perhaps one degree less warmth than usual, but even Wheaton was first class. He was pleased with his daughter and pleased with her prospects; he had applied to her the same principles of conservative integrity that he had applied to Telfair & Company, and he was no less satisfied with the result.

There was, however, one little aspect of Maybelle's character that her father took no account of, indeed knew nothing about. Though she was in every way circumspect and in many ways stereotyped, what he didn't realize was that she had no conception of there being a definite limit to what she would do for her happiness or for the happiness of someone she loved. With him there was a limit, his interpretation of honesty; with her she would perhaps have acted as honestly as possible, but it would have been a secondary consideration. She wasn't independent either socially or mentally, but when she decided what she wanted she was more than likely to see it through. An event that happened during her school days at Richmond seemed entirely unconnected with her real character, but someone with all the facts (there was no such person, of course, except herself, and she was not critical) would have seen in it a definite connection with the apparently inconsistent thing she did that summer; her having had no mother since she was twelve may have had something to do with it, though it was really quite a different sort of thing.

The instructor in English Composition, a girl named Fowler, was a graduate of the school, a pleasant-looking dry-skinned young woman of thirty who did her hair in a severe but not unbecoming manner, wore heavy shoes, and read aloud with a good deal of simple feeling, and Maybelle loved her as she had never loved anyone in her life. She imitated everything about her that could be imitated, the hair, the shoes, the pronunciation, and what she couldn't imitate she admired with unbounded fervor. She stayed after classes to talk to her, she invented excuses to go to her study in the evenings.

Fowler, who had been teaching for seven years, was not unprepared for this kind of thing and she did what she could to discourage it without hurting her. She treated her impersonally and occasionally, in class, with severity; once Maybelle wept, but Fowler didn't relent.

Four weeks later in a faculty meeting in the headmistress's study the situation was discussed perfectly openly and she told them the tactics she was following and remarked that she believed the turning point had already been passed; she said that it was certainly less apparent than before and that from what she had seen of things like this she thought two or three weeks more would probably definitely finish it. "It is definitely on the mend," said Fowler, and the head mistress took off her glasses, nodded sagely while breathing on them, and polished the lenses comfortably with the end of her cravat. A month later Fowler reported that the case seemed to have blown completely over and to be now a thing of the past.

As a matter of fact, though, the 'case' was not a great deal better; Maybelle no longer wept into her midnight pillow at being so disliked by the one person that mattered, but she thought of her the very first thing upon opening her eyes and watched through her window every morning until Fowler hurried across the open space to the dining hall.

Then one afternoon in early February, it was the eighth, she was reading English history in the library in the school building. She was alone in the room; the rest were at exercise, but it was her menstrual period and she had been excused. There was a cold wind blowing from the north and she couldn't even hear the voices from the athletic field.

She had been reading there about half an hour, sitting at a table in the middle of the room, the history book propped against the edge, the clock over the door still ticking in her half-conscious ear. Now and then she lifted her head and studied inattentively the lithograph of the Coliseum on the wall above the bookshelves. Once she gazed desultorily at the shelves. It was a section of miscellaneous record books and she saw for the first time a complete file of the school annual from 1907. She let her eyes run casually over the worn leather backs, the slight increase in size over twenty years, the slight variation in height, in the types of lettering.

Then she suddenly sat up straight. Then she got quickly to her feet, watching the shelf all the while, and walked round the table to it. She found the annual for 1920, took it out, her fingers shaking a little, and dropped into a chair, turning over the pages of the individual photographs and histories. When she reached the 'F's' she moved more slowly, her eyes now on the photographs, not the names. Then she caught her breath and, hardly breathing at all, gazed entranced at the young face of Fowler, practical, full of health. She moved to a chair at the reading table and sank down with the book spread out before her. Slowly now she let her eyes travel from the picture to the paragraph beside it: "Sarah Dean Fowler, born February 9, 1903, Needham, Massachusetts,—"

Maybelle stopped short and read it again. "February 9, 1903,—" Then she breathed in in slowly-mounting excitement, staring straight in front of her, seeing nothing but a calendar somewhere in her mind. February the ninth was tomorrow! Tomorrow was her birthday!

She heard some horses trot by under the window, the sound disappearing into the warm ticking of the clock. A cluster of faint out-of-door voices came to her on a lull of the wind.

She would give her something! Something small, personal. "With love, for your birthday. Maybelle." No. She wouldn't put her name. She didn't want to be thanked. Or was she afraid? Presents were strictly against the rules. No, it was really not from fear of a reprimand, but from not wishing to be thanked. Being thanked had nothing to do with it. It was to make herself happy that she wanted to give something. And to make her happy. That was the extent of it. If she never knew who had given it, it would not matter at all. She herself would know and that was enough. She would have bought something with her own money and given it to her; that would be enough.

But what could she buy? And how could she buy it? The

clock over the door pointed to twenty minutes after four; there was not time to go into Richmond. Besides, it was midweek and they were not allowed off the grounds. Suppose she broke that rule and went anyhow!

But there was not time. It took twenty minutes on the interurban to get into town. Twenty back made three-quarters of an hour, with perfect connections; practically, it would take at best an hour. There was a study hour at five-fifteen, when she would have to be at her desk. She could not go before, that was certain. At six-thirty it was over, but dinner was at seven. She wondered if she could skip dinner. Send word to the mistress-in-charge that she was ill, not feeling well. Someone would come to her room at once! After dinner there was another study hour at eight. At nine, though, she was free until ten o'clock. Would she dare try to make it between nine and ten? If she should be a minute late she would be discovered; at the stroke of ten the housemistress walked down the hall and said good-night at every door and waited for an answer.

She rolled her handkerchief into a ball and clenched it; the idea that had seemed so tentative at first was now planted, fixed in her. It was no longer just an idea; it was part of her, nearly the whole of her. It had to be carried out. Somehow this had to be done. The question had already changed its form from whether to how. Go at ten, then! Slip out, catch the ten-fifteen trolley. But the shops would be closed. Nothing would be open at ten-thirty. Nothing but drug stores—perfume! Perfume from Beam's. Beam's was open at night. Catch the last car back at eleven. And if she were discovered leaving the building, leaving the grounds, or returning, if one of the faculty should be coming back on the car, if somebody should look into her room during that hour—! They would probably send her home. She would get down off the train in Georgetown to a sad-faced father, disgraced. He would never get over it. She would not, either. All in order to give a birthday present, an anonymous birthday present. Was it worth it?

She looked up with surprise to find herself still in the library,

160

the bell in the tower above tolling the four-thirty signal for the end of the exercise hour. She went to the leaded window; she could see groups already returning from the athletic field, sweaters, galoshes, soccer balls, laughing at each other, carefree, with no dishonorable plan making their hearts race. Maybe she would not do it!

At the thought she turned abruptly round, slipped the annual into its place, closed her books, and went downstairs.

From five-fifteen to six-thirty she stared vacantly at the page of a French grammar, seeing nothing but a picture of herself in hat and coat against the wall speechless before the cold eye of the house-mistress standing in her door, a picture of herself waiting for change at Beam's and hearing her name called from behind, of missing the last car, ringing the emergency bell at the gate. The gates were closed after the last car went up.

She could not eat dinner. She tried for appearances sake but the possibilities of failing were multiplying too fast in her imagination. Once she turned half round and stole a glance at her sitting at the head of one of the tables, but she turned back quickly; somebody might see her and suspect something.

All through the evening study hour the chances of failure grew; she began to feel that if she did not get out and move round she would lose her mind. What could she do with the little bottle after she had bought it? Even if she succeeded, how could she get it to her on the morning of her birthday? Perhaps she could come early to the dining hall and hide it under her breakfast plate. No, that would not do. It was unthinkable for her to find it with others round. Slip into the faculty room while she was at breakfast and put it in her coat pocket, put it in her mail box in the school building. No.—But was she really going to do it then?

She turned away from the thought, affirming it with all the emphasis of silence. She saw now that since the thought had first occurred to her, not one of the dangers she ran had shaken her the least bit in her determination. . . .

When she heard the house-mistress go down the hall and

descend the stairs, she hopped out of bed fully dressed, put on a hat and a heavy coat, and opened the door into the corridor lighted now only by the dim night-light over the bathroom. Her nerves began to steady now, the actual problem face to face with her, and she walked down to the banisters in her stocking-feet calmly. She waited by the stair well, listening to the mistress punch out the lights in the common-room on the ground floor and, a moment later, close the door into her part of the house.

She turned up her coat collar and pulled down her hat; there were probably still some upper-class girls not in and she might meet them. She put on her shoes, thinking it might be better to go boldly, and a minute later she was in the main hall pushing against the heavy outside door. The winter night blew cold into her hot face.

She left the curving path and went in a straight line across the frozen grass toward the light in the arch of the gate. When she came from under the trees she glanced at the illuminated clock on the school-building tower. It was ten after ten. The car was never late at night. She began to run. She was out of breath before she reached the gate; suppose it had gone. Sometimes at night it ran ahead of schedule; the motorman wanted to get home. Everything would be ruined.

But as her feet scraped loud on the cement floor of the shelter, she saw the yellow headlight swing like a will-o'-the-wisp out of a cut. It looked bright and cheerful inside, with the glass glittering from the mist and the motorman with the curtain lowered snugly at his back. She sprang up the high step, not looking behind her for fear of seeing someone, and plopped down on a straw seat, turning her face to the glass and the obscure reflection of a wide-eyed, panting truant.

They twisted, screeching, round the corners of emptying streets and into Main. At ten-forty she walked boldly into Beam's, and at ten-fifty she held in her hands a little satin-lined box containing an odd-shaped bottle with a sealed stopper. The clerk supplied her with a plain card and a pen, and she wrote on it

162

with a self-conscious backward slant, "With love for a happy birthday." Then she asked for another card and printed it, tearing the first one into bits and holding the pieces in her moist palm. She put it inside and had the clerk wrap it under her anxious eyes. At five minutes to eleven she was standing small in the glass entrance, watching the car tracks.

When she hopped down at the school station she waited a minute in the deep shadow cast by the light in the shed, clinging to the little package, smiling desperately to herself. She had won. In her hand was the gift of the Magi. All that remained was how she could get it to her. She heard the porter limping down the gravel path to close the gate, and ran.

She was halfway across the broad lawn when the problem reasserted itself. She stopped in indecision, her eyes turning toward the well-known windows across the grass from her own. They were dark. Both her study and her bedroom were dark. She had gone to bed. She was asleep in her warm bed. But her study door was open into the hall; it was never shut.

She made a sudden instinctive move toward the windows, then stopped again. Leave the little box in her study,—leave it on the table in the middle of her study. It was wrapped in white; she could not fail to find it in the morning. Lay it on the table and tiptoe out; there was not even a door to creak, after the big one at the entrance. She sucked in a deep breath of cold air.

It did not seem such an unthinkable thing to do now. After the trip into town it seemed very simple. But she felt that she would not have done it yesterday.

She climbed the two flights of stairs, clinging against the wall where the shadows from the night-lights fell. On the top landing she took off her shoes. The floor was cold through her stockings; she could feel against the sides of her feet the sharp air blowing under the doors along the hall from the open windows in the bedrooms. The air seemed colder than outside. When she stood in front of the open door at the end she was shaking.

It was dark inside the study. She could just see the form of the table with the familiar spherical lampshade and the books. She looked back down the corridor. She couldn't go in; it was too much. She could hardly recognize herself doing all this.

Then she stepped inside and to the table. There was a pleasant odor in the room that recalled her.

Her fingers trembled as she grasped the box and brought it carefully out of her coat pocket. She felt with her free hand for the edge of the table and the surface, not to set it down with any noise. She laid the little box slowly against the base of the lamp, her fingers releasing it in deep relief. Then she withdrew her hand quickly and her coat sleeve knocked a pen off.

There was a sudden move in the other room.

"Who is it?" a voice said coldly.

Maybelle took a terrified step toward the hall. Then she halted as the bedroom light was switched on.

"Who is it?" she said with more asperity, appearing in the door.

Maybelle wanted to answer but she could not.

"Turn on the light," she said in a restrained sharpness. "There, by the door."

Maybelle found the button and pressed it. She felt her eyes on her, waiting for the light to reveal her.

"Close the door," she said.

Maybelle closed the door.

She threw a bathrobe round her shoulders and walked into the study in her bare feet.

"You're up a little late, aren't you?"

Maybelle watched her like a dumb animal; she could not speak. She was in trouble now. This was real trouble. She hadn't known what it was before.

"What do you want?" she said.

If only she would pronounce her name, call her something!

Then she saw the little white package under the lamp and turned inquisitively to Maybelle standing against the wall.

"I suppose you're going to report me," Maybelle said, her voice husky.

164

"Did you bring this?"

Maybelle turned to the door with a quick move.

"Wait."

Maybelle stopped, her lips beginning to tremble. It was all so cold. It was as if she had never seen Maybelle before.

"Tell me, what is in the package?"

"I—can't."

"Tell me, Maybelle."

The sound of her name flooded her eyes. "It's a—it's something for you."

"For me? Shall I open it?"

"No. Yes.—Tomorrow."

"Tomorrow? Why tomorrow, Maybelle?"

"I'm cold. I want to go, please."

"Why tomorrow?"

"It's—it's the ninth."

"Oh!"

There was a pause. Fowler leaned over and picked up the pen.

"I don't care if you report me."

Fowler went to her and took her in her arms and kissed her wet cheeks. In a torrent of tears Maybelle hid her face on her shoulder. There was another pause, then Fowler took the girl's lifted face between her hands and kissed her softly on the mouth.

"I don't care if you report me, I—I don't care at all."

"Go to bed," whispered Fowler. "Run!" . . .

Fowler took a leave of absence for the rest of the year, and when they met again in October everything was different. . . .

Mr. Telfair never knew. And even if he had been told, he would probably have thought it was an outburst of an ephemeral and unimportant phase of her character. It was really, though, a direct antecedent of an incident of more significance.

6. The Finest Whiskey You Can Buy

WITH Mr. Lee Hill the question was not whether he would drink corn whiskey on Saturday night but the relatively simpler one of what time he would begin. The hour varied somewhat according to when he got through at the filling station, but a general survey of his Saturdays over the past five years would have revealed the fact of a more-or-less definite progression; once seven or eight o'clock had seemed a reasonable hour, but now, in the more mature wisdom of thirty-three, this seemed a slovenly procrastination, and he usually reached into his case of Big Boy Dry Ginger Ale and into his lock-up cabinet of whiskey bottles at approximately fifteen minutes to four. The period between then and nine, when he customarily repaired to the Pinetucky Club, was spent in taking a leisurely bath to the accompaniment of whatever program WABC happened to be putting on the air, reading a few pages in the current issues of *The New Republic* and *The American Mercury,* and checking up over the telephone on the latest information as to the subsequent mobilization in Pinetucky. In summer, by the time this was accomplished to his satisfaction, the sun was already burning out in the west and the tepid night already beginning to obscure the varnished patrician austerity of his great-grandfather shrouded in stately dust above the fireplace.

The Pinetucky Club was out in the country about ten miles in a little glen among the low hills, where the great pearly spring that formed the principal source of Spirit Creek had been dammed up with white sand and boards into a swimming pool. It consisted of an unpainted pavilion built against the side of the hill, the upper floor an open-air dance hall with tables and chairs, one railing lined with a bench and looking down on the clear pool and the artificial beaches; there were dressing rooms under the dance floor, and you put on your bathing suit to the

faint music and the scraping of feet over your head. It wasn't
a club in any sense, being open to anybody who was white and
wanted to pay fifty cents toward the support of the negro band;
it was still relatively new and still drew most of its patrons
from Summerville, but there were unmistakable signs that Harrisburg and Pinchgut would before very long come into what was
fundamentally their own.

Mr. Lee Hill, having by then diluted internally two pints of
Big Boy Dry with one pint of corn whiskey, arrived somewhat
like a wrestler entering the ring and saluted the assembly by
shaking his folded hands above his head. He looked round
through the dancers at the tables, then came over to the one
where Austin was sitting with Gwendolyn and Branch Wheaton.
He leaned on the table; "My sister's been carrying insurance on
one of her houses that's been empty for a year and a half and
last night it caught on fire and the God-damned firemen put it
out."

"Hello, Lee," said Austin, rising with a faint smile.

"My God, Austin, do these old eyes deceive me or am I really
looking upon a new face!"

"Mrs. Owens, this is Mr. Lee Hill," said Austin somewhat
stiffly.

"Dear lady, I tremble at approaching you. I have long considered it beyond the fondest dreams of avarice that I might live
long enough to behold a new face—"

"Hello," said Gwendolyn. "Anybody got a cigarette?"

Austin flipped open a silver case and offered it to her.

"These old eyes have looked for so long on Georgetown
faces—"

"Lord, it's hot," she said.

"These old ears," continued Mr. Hill, "have listened for so
long—"

She turned away to Austin to get a light.

Mr. Hill stopped abruptly, made her a bow, and departed.

"What's the matter with him, is he mad?" she said, watching
him cross the floor to another table.

167

"It doesn't matter if he is," said Austin.

"Dear me, will I have to apologize to him?"

"Most assuredly not!" said Austin. "Let's dance."

"It's too hot. . . . Where's your wife, Branch?"

Branch looked at her. "She was dancing with your husband a minute ago."

She expelled a long breath of smoke, then sat up. "I'm ready for a drink. What on earth do they put in this corn whiskey? Or don't you like to think about it?"

"It's the very finest whiskey you can buy in America today," said Austin, "barring none."

"Well, I'd still give my right arm for a drink of bathtub gin."

"There's something very appealing about the whole corn-whiskey traffic. Something sound and good. It is in line with the best traditions of the Renaissance. It is in the tradition of the old Guilds. It isn't warped into something grotesque by advertising. A satisfied customer,—that is the only advertisement. The whole horrible scheme of modern advertising lies has left the industry uncontaminated. I have a friend out here on Spirit Creek who is as proud of his product, as careful and conscientious in what he does, as Simone Martini. He's not a bootlegger; he's a distiller. He makes corn whiskey and rye whiskey and a peach brandy that is in every way comparable to the best cognac in France. In ten years more he would have been producing things of a quality such as this country has never seen. Now they are going to repeal the Eighteenth Amendment and his small hand-made product is absolutely doomed. Patriotic Southerners, in an effort to protect the home industry, will continue to make the South dry, but mass production will force him out of business—"

"Who is that poor man dancing with the woman who paints, what's her name—Tannahill?"

"I don't know," said Austin irritably.

"His name's Pavinovsky," said Branch. "He's a friend of Mr. Applewhite's."

"Oh," said Austin, "is that Pavinovsky?"

168

"They say he's a gigolo in New York," said Branch. "He's old Pavinovsky's son, the shoemaker."

"I'd like to meet him," said Gwendolyn.

Austin looked out at the stars.

"Go ask him over, Austin, I want to meet him."

"I don't know him."

"Can't you introduce yourself to him—"

"Wait until I finish this drink."

"He can certainly have Miss Tannahill for the asking."

"Legend has it that almost anybody can," said Austin.

"Never mind," she said, "when I get that age I think I'll be eating fast too."

"You'll never be that age," Austin mumbled, glaring at Branch innocently making a third. "Let's dance."

"I don't care to, thanks," she said crossly.

He slumped down in his chair and put his hands in his pockets.

"What's your last name, Branch?" she said, ignoring him.

"Wheaton."

"Your wife's really awfully pretty. . . ."

Miss Tannahill looked up at Pavinovsky's face and down. "You dance beautifully," she said.

"It's very good of you to say so."

"How do you like coming back to the home town?"

He hesitated. "I hardly know."

"I was away for about three years once."

"In New York?"

"Yes. I was studying painting."

"If I were a painter I don't think I could do very good work in Georgetown, somehow."

She was silent for a minute, then she said, quietly, "I know."

"I'm afraid I'd get careless. I don't suppose I should if I were great enough. But I'm afraid my ability would be such as to require something outside of myself to keep me up to tempo. The mood of the place infects me. There is something lethal in the air. Do you remember the River of Oblivion? The water made you forget your former existence."

She glanced up at him because he seemed to be speaking so seriously. "I know," she said and was silent again. After a minute she said, "I don't believe I paint as well as I did either."

"Why don't you go away?"

"Oh, I don't know. I guess I don't care enough."

"That's what happens."

She felt that his interest had waned again. "It's too late to go now," she said.

"Well, it's not 'never' yet."

"I hope you're going to be here awhile."

"I don't know how long I'll be staying."

"You ought to stay awhile."

"I've been here several weeks already."

"I'll be sorry to see you go."

He glanced at her, then looked off. "I've been here long enough to lose a fountain pen."

She tilted her head and gazed in his eyes with a young smile, "Maybe if you stay awhile you'll find it."

His expression became again concentrated. "I was walking on the canal bank one afternoon. I took off my coat, it was very hot, and it was in my pocket. Then about five minutes later I saw it was gone. I looked up and down the bank for an hour. I even advertised in the paper."

"That's too bad."

"It wouldn't matter except it was a present from a very good friend of mine."

"You ought to advertise again. It might not have been found until after the ad appeared."

"That's true."

"It might happen."

"I hadn't thought of that."

"Why don't you advertise again?"

"I'll advertise again tomorrow."

"You really want it back, don't you?"

"Oh, yes."

"What's her name?"

"I beg your pardon."

She gave him an arch laugh. "Let's sit down. . . ."

When they circled near the opening in the banisters Eliot said to Maybelle, "Let's go check up on the stars."

She laughed, hesitating.

He put his arm through hers and ran with her down the two or three steps to the sandy hillside. They picked their way gingerly down the hill over the slippery pine needles, the white beach round the pool shining under the stars as bright as moonlight. He took her unresisting hand and put his fingers through hers.

"I can't stay but a minute," she said.

He pulled her, running, down the rest of the slope, catching her in his arms as they stopped. She held him firmly away from her, smiling down at a button on his coat.

"Oh, slip us a little kiss," he begged her with a woeful laugh, his teeth showing white like the sand.

She hesitated a fraction of a second, then shook her head.

"Oh, why not?"

She pushed herself free of him: "Because."

"Why?"

"Branch wouldn't like it."

"I don't want to kiss Branch."

She laughed at him; "No."

"If you say you don't want to—"

"It's sweet of you, but—"

"But what?"

"But under the circumstances,—I don't want to."

"Good Lord," he said. "What's the matter with the circumstances?"

"I mean being married to Branch. I don't want to do something he wouldn't like."

"All right, then. . . . There's the big dipper; if you can see the little star above the third one in the handle, your eyes are O.K."

She reached for his hand. "I do like you though."

She looked down into the pool then turned back toward him; "I reckon you'd better kiss me."

She closed her lips and kissed him quickly on the mouth.

"Now we must go back," she said, putting her palms against his coat. Then, half to herself, "I've never done that before."

He let his eyes rest on her for a moment, then released her. They turned and climbed back up the hill side by side.

"Oh, there's Mr. Applewhite!" she whispered. "Do you suppose he saw us?"

Eliot said nothing and Mr. Applewhite turned away before they reached the entrance.

"What does your husband do?" he said, dancing with her.

"He's with The Georgetown Chemical Company."

"Chemist?"

"No. It's his uncle's fertilizer business. He'll probably be the head of it some day."

"You like him pretty well, don't you?"

"I married him of my own free will."

"And you'd do it again, wouldn't you?"

"Yes. . . . He's really just about the nicest fellow I've ever seen."

"I'm sure he is."

"You mustn't think because of—of what I did that I don't love him."

He laughed outright. "I don't, my dear, I don't. Not for a minute."

"I wanted you to understand that."

"I'd like to come to see you sometime."

"Oh, you must. Branch goes out in the country on business for a day or two now and then, but if you call up first—"

"I meant you," he said, smiling at her. "Not you-all."

She looked away from him at the crowd, but as if not seeing them, her eyes blank, with that expression of not being

172

quite in possession of herself, of being disturbed at the real tumult he caused in her.

"Oh," she said, her shoulders stiffening a little. "I'm afraid you'll have to make it you-all."

"I don't mean to be a nuisance to you, you know, but—hell! here's your beloved husband. . . ."

Mr. Applewhite was getting a little tired. He tried to remember why he had come out to this awful place but he couldn't; he couldn't think of one reason. Maybelle had asked him to drive out with her and Branch, but he could have refused. He was interested in Maybelle, but that was no reason. It was something new to him; perhaps, but after five minutes he had the idea. And there his quiet room was, and his quiet electric fan, and the journal that he was so far behind in. He had better take care to keep that little book under lock and key; he had said in it once, "I hope everything is going to be all right with B and M; something, I don't know what, is standing between them." But to use initials wasn't enough. He might use numbers instead; he had to write about them somehow, from time to time as the thing unfolded; he was interested in them. Maybe he could help them out in some way, later. Youth's young problems! The hardest problems of all. Confused emotional problems. Hoping to live happily. Later it became merely hoping to live, which was a good deal simpler. At any rate when that hope failed you, you didn't have to remember it for so long. . . . Here he was ten miles out in the country with no way to get to his bed; Branch and Maybelle would stay to the bitter end. Still if he hadn't come he wouldn't have seen her with Owens. Was Owens going to be the one to finally separate them? But she had a practical quality of knowing what she was doing; it wouldn't creep up on her unawares. If she encouraged Owens, he thought it would only be after she had weighed the pros and cons and decided that was what she wanted to do. . . . There was Pavinovsky. Absurd he hadn't seen any more of him. He wondered how Pavinovsky was coming out with the shoemaker's boy. Was it his imagination, or had Pavinovsky really lost some of that—that insouciance? Had he really become a little bit the shoemaker's boy? No. Still, people's opinions of you did—

"Good evening," said Pavinovsky, bowing with his heels together.

"Hello, Pavinovsky." He held out his hand.

"I don't suppose by any chance you want a ride back to town."

"Oh, my Lord!" laughed Mr. Applewhite. "I want a ride back to town more than anything in the world."

"Good! I've got my sister's Ford. Are you ready to go now?"

"Perfectly. Are you alone?"

"Oh, yes."

"I thought maybe one of these beautiful girls— Hello, Toombs. You know each other, I suppose. Mr. Toombs, Mr. Pavinovsky."

Austin bowed and in a minute accepted Pavinovsky's outstretched hand.

"Would you—would you like to meet a very attractive girl? Have you met Mrs. Owens?"

"We were just going home."

"Oh, were you?"

"I'd be charmed except for that."

"Come along. She wants to meet you."

"Those are orders," said Mr. Applewhite.

"Well,—would you mind waiting for me five minutes?"

"Of course not. . . ."

In response to his bow Gwendolyn gave him a firm right hand. "You weren't thinking of leaving, were you?"

"I borrowed my sister's car and I was afraid—"

"If you're afraid of something you need a drink."

He smiled. "Would you like to dance?"

"I don't mind."

She walked out on the floor and turned and faced him.

After they had danced a minute in silence she looked at him. "Are you sleepy?"

His cheeks flushed a little. "No. I think you dance beautifully."

She said nothing, letting her eyes wander up from a pair of

174

tan shoes, past a table with a half-empty glass, into Mr. Lee Hill's
face. She beckoned to him with her first finger and Mr. Hill
tossed his cigarette over the banisters, finished the rest of his
drink, and when they had circled conveniently in front of his
table, stood up and touched Pavinovsky on the arm.

She waved at him as he moved away; *"Faites de bons rêves,
M'sieu,"* she laughed.

He returned to Mr. Applewhite and they climbed the hill
through the pines to the parking space on top, Miss Tannahill
looking after them until they disappeared. . . .

"I hear you've got an aeroplane," said Mr. Lee Hill with ill-
disguised animosity.

"Yes. Elly gave it to me for a wedding present."

Mr. Hill sniffed. "Tough."

"It really is tough."

"I said tough."

"But it really is. We can't afford it. We haven't got money
enough to keep it in gas."

"Really?"

"I said really."

"I'm mighty glad to hear that."

"Well!—you are!"

"I was afraid you had lots of money. . . . You're not kidding
me, are you?"

"Listen, I had to go to the dentist and I didn't have money
enough to pay him. We haven't anything until Elly's check
comes. It's terrible to be up against it like that."

"Let's you and I go smoke and drink."

"All right."

"I hate to be a snob, but I can't help being a little impressed
with poverty. . . . *Garçon!* Look round downstairs and bring
up a couple of bottles of the cheapest ginger ale you can find."

"Yes, sir. Big Boy Dry, sir?"

"Indeed he is," said Mr. Hill, "indeed he is."

He acknowledged Gwendolyn's laugh with an appreciative

twist at the side of his mouth. He pulled out a chair for her at an empty pine-topped table.

"I am Lee Hill, madam, in case you've forgotten,—but as the signs along our great highways say, 'God, what does he mean to you?'"

He sat down disconsolately.

"It may be the liquor," she said, "but I think you're pretty funny."

"If what you tell me of your poverty is true, ma'am, I think you are in beauty like the young roe gamboling over the mountain tops."

She smiled at him.

"Tell me," he said. "What do you think of our country? When I opened my eyes at the age of eighteen and a half I wept like anything to see such quantities of sand. . . ."

Austin tried not to see them. But even looking in another direction he was conscious of them. He couldn't believe that she was really amused with Lee Hill; he thought she must be doing it to torture him. He wondered if there were any way to retaliate. He caught sight of the lithe figure of Miss Idis Jesup and followed its sinuously-rhythmic passage round the floor. He finished his drink and walked after her.

"Hello, Idis," he said.

"Hello, Austin."

She put a light hand on his shoulder and they danced without further conversation until strong fingers pulled her unceremoniously away from him and left him standing in the floor alone. He glanced round at the tables and saw that Gwendolyn was watching him.

"Do you want to dance?" he said to her as indifferently as he could.

She nodded with a certain gratifying intimacy and stood up.

When they neared the entrance she said abruptly, "Where's the 'Ladies'?"

176

"I'll show you," said Austin. He thought she was charming.

"Just tell me." She caught his eye and laughed.

He led her out and down the hill to the beach and the dressing-rooms under the pavilion, and smoked a cigarette on the edge of the pool until she returned.

She put her arm through his and stood close beside him looking down into the water. He pressed her arm against his side. Then he stared for a minute at her dim profile and drew her back into the shadow. In silence she put her arms round his neck and kissed him. Then she relaxed and laughed a little; "Poor me!"

"Let's walk up to the spring," said Austin.

She shook her head.

"Why did you say, 'Poor me'?"

"Oh, I don't know. . . . You don't like me, Austin."

"Don't like you!"

"No."

"My God! I can hardly sleep—"

"You don't really like me. You don't think I'm intelligent."

"I think you're much more."

"I knew you didn't!"

"Didn't what?"

"Didn't think I was intelligent."

"You've got something that no amount of intelligence—"

"I want to be intelligent."

"My God, you've got the moon! Do you want sixpence too?"

"I'm not really so unintelligent."

"I didn't say you were."

"I've read a good deal. Just this morning I was glancing through your 'Decline and Fall of the Roman Empire.'"

"But why in Heaven's name do you bother—"

"You make me pretty mad, Austin."

"But why in the name of God do you want to spoil everything by asking to be intelligent!"

"I've got a good mind to slap you."

"Kiss me."

"To hell with you!"

177

She left him standing in the shadow of the building.

From the storm-cloud of music overhead a cigarette twirled, twinkling, meteor-like, through the dark.

7. Wilderness Song

Monday, July 20

THEY drove along the pink road through the brilliant heat.

"The funny thing," said Nora, "is that I really rather like it all."

Mr. Applewhite looked out of the car at a ragged wall of scrub oaks twisting up through the white sand. "You didn't seem to feel quite that way last spring."

"I know. I remember. But it isn't as bad as I thought it would be."

"You don't think it may be just that you're getting used to it?"

"No. I exaggerated it,—exaggerated it so much I could hardly bear the idea of coming back. I thought I just couldn't do it."

"What was it you exaggerated so much?"

"Oh, I don't remember exactly. It was the same sort of feeling I have always had coming back. Only it was stronger, because you see that was my last year. I felt coming back this year was definite."

"And you didn't like the idea of its being definite? I mean, after all, you were coming home."

"I know. But there was somehow a feeling of turning my back on things. I remember that. It was always that way. I remember at Smith everybody talking about what they were going to do that summer, swimming, riding, sailing, getting together again up on the North Shore, on the Cape. I don't know; things were

178

just beginning for them; the weather was just getting to be fun. I used to think it was sort of like walking out in the middle of the show."

"That's about what it was."

"I used to think of all kinds of similes." She laughed. "I used to think, getting on the train, it must feel a little like that to be marrying somebody you didn't love."

"Was it the country? I mean all this sort of thing?" He waved through the window at a green cotton field with a group of earth-colored shacks in the middle.

"Partly, I suppose. It took me awhile to see the beauty of all that."

"Now look here!—That hasn't any beauty."

"It has for me. It really has."

"I'm afraid you're beyond me. I can't understand that."

"I think there's a beauty about these scrub oaks, these sand-hills—"

"This red clay?"

"Yes."

"But, Nora—"

"This country has character."

"But, Nora, if this is beauty, what word do you use in thinking of Devon and Chartres Cathedral and the Hudson River and southern Pennsylvania and—"

"It's a different kind of beauty."

"No, Nora." He laughed.

"But there can be different criterions of beauty."

"There may be different criterions, I'm not sure. People who are very different, like Americans and Orientals, may have what look like different criterions, but you and I belong to the same race and our backgrounds have been, after all, much the same. You may object seriously to an old man's saying he has had the same background as you, but it's only some thirty-five years different and Pennsylvania and Devon and Chartres haven't changed much in thirty-five years. I mean in a general broad way, you and I should have the same criterions of beauty. And

179

I think we have. I don't believe, at heart, that you feel now, any more than you did before, that all this is beautiful."

"You think I'm kidding myself?"

"Well, you must admit that it sometimes happens to people."

"I don't think I am. . . . But suppose I am. Suppose it isn't beautiful. It's home."

"Now, I maintain that's nothing in its favor. That doesn't make any difference. Nobody ought to live in a place if all it has to recommend it is that it's home."

"But—"

"That's an old fallacy. To a person who wants to dig in and become part of a place, establish his family and his name, there is probably no place like home in which to do it. But to a person who is concerned with things of the mind and the emotions, things of beauty and poetry,—an artist, Nora,—the fact that a place happens to be home must be discarded. For what he wants out of life, his home may be the worst place in the world,—probably is."

"There's another old fallacy you have to guard against, you know. That thing about the other pasture always being greener. . . . It's quite a job protecting yourself from all the old fallacies."

"But it's just as great a fallacy to say the other pasture is never greener."

"Perhaps so, but—"

"You might as well say that one seat in the theater is as good as another. You're back in the second balcony here."

"Why not nigger heaven?"

They laughed together.

"Well, yes, nigger heaven."

Then she went on, serious again, watching the road unwind ahead of them, "But where do you think the show is? New York?"

"Not exactly, but somewhere out there."

"You see, I've come to think maybe the show is right here. You're closer to real things here. This woman I get the eggs from. Her daughter teaches in one of the county schools. The

180

farm is owned by a bank in Georgetown; they took it in on an old debt. They advance them a little money to run it; it hardly pays the taxes. Mrs. Dobey wants another room; there are only two rooms in the house. But the bank will scarcely keep it in repair, and as for adding another room, that's just out of the question. The daughter has a 'young man'; but she has seen a little better life and she's ashamed to ask him to the house. There isn't any place to receive him. So Mrs. Dobey is trying to make some money by selling eggs and chickens and things, hoping to get enough some day to add another room off the kitchen. But in the meantime the young man may get away." She laughed. "I don't know that much about any family in New York or Boston."

"But they don't contribute anything to you, Nora. You're a musician. Do they make you want to sit down and play the piano?"

"They make me wonder if playing the piano isn't pretty unimportant."

"But don't you see that's exactly it! That's exactly what I'm afraid of. Music is of very small account to these people and that attitude is bound to infect you. If you stay here, in three years you will have quit playing."

"That's possible, but what of it—"

"With these people it is merely a matter of life and death; with you it's a great deal more."

"That's called sophistry, isn't it?"

"Sophistry the devil! . . . Listen to me. The only important things in the world arise out of a surplus of some kind—"

"Mere living doesn't matter."

"No! It's what you manage to do with your mere living. It's a means, not an end. These people won't do anything with theirs. Can't. They haven't any surplus. But you have—"

"I think you're just plain wrong, that's all."

"You didn't think so last spring in New York."

"Maybe I've learned something since then."

"Maybe you've forgotten something. . . . Look here, Nora! What's really at the bottom of all this?"

She glanced at him. "All what?"

"All this championing of mediocrity. What's keeping you in Georgetown, anyhow? What's really keeping you? I wouldn't talk like this, but I'm interested in you. I think you've got something, something that these people haven't got, and I want you to make the most of it. I think you'll be happier that way than if you look back some day and see you didn't give it a chance. I want you to go away for two or three years and see what happens; if nothing happens, then come back home. But I think you ought to go. When I saw you in New York you wanted to go too."

"I said then I didn't feel like leaving mother and father."

"But that's not the real reason. . . . In other words, my dear,— are you in love?"

"Why—why should you ever think that?"

"Well, it does happen sometimes, you know. And with strange effects, they say, even on a wilderness."

"This isn't a wilderness—"

"And besides, you have a good deal of a very rare kind of beauty."

"The local bachelors are very elusive. They hardly ever let me get my eyes on them. In fact I think they're a little suspicious of me."

"Why?"

"Oh, I don't know. Piano, I suppose. I'm what they call serious-minded."

"That's the other thing! Really the biggest thing of all. The effect on you yourself of these people's opinions. They do affect you; you can't help it. That would be all right if they were capable of judging. But they aren't. They are elemental. They have only the most elemental instruments to measure you by. It's like saying that a certain edition of the *Odyssey* weighs about half a pound. Shaw used a good phrase when he spoke of a 'frame of reference'; most provincial people have no frame of reference at all, but it's a little different with Southerners. I feel that they have a very positive frame of reference, but it's outmoded; it went down quickly about—oh, about the time Hobson sank the *Merrimac*. It no longer works. It almost necessarily follows that your best qualities are the very ones they will like the least; they will be suspicious of every way in which you show yourself not provincial. They will admire your provincialities, the very things that will work most against you elsewhere. And what is the result? Unconsciously, you try to become provincial. . . . Either that, or you shut yourself away from them and cease to be anything—"

"Well, here we are."

8. Pity the Blind Man

Monday, July 20

ON Monday morning Dream went after Mr. Austin's wash. He didn't leave too early because it took Uncle Oregon a while to count it out and get the basket down to the basement. If he left Cobb Street about twelve o'clock everything worked out pretty well; he could take plenty of time on the way and still roll into Mr. Austin's backyard long before dinner. About three o'clock Uncle Oregon would fix him a plate and call him easy-like from the kitchen door, "You, Dream! Git your dinner." After while Uncle Oregon would go in the house and come back with the fifteen cents Mr. Austin paid him for coming after the wash. That and the dinner was more than enough for all the dangers. Then they would put the basket on the middle of the wagon and he would push off. It was fun in a way, exciting anyhow; it was like driving one of the big G. & S. A. engines up to Atlanta and

183

back. He had painted G. & S. A. No. 10 on the side of the hood and made a smokestack out of a tin can.

It took most of Monday morning to get ready for the trip,—an hour alone to get the wheels off, put some bacon fat on the axles, and get them back. When everything was ready he turned the visor of his cap behind, said "Dang-dang," and pushed off.

He left the depot slowly, swinging round on the track by the wash tubs and down along the fence, sitting sideways in the cab, shoving with his right foot and keeping a sharp lookout ahead to see that the track was clear and the switches right. Once out into the country beyond the gate and he could open her up.

For a while the track was pretty rough, what with the tree-roots across the sidewalk and the occasional stretches of worn brick. The crossing at Gwinnett Street was a little difficult too; the black dirt sidewalk had a granite edge and there was a high drop to the cobblestones; it wasn't like the corners on Green Street with the iron slabs over the gutters. The track was round the base of the sycamore tree before the granite began, down the hill with a rush into the gutter of Cobb Street, out beyond into the road and the sun. The sun hit you hot in the eyes and for a minute you couldn't see.

You towed across the cobblestones of Gwinnett quickly; they burned your feet. On the other side you sat in the shade for a while and looked at the people passing now and then. They were all black and brown; after a time most of the people passing would be white. You liked the black ones better; they had a friendly smell; you didn't feel as much like running away.

When he came to the top of the canal bridge there was the terrible roar waiting; it was like going by Miss Zinn's gate with the gray bulldog looking through at him. A white man had walked out on the ledge once, over the churning water where the iron wheels and levers were (Ollie had showed him where) and jumped in with his clothes on. Uncle Oregon said he was crazy; that proved right then he was crazy; white folks did crazy things sometimes.

He didn't stay long on the top of the bridge; he held every-

184

thing tight and closed his eyes as much as he could and shoved on right away, over the hill and down the slope, faster and faster, quieter and quieter, safer and safer. Two blocks farther on was the telephone pole where the woodpecker's nest was.

Everything was always quiet on Green Street; there was a peaceful feeling of space. The pavement in front of the Baptist Church widened out behind the black iron fence to the steps and on one side continued round through the green grass to the Sunday School building at the back. After crossing the rough gutters and the street-car tracks it was pleasant to roll smoothly into the gate and up to the steps. Then you backed round carefully into the space at the side, minding to keep the front wheels off the grass as they swung out; in the afternoon there was a deep shade from the wall at the edge of the steps, and you lowered yourself backward into it like crawling into a hole. In the morning, going in, the shade was on the other side and you stopped there. Then you climbed down from the engine and stretched your legs and took a drink of water out of the milk bottle. You felt a certain tingling enjoyment in the crooks of your arms and legs at having come so far from home by your own power, in a machine built with your own hands; there was a sense of satisfaction, of doubt, of peril. Sometimes you lay out on the grass and gazed for a second into the blinding sky, and when you did that you lost sight for an instant of the machine that had brought you there and was going to take you home, and a great worry descended over you suddenly that when you looked back it would be gone. If you looked away, it was better to reach behind and keep a finger on the wagon. In the afternoon when you came back if you took a running start and hopped on board just as you passed under the little black and gold sign hanging at Dr. Abercorn's gate, you could coast all the rest of the way to the church, maybe even having to drag your feet as you swung up to the steps. But you only stopped a minute or two then on account of having the wash; as soon as you caught your breath you went on.

Now and then some very unpleasant things happened. The gang of white boys that hung around in the courthouse block,—

185

sometimes you sat on the corner for half an hour wondering whether you were more likely to run into them going by Washington Street or Ellis. Sometimes if you were half way down the block and ran into them you got through by summoning all the courage you had and not pushing any faster; once he had begun to push hard and tried to get away and they had chunked him for a block and a half. Ollie said they tied one boy up to a tree like an Indian and scalped him.

There were other things too. Dogs barking and coming at you like murder, the man in the blacksmith shop, policemen creeping up on you with their motorcycles and their terrible whistles, standing there on the corner in front of you when you happened to look up.

The last thing was the blind man. That was the worst of all. There was something really like a nightmare about that.

He had the wash and was going home. It was getting late. He pushed with a thunder-like rumble across the iron slab over the gutter at the corner and went on. Then just as he came in front of Dr. Abercorn's office he looked up and saw him. He was standing by the fence post in front of the Baptist Church, black glasses, a greasy stick, a sign, and a tin cup; he hadn't seen him against the black iron post. When he saw him he felt suddenly faced with a crisis; to get to the church steps he had to go right by him, and even if he didn't go in, even if he went on down the sidewalk to some other place, he had to pass within six feet of him,—and he was getting closer every second!

He dragged both feet on the pavement and swerved into Dr. Abercorn's driveway; the shiny iron tread of his front wheel bumped over the stone in the ground where the double gates latched. He sat there for a minute panting.

When he got over the start he had had, he rolled slowly back until he could see him; the blind man was looking straight ahead of him into the street, not moving except now and then to mumble something with his lips and shake the tin cup. Dream watched him with a fascinated dread. He didn't know what he could do; it was out of the question to go to the steps. The steps were not the same now. Nothing was the same; a strange un-pleasant shadow lay over the whole corner. He would have to go farther on to rest. But how could he get by? He felt like weep-ing. He wondered if he hadn't better go back to the other corner, cross the street, and go down the other sidewalk. But that was a long way.

Then he saw a young white gentleman getting out of a car in front of the doctor's door with a black satchel in his hand. He wondered if the white gentleman might be walking up by the church; he thought he wouldn't mind the blind man so much if he could go past him with somebody. There seemed to be nobody else in sight.

But the white gentleman walked quickly across the sidewalk and into the office without even seeing him. When he disap-peared under the front steps Dream felt more alone than ever; that brief moment of hope and disappointment brought empti-ness after it.

His distress was once more beginning to mount when he saw a colored lady come out of the back of Dr. Abercorn's house and walk down the alleyway toward him. When he first saw that she was colored he thought he might speak to her, but as she came closer something in her face made him decide he wouldn't. She looked like she was worried about something; she seemed to be in a hurry and her shoes scraped the gravel several times.

But when she turned toward the corner where the blind man was standing he made up his mind in a second that he would push his wagon along beside her and pass the blind man with her between them.

He shoved off after her slowly, keeping his eyes fixed on her heels and on the edge of the sidewalk. In a minute he could hear what the man was mumbling.

"Pity the blind man, pity the blind man!" he said, shaking something in the tin cup.

His heart rose into his throat as they came abreast of him. . . . Then they were by.

187

In great relief he pushed ahead of the colored lady and rolled up to the curbstone on the corner. There was no bridge over the gutter on this corner, and when he stood up to lift the wagon into the street he looked back.

For a moment nothing unusual seemed to be happening; the colored lady was walking toward him, almost to the corner now, apparently never having seen him, and beyond her was the blind man looking after them.

But then the blind man left the post and began shuffling in their direction!

Dream pulled the wagon and the wash banging down the curb, dodged an automobile, dragged the wagon frantically in front of a street car, and ran across.

When he got to the far corner he looked back; the blind man had apparently given up the chase. The street car was slowing down and the colored lady was waiting by the track; the blind man was standing on the curb behind her, tapping the stone with his stick.

Then the street car came between him and the other two. He got ready to push off in haste if, when the car went on, the blind man should suddenly appear crossing the tracks after him. But when in a minute the car passed, the colored lady was gone and the blind man was gone; they must both have got on the street car.

He felt a great surge of relief rise up in him; he was safe again. It was like the delicious moment of finally crossing Center Street and leaving the gang behind, of getting round a corner from the policeman, of passing the gray bulldog. He pulled up beside an old brick wall, sat for a minute in beautiful peace, then reached inside the hood for his bottle of water. It had turned over and was empty, but he didn't care.

9. Pay as You Enter

MRS. MATTIE SMALL was leaning on her gate in the still heat of a mid-July twilight, looking ruminatively upon the passing world and occasionally exchanging a greeting with somebody going home along the other sidewalk. In the privacy of her backyard she smoked a brown clay pipe with a reed stem in it that her teeth slipped on; but when she came out to the gate in the evenings she left the pipe behind on the stand that held the washtub and cut herself a sliver from her plug of tobacco and put it under her lip. Now and then as the world passed by she leaned over clear of her broad skirt and spat vertically into the dust.

The twilight was growing dim when, folding her arms and glancing down the dirt sidewalk, she saw a passenger get off the street car at the crossing by Glover's Drug Store at the far end of the block. It was a stranger; she had been in that neighborhood long enough to sense an unfamiliar figure, and besides that, the girl looked about her and read the name of the street on the blue sign.

Mrs. Small sauntered across the sidewalk, spat into the road and returned, glancing at her house number tacked with tin numerals on the gate post; there was something in the general aspect of that girl that made her think she might be looking for her. She left the gate and wandered through the yard path and round the corner of the porch to the back of the house. Here she rinsed her mouth out from a dipper, sat down on the back steps and thoughtfully cut some shavings from her plug of tobacco, molded them in the palm of her hand and mashed them into the bowl of her clay pipe.

When the girl appeared at the corner by the hydrant it was quite dark.

"Any-anybody home?"

189

Mrs. Small leisurely expelled the pungent smoke. "Who you lookin' for, sister?"

The girl jumped. "I'm lookin' for Mrs. Mattie Small."

"Here I is, sister. Come on round, there ain't any dog."

The girl came round into the deeper darkness, moving her hands about meaninglessly.

"Sit down on the step, sister. Make yoursef easy. You ca'y yoursef like you tired."

She sat down and wiped the perspiration from her lips with the back of her sleeve.

"What for you lookin' for Mrs. Small for?"

"Somebody told me—I heard you would—might help me out."

"Hep you out? Hep you out how, sister?" She enjoyed making it a little difficult.

There was a silence during which she could hear the girl breathing.

"I'm—I'm past due."

"Past due? . . . What you mean, sister?"

The girl put her palms nervously on her knees and patted them. "I—I think I'm going to have a baby."

"Oh, I see. . . . And you want me to hep you."

"Oh, God, yes!"

"But, sister, it ain't time for my hep yet. I can't born it now. You come back to me next spring—"

"But I can't have it! I—I've got to get rid of it. I—I—"

Mrs. Small drew herself up slightly. "Sister, I'm afraid you're in the wrong pew. You're in the right church, but the wrong pew. I'm a obsteprician. I don't do nothing like that. That ain't right. Not at no price."

"I'll give you anything. I'll give you ten dollars, fifteen dollars."

"I couldn't do it for nothing like that—"

"How much then, how much?"

Mrs. Small held the stem of her pipe between her fingers and sucked on it two or three times.

"How much? What's your price?"

"I feel sorry for you, sister. I'm gonna hep you."

190

"Thank God! I knew you would."

"I might could do it for thirty-five dollars, but if you wants the best treatment, everything clean, antiskeptic, the cheapes' I can do is forty-five. It's wo'th the difference—"

"Oh, my God! Forty-five. . . . All right. I'll get it somehow. I make seven dollars a week. You can give me a little time and—"

"Oh, no, sister. This here's a pay as you enter."

"But I haven't got forty-five dollars."

Mrs. Small raised her hands. "Now that ain' my lookout now, is it, sister?"

"I'll pay you something every week. I'll give you half my wages every Saturday night."

"You ain' payin' for this yoursef, is you?"

"Yes."

"But, God-amussy, sister, why don't *he* pay for it? He done it."

"It don't matter who pays for it."

Mrs. Small looked at her. "You told him, ain't you?"

"That don't make any difference—"

"Lord-amussy, you ain't told him!"

"That don't—"

"You go tell him. You tell him; he give you forty-five dollars and no questions asked. I know. He's a married man, ain't he?"

"All that don't matter—"

"Ain't he married?"

"No."

"God-amighty, has you got yoursef a baby by a unmarried man! He go off and leave you. You won't get nothin' out of him. Don't you know no better—"

"That don't matter. I'll pay you. I swear I'll pay you."

"What your name?"

"Mary."

"Mary what?"

"Mary Glover."

"You any kin to the drug store Glover where you got off the street car?"

"No. Oh, no."

"What your real name, sister?"

"Mary Glover. That's my real name."

"Where you work, Mary Glover?"

"At the hospital."

"At the hospital? Can't they do nothin' for you?"

"I don't want them to know. . . . What difference does it make where I work?"

"You get seven dollars a week?"

"Yes, ma'am."

"That's good money. . . . You got inshorance, ain't you?"

"Yes."

"Here what you do. You take your inshorance to Mr. Jeff Hooks. I tell him you all right. He give you the money."

"No, I won't do that—"

"Sister, it ain't up to you no mo' what you will do or what you won' do. You be gettin' the sick spells soon. You got a ma; what your ma gonna say? You got a pa; what your pa gonna—"

"I'll pay you! I'll pay you five dollars a week till it's all paid."

"I done told you, sister, this ain't that kind of a job. This here is strikly cash on the barrelhead."

"I know what you mean," said the girl, half to herself.

"I mean it's strikly cash on the barrelhead, that's what I mean!"

"You mean sometime something maybe might go wrong and then where your money gonna come from—"

"I mean I don't lift my hand to touch you tell you pay me. That's what I mean and I mean it. Now then!"

"Tell me, when I commence to get the sick spells?"

"Right soon now—"

"Where in God's world can I get forty-five dollars!"

"Here what you do. You don't like Mr. Jeff Hooks, well, you go to your man and you tell him he got to give you forty-five dollars. Tell him he got to give you fifty dollars; you can keep five dollars for yourse'f. Tell him, don't, your pappy gonna make him marry you—"

"I don't want him to marry me. . . . He can't marry me anyhow."

"That don't matter you wantin' it. You tell him so. . . . How come he can't marry you? He ain't married already."

She was silent for a minute. "He just can't, that's all."

"You don' mean he white! Great God-amighty, you don' mean he white man!"

She wiped her face. "I don't mean anything."

"I has to charge seventy-five dollars for a white baby."

"Oh, God! I didn't say he was white. . . . Forty-five dollars is all I can pay. . . . If it costs more than that, I'll just—I'll just have to go to the canal—"

"Wait a minute, sister—"

"I will! I'll just—"

"All right now, sister. Don't rile yourse'f. I'm gonna hep you. You just bring me forty-five dollars here and I'll take care you. He don't give it to you, you go see Mr. Hooks. You bring it here to me tomorrow night."

"How—how long it will take, Mrs. Small?"

"Oh, not long."

"Can I get home by ten o'clock? My mother make me get in by ten o'clock."

"More'n likely, sister, more'n likely. . . . You're a good girl, ain't you?" Mrs. Small spat ironically into the black yard. "Where you live?"

"Oh,—near the hospital."

"You live on Grinnett Street, don't you?"

"No."

"You been to school, ain't you? I can tell."

"I been a little."

"But they never learned you much, did they, sister?"

"Is there anything I can take to help me?"

"You take that inshorance to Mr. Hooks and bring me the

193

money. . . . You gonna be all right. But don't you go foolin'
with them folks at the hospital. You come to me."

"It's sort of dangerous, isn't it?"

"You leave it to me, sister. I been doin' it for fifteen year."

"Well, I reckon I'll be saying good-night, ma'am."

"I'll be lookin' for you this time tomorrow, sister."

When the girl went out of the yard, Mrs. Small entered the
house and watched her through a broken slat of the front shutters. In a minute she was gone and there was nobody in the
street but a blind man; she watched him go by, tapping on the
tree roots with his stick.

10. Local Page

FINE TALK FEATURES MOTHERCRAFT
PROGRAM AT WOMAN'S CLUB LUNCH—

MINISTER OFFERS
PRACTICAL REMEDY
FOR COMMON ILLS
"YOU CAN'T LOSE ANY-
THING BY TRUSTING,"
SAYS DR. RILEY ALL—

GEORGETOWN COTTON DECLINES 9 POINTS AT CLOSE

*GENERAL COTTON
DROPS FOLLOWING
WEATHER REPORT—*

FAIR AND SLIGHTLY WARMER
GEORGETOWN'S MENU FOR TODAY—

194

KLAN READY TO REORGANIZE;
GEORGETOWN IS INTERESTED
If the Ku Klux Klan will send its trumpeting riders through Georgetown, plenty of white robes will be pulled from their resting places by those who are anxious once again to cluster about the burning cross—

COUNTY OFFICERS
SEIZE TWO STILLS—

CONFEDERATE VETS OPEN
REUNION AT VALDOSTA, GA.—

ONLY SIX BIRTHS
ON WEEK'S RECORD
FOURTEEN CASES OF
MEASLES—

LEGAL BAN MAY
BE TIGHTENED ON
PISTOL CARRYING—

GEORGETONIANS SEEK DIVERSION DURING HOT DAYS

INDOOR AND OUTDOOR SPORTS
APPARENTLY ARE FAVORITES;
CROCHETING WILL BE POPULAR
GOLF, TENNIS, FISHING, HIKING, BADMINTON,
CONTRACT, SWIMMING—ALL HAVE PLACES
IN SUMMER'S WHAT-TO-DO MENU
Georgetonians are preparing to ride their hobbies hard—now that vacation time has come on. Of all seasons, the lazy summer heat has a way of making people relax, take it easy, and—contrariwise, spur some to additional activities. A casual checkup shows a diversity of opinion as to how Georgetonians will play this summer.

195

One of the most favorite of local summer sports seems to be to get with a group of congenial friends on a cool veranda, and crochet.—

PASTOR COMPARES
FEAST IN BABYLON
TO LOCAL PARTIES

King Belshazzar's feast, given in Babylon 2500 years ago was not unlike some of the—

CHAPTER FIVE

1. Isobaric

SIX weeks after the Sanctified Baptists on the hill above the third fairway began their melodious efforts to contact the Almighty on the subject of rain, the Congaree River had dropped eleven inches more at the Sand Bar Ferry Bridge and Brier Creek had sunk listlessly into the bottom of its black and shadowy trough. Jesse Blue, a negro who ran two plows on the edge of the swamp, reported that he had seen the Brier Creek crocodile with his own eyes; the fact that he had met him sitting in the middle of the big road as he came home on a Saturday night from having bartered a sack of Red Cross flour at the local distiller's is not of any significance; he never resorted to the distiller's except when plagued by worry as to his crops, and the appearance of the crocodile was taken in his neighborhood as more or less the official recognition of the times' being out of joint.

The churches out in The Terry took it up.

"There have been sin among you," said Deacon Brooks to the crowded Tabernickle, "and the Lord he gonna dry you out. He gonna dry that sin right on out of you."

"Ain't it the truth!"

"Hit ain't never gonna rain no more twel you come up here and shake that sin away. Repent you, saith the Lord. Gimme the Bible on that. Gimme Matthew four, seventeen. Read it."

His lieutenant found the passage and read: " 'From that time Jesus began to preach—' "

"There it is! Read it again."

" 'From that time Jesus began to preach and to say, Repent ye, for the kingdom of heaven is at hand.' "

" 'Repent ye, for the kingdom of heaven is at hand!' Repent ye, said the Lord, and he mean what he saith. If there is any of you sisters that has done a sin, come on up here and repent ye now, so hit can go on and rain."

"Amen!"

"Eat 'em up, daddy!"

"I feel they has been a sin among you. A sin don't nobody know but that poor sister and that old red devil. And that's why it ain't come on to rain. That's why the cotton is burnin' up. That's why the corn is burnin' up. That's why the cane is burnin' up. And that's why you *all* gonna be burnin' up. Come on up here, sister, so hit can go on and rain!"

"Eat 'em up, daddy!"

"Hold 'em in the road!"

"Thang God the Bishop's comin'!" said the deacon. "It won't be long now."

"Then you said it!"

"He's comin' soon. And when he rise up and ask for rain, why, then, hit's bound to rain. Ain't that right?"

"That's right!"

"Sho it's right!"

"Amen!"

"Gimme the law on that. Gimme James five, sixteen. Listen to the Book. Read."

" 'Confess your faults one to another and pray one for another that ye may be healed.' "

"Pray one for another! Read."

" 'The effectual fervent prayer of a righteous man availeth much.' "

"Hear him! Did you hear him?"

"We heard him."

"The prayer of a righteous man availeth much! Hear him again! Read. . . ."

198

Over the burned hills, over the jade forests, the hot wind shifted now west, now east. The dark clouds gathered ominously in the southwest, made their empty threat, and turned off clockwise to the river valley on the north. The still nights were pale with stars and the sun came up clear and burning.

2. Sentimental Journal

Monday, July 20

MR. APPLEWHITE felt within himself that subtle stirring of life which an animal senses at the first break of spring or a young man at the thought of his mistress, but which had come to be associated in his consciousness with a change of mind. Maybe Nora was right! Maybe, after all, it was better to 'stay put.' Maybe it was broader common sense to stay put and establish your family than to go on your pilgrimage and establish yourself.

He sat by his window looking out southeastward over the town, watching the great shadow of the hill grow out over the plain and rise like a dark mist evenly up the church spires and the dome of the court house and the Cotton States Building as the sun went down behind him. A cloud of steam went up from the railroad station, mounting dull and gray through the shade and bursting suddenly into a snowy light.

Maybe he was wrong. If he condensed all his doctrine into a word and said to her, "Get out into the world, make a name for yourself," she could have replied with cogent finality, "But I already have a name." That was it. Pavinovskys went out; Noras stayed put. And there was a certain dignity that arose from doing nothing in the world but staying put; when your family had simply lived on one piece of ground for four or five generations it acquired a prestige that the mere failure of one or two of the descendants could not shake in the least. Then individual failure or accomplishment didn't matter very much, didn't matter any more than in an individual's career a—a casual solecism mattered. Maybe she was right. Maybe she was not in love, but just wise. Maybe he had come all the way down here with counsel that was, after all, bad. Was it even, perhaps, adolescent? That was a little alarming. Still, whether she was right depended on the man, on what he had on the ball, as people used to say. You couldn't maintain that Shakespeare should have stayed in Stratford. But how about the James Lane Allens and the Henry Wadsworth Longfellows? Might the world not be better off if they left nothing but well-bred progeny, deeper and deeper rooted in their natural soils?

He sat for a minute listening to a bird singing among the packed leaves of Mrs. Eubanks's magnolia tree. Then he leaned over his journal, open on the table beside him:

"I have always felt that if you want to do something with your life you must first get away from home. But there is another side to it: how important is it that you do something with your life? Suppose, instead of 'doing something with it,' as we say, you simply entrenched your good name a little more firmly in your native soil, built your family a little more strongly in an honorable tradition; suppose, instead of spending your life on yourself (a highly speculative investment), you conserved it and put it, so to speak, in the good name of your family in the community, —what then? Haven't you done a little better with your time? Haven't you built up something that will last a little longer against the future than one short, however glamorous, life?"

He drew a line under the paragraph, feeling easier in his mind from simply having stated it; he would come back to it again. He turned over to a new page.

"I don't feel exactly right about S. P. Something happening to him. Don't know what. Sensitive. To be sensitive is to be vulnerable. A man ought to be taught invulnerability,—but then he will become the president of a corporation. Don't know what you

200

ought to teach a man. Seem to know less and less,—seem to be unlearning several things on this Sentimental Journey. Probably ought to have stayed home."

He walked out under the shade trees to the corner and heard a street car droning up the hill. When it came in sight he saw the sign on the front: BROAD STREET VIA THE TERRITORY. It must go round the top of the hill and down the other side. It didn't matter; it would be cool riding. He signaled it and got aboard.

He didn't feel just right about Maybelle, either,—but, Lord, who did he feel just right about? . . . Maybe he ought to go to New York. He had been there nearly five weeks. It was time for him to be going. And yet he thought somehow he was going to miss the place. That was hard to believe; he comes down with a hatred of the place and now somehow rather likes it. You start out in one direction and end in another. You meant to do one thing and you did another. Or did nothing. He had come down there to save Nora and now— Maybe it was just the anesthetic getting him too! O, rest ye, brother mariners, we will not wander more. . . . Absurd! . . .

There were placards all over The Terry announcing the coming of the Reverend Bishop Divine on the seventh of August for two weeks of revival meetings. "Friday the twenty-first: MIRACLE NIGHT."

3. In His Infinite Wisdom

Monday, July 20

BACK in the angle behind the iron fence and the green lawn (the grass was watered every afternoon from May to October and was always a fine green, aside from the fact that The Georgetown Chemical Company accepted every spring the opportunity Dr.

All extended to it of sacrificing two sacks of its G. C. Special 7-5-5 Superbone in a free-will offering to the Lord God) was the Saint John Baptist Sunday School and in the rear where it was shady was the pastor's study. In the great chair at the mahogany desk, his feet on a low stool beneath because his legs were on the short side, sat Dr. Riley All, his face bearing the marks of unusual concern. He took off his glasses and manipulated the skin over his upper forehead with the balls of his fingers.

After he had sat there for some time in a rather sad pensiveness he stood up and removed his linen coat and hung it on a mahogany stand in the corner. Then he returned to the desk, changed the vortex of his fan so that it fell upon the seat of the chair, and knelt in front of it, his eyes closed, his moist hands clasped. He waited until a street car from Summerville went by with its iron clatter, then began:

"O Lord, maker of heaven and earth, in Thy infinite wisdom, I pray Thee hearken to Thy servant's special prayer. . . . For all Thy mercy, Lord, I humbly thank Thee, for all Thy loving-kindness, for all Thy watchful care. For bread and meat I thank Thee, for strength to carry on Thy work. . . . But, Lord, I pray now specially in behalf of one of Thy children. One of Thy poor children, in her darkness, has strayed from the fold; she has listened to the honeyed counsel of the Evil One and turned away from the narrow path. Many times, as Thou with Thy all-observing mind well knowest, I have pleaded with her to turn to Thee, and some progress with her in Thy mercy Thou hadst granted me to make. She paused to look back upon the primrose path by which she had come, the bed of roses on which she had lain, and she saw that it was vanity, all was vanity. 'Some day,' she said to Thy servant, 'I will leave these evil ways. I will forsake the paths of the ungodly. I will turn away from the ways of the sinful.' . . . But seeing that he was about to lose her, the Evil One called his disciples that were walking to and fro upon the earth and appointed one, a Russian, passing under the name of Pavinovsky, to win her back. Almost I had persuaded her, when he appeared. With strong drink he tempted her, with lusts

202

of the flesh he besieged her spirit. He hardened her heart against righteousness. Today when I visited her, her heart was hard. Such was her state that she scoffed at Thy eternal love. Forgive her, O Lord, for she knew not what she did. . . . O Lord, I pray Thee, visit her in her iniquity, reveal to her eyes the error of her ways. Remember, Lord, I pray Thee, the words of Thy Son when He said, 'Verily I say unto you, that likewise joy shall be in heaven over one sinner that repenteth more than over ninety and nine just persons which need no repentance.' Visit her, O Lord, and cause Thy face to shine upon her. Give her strength to resist. Give her, Lord, more than strength; give her the will to resist. . . . And give me strength, O Lord, and teach me words to persuade her, words to harden her heart against the ways of evil—"

4. Gayly the Troubadour!

Monday, July 20

MISS TANNAHILL was worried. Something had happened to her. Her life seemed suddenly to have become vivid. She hardly knew whether she was very happy or very unhappy, but she knew that she was now awake. It all startled her a little. Looking back on the years that seemed now to have come to a close, she could see herself in a long sleep, numb with a drab unconsciousness,—years that seemed to have passed, looking back on them, in a moment like a night's sleep, straight level years without hill or turning to give a sense of distance. She could look back across them at New York and Sheridan Square almost as if they were yesterday; things had happened to her since then, but they were slow things like the nearly-imperceptible drying out of the skin on the backs of her hands which she noticed sometimes when she was painting (it didn't help the job much, either).

Now things had changed; everything had changed. She had felt sometimes as if she were waiting for something; she felt now that this was it, or anyway that she might make this it. She didn't know how he felt about her. He probably hadn't thought about her again. Yet he had danced with her; yet he had remembered their conversation. It had meant that much to him anyhow. She knew he had remembered. She had proof of that. This morning when she had turned feverishly to the Want Ads in the *News* and looked among the Lost and Found, it was almost like getting a message from him; there was the advertisement that she had advised him to reinsert. He had remembered what she said at least until Sunday. Maybe he still remembered. And if he got the pen back now she would be in a measure responsible. He wouldn't have put the ad in again if it hadn't been for her. And when he had turned to that page this morning, as he surely had, his eyes had read every letter of those lines just as hers had done and he had probably remembered a little of what they had said to each other. . . . She thought she would go downtown and see if she could find a blue straw hat.

That was the kind of thing that had changed; she hadn't thought of a new hat with that sort of interest in years. Last summer she hadn't even bought one. And her rooms! She couldn't recall when her two shady rooms had seemed so living, so intense. It was a little like what happened to a canvas when a lucky stroke of her brush suddenly gave it depth, like the blue haze that she applied to her distant mountains to push them back. The future, from a desert, became a vista; she didn't know where it led, but it led somewhere.

What could she do about it? That question puzzled her a good deal. The first thing to do was wait. There was really nothing else; wait until he telephoned her. She couldn't possibly telephone him.

But suppose he didn't call her? Suppose she waited even two days and he didn't call her? Then she would have to make some

204

move. She couldn't imagine her calling him. She had never done that. She hoped she wouldn't have to. She couldn't do that; she was a lady. She thought she might even let the waters of her pool settle into their old quiet rather than do that. But if a week went by? So much of her life had flowed behind her now. Perhaps she would call him if a week went by. There were not many more years between her and the time when no one would look at her; not many men looked at her more than casually now, if she would confess the truth, young men. There might not be another. . . . And what if all this came to nothing? What if she was misinterpreting him? But she didn't ask very much of him. She didn't want him to marry her particularly, or even to sleep with her; that wasn't intrinsically what she wanted. She wanted approval. The means that he might take to show it didn't matter. But if something came between them now,—she hardly knew what she would do. And how likely was it that such a personable young man should be unattached? Hadn't he even referred to somebody else—

She went to the great mahogany wardrobe and took down a hat; there was no use in moping about the possibilities of unhappiness; he had danced with her and remembered what she said; it was not finished, it was just beginning. Before it was finished perhaps she would have felt the tight muscles of his arms strong round her shoulders, perhaps she would have seen his eyes break through their guard and stand naked before her— Only his approval? It was idle to think that was what she wanted. She wanted to be a part of his life, she wanted for a few hours to be his life. For a few hours, if for no longer, she wanted to feel that nothing in the world mattered to him but her. And she wanted it more than anything, more than peace, more than self-esteem. Give him up for the empty pride of not calling him? Not today, but sometime, if she had to? She looked straight into her eyes in the mirror and knew that she would go to any lengths to have him. I'll come to thee by moonlight, Though hell should bar the way. . . . She laughed but she meant it.

She went out on the back porch and called the disheveled servant. She said with extreme nonchalance, pulling on some white cotton gloves, "If anybody should call me while I'm out write down the number. Say I'll telephone them about two o'clock."

At a few minutes after twelve she went into a hot booth in the United Cigar Store on Broad Street and called her number. After a long wait Nancy answered.

"This is Miss Sue, Nancy. Has anybody called me?"

"No, ma'am, the phone ain't rang at all."

She hung up and stood there looking at the soiled wall of the booth, the perspiration gathering on her forehead.

Then she breathed in deeply through her nose and called him. A negro's voice said that he was out.

5. Lost and Found

Monday, July 20

MR. McFARLANE was standing once more in the tantalizing proximity of Miss Idis Jesup when a Chinaman in his shirt sleeves, with an old straw hat sitting on the top of his round head came through the open door, took off the hat, and smiled.

"How are you?" said Mr. McFarlane for the benefit of Miss Jesup.

"Pletty good," said the Chinaman.

"You're looking fine."

"How?"

"God knows."

"How?"

"Can we help you out in some way?"

"I see ad this morning you lose fountain pen."

206

"We ran an ad for a fountain pen about three weeks ago,"
said Mr. McFarlane.

"I see ad this morning."

"Your paper must have been late."

"He telephoned in yesterday," said Miss Jesup, "and said to
run it again."

"Pavinovsky?"

"Yes."

"You found the pen?"

"I find him last week, but—"

"Let's have a look."

The Chinaman, still smiling, opened an empty Zu-Zu box and
unwrapped the pen from a strip of newspaper.

"Get Pavinovsky on the phone, will you, baby, and tell him
we've got his pen."

Miss Jesup searched among some scraps of paper in a drawer
and went to the telephone.

"Where'd you find it?"

"I find him in the glass on the canal by the blidge."

"What's your name?"

"Name Lim Tom."

"You live out in The Terry, Mr. Lim Tom?"

"I keep glocely store on Kollock Street near the blidge. When
I find him I look in the paper for ad, but no ad. I look every
day—"

"I understand."

"Then today I see ad."

"I understand."

"He's coming right up," said Miss Jesup.

"Coming up here?"

"Right now."

"What's this fountain pen made out of, anyhow!"

"He didn't say," said Miss Jesup, sliding her figure under the
typewriter.

"He'll be up here in a few minutes," said Mr. McFarlane.

"Just consider yourself at home. . . . Are you a regular sub-scriber to our little paper, Mr. Lim Tom?"

"Once in a while," said Mr. Lim Tom, still smiling.

"Indeed? How do you like it?"

"Me? Very good."

"I'm glad to hear you say so. We try to make it a good paper." Mr. McFarlane hitched up his Palm Beach trousers over his almost concave abdomen. "It's a better paper than it ever was before."

"Very much."

"That's very gratifying, Mr. Tom."

"You put me in the tomollow paper?"

"Why? . . . Have you bitten any animals?"

"How?"

"Have you committed any news?"

Mr. Lim Tom laughed; "I find pen."

"That's not news, Mr. Tom. If the pen had found you— Or if the pen belonged to somebody,—say, sister, who *is* this Pavinovsky?"

"The only Pavinovsky I ever heard of was the shoemaker."

"No, this boy's a stranger." Mr. McFarlane rubbed his upper lip with his forefinger. "But I've seen that name somewhere."

"If you've ever bothered to have your shoes repaired—"

"No, baby, I somehow don't associate it with shoes." He frowned for a moment at the bright sun spots in the shady street beyond the door, then he took a fold of copy paper out of his pocket and scribbled 'Pavinovsky' on it. It was a funny place for somebody to go walking. Strangers did funny things, though. Hardly a story in it really, anyhow, no matter who he was. He put the paper back in his coat. The printer's boy from the afternoon paper came in with the morning's A.P. reports and Mr. McFarlane glanced at his watch.

"Tell me not, Sweet, I am unkind," he sang, turning away and mounting the steps to the editorial offices, "That from the nun-nery Of thy chaste breast and quiet mind—"

Miss Jesup spun a sheet of paper into her machine and cast a disdainful eye at her shorthand pad. . . .

He sat down on a corner of his desk, shook a cigarette out of a pack and ignited a long wooden match with his thumbnail, running a professional scrutiny meanwhile over the make-up of the afternoon paper's smooth front page. After a time he turned over and appraised the crop of locals.

When he had finished he stared out of the window for a minute or two, then crossed the floor and leaned against the sill of a door marked 'Society.'

"Miss Minnie," he said, "in your peregrinations among the Four Hundred have you ever run into a guy named Pavinovsky?"

"The shoe—"

"No, this guy's not a shoemaker. This guy's got some side."

"There's a Miss Pavinovsky that works for Telfair & Company—"

"No, this guy's a man."

He paused a minute at the worn newel post, then skipped down the stairs. "Has Pavinovsky come yet?"

"Just gone. . . . What do you suppose the reward was?"

"Oh, thirty-five cents—"

"Five dollars."

"Five dollars! My God, he could buy the state legislature for that!"

"And who do you suppose he is?"

Mr. McFarlane stared at her.

"He's with The Metropolitan Opera Company."

"Are you kidding me? . . . What does he do, shift scenery?"

"I don't—"

"No! His picture was in the *Times* six weeks ago! That's where—" He reached for a telephone and called a number. "Police headquarters."

"Hello, chief. This is Mac. Is my boy, Dewey, round there?"

There was a minute's silence then Dewey came to the phone.

"Dewey, I want you to get in touch with Sergey Pavinovsky.

Sergey Pavinovsky. His telephone is—what's that number, baby?
—3057-J. If he's not there keep on till you get him. He's something with the Metropolitan Opera Company. Find out what.
Get a story from him. How does he like the South, Southern
womanhood, Coca-Cola? What does he think of the drop in
cotton? You know. Half a column. I think we've got a scoop.
. . . Anything going on round there?"

"Yeah. Plenty. I just drew a king high full against Bobo standing pat with three aces—"

"Well, suppose you just tear yourself away and—"

6. Amateur Golfer

Friday, July 24

THEY played golf every morning after the high school closed
for the summer, no matter how hot it was. They carried their
own bags and went round hatless, contemptuous of ninety-seven
and eight degrees. They played in white shirts with the sleeves
rolled up to the shoulder, and Elbert himself usually wore a
pair of khaki pants that he had ripped off with a pocket knife
to the length of bathing trunks, his legs burned very brown
and hard. . . .

The one-o'clock sun beat down through the elm trees along
the sidewalk leading from the Country Club; the crape myrtle
bushes drooped in the bright heat. But it weighed lightly on
Elbert's shoulders. The State Amateur was getting close and he
had just shot a seventy-two. He should have had an even seventy,
or better. He had missed three easy putts; the one on the fifteenth
he would certainly have made if that darned aeroplane hadn't
swooped over his head. It was practically a gimme. It wasn't two
feet. He wondered what that plane was trying to do; it looked

210

like it wanted to land. It swooped over them on the fifteenth, then sailed up in a wide circle above the woods and came back over as they went to the sixteenth. The pilot in a white cap and goggles leaned over the side and lifted a hand. He was a little sore at having been made to miss a two-foot putt, but he waved back; you somehow always waved at aeroplanes. But when it came over again, as they walked to their drives halfway up the seventeenth, he stopped where he was, threw down his driver and yelled at it through his hands as it roared over, "Beat it, you big bum!" It rose in a coquettish bank, swung round, and began to climb. When they left the eighteenth green it was a fine black cross motionless against a cloud. "Bet it's nice and cool up there! Oh, boy!" He wiped his hand across his wet forehead while the perspiration trickled down his legs and into the tops of his rubber-soled shoes.

But he would have had a seventy-one if he hadn't three putted the fifteenth; that kind of golf would make any tournament sit up and listen.

7. Evening in Granada

Wednesday, July 29

"WELL, I've got to go down to South Georgia," said Branch Wheaton to his wife, in explanation of his returning from the office at eleven o'clock in the morning. He laid his hat attentively on a hall table and kissed her.

"Now?" she said, a wave of emptiness sweeping over her.

It was always like that. Whenever he told her he was going, for a black moment life suddenly became a void. It was easier now than at first; at first tears invariably shot into her eyes. She was glad that didn't happen now; it wasn't fair to make it

211

hard for him. Nowadays, with a little effort, she could summon a convincing smile; he was never gone for very long. And after the five minutes of his actual disappearance, it wasn't so bad. Things turned up; she managed well enough, watching the time of his return work its way slowly nearer.

"I'm going with one of the salesmen and he's waiting for me at the office now."

"I reckon you want to pack then."

"I won't need much. I'll only be gone a couple of days."

She wiped his suitcase off with a dustcloth while he brought his toothbrush and razor from the bathroom.

"When are you coming back?" she said with an appearance of cheer.

"I'll probably be back Friday night. That'll just be tonight and tomorrow night."

She sat down on the bed. "I'll miss you. . . . But don't worry about me."

"You'd better go over to your Aunt Maggie's. Or get somebody to come stay with you here."

"I'll see. I'll be all right. How many shirts do you want?"

"Oh, one is enough. Put two, though. . . . I'm not taking the car. We'll go in Forshaw's car. You can drive me down and bring it back. . . ."

They were turning into Broad Street when he said, "Oh, I ran into Owens on the street this morning."

"Really?" She thought it was funny that she couldn't say that with absolute naturalness; just because she had kissed him once casually, whenever his name was mentioned her tone changed a little.

"He wanted us to come down to Austin's tonight."

She didn't say anything.

"We must have them up to the house before they go."

"Did you tell him you were going away?"

"That was the best excuse I could think of."

She looked straight ahead of her.

When he drew up in front of his office she reached suddenly

for his hand: "Do you really have to go? Today, I mean. I mean couldn't you wait until next week or—"

He laughed. "What's the matter?"

"Nothing. I don't know."

"I'll be back before you know it."

She drove slowly home, hardly conscious of the external world, of the warm green foliage arching above her in summer extravagance, the barefooted boys walking on the canal bank, the dusty wagons in from the country peddling watermelons. . . . If he telephoned her, what was she going to say?

He did not interest her really. She didn't care if she never saw him again. If somebody should tell her he had gone back to Philadelphia she wouldn't feel anything; it wouldn't matter. Perhaps she would be even a little glad. Not glad, exactly, though. Just somehow, maybe, a little relieved. . . . But why should she feel even that? Was she being honest with herself? Perhaps he interested her a good deal. Perhaps she was in love with him. She smiled and shook her head. She was not. She knew enough about love to know that; she didn't know much, but she knew that. Perhaps, though, she ought to confess that he interested her. Maybe he did; she was gladder to go somewhere if she thought he might be there; his impudence was amusing. But it was no more than a kind of amusement; of that she was very positive. It was not the kind of interest that would grow into love. It wasn't like the interest she had begun by feeling for Branch. That had gone quickly into love; this wouldn't. No fear. She knew enough about love to know that.

How much did she know? She thought it wasn't very much. She didn't know much more now than before. Sometimes she wondered if something was not the matter. She had never been taught anything. Once she would have protested with all her heart that there was anything to teach, but now she wondered a little. It looked sometimes as if her elders had purposely trained her to inadequacy as a wife; they had taught her a few things about folding linen and arranging flowers, but the nearest they had ever come to love was chastity. She had heard a good deal

213

about chastity; it was the most important thing in her life; if she gave it up she would be doomed to misery; if she clung to it she would be happy. After she had been married a few months she began to wonder if her chaste elders had been happiest; she had clung to chastity and she was almost miserable. Perhaps chastity had nothing to do with happiness, perhaps it was even a barrier. It was like equipping a person for the Maine woods, then sending him to the tropics.

She was no longer very unhappy, superficially. She had heard people say that love wasn't everything and she was sure that many of these would have said to her now that she was better off as she was. But it was the discrepancy between her love for Branch and expressing it that sometimes oppressed her; she wondered now and then if it might not eventually come between them. She wondered if perhaps that wasn't what her Aunt Maggie had had in mind when she advised her to have a child. "It will keep you together," she had said bluntly. But she didn't want to be kept together by a child; she wanted love to do it. And she knew so little of the language of love. She had thought once that all that mattered was the inner feeling of love for a person; but that was like saying that only what you thought mattered, not what you said,—when often you only thought something after you had said it. They went hand in hand, those things—

But what had all that do to with her today? What had that to do with Branch's going to the country? With Eliot Owens's knowing he had gone? Nothing. Her world had suddenly shifted a little with her being left alone; it made her more conscious of it. It set her thoughts moving. That was all. . . .

As she was parking the car under a shade tree the telephone in the house began to ring. Her cheeks flushed. She knew who it was; she knew what he was going to say.

She walked up the front steps with deliberate slowness. If it stopped ringing that was all right.—

"I can't make it," she said.

"But you've got to. I'll come and get you."

"I'm going to supper at my aunt's."

"I'll come there for you after supper."

"No."

"I want to see you."

She picked up a pencil on the telephone table and twisted it in her fingers, saying nothing.

"I want to see you. I'm going away next week."

"You are?"

"How will eight-thirty suit you?"

She balanced the pencil on the eraser and licked her lips.

"Make it a quarter to nine," she said. . . .

She went about the rest of the day with two voices speaking in her, each offering a motive for what she was about to do; one she clung to, the other she feared. They didn't bring up a question to be decided; she had already decided. She was going. But why? A sort of exhilarating terror swept through her veins when now and then she stopped and looked at it face to face; she could hardly imagine herself even contemplating it. What would her aunt say? Her father? The whole town? If they knew. But they wouldn't know. She would never tell anybody. Not anybody. She could keep a secret. She had kept one before.

Of course, though, they might find out, somebody might see them, somebody might guess. Mr. Applewhite! He might already suspect something. He might guess. He might tell Branch. If Branch found out! That would be deplorable, simply deplorable; he couldn't understand. Who could? Everything would be lost then, everything that she was trying to gain, and everything that she already had besides. If he found out, she would have to leave him; things would never be the same between them again.

But if he didn't find out! Then everything, she thought, would be immeasurably better. They would be happy then; that was all that was standing in the way. She would bind him to her then. It would not be a marriage that was lasting simply through laziness; it would be something real and strong. The body and the soul were so inextricably interwoven; she remembered

215

vividly the first night she had lain down beside him, but with an even greater vividness she remembered the next day and the deep yearning in her soul just to be with him, just to walk with him, listen to him, look at him, a deeper yearning for those things than she had ever known before. Now it was different, but it was different just because they were both such children; she had thought about it a great deal and she was sure. She had said to herself on many a restless night, that if the chance ever came by which she could become a little less of a child about all that she would not hesitate. . . . Now it had come.

She had no feeling for Eliot at all, beyond a sort of clear liking for him, for the child in him of another kind, imp perhaps. He had a sort of irrepressible exuberance about him toward any girl with a good figure; she knew that was all he saw in her. But she didn't mind in the least; in fact that was exactly as she would have ordered it. He had put his arm round her with a mixture of impudence and real tenderness that no girl could possibly pretend to be offended at without laughing. There was a pleasant lightness about him in regard to her; it was not levity so much as a sort of tacit taking for granted that she, the good figure in question, understood and he understood that this was not something to wreck their lives over but, at the same time, being one of the buds of summer, it was worth anybody's special consideration.

But the voices in her head kept trying to confuse her motives. This was a business proposition, as her father would say. Something had to be done about her and her husband; she loved him, she loved the potentialities of their being together. She knew what ought to be done, and she was going to do it. She understood clearly, without ever saying it to herself, that if it hadn't been for her and her husband, Eliot would not have been of the slightest interest to her, more than as amusing company in a crowd. . . . And yet, was that true? Was she really doing this because she loved her husband? Did she really believe that? And if she did, wasn't she just fooling herself? Wasn't she just trying to justify something she wanted to do anyway? No. No!

She was as sure as she had ever been of anything. She had counted on their marriage, put everything on it. It wasn't working out; she was going to do something about it. She wouldn't only do this, but almost anything. Anything! There were no limits to what she would do for her love. She thought of school and the February night she had broken all the rules and gone to Richmond for a birthday present; she smiled at the danger now, but then it had been intense. That was a real love then, and she had acted for it. This was her real love now. . . . She looked at a calendar. There was a moon in the third quarter; it would rise about ten o'clock.

Austin's grandmother had left him a great black tray with a wide border and fluted edges and garlands of demure flowers painted on it. He had Oregon put it on the porch table before he went home, filled with tall glasses and a large bowl for ice and bottles of ginger ale and charged water; having observed Oregon over some twenty years, he attended to the detail of the corn whiskey himself.

He was in the pantry decanting the whiskey from a fruit jar as carefully as possible to keep any blemish off his brittle white suit, when Gwendolyn strolled in from the dining room with an unlighted cigarette that looked very clean and washed amidst the pearl and carmine of her fingernails.

"Got a match?" she said.

Austin put down the jar and the decanter and felt in his stiff coat pocket. He lighted her cigarette, looking at the smooth fair strands of her hair as she bent over. A host of things he wanted to say to her stampeded into the front of his mind and jammed.

She stood up, glanced at the smoke cloud, and opened the icebox.

"Hungry?" he said.

"Thirsty."

He poured two drinks.

217

"Has Eliot gone for Maybelle?"

"Yes. . . . You know, Eliot's got quite a yen for that girl. I don't know what I'm going to do about it."

Austin turned back to the fruit jar. "Do you want my advice?"

"What?"

"Get even with him. Pretend you've got quite a yen for—somebody else."

She laughed. "Who?"

"Oh, there're lots of people."

"Oh, Austin! . . . I *am* fond of you, too." She came over beside him and patted the hand holding the neck of the decanter. Then she lifted the corner of a damp cloth that covered a silver platter. "Sandwiches!"

Austin had been about to stammer something, but her irrelevant discovery of the sandwiches offended him. He put the stoppers in the bottles and carried them into the dining room in silence. He returned to the door and said to her somewhat formally, "Shall we go outside where it's cooler?"

She bit a sandwich in half and as she passed him held the other half out to him. For a very brief moment he considered saying No-thank-you, but he decided against it almost at once and was glad. She popped it into his mouth.

They walked out on the porch.

"I'm glad Nora isn't coming," she said.

"Don't you like Nora?"

"No. . . . I'm jealous."

Austin laughed with a film of bitterness. "I don't believe you-all know what jealousy means. I had a little talk with Eliot this afternoon. He brought up the subject. He said, 'Well, how do you like Gwen?' I was flabbergasted, you know; feeling as I do about you, you know. I didn't know what to say. I didn't like to say I loved you; I didn't know just how he might take it. I was born and raised down here in Alabama, which ranks, in just about any list you can find, either at the bottom or next to the bottom, with Georgia and South Carolina running neck and neck. I mean this is a backward country; we still think of a

218

husband's getting a little angry if someone says he loves his wife. I didn't want to make him mad. I said, 'I think she's beautiful.' Then he said, 'I rather had an idea you fancied Gwen.' When he put it that way, I said, 'Well, now that you mention it, I rather do.' He said, 'I thought so.' I didn't know just how he meant that; I didn't know but that he was getting mad, but I thought I'd better make a clean breast of it now that it had gone this far, so I said, 'As a matter of fact, old fellow, I'm in love with your wife.' And he said, 'Everybody is; she's never yet made a try for a man and missed.' . . . He's mighty proud of you, Gwendolyn."

She laughed. "Of course he is."

"But doesn't jealousy mean anything in you-all's lives?"

"Certainly. I'm jealous of Nora."

"Why are you jealous of Nora?"

"Because you like her."

He laughed incredulously, trying to make the incredulity hide his contentment. "Why, I've never thought about Nora for two minutes in my whole life!"

"You like her just the same."

"Of course I like her. She's so absolutely A-one you have to like her, but—I don't know."

"I know. . . . She doesn't give you goose-flesh the way I do."

She allowed him to pull her toward him with a half-resisting smile.

"Maybe so."

Then she pulled back. "Well, I'm sick of giving people goose-flesh."

"Don't be silly."

"I am. Sick of it!" She freed herself petulantly. "I'm sick of being propositioned by every pair of male eyes I run into."

Austin thought bitterly of all the male eyes in Georgetown. "No resistance at all?" he said, with some irony.

"No. . . . Practically none."

"Who's the practically none? . . . Mr. Applewhite?"

"I'm not going to tell you."

"Well, of course if you're going in now for octogenarians—"

"You're making me mad again, Austin."

"Who is this man with the iron will?"

"You'd like to know, wouldn't you?"

"Yes."

"Nothing you could possibly do would make me tell you!"

"Well—"

"I'm not in love with him. I just appreciate somebody's looking at me as if I were an honest woman."

"But how do I look at you?"

"Spare yourself being told!"

"Oh, wait a minute. I look at you as if you were a human being. Have you ever read *Anna?*"

"There's somebody coming up the front steps. Maybe it's Eliot and that girl."

Austin went to the iron railing and looked down. "Hello, Lee," he said unenthusiastically.

"Austin," said Mr. Lee Hill, "I've just discovered what's the matter with Georgetown.—Good evenin', ma'am.—There's no place to sleep in Georgetown. Now and then a lady will invite me to supper, but that's all. I break bread with her and go my way. And yet our Savior himself has said, 'Man cannot live by bread alone.' . . . I'm a po-o-or little sheep with no place to sleep—"

"There they are now," she said.

"Who is that, ma'am?"

"Eliot and Maybelle."

"Fix yourself a drink, Lee."

"I'm a po-o-or little sheep—"

"I'm glad to see you," said Mr. Applewhite earnestly to Pavinovsky as they walked out of Mrs. Eubanks's white gate and got in Pavinovsky's car; he thought the boy seemed a little subdued. "How are you standing the summer?"

"Um,—I don't like it. I'm sorry, but I really don't like it. I don't think I like small towns."

"You'd better be careful how you say so."

"You have no privacy. It's like living in a boarding house."

"That's true."

"Excuse me if I—"

"Don't mention it. If I weren't living in one I might not realize how right you are."

"I don't like strangers to be so close to me."

"When are you going back?"

"I don't know. It's a little indefinite. Not for some time yet. . . . My sister shrugs her shoulders at all that, but I can't do it."

"You aren't used to it."

"Their attitude toward me, toward my art,—but let's not talk about it. . . . I'd like to have you meet my sister."

"I'd like to very much."

"I thought perhaps we might go to see her tonight if—"

"I'd be delighted. . . ."

They sat out in some canvas chairs under a hackberry tree in the backyard. Judith brought a tray with some cake and a bottle of sacramental wine.

"I'm afraid we're going to have to do something about your brother," Mr. Applewhite said with a disguising laugh.

She looked at him quickly.

"I think he's had about enough of Georgetown for the time being."

"No," said Pavinovsky, laughing; "when I've had enough I'll go."

"But do you know your capacity?" said Mr. Applewhite.

"Intimately."

"All right, then. All right."

"It isn't very exciting," Judith said. "Nothing ever happens. There's not much for him to do—"

"You probably have plenty to do."

"Plenty."

"You work round on Cotton Row, don't you?"

"Yes. I work for Mr. Telfair."

"Do you like it?"

"Well, I never thought of it exactly that way. I've been there going on sixteen years. I wouldn't want to change, if that's liking it. . . . You probably know Mr. Telfair."

"No, I don't. I know his daughter, Maybelle."

"He's my idea of a real Southern gentleman. He has made lots of money too. Things are kind of slow right now, but we *have* made it. Georgetown used to be the second biggest inland cotton market in the world. Then the river began to get so full of sand they had to take the boat off and the railroads raised their freight rates to favor the ports. We still do a fair business though."

"The cotton farmer seems to have had a right tough time. It seems to cost them more than twelve cents to raise it."

"They don't know what it costs them to raise it. They don't know what a book-keeping system looks like. They're always complaining. They could get a dollar a pound and they'd still complain. It's such a gamble. They always think that maybe next week the market's going up. We store it for them, you see, until they are ready to sell it. We lend them money against it. Sometimes they hold it for a year or more. There's one old customer of ours up at Due West that's still got his 1930 crop. He could have got twenty cents for it in 1930 and now he can't get nine; he couldn't get seven with the warehouse charges against it and insurance. But he won't take his loss. He says it's going up again. It don't look to me like it ever would go up again."

"What happens when you can't sell it for what you've loaned him?"

"When it gets to a cent of what we've loaned him, he has to put up more against it. If he can't do that we have to sell it."

"You can't lose then."

"Can't lose! Mr. Telfair owns three thousand acres of farm lands he has had to take in on part payment. Not counting a clay mine. One of these farmers, old man Jim Baker, put up a

222

clay mine as security and Mr. Telfair had to take it. He runs it too. Some people would let it sit idle, but Mr. Telfair don't believe in that.—But now he won't credit anybody named Baker."

"A clay mine?"

"You know, chalk, kaolin. They use it in making tires some, but most of it's used in making paper."

"Paper?"

"Oh, Lord, yes. His biggest customer is The Great Lakes Paper Company. They own the *Daily News.*"

"Oh, I see."

"Yes, they own papers all over the South—"

"Business! Business!" said Pavinovsky. "If you don't stop I'll go jump in the river."

She put out her hand and patted him on his bare forearm. "Of course, they don't buy the clay they used to."

"I've never seen a clay mine."

"Haven't you ever seen a clay mine? Mr. Telfair would be glad—"

They drank the sacramental wine while the moon sailed through the hackberry tree and the street noises died away. He liked them. He didn't know why; he hadn't very much in common with them. But they were pleasant to sit round with.

"No, sir," she said, "Mr. Telfair won't credit anybody named Baker. There was a man named Baker once, he wasn't any kin to old Jim Baker, his name was Bill Baker. He lived over in middle Georgia at a little town called Sautee, and he owed Mr. Telfair seven hundred and fifty dollars. I remember the account well. Mr. Telfair had financed him one year and his crop failed; they had a cyclone that year and he didn't make anything. But the next year was a good year; everybody said the cotton all through that section was the prettiest you ever saw. Well, September and October came round and the crop was gathered and sold, but we didn't hear anything from Mr. Bill Baker. We began to get a little worried that maybe we wouldn't ever get our seven hundred and fifty dollars. Once they get behind with you, you know, they're more than likely to quit you and start

223

doing business somewhere else. So Mr. Telfair thought maybe we'd better send somebody over there and see if Mr. Baker couldn't pay us something.

"'Why don't you send Mr. Randolph Wesley?' I said.

"'Randolph don't know that country,' Mr. Telfair said.

"'Maybe that would be a good thing,' I said. 'Sometimes, you know, a new man can do more with a thing like that than an old one.'

"He thought a minute, then he said, 'Get Randolph on the telephone there, Miss Judy. Tell him I'd like to talk to him first chance he gets.'

"I called Mr. Wesley's house, County 1122, and left word with one of his grandchildren. They said Mr. Wesley had gone out to see about a load of wood. It was November. I remember it was raining too.

"But a couple of hours later Mr. Wesley came in the office. He hung up his rubber coat and Mr. Telfair told him to sit down.

"'What do you think about the weather, Randolph?' said Mr. Telfair.

"'It don't look so good, Mr. Telfair,' said Mr. Wesley.

"'I don't reckon the roads over in middle Georgia are anything to brag about after all this rain.'

"'Oh, I reckon you can get through, Mr. Telfair.'

"'Well, Bill Baker over at Sautee owes me about seven hundred and fifty dollars and I think he ought to pay us something. Do you reckon you could go over there and find him and have a talk with him?'

"'I don't know any reason in the world why I couldn't.'

"'Do you know that country over there?'

"'No, sir; but I can find him.'

"'Well, I think you better do it, Randolph. We ain' got any security. He might be fixin' to put his property in his wife's name—'

"'Yes, sir.'

"'You see him and if he'll give you six hundred dollars cash money—I reckon you better take it.'

224

" 'He be standin' very much in his own light not to accept that. 'Course you know they want the world and a wire fence around it.'

" 'Well, Randolph, suppose you just get in your car and go over there and see what you can do.'

" 'All right, sir,' Mr. Wesley said, and he put on his rubber coat and went out in the rain.

"Well, Mr. Wesley said it looked like he never would get to Sautee. First one thing came up, then another. He hadn't gone twenty miles when he got a flat tire. Then, going up that long slick hill outside of Early Branch, he slipped off in the ditch. He had to get a pair of mules to pull him out and by that time it was getting on to night. He spent the night at Early Branch; he said he thought it might break his luck.

"But it didn't seem to do any good. The next morning it was still raining and about twelve o'clock he had another flat tire. It just looked like everything was going wrong. Then in the middle of the afternoon, just when he was getting in the neighborhood of Sautee, he ran into a funeral. He saw some cars stopped in the road up ahead of him and when he came a little closer he saw it was a funeral. The hearse was standing in the road all right, but the other automobile, the one the family was in, had slid off in the ditch. The widow and her two grown boys and the preacher were standing round in the rain.

"Of course there wasn't anything to do but pull up and see if he could help. So Mr. Wesley stopped and got out and asked them if there was anything he could do to help them. The car looked like it was stuck in the ditch good and proper.

"Well, Mr. Wesley had a cable in the bottom of his car he had used the day before when he was in the ditch himself, and he told them if they would fasten it on to the front axle he would see if he could pull them out. They did that and he tried, but the road was so slick he couldn't get any hold; with that extra load his wheels spun around and it looked like he might even get over into the ditch too. All this time it getting darker and night coming on and he not getting any closer to Sautee. Then he got out and told them that if they would all just come get in his car he would ride them on to the cemetery behind the hearse and glad he could do something to help them out.

"At first the widow didn't want to do it, but they persuaded her and they all got in. The cemetery was about two miles up the big road and he drove along after the hearse through the rain, nobody saying anything but the preacher, who was reading now and then out of the Bible.

"When they got to the cemetery Mr. Wesley helped them get the coffin out and then stayed and helped them lower it in the grave. The rain was slacking off by this time and it was beginning to turn cold. But he stayed on until the service was over and then took the widow and her two boys back to the farm.

"'Can't I take you to your home, sir?' he said to the preacher; it was almost dark by then but he knew he couldn't do anything in Sautee until tomorrow anyhow. So the preacher got back in.

"As they rode along he said to the preacher, 'I'm a stranger in this county, I wonder if you could tell me, sir, whereabouts I can find a Mr. Bill Baker. I believe he lives in this general neighborhood—'"

"'But, brother, you just buried him,' said the preacher. . . .'"

It was three-thirty when Pavinovsky set out to take Mr. Applewhite to Summerville. Mr. Applewhite was tired but he again brought up the subject of home.

"I have always felt very strongly," he said, remembering his journal, as they drove swiftly along the empty streets through the tepid daybreak, "that if you want to do anything with your life you must get away from home. But there is another consideration to it: Is it terribly important to do something with your life? Suppose, instead of 'doing something' with it, which may be after all a rather childish ideal, you simply entrench your family a little more strongly in an honorable tradition; if, instead of spending your life on yourself, you conserved it and invested it, so to speak, in the good name of your family in

226

the community, what then? Haven't you done a little better with your time? Haven't you built—"

He paused for a moment as his eye caught the figures of a man and a woman moving slowly across an open hill of the pale golf course. A fine arrow of sadness shot through him, through the tall ghost of his youth, and was gone.

"Haven't you,—dear me, where was I? . . ."

At Mrs. Eubanks's gate he gave Pavinovsky a quick good night and saw him disappear down the glowing street.

Then he walked pensively through the yard and up to his room. He went to the window and leaned with both hands on the sill, looking out over the town but not seeing it: there had been a light burning in the Wheatons' hallway.

8. Local Page

Friday, July 31

WARREN CO. BAR
PRESIDENT LAUDS
SOUTHERN WOMAN

The Hon. R. M. Kelly, president of the Warren County Bar Association, in a silver-tongued address of welcome to the members of the State Bar Association yesterday, delivered an inspired panegyric on Southern womanhood. After praising the Southland and its contributions to civilization, Judge Kelly concluded his oration as follows:

"Now what of the ladies? When God made the Southern woman He summoned his angel messengers and He commanded them to go through all the star-strewn vicissitudes of space and gather all there was of beauty, of brightness and sweetness, of enchantment and glamor, and when they returned and laid the golden harvest at His feet He began in their wondering presence the work of fashioning the Southern girl. He wrought with the gold and gleam of the stars, with the changing colors of the rainbow's hues and the pallid silver of the moon. He wrought with the crimson that swooned in the rose's ruby heart, and the snow that gleams on the lily's petal, then, glancing down deep into His own bosom, He took of the love that gleamed there like pearls beneath the sun-kissed waves of a summer sea, and, thrilling this love into the form He had fashioned, all heaven veiled its face, for, lo, He had wrought the Southern girl." —

COTTON DECLINES
TWENTY POINTS ON
LOCAL EXCHANGE
CONTINUED DRY WEATHER
REDUCES RAVAGES FROM
BOLL WEEVIL—

CHAPTER SIX

1. Isthmus

"I SHOULDN'T be surprised, Austin," said Dr. Abercorn, looking up at the fiery little points of the Big Dipper burning steadily in the northwest, "if, in beating your way through your jungle in quest of truth, dead or alive, you found you could shed a faint light in the darkness by considering questions of morals and ethics as if they were human beings, or even animals or plants. There's no reason to think they're a law unto themselves; we can't create anything except in our own image. Grant them, I mean, powers of reproduction and growth and natural death,— being careful to give the power of reproduction its accredited place at the front. You might decide they had evolved into highly complex organisms from very simple ones. They've done a lot of reproducing since the foundation of the species, probably not many thousand years before Moses, and it's sometimes hard now for an intelligent man to trace a question's genealogy, hard to know who it's grandparents were. But if you consider that the evolution of these questions is analogous to the evolution of life, you might, by examining a little of what we know about that, make one or two deductions about 'em that would give off a sort of mild phosphorescent illumination,—something about like this starlight, not telling you very much but still maybe keeping you from breaking your neck as quick as the other fellow.

"For instance, these plants and animals and human beings, I

229

figure they make up a kind of archipelago of life, islands of life, kingdoms, animal, vegetable, mineral. You find many things on one island you don't find on another, but now and then you find a pair of widely-separated islands that have one or two curious things in common,—a little like the pyramids you find in Egypt and Mexico. Such a pyramid might be, say, the elaborate precautions taken in both the animal and vegetable kingdoms against inbreeding. . . . Of course, in all this, Austin, I am presupposing in you a rather highly-developed ignorance."

"I'll try not to disappoint you, sir," said Austin.

"Well, these little islands may seem at first glance to be just thrown up there casually, as you might think the West Indies just happened to be thrown up there or the Philippines. But if you stand back a little you can see there isn't much difference between the Isthmus of Panama and the Lesser Antilles; the ocean wouldn't have to drop but a few feet more to give you an isthmus connecting Florida with Venezuela. The Philippines are a continuation of the China coast and Australia of the Malay Peninsula. And if you stand back these other islands connect up too; you can go practically dry-shod all the way from the human intelligence to a—camelia bush. You can go anywhere.

"Suppose you begin with the very last word in evolution, the most up-to-date thing on the market, the human intelligence. Call it an island, a volcanic island. It is continually in modest eruption, pouring down lava streams both tonic and toxic, though scientists have conducted expeditions to the edge of the crater. There is a good possibility that it will explode some day in a fine intelligent war and blow this end of the archipelago off the map, but anyway,—when you look around you from this pinnacle the closest thing you see is what looks like another island, the human body. It's a very different sort of place, tough and solid, nothing volcanic about it; it don't seem to have anything in common with volcanoes. You are looking from what may be called the soul over to the body and you may, at first look, think they don't connect. But they do; round here on one side is a sort of isthmus: you lie down on your back in a quiet room and

230

relax your muscles. You know how you feel riding in a buggy up a hill, how you try to make yourself light? Well, try to make yourself heavy; begin with your fingers and your hands, then go on to your arms and legs and chest, make everything heavy. You can't do it at first, but if you try every day for half an hour, after a month or two you'll be able to do it pretty well. You'll be able to relax your eyelids and your eyes and your throat. Then one day if you watch yourself you'll find that when you relaxed all your muscles as far as they would go, you weren't thinking. There is good reason to believe that every thought sets up a minute muscular response, probably in your throat; and some people maintain that if you could measure this response with an instrument you could translate thought into a graph or even into sound. But anyhow, you don't think when your muscles are relaxed. There's got to be a muscular tension. . . . So here you are, with dry feet, on the other island, on the human body, the vertebrate.

"There's nothing sleight-of-hand about all this, Austin. The idea is not generally accepted, but I believe it goes in the right direction and I believe if it is disproved sometime it will be because some even stronger connection has been found.

"But here you are now on the biggest piece of land in the archipelago, the vertebrates, and you wander back along the ridge, back along the backbone, back and back, until you finally come to what looks like the jumping-off place, the end of the backbone. This seems to be as far as you can go. The nearest dry land you see is a long way off and they are the animals without any backbone, with the skeleton on the outside, the shell-fish. There may not seem to be, at first, any way of getting across there. But round here at the side is another little isthmus, a creature called the ostracoderm. This little animal, which was once around in great profusion, has the upper part of his body encased in a shell, but his tail has a very delicate cartilaginous backbone inside of it. You can get across the gulf quite easily on him, and the first thing you know you are in the land of the invertebrates, the crustaceans. . . . Things are getting simpler and simpler all this time and you probably feel pretty good about it.

"You can see from here quite a large piece of land off to one side, the vegetable kingdom, the plants. There doesn't seem to be any way in the world to get over to the plants. They haven't any skeleton at all; they don't seem to have anything in common with the rest of us. But if you look round a little bit you'll find this sort of instinct against self-pollination, which has a familiar ring to it, and also a curious little thing called a carnivorous plant. It eats meat. If an insect lights on one of its leaves it closes up so quick it can catch it. If you touch it with a pencil it doesn't do much; you can even put a few grains of sugar on the leaf and it won't pay any attention to it. But you put a little piece of meat on there and it grabs it. . . . And there's also another very curious little thing called a diatom. It's a sea plant, but it can crawl around on the bottom like a snake. And there are the bacteria, too, which are plants and, so to speak, carnivorous.—You can get across, then, somewhere in here, to the vegetable kingdom, if not absolutely dry-shod, at least your feet aren't *very* wet.

"All these things are kin. You can even get over into the mineral kingdom by way of the coal deposits, which you might call vegetable cemeteries. All these things came out of one. There was one cell and it divided in two. Then these two grew up and divided. And after a while the temperature changed and it got more complicated. Then something else changed and it got more and more complicated, until after a while, it got into plants and animals, vertebrates and invertebrates, body and mind. But what I'm getting at is you can go back and forth all round this archipelago with practically dry feet.

"And I think it's the same way with these ethical organisms like good and evil and the rest of them. The same thing happened to them. They began as mental bacteria or algae and divided, then reproduced by dividing again, and after ten or fifteen thousand years (their existence as an independent kingdom is relatively recent) they come down to us as distinct species. But they go back to one, just like the rest of us. I don't know what that original moral cell looked like, but if you can convince yourself, Austin, that there was such a cell, that these things are only human and have somewhere a common ancestor, you may, as I say, stir up a sort of starlight in the darkness and be able to find your way along a little more readily than the next man—"

2. Sabbatical

THE Reverend Dice Alexander, from his room in the second-best hotel in Yokohama, wrote a letter to his old friend Riley All in Georgetown, Alabama, in which he covered with some detail the following events of his soul-shaking pilgrimage among the heathen.

He and Mr. Wu Fu took the afternoon train from Shanghai to Hang-Chow and he spent three days with the little China-man's family. He would have stayed longer, for he was having a thoroughly agreeable time, but his boat was sailing from Yokohama a week from the following Saturday and he had just time to make it.

Those three days, however, he enjoyed keenly. They were met at the railroad station at the end of the Great Street by two of Mr. Wu Fu's younger brothers and escorted enthusiastically to the compound. Mr. Wu Fu had apparently written his family in detail of the Jerusalem episode, for his grandfather, an aged man with skin the color of an autumn leaf and a scanty white thread of a beard, sat waiting for them in The Hall of the Formerly Ardent Ones wrapped in voluminous waves of embroidered silk, a hat on the back of his ivory head with a pale

233

green mandarin's button on the top. He looked as if he had been sitting there for several weeks.

When Dr. Alexander and Mr. Wu Fu came in the old man rose slowly, his hands still tucked away in his silk sleeves, and made Dr. Alexander a profound obeisance.

"Is this your grandpa?" said Dr. Alexander.

Mr. Wu Fu presented him, and they stood in front of the chair while the old man delivered a long speech in a high but solemn tone, looking over their heads with his pink eyes at the back of the room; when he had finished a servant entered bearing a porcelain vase of the Ming dynasty, which he took and presented to Dr. Alexander. After that they sat down in some high carved chairs on each side of the old man's throne and had some tea. He thought it was very nice of them to give him a vase; he didn't like vases much and he thought this one was a little gaudy, with its teahouses and flowers and young men and women with shiny black hair dressed in green and blue and red against a white background, but he thought if he could get it home without breaking it he could find something to do with it. Anyhow, it was very nice of them; he told Mr. Wu Fu to tell his grandpa he appreciated it very much. The old man replied, according to Mr. Wu Fu's translation, that it was just a trifling thing that they offered in abysmal humility to the august light of his countenance. Had he not been a sentimental man, Dr. Alexander would have decided it was hardly worth taking home.

They were just finishing their tea when they were aroused by a brazen racket in the street outside. It was reminiscent, to Dr. Alexander's increasingly nostalgic brain, of the Georgetown High School Band at one of the first rehearsals of the season. Mr. Wu Fu stood up and requested him to lend the morning sun of his presence at the front of the house.

Dr. Alexander, in some mystery, straightened his white tie and they went out. It was a parade of some fifteen or twenty coolies in livery, carrying between them banners and scrolls covered with large Chinese hieroglyphics; as they strolled along

234

they turned the letters to one side of the street then to the other so that the crowds which the band was drawing out of every by-way, crack, and crevice could read the legends. The band was in livery too, which gave it a feeling of homogeneity somewhat lacking in the styles of their American horns, if not in the tune itself. The consensus of melody, however, Dr. Alexander thought, seemed to be in favor of 'Johnny, Get Your Gun.'

"I don't know exactly why," said Dr. Alexander mistily, "but that takes me back to one of old Cliff Gowdy's Fourth of July barbecues way back in Georgetown, Alabama, where I come from."

Mr. Wu Fu explained to him that it was just a slight gesture on his family's part to explain to Hang-Chow a few of Dr. Alexander's less dazzling virtues. "The one in front says, 'Gorgeous and illustrious offspring of the Far East—'"

"What do they mean, Far East? I come from the United States."

"That's the Far East, reverend."

"Well,—" began Dr. Alexander in protest, but it seemed an upset hardly more striking than the one he thought was taking place in his spiritual life, so he desisted. . . .

On the third day he bade Mr. Wu Fu and his family an affectionate farewell, went down to Shanghai and boarded a small steamer to take him the thousand miles to Yokohama. He pondered continually during the four-hour train ride to the coast on these strange heathen people and their strange heathen beliefs and customs, their strange heathen religion. They didn't know what baptism was; Mr. Wu Fu had never heard of the efficacy of complete immersion as a spiritual insurance. What did it mean? Were they all damned? Or, heresy though it was to utter it, was complete immersion not as important as he had been taught to believe! As they struck out into the Yellow Sea he lowered his head in prayer.

It was a beautiful summer day and he sat down on deck and opened his limp-leather Bible to the story of John the Baptist. There was a Chinaman sitting in the chair next to him, his eyes

235

half closed, looking straight ahead of him out through the railing at the warm-tinted surface of the Hwang-hai, his hands in his sleeves. All that afternoon Dr. Alexander read on,—John the Baptist, The Gospel according to Saint John, The Revelation of Saint John the Divine (the matter of baptism was on his mind). The Chinaman just sat there looking at the Yellow Sea, not doing anything. It began to worry Dr. Alexander after a while that the man should be content to sit there in such lazy indolence, not even trying to improve his mind by reading a book. A little before sunset he said to the Chinaman, "Pardon me, sir, but maybe you would like a book to read."

The Chinaman turned to him with a peaceful smile. "Oh, no, thank you," he said. "I've read everything worth reading and I know most of it by heart."

Dr. Alexander went below and began a letter to the Reverend Riley All; he felt again that a great change was coming over him. "Some things have puzzled me, brother," he wrote. "I have looked upon sights I do not understand; I have listened to words I do not comprehend. Remember me in your prayers."

3. Precipitation .09

AT two o'clock on the fourth of August Mr. Estill went up to the roof of the Post Office Building and looked aloft at his wind gauge. The cups were hardly turning, but the arrow lay a little to the east of southeast; it had shifted about ninety degrees since noon. Twenty degrees more and it would be blowing clockwise into the low-pressure area over Louisiana and Arkansas. Perhaps at last the "low" was moving east.

He crossed the hot faded boards to his blistered rain gauge

236

and lifted off the funnel top. It scorched his fingers, and he set it down quickly on the railing. He made sure that the cylindrical receptacle beneath was dry and clean; the blue sky was brilliant and empty except for an innocent-looking cluster of high fleecy clouds to the southwest, but if the wind shifted any farther he thought there might be rain before dark.

When he put back the funnel top and took another look at the wind before returning to the vortex of his office fan, he saw that the vane had shifted two or three degrees more to the east. . . .

At four o'clock, Oregon, having mixed Mr. Austin and his company a bowl of shrimp salad and put it in the icebox beside a china pitcher of fresh tea, rolled four pieces of cold fried chicken into a newspaper with eight beaten biscuits, three sticks of cornbread, and a hard-boiled egg, put on his broken-brimmed straw hat and started home. When he climbed circumspectly into the rear seat of the open street car he tipped his hat and observed politely to Mrs. Beaseley's maid, "Look like, ma'am, we might get a little shower before dark."

"It do, Mr. Oregon. But I seen it look like this the odd time and ain' no rain."

"Yes'm, ain't it the Lord's truth, ma'am. . . ."

Shortly after four-thirty the clouds began to grow over the west. The warm wind subsided into a motionless heat and the dusty leaves above Kollock Street hung heavy on their stems without a tremor. The sunlight, shining down the lower blue surface of the cloud wall, reflected outward in a steely glow. For a few minutes the storm, as if in final indecision, seemed to pause.

Then the cloud-bank, instead of shifting northward over the river, began to climb.

Out in The Terry the tempo of living increased. Sidewalk conversations were broken off; clothes were dragged helter-skelter off the backyard lines; shutters were pulled to. A twister pirouetted in the Kollock Street dust. . . .

Mrs. Mattie Small peered out of her kitchen window at the

bruised sky beyond the fig tree, withdrew her head hurriedly, and less than a minute later, just as the topmost leaves along the sidewalk began to turn up their gray undersides in the freshening wind, opened her rarely-used front door and pushed on to the porch a small-sized clothes basket covered with newspaper. She dragged it after her to the edge of the porch, straightened up, and lighted her pungent pipe. Then she went down the steps to the ground and lifted the basket to her head; she steadied it, shifted it for balance, then put one fist on her hip and walked through her gate. The wind had descended to the lower limbs now and there were swirls of dust down Kollock Street toward the town; toward the canal bridge, though, it was still quiet. Anyway, she had to go now rain or shine; she had already waited too long.

"Where you goin' to, Sister Small? You gonna get drownded."

"I got to ca'y these here figs to a lady. They be spile by in the mornin'. I don't spec it's gonna rain, nohow. It's jest a threat."

She turned her head slowly away and walked toward the canal, her shoulders steady, her heelless shoes scraping the ground. . . .

She didn't feel the first large scattered drops on account of the basket above her face, but as the bright lines began to lace across the dark foliage ahead she felt it on the back of her hand. She frowned, took several quick pulls on her pipe, and increased her pace a little.

It was beginning to rain quite hard as she passed Lim Tom's Grocery Store. Mr. Lim Tom, standing in the doorway in a pair of shapeless cotton trousers watching the shower, said to her, "What the hully, Sister Small? Come in from the rain."

"These here figs'll spile," she said, and went on.

She was nearly to the canal when a sudden clap of thunder cannonaded over her head and the clouds opened. The water descended in sheets with a noise like escaping steam. It was as if the stored-up rains of all summer were now loosed. Puddles collected at once in the road and sidewalk, the surfaces bubbling high with the splatter like boiling water in a kettle. A trace of alarm shot into her eyes, then melted away.

238

She paused under the poor shelter of a sycamore tree and stood there with the water beginning to leak through the basket and run down her face. She wiped it off with the pale palm of her hand, shuddering a little; enough was enough. Her skirt was already black wet in front and her pipe was out. She looked out from under the worn wicker bottom with a slight frown on her eyebrows; enough was enough.

Then someone dashed panting under the tree from behind her. She turned round so quickly she nearly dropped the basket.

It was a negro man with a newspaper package under his arm and he brushed at the rain on his sleeves and trousers as if it had been dust.

"Ain' she rainin'!"

Mrs. Small said nothing. He had scared her, running up there like that. She steadied the basket and moved coldly to the other side of the trunk.

"Don' let me discommode you, ma'am."

"You ain' discommodin' me."

A boy bolted by, his head pulled down between his shoulders. Mrs. Small followed him with her eyes without turning her head, the water trickling off the end of her blunt nose unheeded.

"You better come round on this side the tree, ma'am. This here the dry side."

"Ne'mind," said Mrs. Small and looked out at the deserted street now disappearing into gray toward the bridge.

One or two of the porches were occupied by people watching the rain. "You, sister!" somebody called to Mrs. Small. "Y'all come over here on the porch."

"Hit ain' gonna last," said Mrs. Small. "Thank you, ma'am."

She turned away from them toward the man under the tree; he was looking round him inquisitively.

"Look like sumpn don' satisfy you," said Mrs. Small impatiently.

"Don't it seem like to you sumpn smell kinder funny round here—"

239

"I ain' smelled nothin' funny till you got here," said Mrs. Small.

"I don't intend anything personal, ma'am."

"Ain' nothin' tyin' you to this here tree, is they, beein's you don't like it?"

"No, ma'am. No, ma'am, ain' nothin' tyin' me."

"Who got this tree first, anyhow?"

"You, ma'am, you. No harm intended."

Mrs. Small turned away again. "Well, look like hit's lettin' up," she said. "Reckon I'll be pushin' along."

"I don't see no lettin' up—"

"Course it's lettin' up. What make you so onery!"

She walked out into the full rain, the basket, streaked with black down the sides, balanced on her head as level as a sun dial.

On the corner below the bridge, where the approach began to slope upward, she passed the front of an empty store, the wooden bench in front of the window gleaming under the rain.

Then in the recess of the doorway she saw a patrolman. She saw him with the tail of her eye, his dark trousers, his blue shirt, and the black holster at his belt; he was swinging his stick so that it wound up on its thong, then unwound, looking idly at the rain, standing on his heels.

When she saw him something inside of her caught her breath. She passed him without breathing, looking straight ahead. Then just as she was almost by, she saw the stick tumble down to the end of its thong and hang there as if something had surprised him. She could feel his eyes ominously on her back.

Then she heard somebody running toward her from behind, and her reason went suddenly black. Her legs sagged and for a moment she wavered. Then she hauled the basket off her head with a wild sweep, dropped it with a muddy thump, and fled down the canal bank.

4. 96 pt. B B Caps

THE rain ended in the two-hundred block of Kollock Street. Dewey Selph, telephoning in from the pay station in Glover's Drug Store, told Mr. James McFarlane, sitting with his feet just out of the bright spot of sunlight on his desk, that it was raining pitchforks. Mr. McFarlane tried to break into the flow of words to tell him he was drunk, but failed to dent the narrative pouring in from the other end.

Mr. McFarlane's shoes came down with a bang. His right hand shot to a pile of rough copy paper while his left, with almost amorous passion, entwined the receiver and mouthpiece. His right foot, brushing against the spittoon with which Major Bain thoughtfully supplied his boys, kicked it careening across the office floor as he planted his telephone arm on a corner of the copy paper and began a flying pencil scrawl.

His sports editor stopped on the threshold and stared at him; he hadn't seen such a spectacle before.

"Get Tom!" said Mr. McFarlane, wiggling his middle finger at the door leading into the composing room. . . .

Tom was fishing in a tin tub of icewater for a bottle of Coca-Cola, a batch of market reports under his arm. In front of a window one of the machines was running, clanking and chinking as if it were counting money. He pulled out a dripping bottle as the sports editor touched him on the arm.

"Mac's got a must," said the sports editor.

They entered Mr. McFarlane's office as he dropped the receiver down and snatched the cover off his typewriter.

"Get out an extra!" said Mr. McFarlane. "Has that green paper come in yet?"

"Just come up from the depot this—"

"Run your front page off on green. Here's your streamer. Ninety-six point B B caps—"

5. Former Nurse

DR. ABERCORN stirred the ice in his corn-whiskey-and-plain-water with his first finger. "But I'm an old man," he said. "What's good for me don't matter if it isn't good for you. How do *you* feel about coming back to Georgetown?"

"On the whole," said Lucian, "I think I rather like it."

They were sitting in the twilight in their shirt sleeves with before-supper drinks.

"Is it big enough for you?" Dr. Abercorn said, apparently ignoring Lucian's answer, intending vaguely to hide his relief. "You know, there's a good deal to be said for a place like Georgetown. I think life flows at a better pace than in the big cities. There's time for things to sink in, time to get a little understanding with all your getting. I believe you'll find a better quality of wisdom in a place like this than in New York or London or Paris. The environment is not so obtrusive. In a big city you are always in some kind of petty conflict with the physical world. Why, you can't even cross the street without giving it serious consideration.—But, more than that, there is a crowding and confusion of ideas in a city. The mental traffic is as bad as the physical. And there are no policemen to direct it; there is a mental jam at every crossing. The friction generates a good deal of sparks, but there isn't much power; an idea doesn't get a chance to grow up. Using a sexual metaphor, there is too high a ratio of fornication to reproduction."

"There's something in what you say—"

"I was a little afraid you might not be satisfied down here. We are behind the times, we are very conservative. But those things aren't so bad. Truth is much more likely to lie somewhere near the middle of the road. The nigger makes us conservative; he is pretty good ballast; we don't like to take any chance of an upset. He holds us back from the latest improvements, but he also holds

242

us back at the same time from the latest errors. It doesn't make much difference to us whether it's 1930 or 1932. And that's a good attitude. It's sane. I happened to see the other day in the New York paper a piece discussing a book by—somebody or other, I've forgotten. The man apparently reads a book every day and some days he reads two or three. That is utterly inconceivable to me; my mind, as far as I can see, is as good as it ever was (and that's pretty good), but I've been reading *War and Peace* for six months, and *Tristram Shandy* more or less all my life. But the really amazing thing about it is what this fellow said; (I don't usually read these book articles, so it may not be as amazing as it seemed to me.) He was talking about this book and its attitude and its arguments and he referred to one pessimistic argument that the only way to unite Europe was to fuse it in one strong hate for Asia and America. Then he adds deprecatingly, 'But this is 1932!'—Things up there move so fast that before an author can get his book through the press it is out of date. The book might have been all right, apparently, in 1931, but the 1932 literary standards—"

"What's that?"

"What?"

"Out in the street. Is it an extra?"

"It probably is."

"Shall I go get one?"

"By no means. By no means. . . . That's exactly the sort of thing I'm talking about. I can't imagine a piece of public news that I would be any better off knowing tonight instead of tomorrow. Even if those boys were proclaiming the perfection of a cure for cancer, tomorrow morning would be plenty of time for me to know about it. . . ."

When Lucian came in to breakfast his father was eating a hot biscuit with jam on it.

"There's your news," he said. "A hacked body, sir, shook the world yesterday by being found in a basket." He drank his coffee and got up.

Lucian glanced at the headline: HACKED BODY FOUND IN BASKET, Woman Flees—

"Of all the damned things," said the doctor, "to spread across the front page of a newspaper! I've got a good mind to get Miss Cope to write Major Bain a letter. It ain't worth printing at all, a lot less spreading it over the front page—"

"Oh, that's news, pater," said Lucian, pouring some cream on his fresh figs.

"It's yellow journalism."

"I'll bet you read every word of it."

"Well, you lose!" He bit the end off a cigar and went to the door. "Come downstairs when you finish your breakfast; Miss Cope brought in those pictures." He went out.

Lucian laid the paper beside his plate and glanced through the first two or three paragraphs of the story as he ate his fruit. Body alleged by Mattie Small to be that of Mary Glover, 22,—had declared, according to testimony of Mattie Small, she had been working at hospital,—no record at hospital of Mary Glover,— late hour last night body not identified,—

He turned away to Brisbane's column and read a paragraph. Then he pushed the paper away, thinking of Cope bringing in the X-ray pictures. She irritated him somehow; she always agreed with everything he said. Sometimes he tried to make her disagree. She wasn't even efficient; his father didn't seem to notice it, but she wasn't. He thought he would suggest sometime getting somebody else, a younger woman, a white girl. It was funny why the colored girl had left; just walked out one afternoon and that was all. The way they did you, though, his father said. But perhaps it wasn't so strange; after what had happened it was probably a good idea. He had been glad enough when she failed to show up. They had managed all right during the week before Cope got back; he wished she hadn't got back at all. They could manage a lot better with a young white woman—

Body not identified! Mattie Small held on charge of first degree murder, performing illegal operation—

He felt his face all of a sudden begin slowly fading into a sick

244

gray, then becoming damp. Then the conviction broke over him like a wave that it was the colored nurse who was dead! It lifted him to his feet and he stood there for a minute straddling the chair and staring at the musty wall. He felt nauseated.

He pushed back his chair and went out.

When he came back he was still pale. He took the paper to a stiff chair by the window, sat down on the edge of it, and read the story through from beginning to end. At a late hour last night the body had not been identified. Body not identified.

He heard a step in the hall and stood up, putting the paper aside. It was Cope.

"The doctor's waiting for you, Mr. Lucian."

"I'll be right down. I'll be down in a few minutes."

"All right, sir." She went back downstairs.

How long before it would be identified! It was probably identified now. It was almost nine-thirty. The afternoon paper was probably setting up its headline now: FORMER NURSE OF PROMINENT DOCTOR—

Telephone the paper! Know the worst. . . . There was a New York train at eleven-fifteen. . . . Use the extension by his father's bed. Somebody downstairs might— Go out. Go out for a package of cigarettes.

He went downstairs. Miss Cope was in the waiting room. He put one hand in his pocket and said to her casually, "Tell the governor, will you, I'm running out for a package of cigarettes. I'll be right back."

There was a telephone booth in the drug store on the corner. His wet fingers stuck to the pages of the telephone book as he ran through it for the number; then he dropped in a nickel, put his lips close to the warm mouthpiece, and called the editorial rooms of the afternoon paper. He thought that probably one of the reporters or the city editor would answer; they would know, he could ask them. He thought he had better come right out with it boldly, professionally, as if he wanted to know for business reasons—

"Georgetown *Chronicle*."

245

"Can you tell me if the body of the murdered woman has been identified yet?"

"No, and it ain't likely to be either. . . . Who's this talking?"

Lucian hesitated for a fraction of a second; if he gave his name— He hung up.

He stood for a minute under the ceiling fan in front of the soda fountain, weighing the importance of this information; slowly he began to be conscious again of the bright morning and the sun outside pouring into Green Street. He lifted his shoulders in relief and breathed in deeply through his sensitive nostrils.

6. If This Were China

Wednesday, August 5

NORA hung a tapestry bag on the arm of one of Austin's porch rockers and looped a thread of brown yarn round her first finger.

"What are they *doing* out at the airport, Austin? You don't suppose they have flown the coop, do you?"

Austin leaned his elbows on the bridge table in a temporary manner and dealt himself a desultory hand of solitaire. "They'll be along directly. Don't be impatient."

She crossed her feet against the banisters and started knitting. Austin turned up the seven of diamonds, searched the table, and put it on the eight. The fan buzzed somnolently on the floor by the wall.

After a silence she said, "Take off your coat, Austin. Take off your tie. You're among friends."

"Quite comfortable, thanks."

"You always used to take your coat off."

He lifted his eyebrows. "There's another deck. Deal yourself

246

a little Napoleon. Time seems to be hanging heavy on your hands."

"I'm quite comfortable, thanks."

"Do I have to amuse you?"

"You do, darling."

He stared patiently across the cards at her as her smile broke into a laugh. Then he turned indifferently back to the table and studied the array.

"I do, do I?" he said with active unconcern.

She laughed, biting her lower lip, watching the shining points of the steel needles.

He flipped over the ten of spades. "Well, I'm glad you're amused."

She didn't say anything, but went on smiling at the wool in her lap.

He came to the end of the deck, picked up the discards, tapped the edges three or four times with his fingers, and started through again.

"What is it about me you find so funny?"

"Oh,—I don't know—"

"I would have bet hundreds of dollars you would say that. Hundreds!"

"No; I really don't know. It isn't malicious,—or not very. . . . When's your company going, Austin?"

"They're talking about going next week. I tell them that's absurd."

She straightened out the bottom of the sweater, which was getting twisted. "She's good looking, isn't she?—Nice legs."

"You know, there's one thing I really wish in this life." He stopped. "I wish girls wouldn't talk about other girls' legs."

"Why?"

"It's a masculine subject, for one thing. You take all the poignancy out of it. You approach it academically, intellectually. Or try to. You can't quite do it, you know, partly because you aren't intellectual and partly because you can't get rid of a slight bitterness."

247

"I'm not bitter. My legs aren't bad."

Austin glanced at them, horizontally pushing against the banisters.

"Let's not discuss it," he said.

She laughed.

He turned up two or three cards in silence.

After a while he folded the deck in one hand again. "You know, there's a lot to be said for the Oriental way of handling this marriage thing."

"What marriage thing?"

"That's what I mean. You mention legs and to my barbaric Western mind comes the associated idea, marriage. Legs oughtn't to have anything to do with marriage. They have, and that's where we get into trouble. They haven't in China. At the very end of the long ceremony, and not before, the parents lift the girl's veil and the boy sees who he has married—"

"I wouldn't like that."

"But we'd be so much better off if we did that. We cling to the idea of marriage having something to do with sex; it has very little. Look at you and me. If Georgetown were in China, we'd probably be quite comfortably married to each other; had you ever thought of that?"

She laughed. "No, I hadn't."

"It's true. It has occurred to my Uncle Jim and I dare say it has occurred to your father."

"He has never mentioned it to me."

"I don't mean that he is sold on me personally. I may be deficient personally in certain admirable commercial qualities; but my people are all right in their way and I really believe if we had progressed a little further in culture your father would have looked round the town (he would certainly have wanted you to marry one of the local boys) for somebody very much like me. He might have preferred to have me hungry in the cotton business, but, in general, I would probably get by. Uncle Jim, as my nearest kin, would have been looking round the town for a sane young woman of good family, in good health, and I am sure he

248

would have fastened on you. He would have gone to your papa and they would have got a little drunk together and—we would be sitting here now just like this, doing exactly what we are doing, knitting and playing solitaire, in comfortable indifference—"

"And probably waiting for Gwendolyn."

"How do you mean?"

"We *are* waiting for Gwendolyn, aren't we?"

He turned back to the cards.

"The question of legs," she said, "usually comes in somewhere, sooner or later."

"Well, suppose it does— Say, what do you think's up between Gwen and me?"

"Up?"

"Do you think I'm in love with her?"

She met his frown with a laugh. "Yes, darling."

His lips twisted into an unwilling grin. "Don't be silly."

"What does the lady's husband say?"

He laughed, turning up another card and glancing at it. "Would you like to know?"

"Yes."

"He says she's never yet made a try for a man and missed."

"Well!"

"Of course that's just his way of putting it. She isn't interested in me at all,—or no more than on the well-known feminine principle of leaving no stone unturned."

"Why isn't she interested? You're a nice boy. I don't know what kind of Casanova you'd make, perhaps rather too cerebral, but after all—"

"I can throttle that down to six miles an hour."

"What have you tried?"

"I think we might be a little less personal, don't you?"

"Do you suppose it could be possible that she loves her husband?"

"I thought of that. I don't believe it. But let's not—"

"Well, how does all that affect your plans?"

249

"What plans?"

"Oh,—plans for the future."

"I haven't any plans. Any future, for that matter."

She took two or three stitches. "I don't like to hear you talk that way."

"What way?—Look here, Nora, you've been up there in New England; those people have to plan, if for nothing else than how to get the firewood in for the winter. That's the great thing about the South; as far as plans go, you can live down here practically naked. Consider, Nora, the lilies of the field—"

"You've been away too."

"But I've been back, oh, three years now. I brought back a few plans with me when I came, like you, but when I began to study the lilies of the field and realized that Solomon in all his glory, indisputably, was not—"

"Oh, stop!"

"Why, I—I became a Christian."

When she didn't say anything, he dealt himself a card and said, "What are *your* plans?"

"Well—" She hesitated.

"You see?—I give you six months. By January you will be a Christian."

"No. I have plans. They aren't the ones I came down with, but they haven't just evaporated in the sunshine."

"Are you sure?"

"I can follow just what's happened to change them."

"What's become of your piano?"

"That's what I mean. I've been thinking about all that ever since I've been here. I've come to some pretty definite conclusions, if you are interested."

"Go on."

"Well, I figure I am at the point now where, if I am to get anywhere, I've got to sacrifice. I may have passed that point without knowing it, but I think it's now. Up to now, you see, I haven't taken many chances. I was just as well off studying music as anything else. I haven't sacrificed anything; I haven't bet anything. I'm really just a dilettante. And I believe if you are going to gain anything you've got to risk something. You can't win much backing the favorite. The rewards seem to me more or less in proportion to your chances of losing. When I came down here I thought I would stay a few weeks, then maybe go to Europe. But I began to think about what my chances were of winning; and I have decided they are very slight. I'm not a real musician. I haven't the artist's attitude. I'm not inward enough. And I haven't restrictions enough. I'm a little bit overwhelmed at my freedom. Except for leaving mother and father, there are practically no restrictions on me; I'm not restrained. And it seems to me we are like kites; we can't fly without that string. My whole attitude is so diluted by respectability and—and tradition, by—"

"But, why isn't that your string? 'She faced the handicap of her social position without a qualm and overcame those tremendous obstacles of respectability and abject ease. Born of honest parents, she spent her childhood in the thrall of the most degrading luxury, surrounded on all sides by depressing spectacles of comfort and contentment that would have proved insurmountable except for her insatiable desire to achieve the heights of loneliness and misery. Miss Fenwick—' "

She threw the sweater and the ball of wool into the midst of his cards, scattering them.

"So what?" he said.

"So I have decided that it isn't worth it. I've got too much to lose. I'll just hold to what I have. I like it here. I'm just going to stay."

"Well, you've gone through a lot of laborious thinking and reasoning and arrive in the end at exactly the point that I reached instinctively."

"Of course—"

"But, really, I think you're right. You'll be better off to stay here and marry." He picked up the knitting. "You knit too well; you'd be throwing yourself away on art."

"Of course, you know it's awfully hard to be honest with yourself. I tell myself these are the reasons I'm staying here. I don't

know. Sometimes I wonder if they are. Sometimes I wonder if I
even think they are, honestly."

He looked at her, slightly surprised. "What's the real reason?
. . . As a matter of fact, we saw you the other night at the
movies with—"

"Austin, will you get me a drink of water?"

"Certainly. How about a little corn?"

"No, thank you. Ice water. . . . Here they are! I'll fix the
table—"

7. Wait a Minute!

Wednesday, August 5

WHEN Mr. McFarlane arrived it was about noon and the coro-
ner's son, Bubber, heir to the Funeral Home and probably, unless some unforeseen revolution should upset local politics, heir
to the title, was standing on the edge of the low back porch chat-
ting soberly with a few friends. He was neatly garbed in dark-
blue Palm Beach and, in the rôle of host, bareheaded. His face
wore that expression of deep solemnity with which a boy goes
about the springing of a practical joke.

He nodded with cordial seriousness to Mr. McFarlane, who
folded his hands softly in front of his breastbone and approached
him in a manner duplicating his own when entering a 'house of
mourning' and said to him in a melodious sepulchral tone,
"Where is the body, please?"

A quick smile flashed over Bubber's face, then disappeared.
"In the guest room, Mr. McFarlane,—most of it. Won't you just
come in?"

Mr. McFarlane went into the windowless tile room, stood for
a minute in the three-hundred-watt brilliance amid the audible

252

breathing of three or four visitors gazing in rapt silence at the table, then came out into the sunlight. He drew Bubber aside.

"Who is she, Bubber?"

Bubber shook his head.

"Haven't you any idea?"

"Not a glimmer. . . . One person you can be pretty sure she ain't, though, is Mary Glover."

"Yeah. I guess so."

"Mattie's the biggest liar in Davis County."

"She's been up before, hasn't she?"

"The odd time. They don't want to be too hard on her."

"What'll she get?"

"Oh, maybe two years."

"I'd like mighty well to know who she is. I've got to have a story."

"Mattie says now she came from out of town."

"What happened to her clothes? Wasn't there anything that could be identified?"

"Burnt 'em up. She always burns 'em up. . . . There are always half a dozen people it might be, you know. Two mammas have already been here this morning."

"Is that so?"

"Sure."

"You got their names?"

"Sure. Police regulations."

"That keeps them away, don't it,—taking their names?"

"We'd have all The Terry in here if we didn't."

"It might keep the real family away, too."

"It might. They're scared of anything with police on it."

"How about giving me the names, Bubber?"

Bubber took a notebook out of his hip pocket. "Jessica Heath, 1971 Wrightsboro Road. Rosa Clark, 244 Railroad Avenue."

Mr. McFarlane wrote the information down.

"Well, Bubber," he said, turning away, "let me know if anything comes up."

"I'll do it, Mac."

253

"Don't forget and call up the wrong paper."

"All right."

"I'll be seeing you."

"Be sweet. . . ."

At one-thirty Mr. McFarlane went into Home Folks for his dope-and-lemon. He telephoned Bubber from the booth.

"Anything new, Bubber?"

"Not a thing."

"Nobody else come to claim the body?"

"Not a soul."

"Well, keep me posted, Bubber."

"Oh, I was talking to Battle a little while ago."

"Yeah?"

"He says somebody called him at the office early this morning and wanted to know if the body had been identified. He told him, 'No,' and asked who it was and the bird hung up."

"Hhm.—Nothing else?"

"No."

"All right, Bubber. Thanks."

Mr. McFarlane wiped the perspiration off his face, went up to the corner, and caught a street car for The Terry. . . .

He was retracing Mattie's steps after she had left her house and started out for the canal, when something happened. He had gone over the premises with Police Chief Daughtry and walked to the tree under which Mattie had sought shelter; he had lighted a cigarette and taken two puffs on it. Then in the midst of the third his eye lighted on the dingy window of Lim Tom's Grocery Store. Lim Tom? Lim Tom was the Chinaman who had found that fountain pen. Pavinovsky's pen. This was where Pavinovsky had lost his fountain pen! Great God, there couldn't be any connection—no, not possibly. Lord, that would be news, though! International news! It would put the paper on its feet. It would put him on his feet. They would raise his pay. They would probably take him out of this dump. They—wait a minute! Wait a minute!

But it was a funny place for a Metropolitan Opera star to come for a walk. And who was it had called Battle on the telephone! Whoa! Wait a minute!—

8. Local Page

LEGION AUXILIARY
GIVES FISH SUPPER—

DR. ALL TO DELIVER
EARNEST MESSAGE
ON 'HOLY SPIRIT'
BAPTIST PASTOR TO PLEAD
WITH HEARERS TO ACCEPT
JESUS AS THEIR REFUGE—

NO RELIEF YET IN
SIGHT, SAYS GOV.
WEATHER PROPHET—

HOPKINS RITES
TODAY AT FIVE
VETERAN FIREMAN TO
BE LAID AT REST IN
WESTOVER MEMORIAL—

LOCAL BOY WINS CRITICS
PRAISE IN N. Y. OPERA CO.
SERGEY PAVINOVSKY TO
APPEAR IN EUROPEAN
PRODUCTION IN FALL
by Dewey Selph
Garbed in a pair of old white ducks and a blue shirt open at the neck, young Sergey

255

Pavinovsky, son of the late owner of Pavinovsky's Shoe Hospital on Marbury Street, extended a cordial greeting yesterday afternoon to Your Correspondent when the latter called at the Pavinovsky home on lower Green Street and interviewed the young member of a metropolitan opera company on the alleged lack of interest in the Fine Arts in some parts of the South—

"Look here, Dewey, ain't this bird a dancer or something?"
"Yeah."
"Well, Dewey, why don't you just bust loose and call him a dancer, then?"
"I didn't think you'd want to call him a dancer right out—"
"But, sugar lump, that ain't libel."
"I'm sorry. How do you like it except for that?—"

FIRST BALE 1932
COTTON CROP TO
TELFAIR AND CO.—

THREE BOUND OVER
ON PROHI CHARGE—

CHAPTER SEVEN

1. Two Times Two

Saturday, August 8

"IT used to get right lonesome round the house sometimes," said Dr. Abercorn. "I'm glad to have him back."

Austin unscrewed the cap of the bottle of corn whiskey and handed it to him.

"But I really don't know whether he likes it here or not. Things seem a little out of date to him, I reckon. And of course we *are* a long way from New York. I'm hoping he'll like it better, though, when he gets into the swing of things. He's not on to all our little ways yet."

"He'll be getting married first thing you know."

"He's got a good deal of force. And a good deal of ability, I really think. In fact the idea hits me now and then that he might be doing a lot better for himself working with somebody in a big city. He hasn't said so, but you couldn't blame him if he felt that way. After all, I'm just a country doctor."

"Well, you've just about cured *me*, anyhow."

"I'm glad to hear it.—I didn't have anything to do with it."

"What do you think cured me then?"

"Don't worry about that." He laughed.

"It was a miracle."

"The most miraculous thing about it was that you finally quit monkeying with the works. You've learned a little control. I had a patient once over in Clearwater and every time I'd come to see

257

him he'd begin coughing his head off. There wasn't any sense in it. I said to him, 'Look here, you don't have to cough that way.' He was a little offended. He said, 'But, doctor, coughing is a reflex action.' 'But don't you realize,' I said, 'that the whole fabric of civilization is built on people's being able to control their reflex actions?' "

Austin laughed.

"The trouble with you, Austin, is you believe in ghosts."

"I don't know. Maybe I do."

"You'd rather have a wrong explanation than no explanation at all."

"The way I feel about it is, if it's an explanation it's probably wrong. It's almost certain to be incomplete; it don't tell all. . . . Pilate, I think, was a wise man. He had sense enough not to stay for an answer."

"Oh, no!" said Dr. Abercorn. "He ought to've waited! He was in too big a hurry. I can answer his question." He grinned, fishing out a crumpled package of cigarettes and some matches. "Truth is the way to the cheese."

"Yeah?"

"Yeah. You go at it this way." He moved his hands round in the air. "You build yourself a maze, see. Passages going off in this direction and that· direction, lots of passages. And then you toast yourself a nice piece of yellow cheese and put it down at the end of one of the passages. Then you bring on your rat, and you shut him up in there. And he don't know what to do. All he knows is that there's cheese around there *some*where." He rolled one of the cigarettes on the arm of the rocking chair. "In a minute he goes off down this passage,—which you might call Democracy,—and he butts into the end of it and there ain't any cheese. Then he turns round and comes back and goes off down another passage. And there still ain't any cheese."

"What do you call that one, Communism?"

"Maybe. . . . And he comes back and tries another one—"

"Are you sure the cheese is still there?"

"Of course the cheese is still there."

258

"Maybe there's just a good smell."

"There you are again! You want just the ghost of a cheese. The first thing you've got to learn, Austin, is there ain't any such thing as a ghost. It's going to be a big disappointment to you, but you might as well face it like a man. You can't smell cheese if there ain't any cheese to smell."

"I've never *seen* any cheese."

"Of course you have. Thousands of times. . . . Just last night I happened to pick up a piece of cheese. It went like this, I think: Once I sat upon a promontory, And heard a mermaid on a dolphin's back Uttering such dulcet and harmonious breath, That the rude sea grew civil at her song, And certain stars shot madly from their spheres To hear the sea-maid's musick— That fellow found the way to the cheese."

"But wait a minute. That's different. That's coming over into my camp. You can't prove scientifically that that's good poetry. You can't put that into a test tube and get any positive reaction. But the poetry is good just the same. Where does that leave your science? . . . Science is the great delusion of the twentieth century, just as religion was of the fourteenth. Once the prophets wore a surplice, now they wear a sort of white jacket that buttons up the side of the neck.—No; the cheese isn't down that alley, either. What you-all have found ain't the cheese; it's an old piece of leather,—and you can't seem to tell the difference."

Dr. Abercorn laughed, shaking his head.

"There's something else to all of it that you don't take into account. You can't. You can't measure it. You can't tell anything by putting acid on it or by heating it to four hundred degrees Centigrade over a Bunsen burner. So you just say, to hell with it, it ain't so. But it happens to be the heart of the whole question. The real *heart* of the thing you can't tell anything about. You get up on your pillar like Saint Simon and now and then you let down a basket containing a piece of glittering information that everybody knows sounds a little bit phony. You say, 'Conduct is a series of reflex actions.' That's just poppycock. That's just as much poppycock as telling people they've got to

259

eat fish on Friday. You say, 'Energy can't be created or destroyed.' I say, that just don't mean anything."

"My God!"

"To all intents and purposes we can create energy and we do it every day."

"My God! I never thought I'd live to hear this. Go on."

"I was reading the other day about a new kind of automobile. You wind it up. It's got a spring inside. You can wind it up quite easily in a few minutes. Then you get in and it will carry you for ten miles. When it runs down you get out and—"

"Create a little more energy."

"In effect that's exactly what you do."

"I don't know where to begin. I can't go back and show you that two times two—"

"Your story is that it takes as much energy to wind that spring up as to push the automobile ten miles?"

"My story is that you can't create energy and I stick to it."

"But that don't mean anything. It just doesn't take anything like the energy to wind up that spring as to push the automobile ten miles."

"Well, I reckon there's nothing to do but try to drive you out a little into the light of day. . . . Son, in order to move a certain mass from point A to point B a certain amount of energy must be expended. Take our old friend, the lever and fulcrum, to make simplicity double simple. You want to move a five-hundred-pound block of stone. You can't move it with your bare hands, but with a lever and a fulcrum you can move it without any trouble. All you've got to do is apply the energy in the right place and—"

"That's it! That's exactly what I'm talking about! It ain't the energy, it's the application. Right off the bat you're into something unscientific. The application of the energy is skill; that's taste, poetry, art— That's a ghost."

"My God, son—"

2. This Is Western Union

THE grandson of that lean man with flame-colored hair who had gone up the river with Mr. Hy V. Toombs's surveyor in the eighteen-forties and subsequently bought and paid for the old Hardee Place, had grown up on the land, become perfectly competent to take care of himself at the age of fifteen, drifted into a sinewy middle-age before he was thirty, and become 'Old Man Ben Gray' before he reached sixty. Now, at sixty-three, he took care of his farm as vigorously as ever, stood under the trees in the churchyard with his contemporaries every Sunday morning waiting for the women-folks to get through singing and let the preaching begin, drove his truck into Georgetown every spring to hand The Georgetown Chemical Company his personal check for about thirty-five hundred dollars' worth of fertilizer and to inspect the serried ranks of his cotton in the dim warehouses of Telfair & Company. He would walk into the fertilizer office and lean his elbows on the high counter, pushing his black hat off his forehead. "Well, here's your money. Y-all better take it quick. Just a streak o' luck for fellow like me to pay you." After which he would open his mouth wide and everybody would laugh.

He was a little suspicious of Georgetown cotton factors; he had once said of them, sitting on the whittled bench in the afternoon shade in front of Ben Gray & Co., a five-cent cigar in his teeth, his bony freckled fingers round the elastic of his suspenders, "They shuffle the cards and they deal you your hand and then they telegraph you that *you've* lost."

There was nothing personal in this observation; he had never had any suspicious treatment from Telfair & Company. He trucked them his cotton in the fall as it was ginned and instructed them whether to sell it or hold it. His usual policy was to sell right off; holding it cost money. The price had to rise a cent a pound a year for the cotton not to decline in value; insur-

261

ance and warehouse charges slowly devoured it. You put it in the warehouse as yours, but gradually it became less and less yours and more and more the cotton factor's, until at last what you had drawn against it and the interest and the warehouse charges and the insurance climbed up equal to the market price and bang! the cotton factor sold it. He knew; he hadn't every time been able to resist the temptation of holding a crop over on the chance of a possible rise. One crop he had held from ten cents to twenty and picked up about eight thousand dollars. But another crop he had held from twenty-two cents to sixteen and another from eighteen to eleven; this last one cost him sixty-five hundred dollars. That kind of thing was serious; it meant holes in your shoes; it meant maybe jacking up the Ford and rolling out the buggy. It meant a scar, too, on your prestige in the county; you didn't feel quite the same standing in the churchyard or walking into the bank.

These consequences, that summer, were playing about in the front of his mind, for he was holding cotton for the fourth time in his life and the market looked disturbingly weak. Two hundred and twenty-six bales of 1930 cotton lay in Telfair & Company's warehouses; he had at one time refused twenty cents for it, and now it was down nearly to nine. If he sold it now, by the time the storage charges came out he would get about seven cents. He had already drawn about five cents against it, so he would hardly get two cents more. And two cents, by the way, was not exactly a comfortable margin; it wasn't likely, but it was possible for the market to drop down and wipe it out.

He didn't worry about that, though, as much as he did about having refused twenty-two thousand dollars for what was worth now less than eight thousand. He thought about it all through the planting season; the first thing his eye would fall on as he pulled the *Daily News* out of his mail box was the little square in the upper right-hand corner of the front page: MIDDLING COTTON, Yesterday's Close— He thought if he could get thirteen and an eighth he would sell. Nine cents was too cheap for cotton; sometime it was bound to go back to a fair price. If it didn't go back soon, he was tempted to just sit on those two hundred and twenty-six bales until it did, even if he had to sit on them into another season.

In July, though, when the market went to ten cents, he changed his mind. He wrote Telfair & Company to put it on the table. He drove into Due West and mailed the letter.

The next morning, however, when the *News* came, he saw that the market had closed at better than ten and seven sixteenths, and he began to wonder if maybe the turn hadn't come. He sent Telfair & Company a telegram asking them what they thought about selling. He cogitated for an hour over Mr. Telfair's reply: "October stronger this morning don't want to advise because may be wrong but feel generally more optimistic about price outlook." He wired Mr. Telfair to hold it. Mr. Telfair's letter the next day, in spite of a sharp decline at the close, reassured him.

Then the market began to drop again. When it closed a week from the following Saturday middling cotton was eight and a quarter. After several weeks of fluctuations between eight and a half and nine, it declined one Thursday to eight cents flat; in his Friday morning mail there was a letter from Mr. Telfair saying that though he didn't want to embarrass him, due to the extreme weakness of the market, he thought it would be a good thing, just to be on the safe side against any sudden drop, if he would increase his margin a little bit. "If you could ship us, say, about fifteen bales more—" Hell! he couldn't get together two bales; they had all his cotton now. He thought he would try to forget it and go dove shooting on Lush Hulett's mill pond.

The time to go was just before sunset when the birds began flying over the water to roost in the swamp, but when he got through dinner about three o'clock he went to the closet where he kept his Number Twelve, intending to let one of his niggers put a drop or two of oil on it during the afternoon.

He was standing in the hall with the unbreached gun in his hands when his party line rang one long and two shorts. He closed the piece and held it in his right hand while he picked up the receiver.

"Hello?"

"Hello? Mr. Ben Gray?"

"Yes, ma'am."

"This is Western Union, Mr. Gray. We have a telegram for you."

"A telegram? All right, ma'am."

"It's from Georgetown, Alabama. Mr. Ben Gray, Due West, Georgia. Your cotton sold today six five eighths sudden drop in market closed out your margin letter follows. Telfair & Company."

"What's that, ma'am?"

"It's from Georgetown, Alabama."

"All right, ma'am."

"Mr. Ben Gray, Due West, Georgia. Your cotton sold today six five eighths sudden drop—"

Mr. Ben Gray slammed down the receiver.

"God damn the double-crossing bastards!"

The lean hound lying in the shade of the doorway opened his eyes, got to his feet, and sidled hurriedly across the porch. Mr. Gray leapt through the hall and swung an army shoe viciously after the hound's bony buttocks as he scuttled down the steps.

Sold him out! He wouldn't get anything. A thousand or fifteen hundred dollars was the most he could hope for. Fifteen hundred dollars instead of twenty-two thousand! And it was on their advice he had held it. He wrote them to sell, didn't he, and Telfair wired him advising him to hold it! And now they had sold him out. They had dealt him his hand and now they had wired him that he had lost! If they had sold the way he wrote them to, he would at least have netted about forty-five hundred dollars. And he had told them to sell, begged them to sell. They gambled on your cotton, that was what they did. Maybe they hadn't sold it at all. Who had bought it at that price? As likely as not they had bought it in themselves! Then when it went up to fifteen cents they would sell and pocket the difference. It

264

looked like he raised his cotton to sell it out to them at the bottom of the market. It looked like he did all the work and they did all the riding round in limousines,—limousines he had paid for. He ought to sue them. He ought to make them give him what the market was on the day he wrote them to sell. Take it to court. But what chance would he have against all their money? They would take the money that belonged by rights to him and hire some slick lawyer up in the Cotton States Building, and he wouldn't get a red cent. He ought to make them do it himself. There wasn't any use appealing to the law against—

A gust of warm wind fanned through the pines.

3. Pity the Blind Man

Saturday, August 15

BEAVER was in a quandary. The Bishop had told him to stay away from him until Healing Night. He didn't know what to do; that was six days off, and the Bishop meant what he said. But he had to see the Bishop. Something had come up.

He stood in a shadow by the canal bank and listened to the singing and the stamping in the Tabernacle half way down the dark street. He thought he had better chance it; this was something big. He pointed his stick in front of him and shuffled off.

When he came closer he could see round the edges of his spectacles the high open windows and the powdery film from the sawdust floor floating in the yellow beams of lantern light. There was a crowd of men round the Bishop's limousine parked under the trees with the interior lights on. He could see the shoulders of Oscar's gray linen uniform as he leaned democratically against a front fender. If he could get a word to Oscar, Oscar could tell the Bishop.

265

He brushed against a youth on the edge of the sidewalk.

" 'Scuse me, brother. . . . This here the Tabernickle?"

"That's right."

"That the Bishop inside there, ain't it?"

"That's right."

"Thang God! Thang God! They got a prophet in their mist now. . . . Brother, bez that beautiful automobile anywhere round hereabouts?"

"Right yonder in front of you."

"Brother, would you just hep the old blind man over there where he can stand near besides that beautiful thing?"

"Sho."

He took his arm and led him to the edge of the crowd.

"Look out there, genelmen, let the blind man come up close."

"What good that gonna do him how close he get—"

"Gangway there, genelmen, for the blind man."

"Oh, if I only could lay my hand on it, just lay my one hand on it."

"Ain' no harm to that."

"Look out there, mister, let the blind man come up close where he can tech it."

"Where the chauffe'r? Ast him kin the blind man tech it."

"Dispose yourselves backward slightly more, if you please, gentlemen," said Oscar. "Just step yourself back a little there, blind man."

When he took Beaver by the arm to guide him backward, Beaver said close in his ear, "Tell him I got to see him; sumpn's happened."

He waited in the obscurity of an oak tree and after a while Oscar went off through a back door that led up to the stage. In a few minutes he returned; he paused a second on his way back to the car.

"The Bishop say, 'Go wander beside the still waters.' "

"I got to see him."

"He say, 'Be like the chaff which the wind driveth away—' "

"You tell him I know sumpn about that girl that got killed."

266

"Go on sell your papers."

"You tell him when he come out. . . ."

He was led up the back steps of the house the Bishop had rented for his stay in Georgetown and shown into the kitchen. The shades had been pulled down to the window sills.

He waited for some time, his hat and spectacles in his hand, sitting on the edge of a kitchen chair by the sink. There was a nickeled alarm clock on the table, running with a loud martial ticking, and it moved from about twelve-thirty up to nearly one; his eyes kept passing between the door into the house and the black hand, slowly climbing. Once he considered for a minute creeping out and running away; but he knew almost instantly that that wouldn't do. He sat there watching the door and the clock, twisting his hat.

After a while the loose doorknob turned leisurely and the Bishop came in. He was in his shirt sleeves with his collar off and his stiff cuffs turned back, the white shirt sharp between the black of his trousers and his neck.

Beaver stood up. There was a certain easy cordiality about the Bishop's costume but his face was cold.

"Evenin', Bishop, sir."

The Bishop sat down slowly in the chair and laid his hand out flat on the table, saying nothing.

After a pause he said, looking at the upper part of the opposite wall, speaking without any hurry, "I thought I told you, Beaver, to keep away from me." He smiled a little at the wall. "I thought I made it clear to you that under no circumstances were you to come to me before Healing Night."

"Yes, sir, Bishop—"

"Maybe you have forgotten, Beaver"—he looked at him for the first time—"that I mean what I say."

"No, sir, Bishop, but that girl—"

"Hold on a minute, Beaver. . . . You have done something I told you under no circumstances to do."

"Yes, sir."

"What would be your idea of a suitable punishment?" He smiled up at the wall. "And before you speak I ought to remind you perhaps that if what you suggest is not an adequate atonement you will force me to search in my tired memory for something more suitable."

Beaver dropped down on his knees. "I thows myself on your mercy, Bishop."

"You think it over. There's no particular hurry. Tomorrow will do. . . . Now suppose you just stand up over there and explain to me what outlandish situation prompted you to do such a thing."

"It's about Mrs. Mattie Small, Bishop."

"What about her?"

"That is, about the girl. I know who that girl was. I know where she worked."

"You do."

"Yes, sir. She worked for Dr. Abercorn on Green Street. She—"

"Hold on a minute, Beaver; let me get a couple of cigars. You smoke, if I remember right—"

4. Take it at the Flood

Saturday, August 15

THE words "state fair" popped into Mr. McFarlane's brain like typhoid bacteria into a blood stream; a frantic germination set up in that congenial element and an outlandish progeny sprang forth almost at once. Things seemed at last to be coming his way. The tide had turned; all he had to do was watch it and take it at the flood. With the state fair as a bait, he could get the support of the Chamber of Commerce.

268

His tide had stayed out long enough. In the spring, after he had been there six months, he had taken stock of himself and found that he had used every gag he knew and only been able to raise the circulation from about eleven thousand to about thirteen; that could hardly be called putting it over and when, through the early summer, it seemed to hang there he began to give more and more thought to the hard-shelled gentlemen in Woodward Avenue, Detroit, and to his own personal future. His twelve months would be up in November, and if nothing happened before then,—he would just be on the street, that was all.

But something had happened. For two days after the murder they had sold fifteen thousand. His first problem was to peg it there. But it was hardly a problem; the answer to it was staring him in the face: Pavinovsky. That seemed almost too good to believe. But when things came your way, they came in droves. If he handled it properly and it turned out to be true! He would have Woodward Avenue in the palm of his hand.

Some further investigation of Pavinovsky, though, was absolutely necessary before he dared go ahead. That might take a week. Could he keep the ball rolling during that time and not drop circulation? Once he began to unfold that phase of it, the circulation would take care of itself.

He thought the best way of proceeding would be to run a daily news story from the obvious angle of the case, then in three or four days, to run an editorial asking, in the name of civic decency, who was Mary Glover. There was no proof that the woman's name had not been Mary Glover, but that it hadn't been was well within the bounds of possibility, and even a denial of it by Mattie's lawyer would give him his story. He could probably get a denial or at any rate a refusal to talk; one was about as good as another. When that began to exhaust itself, he could raise the question of why the police failed to take any action. In the meantime he would have had time to stack his cards against Pavinovsky.

One phase of the matter, however, gave him some worry: How

269

far could he rely on the support of the town? He was in the South now; this was an inflammable question. There was a chance, even if he could prove Pavinovsky's connection with the story, that the town would turn against exposing him; there would probably be several sharp young lawyers with political ambitions who would jump at the notoriety of defending or attacking such a nationally important figure, but that wouldn't completely nullify a sudden reversion of that section against the paper. What he needed was some sort of civic backing.

When "state fair" popped into his mind, it was like turning up your hole card with an ace showing and finding you had a pair back to back. If he could get the Chamber of Commerce interested in it through the state fair, he had as good as won. And his tide had turned; he thought they would do it.

The hall that pierced the center of the Cotton States Building had for Mr. McFarlane an odor of a peculiarly local blend. The ingredients, in the finished product, were scarcely detectible but he had analyzed it in his mind as being a compound of barbecue hash and cold sandwiches and Coca-Cola from the lunch counter on one side added to a pinkish odor of hair tonic from the barber shop on the other, both of these blended with the three black elevator-boys appearing and disappearing behind their gratings perched dejectedly in white overalls on high stools, all of that blended again with a faint aroma of surgical dressings from patients going to and from the doctors' offices upstairs and again with a still fainter scent of countrymen, that itself being a mixture of bodies washed under difficulties and chicken coops and old clothes. It always reminded Mr. McFarlane, in case he had for the time being forgotten it, that Georgetown was something he didn't intend to subject himself to for one minute longer than was necessary. Not that he was fastidious about odors; it was simply that this particular one carried with it a suggestion of rusticity and amateur urbanity distinctly irritating to his sense of smartness. He usually paused long enough by the elevator to let his soul turn up its nose and recall the brighter females of its metropolitan memories, but today he hurried through a door marked Exit and ran up the inside fire escape to the second floor and the office of The Alabama Automobile Association and The Chamber of Commerce.

He asked a flat-chested young woman sitting near a rack of road maps if he could see Mr. Couch.

"Just go right back. I believe he's back there."

Mr. Couch raised his hand with a certain mixture of punctiliousness and disdain: "Brother McFarlane, I salute you, sir."

He talked to Mr. Couch for some while, now and then following Mr. Couch's eye through the open window to a cinder court where a blue bus ponderously bided its time. Once a negro boy tucked the corner of a soiled apron in the side of his belt, mounted a bicycle with a tray of dopes in one hand, and pedaled away toward Cotton Row. . . .

"But you'd like to see Georgetown get the state fair."

"Oh, sure."

"It would mean a lot to the town, bring a lot of people in."

"Oh, yes. But we've tried. We've done everything in the world."

"Have you ever tried first getting Georgetown into the news—"

"You see, we're a rim town. We're way over on one side—"

"Mr. Couch, would you like to know the real reason why Georgetown hasn't had the state fair? The real reason?"

Mr. Couch looked at him.

"The biggest thing is that Georgetown simply isn't on the map—"

"Well, I wouldn't go as far as to say that."

"I mean people haven't been interested enough in Georgetown. Georgetown hasn't been in the papers enough. If we put Georgetown on the front pages of the state's newspapers for a while you'd see our chances of getting that fair go up like a rocket."

"I don't know what the Chamber of Commerce could do—"

"If Georgetown was the scene of a piece of real A-one front-page news,—why, people would flock to a fair here. Visit the scene of the crime, you know; that sort of thing."

271

"We don't have crimes like that down here, Mr.—er—McFarlane; we don't have any vicious characters—"

"This murder—"

"What murder? You mean about Mattie? That's not a murder. Say, what did you-all play that thing up for like that? It's bad for a town. It gives it a black eye."

"Mr. Couch, it's the best thing in the world for a town! Georgetown isn't hurt. If you could examine Alabama and Georgia you'd find there were more people thinking about Georgetown today than there had been, maybe, in all history. That's good for a town. It's money in its purse."

"I've heard a lot of people complaining about it."

"People never like what's good for them—"

"Well, a lot of people don't like it, right on." Mr. Couch leaned over and spat into a shallow spittoon.

"The biggest part of that news hasn't been printed yet, Mr. Couch."

"You take my advice, brother, and don't go any farther with that thing."

"If I told you who got that girl in trouble—"

"My goodness alive, man! You not going into that, are you?"

"I was sent down here to print the news—"

"Look here, boy, we don't print news like that—"

"Of course we may not print it. I want you to understand that the *News* is acting from purely public-spirited motives in all this. We want to build up Georgetown. We want to make Alabama interested in Georgetown. We want Georgetown to get that fair. And this is my point, Mr. Couch: if we follow this story up, you'll find the fair will practically come to you."

"We don't like monkeying round with that kind of business."

"It would be a great thing for the Chamber of Commerce."

"I don't deny that, brother, but—"

"A great thing. . . . Will you have a cigarette?"

"Thanks. I don't use them."

"What we want to do is to tell Alabama, tell the South,—tell the United States, that interesting things are happening in

Georgetown. And if we tell them, they'll beat a path to our door. And I'd like to have the Chamber of Commerce coöperate with us."

"What do you mean?"

"What I had in mind was this: tomorrow morning or the next day I'll run an editorial asking the question whether in the name of civic decency we can sit by and investigate no further into this crime. And I thought if the Chamber of Commerce cared to send us a letter simply endorsing our stand—"

"Write you a letter!"

"Yes. The idea is to keep this thing alive. Then when the time comes to go before council with a motion about the state fair I'll run it on the front page and people all over Alabama will say, 'Oh, yes, Georgetown; that's where that murder was.' You see?"

"We can't write you any such letter—"

"Don't give me your answer now, Mr. Couch. Turn it over in your mind. I wish I could lay the whole thing before you, but unfortunately I can't. It's all practically in the bag, though, and when I say it's a wow, I mean it's a wow."

"Somebody prominent, you mean?"

"Mr. Couch, would you call Toscanini prominent?"

"Who?"

. . . But when he went out he knew he had failed. He had prevented Mr. Couch from actually saying they would not support him, but their attitude was unmistakable. He had failed. What was the matter with these people? No wonder they were a quarter of a century behind the times. . . . That was the first setback since things had begun to break his way.

5. *Air de Ballet*

PAVINOVSKY was dejected. Sometimes he felt slightly drugged; not sleepy exactly, but as if he could sit in that swing and look straight in front of him by the hour, not thinking of anything. You could look out into this burning sunlight with the blank stupidity of someone gazing at a candle. You sat there staring into the eye of summer, charmed, hypnotized; you had a feeling that, even if you wanted to, you couldn't arouse yourself, that your strength was running away, that you were bleeding to death. . . . What was happening to him anyhow?

He took his watch out of his trousers pocket; there was a mail delivery at eleven. He would be glad when he got back to a climate where he could wear a waistcoat; it offended his sense of neatness having to carry his watch beneath his belt with the chain falling round into a side pocket in a makeshift way and the little white moon deep in his pocket knocking against the knife and some pennies. He wanted it again dangling against the front of his waistcoat; that seemed to epitomize all the reasons he had for going, that was something very definite and specific, implying all the others. He had thought he would be gone by now; he had written him he was going to leave this week. It was funny there had been no reply; still he might have been away on an assignment. His answer might be at this minute in the postman's bag. If it wasn't,—he would telegraph him; his own letter might have been lost.

It was time for him to go. He was a little worried about Georgetown. His pen had been found and one of the reporters from the *Daily News* had come to see him and worked up a story about him. That was all right; that amused him; he cut it out for his scrap book. But now two of them had come and asked him about this other thing. "What do you think about this Mat-

274

tie Small case?" It annoyed him. "I don't think about it at all," putting his chin out.

Why ask him about that? Had he any clews? Of course he hadn't any clews! He had rather his name not be used in connection with that sort of thing; he told them so. . . . He wished he was going today. Or what he really wished was that he had never come; he could hardly imagine himself going, somehow. He stopped sometimes and looked back at Tony and Nikelief and the Paris contract like a diver on the bottom looking up his air pipe; cut that and he was done for. If his name came out involved in something like that—he wouldn't even think of it—. Maybe he would never see him again. Maybe before he saw him again the dream would have got too bad. If something cut that line! If something came between him and Tony, him and his *pas seul,*—if the newspapers printed his name in connection with this,—the New York papers would run a story, Nikelief— He popped to his feet. No; he was dreaming; it was all right. . . . Where was the postman? . . .

When he heard the postman whistle next door he ran inside the house and tiptoed into the front hall. He was standing there gazing at the sun-spangled sidewalk when the postman walked by; he felt his heart rise up in him, then drop a sickening depth. The postman had gone. There was no mail. Now he couldn't hear until tomorrow. Twenty-four hours of emptiness!

He went into his sister's room, shut the door, and sank down in a rocking chair, his eyes wet.

He sat there for a long time, looking at an ink spot on the straw rug; he could feel his eyes focus it, then relax it into a blur; it seemed to be the same thing thinking of his past, it focused then blurred,—the same thinking of his future. It was a blur like a heat haze. He wondered if the heat really had anything to do with it; it did have an enveloping quality, a—what were those things on electric wires?—an insulating quality. Things passing through it, seen through it, lost their clarity, their distinctness, blurred.

He sat down at his sister's narrow desk and wrote him, put-

275

ting a blotter under his hand to absorb the perspiration. He thought he would not telegraph him yet; that was a last resort. Maybe his letter had gone astray. He didn't want to seem too anxious. . . . He went up to the post office on Broad Street and bought a special-delivery stamp.

As he turned away from the mail slot he met an old friend of his father's who was in the wholesale grocery business.

"Hello, Sergey."

"Hello, Mr. Pender."

"Mighty glad to see you're making Georgetown your home now."

"Well,—"

"This is the place for you."

"I don't know."

"It's all right to wander around when you're young, but— how old are you now?"

"Twenty-six."

"You ought to go into your father's business, Sergey, and make a man of yourself. A little honest work never hurt anybody yet."

"I've been working."

Mr. Pender patted him on the shoulder. "Glad to see you back."

He went out into the flaring heat: was he wrong? Had he been wrong all these years?

The sunlight enveloped him.

6. Of Our Worldly Goods

"WELL," said Lucian, putting his satchel on a round table beside a leather Bible, "what seems to be the matter? You don't look very sick."

"The Lord looks after me pretty well, sir," said the Bishop. "I seem to have contracted a sore throat, though."

"Sore throat, eh?"

"Yes, sir. That's why I called you. I thought—"

"You ought to know better, Bishop, than to pick up a sore throat,—a man of your age and experience."

"I don't think this is the kind you have in mind, sir," said the Bishop, showing his white teeth.

"All you preachers have it. You have the pick of the flock and you always pick wrong. Or rather you keep on picking until you pick wrong."

The Bishop laughed good naturedly. "There's a lot of truth in what you say, sir. However, I think mine was caused simply by preaching the Gospel three times a day through the dust of the Tabernacle. I thought if you could give me a spray or a gargle I could get through; I only have two days more."

"Are you leaving us?" said Lucian, turning to his satchel and taking out a pocket flashlight.

"Yes, sir. I'm going back to my home in Jamaica."

"Open your mouth." He pointed the light down a thin stick and carefully round at the Bishop's tonsils and the back of his throat. "There's not much inflammation there."

"It's sore down the right side when I swallow."

Lucian sat down at the table and unclipped his fountain pen. "You spray your throat with this once every hour until you go to bed. You'd better turn in early and get as much rest as you can. Might be better if you didn't preach tonight."

"Oh, I've got to preach, sir. The Lord's work must be done."

277

"Can't you let one of your henchmen run the show?"

"No, sir. I've got to preach."

"Well, your throat really isn't very serious." He took a prescription pad out of his pocket and shook his pen.

"Er, doctor," said the Bishop in a minute, tentatively, changing his tone, "I wonder if you would allow an old nigger preacher to say a few words to you."

Lucian glanced round from the pad and looked at him with a surprised smile in his eyes; then he went back to his writing: "Shoot."

"You may feel that it's impertinent for an old nigger who hasn't had any advantages or—"

"You've had plenty. . . . What college did you go to, anyhow?"

"It's nice of you to say that, sir, but I'm just self-educated. In fact, I'm not educated at all, as you can see very easily, sir."

"Tuskegee?"

"No, sir. I was at Harvard for three years but I didn't get my degree. Most of the little education I have, I gained after I answered the call."

Lucian sat back and smiled at him. "You've really done very well for yourself."

"Thank you, sir. God has been good to me beyond my just deserts."

"He probably has."

The Bishop grinned. "I shouldn't venture to bring up the matter of God and the Church with one of the white brethren except for the fact that there is only one God for everybody, sir, —the Lord God, Jehovah. He is God of the black and of the white. He is your God, sir, and my God."

"All right, Bishop. What are you trying to make me do, hit the trail?"

"No, sir," said the Bishop, laughing. "All I want is a little contribution from you for the church."

"Oh, I see."

"Won't you he'p us out a little bit, as we say?"

278

"You mean about my bill?"

"Oh, no, sir! Oh, no, sir. I'm going to pay your bill myself. This is for the church."

"Sure. I'll give you something." He took a quarter out of his white trousers and put it on the Bible. "Will a quarter be all right?"

The Bishop glanced at it smiling and lowered his eyes to his folded hands. "Well, sir, I confess I was really thinking of a little more."

"You were?"

"Yes, sir. What I really had in mind was something like—well, a thousand or twelve hundred dollars."

Lucian started to force a laugh but his eyes filled with anger; this gave way almost immediately to real bewilderment. Then some of the uncertainty went out of his smile; "You mean you're a thousand dollars in the hole?"

"Oh, no, sir. With God's help we manage to pay our way. But every little bit over is thankfully received—"

"Well, there's a quarter for you," said Lucian, standing up and closing his bag. "And there's your prescription. You can get it filled at any good drug store for about fifty cents. . . . And by the way, there's no use sending this bill to Jamaica,—"

"Just a minute, doctor, sir, just a minute," he begged, laughing and lifting up his hand as if staying applause.

Lucian stopped and looked at him full face; he was beginning to get angry. All this had a peculiar ring to it.

The Bishop went on in a narrative tone: "I'm not a mind-reader, sir, or a fortune teller; I'm just an old nigger going round the country preaching an old-time religion. But God has ways of telling His children things. In nature's great book of infinite secrecy, thanks to Him, a little I can read. And He shows me there a little something about you, sir, doctor."

"What are you talking about?"

"It looks like there that you are worried, sir, that you have something on your mind."

Lucian, wordless, began involuntarily to stiffen his neck muscles.

"I wouldn't say anything to you about it, sir, because your skin's white and mine's black, but in heaven there is only one Father; your God and my God are the same. And when He says, 'Come unto me, all ye that labor and are heavy laden, and I will give you rest,' He's talking to black folks and white folks too. He's talking to you and He's talking to me."

In a remote corner of his consciousness Lucian felt his blood pressure going up.

"He's a mighty fortress in time of trouble, a haven in time of storm. But for this blessed privilege of refuge, doctor, we must give of our worldly goods."

"Well, that's all right, Bishop," said Lucian. "I don't mind giving of my worldly goods. You make such a touching appeal I'll tell you what I'll do. The regular charge for a visit like this is three dollars; I'll just donate my services. I won't send you any bill. How about that?"

"Thank you kindly, sir, doctor. . . . I hardly know what to say. I hardly know how to explain it to you. I preach that a man must give according to his needs; the more he needs God's help, the more he must help God."

Lucian picked up his satchel. "You think I need more than three dollars' worth of help?"

He said it with a specious lightness, but the Bishop answered him gravely, though matter-of-factly. "Yes, sir, I do. Because if it got to the newspapers it might be very embarrassing—"

"If *what* got to the newspapers?"

"I mean this thing that's worrying you, sir; this thing about your nurse dying in an illegal operation—"

Lucian stared in his eyes for a moment, then said in dull simplicity, "If I had a pistol I'd shoot you."

"That would be the worst possible thing you could do, sir. The whole affair would be bound to come out in the papers then."

"So you think you can blackmail me!"

"No, sir, I just think you need God's help. With His help, the papers won't know about it. You see, sir, nobody knows about this but our Heavenly Father; I prayed to Him for a thousand dollars and He told me to come to you. If you will contribute a thousand dollars to the furtherance of God's holy work—"

"I won't pay you a cent!"

"I don't want you to make the contribution, sir, if you don't feel that His help is worth that much. You know better what it is worth to you than anybody else. Under the old management the *News* might not print it, but I'm afraid the present editor—"

"He won't touch it."

"Maybe not, sir. But the church needs the money and if you don't feel like making the contribution there's nothing left for me to do but to ask the *News* if they want to buy the story—"

"They won't print it, I tell you!"

"I'm afraid they'll jump at it, sir—"

"You'll find this country too hot to hold you if you take that story to the paper."

"God will provide for His servant, sir. . . . You consider it at your leisure, sir. If it's worth that to you, just drop me a check in the mail tonight. If it isn't,—well, it isn't."

"Do you know how much time a man gets for blackmail?"

"But that wouldn't do you any good, sir—"

Lucian went out to his car, the perspiration rolling down his burning face.

7. Local Page

MRS. SHIVERS ASKS
"COMMON SENSE" IN
LEGISLATURE RACE—

MAN BOUND OVER
ON PROHI CHARGE—

PELLAGRA CASES
WILL GET YEAST
HEALTH BOARD—

$25 Reward for the capture and return of
Monroe Hickson, who escaped from Chaingang
No. 1 August 17—

WILLET SUGGESTS
SOUTHERN TOWNS
USE DOUBLE NAME—

LOCAL MAN KEEPS RECORD OF
5,000 GAMES OF SOLITAIRE—

COTTON FUTURES
DEVELOP DECIDED
DOWNWARD TREND
DROP IN CABLES AND FAIR
WEATHER PROSPECTS IN BELT—

SUMMER'S MEAN TEMPERATURE
HIGHER THAN SUMMER OF 1931
100 OR HIGHER ON TEN DAYS
CONSECUTIVELY—

MRS. BARKSDALE
  TELLS OF SEEING
    METEOR IN FLIGHT
LOOKED LIKE FLAT DISK
  ABOUT SIZE OF WASH-TUB
    WITH FIERY STREAKS—

                    416 INOCULATED
                    AGAINST TYPHOID—

        75 P.C. ECLIPSE
        OF SUN DUE HERE
        3:41 P.M. AUG. 31
        Get your red and green glasses ready—

    SECOND BOY SCOUT CAMP
    WILL BE OPEN THURSDAY—

                CROWDS THRONG TO
                MUNICIPAL BEACH
                AS MERCURY RISES—

"MISS PERSONALITY"—

            GOLFERS PREPARE
            FOR STATE EVENT
        Golfers young and old throughout the state
        are polishing up their games—

CHAPTER EIGHT

1. Sentimental Journal

Wednesday, August 19

"THE evolution of man," wrote Mr. Applewhite, "is inward. Even today, hardly five thousand years from a state of complete savagery, we exhibit the few remaining relics of well-developed extroversion and pay admission to see them and wonder at them,—specimens which five thousand years ago would have been no more remarkable than dinosaurs in the Mesozoic Era,— specimens which would probably not have survived the battles of a normal week. First, no skeleton; then mobility and a skeleton covering the life inside; then the skeleton moving from the outside inward.

"And now the mind; first no mind, then a mind turned outward at stone and bronze and iron, now a turning in. Over two thousand years the swing is apparent,—away from geometric temples, from sculpture glorifying the physical body, toward the aspiring Gothic, toward symphonic music, toward the overtone in art. Even Shakespeare's world was an outer world of danger and defense; imagery of the visible world, of emotions outward-moving with tangible cause and tangible effect: 'To be or not to be.' A very simple and concrete question.—'As fearfully as doth a galled rock O'erhang and jutty his confounded base, Swilled by the wild and wasteful ocean,'—'Tempests themselves, high seas, and howling winds, The guttered rocks, and congregated sands, Traitors ensteeped to clog the guiltless keel.' Now Daedalus be-

284

side Dublin Bay: 'In long lassoes from the Cock lake the water flowed full, covering green-goldenly lagoons of sand, rising, flowing. . . . Vehement breath of waters amid seasnakes, rearing horses, rocks. In cups of rocks it slops: flop, slop, slap: bounded in barrels. And, spent, its speech ceases. It flows purling, widely flowing, floating, foampool, flower unfurling,'—'Across the sands of all the world, followed by the sun's flaming sword, to the west, trekking to evening lands. . . . A tide westering, moondrawn, in her wake. . . . Behold the handmaid of the moon.' First the skeleton, now the mind turning inward upon itself like an old man sitting by the fire. Two thousand years hence the extro-verted mind will be as unfit for competition in that involuted world as a turtle or a snail,—a museum piece, like a sea tortoise or a horseshoe crab. We must speak soon not of the evolution of man but of his involution.

". . . The fact there was a light burning in the T's hallway proves nothing. Yet I think it was unquestionably she,—wandering unhappily in the borderland, neither outward nor inward."—

2. Nymphs and Shepherds, Dance No More!

Thursday, August 20

WHEN his father left home for the office about nine o'clock, Elbert tore the editorial page out of the *Daily News* and ripped it carefully in half. His mother would look at the paper later in the morning but she had no interest in the editorials; once he had taken the market page, but then his mother had bought the three shares of Dome Mines and told him to take the editorial.

When he was ready, a little after nine, to walk to the Country Club, he went into the lavatory and wet both halves of the

285

page, doubling them up into two spongy balls. As he walked along through the early sunshine, his fresh shirt getting rapidly damp between the shoulders, his bare legs getting rapidly shiny, he squeezed one of the sodden balls rhythmically in each hand, the water oozing out through his fingers. When he started doing this early in the summer his hands and forearms ached before he got to Peachtree Road; now he could get as far as the Arsenal. And his woods had stretched out fifteen yards. It was true he had grown a little heavier, which might have accounted for it, but he thought it was largely owing to the increased strength in his wrists and fingers. He was glad he hadn't told anybody about the exercise, glad he could keep a secret; now he was almost always out in front.

His distance was all right. What he thought could be polished up a little was his medium irons; they flew too straight. He wanted to develop a fade on them, make them come into the green with a cut. Just a trace of a fade. Control them better. He thought he would go out on the course somewhere and practice awhile; he wouldn't be in anybody's way; no one ever played in the morning. . . .

He was standing on the edge of the thirteenth fairway, working one of his flock of practice balls into a good lie on the sandy turf with the toe of his No. 2 iron, when he heard the plane. He went on and hit because it was still far away and he thought nothing of it. But by the time he was ready to swing again the plane was circling over the green woods and coming toward him; he stopped while it passed over his head, the sun shining through its pale wings. He waved; it looked like the same plane that had come over a few weeks ago and made him miss that putt, but he always wanted to wave at a plane going over. It looked nice and cool up there.

He watched it tip over on end, mount in a rising arc, and come back. He waved again at the goggles that looked down at him out of the swift roar.

Then it swung off once more toward the church of the Sanctified Baptists, tilted up on the other wing, and came round.

The noise of the motor suddenly subsided into a kind of hissing and the plane slipped sideways and down over the chinaberry trees; there was a spurt of noise, a straightening up, a skimming over the trap on the fifteenth like a long brassie that just carries, and a puff of dust from the stick. It came up opposite him beyond a young pine thicket and stopped, the motor idling over with a rushing sound.

He dropped his iron among the practice balls and ran across the tangled rough.

"Look out for the propeller!"

The voice surprised and somewhat disappointed him. It was a woman's voice; he had thought the pilot would be a man, lean, fair-haired, with maybe a squint. He stopped running, put his hands in his pockets, and walked round the wings; he looked up at her as she lifted the glasses.

"Sorry to land on your golf course," she said, smiling at him slightly.

"That's all right, ma'am," he said; he thought her lips were too red.

"You probably want to shoot me."

"It don't matter at all, ma'am." Then he grinned, "Nobody to see you anyhow. There's nobody out this morning."

"Are you playing by yourself?"

He looked down, then up; "Just hitting a few."

"You look hot."

"Yes'm," he smiled. "It's right hot." He wiped his face on his rolled-up sleeve.

"You probably wonder why I came down. But—but I'm trying to find the airport."

"It's right over there."

"Where?"

"Right over yonder by the reservoir."

"Funny I couldn't find it."

"You been lookin' for it ever since last month?" he said, looking at her.

They laughed together.

"I—I landed at one field, but—I thought there was another."

"No'm, there isn't but one."

"Oh, really?"

"Sure."

"Silly to keep on looking then, I guess."

They laughed again and he glanced down and scratched his leg.

"Well, thanks," she said. "I guess I'll be going. . . . Want to go up for a ride,—cool off?"

He hesitated. He had come out to practice; he wasn't getting enough right wrist into his irons and the State was only two weeks off. But she was pretty in a disturbing sort of way; he somehow didn't want her to leave him now.

"I don't care," he said.

"Come on then."

"How about my clubs and things?"

"I've got a car; I'll bring you back."

"I hate to bother—"

"Don't be silly."

"All right."

"Climb up front."

He laughed nervously and reached for the step.

"You don't remember me, do you, Elbert?"

He flushed a little; he had never seen her before. But it was pleasant to hear her pronounce his name.

"I saw you over at Nora's one afternoon. I'm Gwendolyn Owens."

"Oh!" he said, giving her a quick scrutiny. "Mrs. Owens. I didn't know you with your—your—"

"Mrs. Owens! You make me feel so out of date. . . . Well, come on, Mr. Meigs."

He grinned at her, blushing, then hastily climbed aboard.

They rolled up to one end of the long fifteenth and turned round.

"Ready?" she shouted, hardly audible above the motor.

"Let her go!"

288

The motor doubled its roar and they began to move. The plane lifted its tail with a certain amorousness and a minute later rose into the southwest wind. . . .

When they pulled up in front of the hangar Elbert picked his way down the steps and hopped to the ground. "That was fine!" he said, beaming.

"Fun, isn't it?"

She stripped off her cap and shook her hair. Then she stood up and threw one sand-colored leg over the side, feeling about with her white shoe for the step.

Elbert saw the hem of her linen skirt stretch tight above the top of her round garter; he moved a few steps away and glanced at the hangar.

"Don't let this embarrass you," she laughed. "There's no other way out."

She half turned her back and put over the other leg, looking down for the step; she found it and jumped the rest of the way, leaving Elbert with a bright picture on his retina of a flash of stockings and tan skin. "Sorry!" she said with a laugh, not looking at him.

They turned away from the plane together and she said, "I've got Austin's car. I'll take you back to your sticks."

He sat silent most of the way; he felt peculiarly naked somehow with his bare knees and his sleeves rolled up to the shoulder. She was silent too, guiding the car attentively round the short turns of the sand road. Once as they mounted the hill between the fifth fairway and the woods she glanced at him covertly; he was gazing straight ahead, his hands folded in front of him.

When the road entered the shade of the pines she put out her hand and laid it on his knee, turning her face toward him for a second with a tremulous smile. He clasped her hand suddenly in both of his and held it tight.

"Would you—would you mind if—if I kissed you?" he said, gazing at the rim of the steering wheel.

She waited a minute, then stopped the car abruptly, the tremulous smile still on her lips. He leaned over and kissed her inexpertly on a corner of her mouth. She remained passive for a moment, then the smile disappeared and she turned her head to him.

In a minute she drew away from him and got out. He stayed where he was a second, then slid under the wheel and out the door. "I—I think you're beautiful."

She looked away through the trees, then said, "I feel pretty much the same way about you."

"There's a nice cool spring down in the bottom there—"

"Don't you think you'd better go back to your golf?"

"I can play golf any old time."

"You could probably take girls down to the spring any old time too," she laughed, glancing at him. "Though I don't believe you realize it."

"Realize what?"

"You lead the way."

"This weather makes you thirsty. It's fine cool water."

He led off down a steep path, slippery with pine needles. She followed him through the heavy foliage, picking her way among the roots and vines. At the bottom he stopped on the matted leaves and looked back.

She sat down on the grass watching him while he bent over gazing into the spring.

"I don't know what you can drink out of," he said.

She crawled over beside him on her hands and knees.

"I know what I can drink out of."

"What?"

She opened her hands. "The spring!"

She lay down, laughing, and put her face down in the basin. When she lifted her head she laughed at him through the smear of water and brushed it out of her eyes with her fingers.

"I've got a handkerchief but I'm afraid it isn't very clean," he said.

"I don't want a handkerchief."

He leaned over the pool and drank in the same way.

290

Then he sat back on the leaves apart from her. "Nice place, don't you think?"

"I've never been to a more beautiful place."

"I'm glad you like it."

"Do you bring all your little girls here?"

"You're the only girl I've ever brought here in my life."

"You're a sweet boy!"

"Can I kiss you again?"

"Does anybody else ever come here?"

"No. Nobody comes here."

"I'm going to take off my socks."

She peeled off her stockings before his rapturous eyes and stuffed them into her shoes. When she looked at him he was leaning on one stiff arm pulling off blades of grass.

Then he said to her tensely, gazing at her shoulder, "I reckon I ought to tell you—now—the only reason I brought you down here was because I wanted to—to—I reckon I wanted to take advantage of you. You better get out now while—before it's too late—"

She put back her head and laughed whole-heartedly into the pines. Then, even before she had finished laughing, she pulled herself toward him over the grass; then she fell in his lap and worked her arms about his waist.

"Don't look so scared," she said with a short laugh.

3. He Knows Everybody

Friday, August 21

JUDGE FULWOOD was on the bench of the Superior Court of the Congaree Valley Circuit and his claim that he knew every dog from Tennessee to the Gulf of Mexico was in spirit

291

essentially true; he knew every fish pond in a hundred miles and every camelia bush in two states. He was the only male member of the Sand Hills Garden Club and when that organization built a brick wall round its headquarters on Telfair Street and held a meeting to go into the question of how they could get their hands on a pair of wrought-iron gates to hang in the entrance, it wasn't surprising that they should have decided to appeal to him.

"We've just got to have some nice gates, judge," they said.

"I ain' got any gates," said the judge.

"You must know some round here."

"How much you willing to pay?"

"How much! Goodness! Don't be silly, judge."

"But, God-amussy, sister—"

"We can't *pay* anything, judge."

He twisted up a corner of his mouth, combing out his right eyebrow with his fingernails. . . .

He knew of a pair of gates out on the road to Due West before it crossed the river out of his bailiwick. He had often admired them. Before 1925 he had often driven through them on summer evenings to sit awhile with Jim Marbury and his wife; he knew all about the gates. They had been made over in Charleston and brought to Alabama by Jim Marbury's father. When hard times overtook Jim Marbury and the place was offered for sale the gates were quite an item. It was on the market for nearly three years and people in Georgetown thought there was nobody in that section with money enough to buy it. Then one day the real estate agent received an offer of two-thirds and Jim Marbury, needing the money, sold.

The purchaser turned out to be Mr. Speck Hayes and he paid cash. Up to then Mr. Speck Hayes had been noted chiefly for the quality of his locally distilled whiskeys and his Bacardi; his Scotch was also considered first class by the few who could afford it, and for his most discriminating clientele he carried on hand two or three bottles of sixty-year-old Courvoisier Brandy. He had not, up to then, been taken seriously as a property owner

292

and tax payer. Judge Fulwood numbered him among his exhaustive acquaintance, having even met him officially in his own court room (the jury acquitted Mr. Hayes, responding unanimously to his lawyer's plea that it was on the face of it absurd to think the defendant would manufacture whiskey for sale when, as everybody in Davis County knew, he had a hard enough time getting enough for his own consumption), but after the gates changed hands he had confined his admiration of them to the outside.

A few mornings after his fellow members of the garden club had appealed to him, he got in his Ford coupé and drove out the Due West road. He stopped at the gates and examined the hinges: they were simple affairs, pinions working in sockets that were cemented into the brick pillars. He returned to his car and continued on round the circular drive to the house.

There was a negro boy standing on a ten-gallon keg clipping the top of a privet hedge.

"Is Mr. Hayes here?" said the judge, cutting off his motor.

"I think he in the house, sir."

"Ask him if I could see him for a minute."

The boy disappeared round the back of the house and Judge Fulwood got out of the car and strolled to the edge of a cotton field. He was casting an appraising eye over the level expanse when Mr. Speck Hayes sauntered round a corner.

"Why, hello, judge."

"Hello, Speck."

The judge advanced toward him, one forearm behind his back, and they shook hands.

"Won't you come inside, judge, out of the sun?"

"No, thank you, Speck. I was just driving by. Your cotton looks good."

"Yes, sir, it's done pretty well,—what there is of it. I just put in ten acres this year."

"Had any boll weevils?

"Few down near the creek, judge. I've been spraying."

"Spraying helps."

"Oh, yes, spraying helps."

"You'll have to pick it over again soon."

"Yes, sir. I'm planning to go over it again first thing next week."

"How much you going to get?"

"I reckon I'll get about seven bales, seven heavy bales."

"Good land."

"Yes, sir. And I put a ton and a half of 7-5-5 on it."

"Fertilizer pays."

"Yes, sir, it pays."

"Oh, by the way, Speck."

"Yes, sir, judge."

"The ladies down at the garden club asked me the other day to try to locate a pair of gates for them. They've built themselves a kind of wall around their place and now they want a pair of gates."

"A pair of gates, judge?"

"Yes, they seem to kind of want a pair of gates. I searched in my memory, but I couldn't think of anybody with a pair of gates, and then—"

Mr. Speck Hayes lifted his eyes to the top button of the judge's black alpaca coat.

"And then I remembered you. I thought maybe you might like to donate those gates down there to the garden club."

"Them gates down there, judge?"

"Yes; old Jim Marbury's gates."

"Those the best gates in the county, judge."

"I know it, Speck."

Mr. Hayes let his eyes run off over his cotton field. "You think I ought to—"

"You know best, Speck."

Mr. Hayes looked down his drive for a long minute, then heaved a sigh:

"They're yours, judge. . . ."

Judge Fulwood was halfway back to Georgetown when he overtook an old high-topped open car with pink dust covering its dingy rear. He swung out to the left, and as he passed it, raised his hand in salutation.

"Howdy do," he said, glancing over at the upper foot or two of a double-barreled shotgun propped up in the front seat beside the driver. Old man Ben Gray from up round Due West. A regular Bulloch County farmer; couldn't raise a damn thing but cotton, but could raise a bale of cotton to an acre. Looked like he had something on his mind.

4. Black Maria

Friday, August 21

AS a rule Miss Judith Pavinovsky got back to the office from dinner a little after three; she usually walked up the shady side of Cotton Row, crossed over diagonally in front of The Georgetown Chemical Company, skirted the arm-chairs under the trees, and entered the sky-blue outer office calmly, even serenely, with that almost palpable peace-of-mind popularly considered the exclusive property of ladies of impeccably Christian morals. She usually then proceeded with her exhaustive search of the morning paper or carried on with a piece of embroidery, while Tucker crossed his ankles, leaning against the wall phone, and called the soda fountain in the Cotton States Building.

"Send two with lemon to Telfair & Company."

"Tell 'em to make 'em nice and strong."

"They know by the tone of my voice I mean strong."

If Mr. Telfair came back in the afternoon she might take down two or three letters.

On this particular Friday, though, everything was different. It was after four when she got back and she hung her hat and pocketbook askew on the hook. Then she sat down and bit at the side of her fingernail, her eyes wandering about between the little clock on Mr. Telfair's desk and the front door. It looked as if Mr. Telfair weren't coming back.

At four-thirty she got up suddenly, sat down at Mr. Telfair's desk and called his house.

He had left about fifteen minutes before.

"This is the office. Do you know where he is?"

"No, ma'am, I declare I don't."

"Has he gone to play golf, you think?"

"He never said, ma'am."

As she hung up Mr. Telfair walked in the door. He stopped a minute in the entrance to glance at his thermometer.

"It's right warm today, Miss Judy; right warm." He laid his hat on the top of his desk and sat down, taking a box of Havana cigars out of a drawer as if he had been thinking about them. He picked the band off one of them and, getting no reply from Miss Judy, glanced at her. "What's the matter, what's the matter?"

"I want to talk to you, Mr. Telfair."

"What's the matter?"

She seriously drew up a chair. "I want to ask your advice, Mr. Telfair."

Mr. Telfair's eyes brightened. "You mean about Jebby?"

"No, this is about my brother, Sergey. . . . I don't know quite where to begin. . . . You remember him."

"Yes," said Mr. Telfair, pausing as he was about to srike a match on the side of a drawer.

"Well, they're trying to—to—they're trying to—"

"To what? Who is?"

"They're trying to involve Sergey in this—this Mattie Small thing."

Mr. Telfair looked at her in some surprise and noncommittally struck the match. "Who is?"

"The *News*. They tried to get him yesterday but Sergey wouldn't go to the phone. He sent word he wasn't feeling well; and he wasn't. I don't know what's the matter with him. He

296

seems depressed. I'm a little worried about him. . . . But anyway, today this McFarlane, he's the man the paper company sent down here last year, he came in as we were eating dinner. Sergey was nice to him; he's used to newspapers, you know. Well, in a few minutes (I heard them from the other room) the man started talking about that colored girl again. He had been down there once before. He asked Sergey if he would care to endorse the paper's stand, or something. Sergey told him politely as he had told him before, he didn't know anything about it, hadn't thought anything about it, and positively would not consent to be quoted in connection with something like that. Then the man mentioned Sergey's fountain pen."

"Fountain pen?"

"Sergey was walking on the canal and lost his fountain pen. It was six weeks ago. More than that. He advertised for it in the *News*. And now this other thing comes up and McFarlane remembers it. He lost it, you see, out near that woman's house—"

"Oh."

"There's no connection in the world, Mr. Telfair—"

"They ought to have better sense than to print it anyhow."

"But there's absolutely no connection—"

"That don't matter, Miss Judy. It's been done before. Sherman's army's responsible for nine-tenths of it. What hasn't been done before is putting it all in the newspaper."

"I'm afraid they may put something in tomorrow."

"They won't put anything until they can substantiate it. That would mean a libel suit."

"But they might say that Sergey refused to make any comment. And if they even mention his name in connection with it—I—I don't know. He's so sensitive. Something like that might—"

"If they make a misstep he can go to court."

"But his career. That's everything to him. The harm would be done. If they print his name—I—I don't know—"

"What do you want me to do?"

297

"Just tell them, Mr. Telfair, they mustn't print anything about Sergey now—"

He looked toward the top of his desk and picked up his hat by the stiff brim. "I'll step round there and talk to Major Bain—"

Something moved in the front door. She glanced round and caught her breath.

"Who's that!" She said it almost in the tone of someone calling out at night.

He stared at her for a second before he realized that something must have happened behind his back. Then he turned about, his starched shirt creaking a little, and saw old man Ben Gray standing in the door from the sidewalk, steadying himself with one hand against the stone frame. He couldn't see all of him on account of the solid wainscot of the glass partition between them, but he could see the upper foot or two of Mr. Ben Gray's black shotgun which he was dragging by the barrel.

Miss Judy put her hand on his knee.

"Get out the back way," he heard her mumbling to him. "Get out quick. He ain't seen you yet. He's drunk. He means trouble. Get out in the warehouse. I'll tell him you're out of town. I'll call the police—"

He didn't know exactly what to do. It was easy enough to slip out the back door into the warehouse, but he didn't like being forced into something like that; there wasn't much dignity to it. On the other hand this cracker had a gun. The chances that he would really fire it were not very strong, but at the same time these countrymen sometimes did shoot. There was a good Yale lock on his private cabinet in the warehouse—

Old man Ben Gray took two strides into the sample room and Mr. Telfair, watching him, felt behind him in the drawer and found the key with the Dennison tag on it.

"I want to see Lamar Telfair!"

Miss Judy pushed Mr. Telfair out of the office toward the back door.

"Mr. Telfair is not in," said Miss Judy, walking forward, her voice a little shrill. "Is there something I can do for you—"

"Hold on there, Telfair, you damn rascal!"

Mr. Telfair sprang out of the door into the dark warehouse and bolted through the dry hot air to his cabinet. He jabbed the key against the side of the lock and dropped it.

"Jesus Christ!" said Mr. Telfair, ducking down on his knees and patting his hands about on the gravel floor in the darkness.

Voices came to him from inside the office, faint for a moment, then suddenly loud as the door was thrown back and a sheaf of daylight was flung into the dusk. He leaped behind a row of upright cotton bales as Miss Judy squealed.

He was sure that old Ben Gray had failed to see him and that he was safe for the instant, but just how to take advantage of this pause he couldn't quite decide. There were only eight or ten bales of cotton in the upright row and they were standing by themselves in an open space waiting to be trucked out. Beyond the far end was a break of several yards before the beginning of the stepped-up tiers of bales on their sides mounting up to the roof. He had climbed those things many a time when he was a boy; he could climb this one now. The principal difficulty was in getting across the break. And then too if he climbed to the top and old man Gray saw him and climbed after him, that would be about all there was to it; there was no place to go up there. And aside from that, too, the target he would offer as he heaved himself up the tiers would be something that no rabbit hunter in the South— He pulled a pinch of lint out of one of the bales in front of him and felt it. Strict low middlin', he thought in desperate calmness.

"Which way'd he go, ma'am?" said Mr. Ben Gray.

"I—I couldn't say, Mr. Ben Gray," said Miss Judy. "If you'll just take a seat he'll be back in a few minutes. Or if you'd like to leave a message—"

"Thank you, ma'am, I reckon I'll just go roust the son of a bitch out myself—"

"I'll thank you to refrain from using such language in the presence of a lady!"

"Excuse me, ma'am."

"The idea of anybody who calls himself a Southern gentle-man—"

"Excuse me, ma'am; I forgot myself."

"Well, kindly recollect yourself. What do you mean anyhow, coming in this office with a shotgun! Don't you know I can call the Black Maria and have you arrested? Give me that gun."

"Take care, young woman!"

"Give me that gun or I'll call the police."

Mr. Ben Gray, who for a moment had seemed surprised into a sort of tractability, at the prospect of surrendering his weapon, relapsed into belligerency. "Don't trifle with me, ma'am! Which way'd he go?"

There was a pause, then Mr. Gray apparently caught sight for the first time of Mr. Telfair's private cabinet in the corner. "What's this here place?"

Mr. Telfair thanked God subconsciously for the dropped key and crept farther away toward the end of the bales.

"There—there's nobody in there," said Miss Judy, her voice shaking. "It's all locked up."

"Get me the key, please, ma'am."

"The key's lost, Mr. Ben Gray. There's nobody in there. Why—why don't you look round on this other side first—"

Mr. Telfair glanced round him bewilderedly, damning his stenographer's solicitousness and trying to settle in his mind where his imminent retreat was going to lie. He let his eye run up the nearest tier, measuring the muscular strength it would take to climb those tall steps and the chances of his being able to reach the top.

He lowered them, because that was what he had uncon-sciously meant to do, but then he frowned and looked aloft again; he thought he had seen something move up there. When he looked up he began to frown a good deal more, for what he saw up in the dim heat was the upper halves of two black heads just visible over the gray rim of one of the topmost bales, the four eyes staring in white terror down into the arena. . . .

300

It was at just about this moment that Mr. Applewhite, wandering desultorily about the town, paused in the shade of The Cotton Exchange to watch a brown squirrel gingerly crossing Cotton Row on one of the high black wires of The Southern Bell Telephone and Telegraph Company. The squirrel darted out a few feet along the wire and paused like a Japanese acrobat taking a curtain call. Then he flipped his tail out flat behind him and scampered over the middle of the street; here he made an abrupt halt, his agile tail curled on his back like a question mark. He seemed to be hesitating whether to go on or turn back. Then Mr. Applewhite saw him all of a sudden become as tense as a drawn spring, then spurt off along the wire as if for his life; as nearly as he could remember it afterward, the squirrel had gone a yard or so when the gun sounded. He thought he must have been mistaken, but he could recall definitely seeing the squirrel set out and yet the instant he heard the report he turned his gaze in some alarm to Cotton Row. He forgot the squirrel completely, for it was quite a loud noise, coming in the midst of the somnolent afternoon.

Mr. Applewhite looked up and down the street; he thought it might have been a backfire from some truck, though the explosion had had a slightly different volume to it and there was no truck in sight. Everything went on as usual; a white employee of the city climbed out on the side of his water wagon and fumbled with the hose of the tall faucet on the corner; on an upper porch over a cotton office down nearer the river a group of negroes continued cheerfully clipping each other's hair. Three cotton-flecked drays thundered matter-of-factly by him, the drivers standing in the middle with whips over their shoulders, balancing themselves against the heavy jolting with the help of the long black reins from the trotting mules.

Mr. Applewhite turned away; it must have been a truck either round on another street or back in one of the warehouse yards. He was about to move on when he happened to glance down the alley that led past Telfair & Company's office into their warehouse; here he saw the anomalous sight of a negro girl in flowered

301

beach pajamas, a closed purple umbrella in her hand, bolting across the court toward the river like a cat with the dogs behind her. He was trying to connect this vaguely with the fact that the backfire might have come from that general direction, when he heard the siren of Georgetown's Black Maria and saw it bound out of its garage a block to the west and swing round in his direction, the siren rising into a scream.

The squirrel shot up the pole to the top insulator and bared its teeth.

5. Long Distance, Please

Friday, August 21

THAT was a day of days for Mr. James McFarlane; he came out of it as limp as a half-drowned rat, having been knocked so often and so violently from ecstasy to despair, from despair to ecstasy that he hardly knew at the end which extreme he was occupying.

When he left Pavinovsky's house on that Friday it was about three o'clock; he went straight to his office, rolled up the sleeves of Thursday's shirt, opened his collar, tucked a handkerchief between his pale cotton tie and his perspiring chin, and spun half a dozen sheets of copy paper into his typewriter. He glowered at it for a minute, rubbing his finger-points with his thumb, then suddenly hammered out with two expert fingers the title of his leading editorial for the next morning: "We Do Nothing." He hesitated a minute, drumming on the iron frame, then went on: A negro girl who had given her name as Mary Glover had been killed; the Georgetown *Daily News* had taken the position, the only humanitarian position that could be taken, that this was an outrage against the citizenry of the town, a blot

302

in Georgetown's stainless 'scutcheon. He turned the paper back, changed the title from We Do Nothing to A Blot in the 'Scutcheon, and went on. The *Daily News* was going to insist that justice be meted out to her slayer; and it was going to do more; it was going to press on in the pursuit of truth. There were reasons to indicate that the name of the victim was not Mary Glover; who then was this girl? What had been her employment? Who was her seducer? What was her story? The *News,* in the name of civic decency, wanted to know.

He pulled the paper out, proof read it, changed the title with a pencil to Who Was Mary Glover?, folded it once and stuck it on the hook.

The next thing was to write out an interview with Pavinovsky. The interview itself hadn't been very satisfactory; Pavinovsky had refused to be quoted. But he thought if he gave Pavinovsky half a column on an entirely different subject that the same purpose of association would be achieved and that Pavinovsky would consent. He put the paper in the machine and began: "The Southland gives signs of being on the eve of a great artistic revival," Sergey Pavinovsky, noted member of The Metropolitan Opera Ballet, said to a *Daily News* reporter yesterday. Mr. Pavinovsky, who—

He was at just this point when his man, Dewey, came into the outside office and turned on the ceiling fan. This distracted him enough to remind him of cigarettes and he took a crumpled pack out of his trousers pocket and inserted his finger, staring at the last line in the typewriter. The pack was empty.

"Got a cigarette, Dewey?" he called.

Dewey came in without much enthusiasm and handed him one.

"Anything going on round at headquarters, Dewey?"

"Headed round there now. Been down to the jail house."

"Get anything from Mattie?"

"They won't even let you go in the block."

"Get anything else?"

"Not a thing."

"You better beat it on round to headquarters. I've got a hunch something's gonna break."

Dewey started out then turned round. "Oh, say, I've got a piece of news for you at that."

Mr. McFarlane struck a match under his desk, looking at the paper in the typewriter.

"This is gossip but it's straight—"

"Go on, let's have it. I've got work to do."

"Well, you remember this guy Pavinovsky?"

Mr. McFarlane looked up. "Do I remember—"

"Well, I just find out that Pavinovsky's a canary."

Mr. McFarlane didn't say anything for a minute; he just sat there with the smoke drifting up his forehead. Then he looked up with an almost burlesque frown. "Did you say canary?"

"Yeah—"

He got to his feet and leaned both palms flat on the desk top, staring with a ludicrous intensity into space. Then he said slowly, in almost a whisper, "Great God of hosts! I'm ruined!"

"What's the matter, Mac?"

Mr. McFarlane explained to him with both hands what the matter was. "Where's the story now? Who gives a damn about Mattie Small and Mary Glover? It ain't news any more. What's going to become of the circulation,—hell! what's going to become of me? They're going to kick me out on my ass, that's what's going to become of me,—look here, Dewey, it ain't so. This guy,—you're kidding me. Say you're kidding me, Dewey—"

"I may be wrong, but I ain't kidding you."

"But that knocks the whole bottom out of everything, it blows the dam, it—and you ain't wrong either. You're right. I see it. I see it as clear as daylight now. My God, Dewey! where have I been all my life that I can't tell— Who's that out there?"

Dewey went to the door and looked out.

"It's the Bishop. You want to see him?"

"Christ, no! . . . Tell him this ain't a Sunday School paper. Tell him the free publicity's all run out. Tell him I'm out of town."

When Dewey left him he sntached the beginning of Pavinovsky's interview out of the typewriter, wadded it into a ball and threw it at the round belly of the little black stove. It was true, of course it was true! And where did that leave him? It left him without a story, that's where it left him. It left him up bitch creek without a paddle. It left him with fifteen thousand circulation that would drop back in a week to twelve. And what would The Great Lakes Paper Company say to that? He knew damned well what they would say! He was on the street. He was as good as on the street. A whole year in this lousy burg for nothing. And just when everything—

His eye fell on the editorial hanging on the hook ready for Tom. He ripped it off and threw it after the interview. He was slouching in his chair with his fists above his head when Dewey came back.

"He says he's got to see you. I told him you had shut up and gone fishin'. He said he had some dope on Mattie Small, but he wouldn't tell anybody but you. He wanted to know when you were coming back. I believe he knows something. I told him to wait a minute."

"But we're through with that story, Dewey! We don't print anything else about it at all. I don't want to *hear* anything else about it. I've forgotten it. Tell him to go away."

"Don't you want to see what he's got, Mac?"

"No! . . . Bring him in. But tell him I've got a ton of work on me and can't give him but a minute."

The Bishop came in with easy dignity, his black hat in his hand, his long bald head shining with perspiration.

"Good mornin' to you, sir."

"What can I do for you, Bishop? I'm up to my neck."

"I won't take up but a few minutes of your time, sir. I'm going away tonight and much of God's work still remains to be done. I'll come straight to the gist of the matter." He smiled with his white teeth. "In my work out there in The Terry among God's poor black children He has led me upon some surprising information relative to Mattie Small. You know who I mean."

305

"She's the one held for the death of that girl, isn't she?"

"Yes, sir. Now who was that girl?"

Mr. McFarlane shifted the angle of his slouch.

The Bishop went on: "The papers say her name was Mary Glover. But that's wrong."

"How do you know it's wrong?"

"Because her real name, sir, was Laney Shields."

"Did you know her?" He wrote down the name, hardly able to bring himself to trust these signs that kept telling him louder and louder that after all everything was not yet lost.

"No, sir, but Laney Shields was followed from the place she worked to Mattie Small's and she was never seen again—"

"Where'd she work?"

"That's the interesting part, sir. She worked as a nurse for a certain young doctor on Green Street. . . . You get the idea, sir, I am sure."

"Well, Bishop," laughed Mr. McFarlane deprecatingly, though he could hardly hold himself in his chair, "this is all very well, but how do you know it's so,—how do I know it's so?"

"I suggest, sir, you telephone Dr. Lucian Abercorn—"

"Dr. Lucian Abercorn?"

"Yes, sir. Telephone him and ask him if he had a nurse working for him by the name of Laney Shields—"

"But Laney Shields may have disappeared too. It happens all the time. That doesn't prove she's the one Mattie killed. Laney Shields may have gone off to Birmingham with the elevator boy—"

"Call Dr. Abercorn, sir. See what he says. Just say you're trying to locate Laney Shields and heard she worked there."

Mr. McFarlane indulgently reached out for the telephone book.

"It might be just as well, sir, not to mention me; I'd rather the church didn't—"

Mr. McFarlane found the number, called it, waited while it buzzed irregularly. After a while a woman's voice answered.

"I'd like to speak to Dr. Lucian Abercorn."

306

There was a pause of several seconds, then the woman said, "Dr. Lucian Abercorn's out of town."

"Will he be back this afternoon?"

"No. Dr. Abercorn's gone to New York."

"New York!"

"Ask her when he went away," said the Bishop, watching a fly crawling over the window pane.

"When'd he go away?"

"This morning, about eleven. Is there any message?"

"When do you expect him back?"

"I don't know, sir."

Mr. McFarlane hung up.

"Does that satisfy your mind, sir?"

"That's very interesting, Bishop. Thanks for the tip. There's probably nothing in it; we'll have to do a good deal of checking up. . . . Get you one of those paper cups over there and I'll give you a drink of good corn whiskey."

The Bishop smiled his refusal, thanked him, and went out. At the door he paused to look at the pottery vase on Miss Minnie Posey's desk. "Those are beautiful petunias, sir," he said to Mr. McFarlane.

Mr. McFarlane, though, didn't hear him; he was down on his knees beside the black stove searching among the balls of copy paper for his editorial, "Who Was Mary Glover?" . . .

At about five o'clock that afternoon Mr. McFarlane was back in the office contemplating with almost fervid satisfaction the new and firmer foundations of his success, the pleasure of looking upon them enhanced many times by the sudden terrible glimpse he had had of disaster. For a moment it had looked as if everything were melting into a jelly; then everything had suddenly taken shape again. He had been out making a few investigations. He had talked to Dr. Abercorn's cook; he had asked to see Dr. Abercorn, but the cook said he hadn't been feeling well and had gone to bed. He had found out what he wanted, though. It was all right this time; go ahead. He had hurried back and read the proof of the editorial. He thought he would let that go in the regular morning edition; then at about two o'clock, just before everybody started home for dinner, he would put an extra on the street with the streamer, "Girl's Body Identified." He had been a little worried that perhaps the other paper might get it, but the edition was out now and there was not a word about it. He thought before he got through with this thing he would rate a rise in pay, would probably get promoted all the way out of the South. He sat down at his desk and started hammering out the story of how the *News,* following on the scent of certain clews of its own, had at last unearthed the hidden identity of Mary Glover. He was writing the last paragraph: "Young Dr. Lucian Abercorn, in whose office she worked, could not be communicated with at a late hour last—"

This was the point at which the telephone rang and Dewey Selph told his chief that a gang of hoodlums was running amuck on Cotton Row, had desperately wounded Lamar Telfair and his stenographer and several other prominent Georgetown business men. The wagon had just gone down to Telfair & Company's cotton office, the scene of the disturbance—. Mr. McFarlane, being sociological to the extent of believing firmly in the breeding possibilities of high temperatures on news, and superstitious to the extent of believing just as firmly in the gregariousness of front-page items, clapped on his Panama hat without much surprise and proceeded at a quick walk to Cotton Row.

He hurried past the half dozen people gathered round the ambulance and the Black Maria, nodded with esoteric camaraderie to the policeman in Telfair & Company's entrance, and went inside. The only person with a scratch that he could find was a negro named Pleasant Showers, 989 Third Street, who was lying with wide scared eyes in a corner of the floor under the fingers of the ambulance surgeon; he was wounded with three or four buckshot in the top of the right shoulder. Lamar Telfair and the stenographer, though excited, were perfectly whole. Ben Gray of Due West, Georgia, stood between two policemen, his hands behind his back, his glazed pink eyes blinking now and then perplexedly.

Mr. McFarlane sent his man Dewey to talk to Telfair and concentrated his own attention on the disturber of the peace and the victim; he rode up to headquarters with Ben Gray and talked to him for some time.

It was nearly six o'clock when, with a handful of notes on holding cotton and margins and telegrams and declining prices, he finally left the cell and returned to the office. It looked as if everything were breaking his way after all. Here was enough news to float a battleship. And it was not just news for a day, either; there would be reverberations,—Mattie would come to trial, the Grand Jury would find a true bill against Ben Gray, stories from Lamar Telfair, from the stenographer, from— My God!—Pavinovsky, brother of—three-column cut of Metropolitan Opera House, New York, where stenographer's brother, Sergey Pavinovsky (inset)—

He bounded up the steps and Dewey met him at the top.

"Lamar Telfair's in your office."

"Good. . . . Hold your story up a few minutes, I may want to add something."

Dewey lifted his hand as if half thinking of saying a word or two further, but Mr. McFarlane was already nearly to his door.

Mr. Telfair was moving about between the stove and the window, his stiff collar and white shoes lending an air of somewhat incongruous consequence against the informal background of calendars and posters and photographs of very much *au courant* young women; he had laid his hat on a table among the exchanges and was walking about with his hands in his pockets jingling his silver money with a certain cadence.

"Good evening, Mr. Telfair. I'm McFarlane."

"How you do?" said Mr. Telfair, giving him a leisurely hand.

"Glad to see you, Mr. Telfair. There were one or two things—"

"It's been hot today."

"Yes, it has."

"I see your weather man up there," said Mr. Telfair, nodding at a printed card in a slot on the wall, "says it was ninety-nine."

"Yes, that was at one o'clock."

"That ain't on the street either. The thermometer in my office at four o'clock was a hundred and three."

"I should think it would have registered at least that," laughed Mr. McFarlane good-naturedly, but Mr. Telfair was apparently deaf.

"September's one of our worst months down here."

"Will you have a cigarette, Mr. Telfair?"

"No, thank you."

"It's mighty nice of you to come by."

"I just thought I'd stop in and have a little chat with you about that—that affair round at my office awhile ago—"

"I'm delighted to see you, sir. I wanted to ask you particularly if there had been any trouble before this between you and Mr. Gray—"

"Now just a minute, youngster," said Mr. Telfair, walking by the back of a chair with a pleasant jingle. "This little thing this afternoon was too bad. I regret it very much. And I know old Ben Gray regrets it. He's an old customer of mine. I've been doing business with old Ben Gray for fifteen years. I've been fishin' and huntin' with him the odd time. He'd been drinkin' a little too much, that was all; he had nothin' in the world against my nigger Showers."

"Mr. Telfair—"

"Knowin' how you young fellows are, impetuous and all that (you-all went pretty far with that Mattie Small thing, you know), I thought maybe I better just step by here and get you to go kinder easy on old Ben Gray. If you want to run two or three inches about it on an inside page, why—go ahead; that's all right. I don't want to be unreasonable about it. Go on and run your story. I'd rather you didn't mention it was my office, but go on and run your story."

"But, Mr. Telfair—"

"I was afraid, seeing how you-all wrote up this other thing, you might just take it into your head to put this on the front page and I just thought I'd stop by and see you." He reached for his hat.

310

Mr. McFarlane shook his head with a smile of regret. "I wish I could help you, sir."

"I thought maybe you might not understand that this would hurt business, and anyhow, what happens between old Ben Gray and Telfair & Company is—well, between him and the company."

"I'm sorry to say so, Mr. Telfair, but I'm afraid I can't help you."

"How do you mean, son?"

"Why, this is a big piece of news, Mr. Telfair. I couldn't think of dismissing it the way you suggest, as much as I'd like to accommodate you personally, sir. You must see my position; I was sent down here to get the news and print it. I can't show any special favoritism—"

"Excuse me for interrupting you, but my nigger Showers is out at the hospital and I've got to run by there and see him before I go home. I'm in kind of a hurry and I haven't got time to argue about it—"

"I'm not trying to argue, Mr. Telfair—"

"If you don't feel like you've got the authority to dismiss this thing, I better—"

"I've got the authority, Mr. Telfair. The whole thing's on my shoulders. That's why I can't afford to let myself be told what to print and what not to print. If the paper goes in the red I'm the one they ring for. This is a newspaper, Mr. Telfair; we can't show any favoritism about what we print—"

"May I use your phone?"

"Certainly."

"I'll see if I can get you some more authority."

"If you're going to call Major Bain, it's a waste of time. I'm not responsible to anybody but the people that employ me—"

"Long distance," said Mr. Telfair. Then *sotto voce*, "Would you mind just shoving that chair a little—thank you. . . . Long distance, I want to talk to Mr. Charles Snelling at Detroit, Michigan. You'll find him at the office of The Great Lakes Paper Company, yes,—and if he's gone home, why, try his house, please, ma'am. This is Mr. Lamar Telfair speaking and I want you to put this call on Telfair & Company's bill."

Mr. McFarlane shook out a cigarette and struck a match with a flourish on the stove. "Let me talk to Mr. Snelling when you get through."

"That's what I have in mind. I want you to talk to him yourself."

"Is Mr. Snelling a friend of yours?"

"I never saw him in my life."

"They can't afford to do this for you, Mr. Telfair. They own a dozen papers all over the country and they can't afford to dismiss a piece of hot news just because it concerns a prominent citizen. Where would the newspapers be if they canned everything—"

"Hello. Yes, I'm waiting."

"You can't expect Mr. Snelling to do something like this for you as a personal favor."

"Son, I never ask personal favors. This may look to you like a personal favor, but it ain't. I don't believe there's any personal side to business; you do business with a man because it's profitable to you, not because you think he's a nice fellow.—I'm waiting.— You're wasting your time being friendly with the head of a bank, for instance. He ain't going to lend you any money because he likes you, and if you're a good loan he'll lend it to you even if he thinks you're a bastard—yes, hello. Hello! Hello, Mr. Snelling?"

"Hello, Mr. Telfair," said Mr. Snelling. "How are you?"

"I'm fine. How are you?"

"Things are pretty slow, Mr. Telfair. You're not getting impatient, are you?"

"Not a bit in the world, sir."

"The security we gave you—"

"We're not worried about that. It's a good loan and well secured. No, sir, it's about another little matter I wanted to talk to you."

"All right, Mr. Telfair."

312

"You sent a young man down here about a year ago to run this paper, named McFarlane."

"Who?"

"McFarlane."

"Oh, yes. I remember. McFarlane."

"Well, we had a little trouble around here this afternoon. One of my niggers round in the warehouse accidentally got shot. I'd rather that didn't come out in the paper; that sort of thing, you know, don't help business. We have a hard enough time making a living without—"

"Sure, Mr. Telfair. Tell him I say not to print it."

"I thought maybe it might be better if you talked to him—"

"Be glad to do it, Mr. Telfair. I'll call him right now."

"He's here in the office, Mr. Snelling."

"Good. Put him on."

"Just a second before I put him on. There's another piece of news that's embarrassing us a little—"

"Let me talk to him, Mr. Telfair."

"You see, this ain't like Detroit down here, Mr. Snelling. This is a small town and it's bad to have the newspaper always embarrassing—"

"I understand perfectly, Mr. Telfair."

"This youngster doesn't use any discretion—"

"Suppose I send somebody else down there?"

"He's a good boy but he's got a lot of ideas about—"

"I'll send somebody else down there tomorrow."

"Well, I reckon that'd be about the best thing to do at that, Mr. Snelling."

"Let me speak to him, Mr. Telfair."

Mr. Telfair handed Mr. McFarlane the receiver, put on his hat and walked out.

6. In His Infinite Wisdom

THE news about Pavinovsky sank into Miss Tannahill's consciousness slowly. She learned it after the early movie, about nine o'clock, sitting in a Dodge sedan in front of Dunovant's Drug Store with two of her friends; she had denied herself a chocolate malted milk and ordered tomato juice on account of her figure. She was sipping it contentedly when his name was mentioned and the fact came out. She stopped almost in the middle of a swallow; it seemed to close up her throat. She hardly heard any more of what the girl was saying, hardly noticed how she was saying it except to hate her smile. She thought she must be turning pale; she could feel something happening to her cheeks. She thought it must be like this when you realized some day that you were about to die. She stirred the shaved ice in her glass with the straw. In a few minutes she noticed that she had become silent. This won't do, she said to herself, they'll think you're in love with him. She found something to say.

But when they left her at home things began to change. She lighted a cigarette on the steps as they drove away; if they glanced back they could see that the news was nothing in her life. She smoked it while she unlocked the door of her rooms, stood for a minute in the dark, then turned on a lamp. But when she heard the gears shift at the corner and die away up the car track she tossed it in the fireplace. She hardly ever did that because she liked her rooms to be neat and the servant never cleaned the fireplace in summer; she usually put her cigarettes in a brass Chinese bowl and before going to bed emptied it into the toilet and wiped it out with a piece of paper. She saw it spatter a dry flurry of sparks as it hit the sooty brick. She walked round an empty easel, sat down in a rocking chair, got up, went to a window; everywhere she turned was this new and sinister guest that had come to live with her. The hopes she had gone out with, sat through the movies with, ordered her tomato juice with, frail though they had been, were living hopes; now they were dead, every one. There was none left now, not one. She faced into the room and leaned against the side of the window, smiling a little. If she were an outsider the situation might seem rather funny; for years she had carefully nursed her innocence, then for years she had as carefully tried to hide it, now finally as a last— It wasn't true! It was malicious gossip!

But she knew it was true. It explained too many little things. It explained about the fountain pen; it explained— It was true, every word of it. Her love was hopeless. As hopeless as if he were dead. Worse than that; dead, she could steal away sometimes and go look at his grave, she could think of how different it would have been if he had lived, she could take somebody into her confidence and tell about it. She couldn't tell about this; they would laugh. There was something funny about this; there really was. Where was she going to find solace? What was she going to do when tomorrow came? Tomorrow, and the long dusty days that would follow. What was the hope she was going to live on now? A person needed a hope. He would never tap lightly on her door now. She would never wake now to hear him tossing gravel against her window pane. He would never lie down beside her now. She was dead to him. She had always been dead to him. She was dead to herself now; all her hopes of beautiful sin had vanished like a rainbow. And tomorrow was coming, interminably long. . . . Mrs. Eubanks kept a pistol in the hall table upstairs.

She turned away from the window as if the pistol had been lying there. She would have to watch herself; she was taking this thing too seriously. What difference did it make? Three months ago she had never heard of him.

She lifted back the pink bedcover and folded the edges of it neatly together; then she hung it over the back of an antique mahogany chair and took off her clothes. She stood for a minute naked, then dropped prone across the warm sheets, her arms stretched out. . . .

When the bell in the Arsenal started striking she listened. She didn't know how long she had been there; she thought it must be three o'clock, or later. But it kept on striking, three, four,—morning? Daylight? Five, six,—ten, eleven, twelve. Twelve! The night had just begun. The last car hadn't even gone down yet. Eight hours before the house would begin to stir, eight hours to be alone. At seven-thirty she could get up and put some cool water on her eyes and walk down the bright street to the other house to breakfast. She didn't think she would eat anything. Maybe she wouldn't even get up. Just lie there, lie there feeling the room get warm. There was no reason to get up. How long would it take to die of starvation? That fellow in India had lived for three or four weeks. That was too long; when you wanted to die you didn't want to have to wait three or four weeks. Sometimes people took an overdose of sleeping powders. She didn't have any. There was none in the house that she knew of. The drug store was closed. . . . But—

She took a Chinese kimono out of the wardrobe and wrapped it round her. If anybody came out in the hall she would say she had thought she heard somebody down in the basement. She would put it in her sleeve and bring it back to her room. And she had better put on some clothes too.

She tiptoed out in the hall in her bare feet and felt her way to the smooth round newel post. When she stepped on the third tread it creaked, dry old stairs, every drop of moisture drawn out by heat, heat. She moved over against the wall and climbed another step. It cracked like the other and she moved on tiptoe to the other side and tried with both hands to lift most of her weight by the mahogany banister, glass smooth, tepid, lowering it slowly on the next tread.

Half way up she thought she heard a footstep in one of the rooms upstairs. She waited a minute, then went on. As she reached the top she heard a quiet click like a bolt being let into place. If anybody came out in the hall she would say, Sssh! I think I heard somebody down in the basement.

It was heavier than she had thought it would be. It wasn't very

316

large, but you had to take a firm hold of it to lift it. She picked it up in both hands and closed the drawer. If she stumbled on the way back down it would probably go off.

But she didn't stumble. When she reached the bottom she looked back up to see if there was a light, but apparently she hadn't awakened anybody.

She shut the door of her bedroom behind her and locked it. She laid the pistol on the glass top of her bureau, her fingers shaking a little. He would never know the truth about it. He would see it perhaps in the paper but he wouldn't connect it with himself; he would go away and never think again about that girl—that woman down in Georgetown who one summer night— Why not just walk over there to the bureau and quit all this worrying?

She glanced toward it in the light from the street lamp on the corner and saw the shiny back of her silver hairbrush. She hadn't any clothes on. It wouldn't do to be found like that. She started dressing. When she was half dressed she stood in front of the mirror in the pale light and brushed her hair; it was wet above her ears; the bristles always seemed stiffer in summer when your hair was damp.

She heard a noise and paused; then she went on brushing her hair. It was the last out-bound car grinding patiently up the hill. When she was going to town that was the signal for her to get her things together. She could just make the last car down if she wanted to.

Of course she didn't want to! Why should she want to go to Broad Street? But it went on down Broad Street. It passed within two blocks of the house where he was living. She could take that car and walk to his house and—

No, she couldn't do that. That was murder. Just wait a minute. She was dressed now; just sit down on the bed and wait a minute, wait until the down car passed. As its gold-lighted emptiness passed her window—go ahead. It would be very easy. With one slight pressing of her finger she would destroy—destroy tomorrow. Destroy futility, loneliness, chastity, destroy in her own

317

way all the things she had thought he would destroy. It would be strange to be without loneliness, it had been a boon companion for so long. Maybe there was loneliness afterward too. Maybe you couldn't destroy loneliness. If he were going to die too— No, leave him to life. Leave him to lie down in the arms of life. Let life take her place beside him, let life lie down upon him— No! *No!* Take him with her!

The grinding of the car died out up the hill. From where he was now the motorman could probably see the down car waiting, its headlight orange like an old kerosene lamp. . . .

When the orange lamp came over the break of the hill she stepped down from the curb where she had been standing and crossed the road to the track. There was nobody in the car windows. Thank God for that! She might have lost her nerve.

As she climbed aboard the motorman looked at her and she put her purse in her other hand. She held out a dime.

"In the box, please."

Of course. She knew that. She rode on those cars every day. What was the matter with her?

She dropped it in the box, wondering if he had thought it peculiar that she had had the fare ready and not had to look in the purse for it.

"You go down Broad Street, don't you?"

"Yes'm."

He seemed sleepy. She wasn't sleepy at all. Her eyes seemed to burn inside but she didn't feel sleepy.

There was nobody in the car. If there had been, she thought she would have got out; she felt as if anybody could look at her and know what she had in her purse and what she was going to do.

"Candor of soul," said Lee Hill to his image in the bathroom mirror; "if you could just meet a woman with some candor of soul." He picked up his last quart of corn whiskey in his wet fingers, felt it skidding, grabbed at it with the other hand, dropped it with a musical smash against the tile floor.

318

He considered the wreck for a moment in silence, then poured out upon it a slow cascade of earnest profanity. That was all the whiskey there was in the apartment. There wasn't any more. That was all there was!

He salvaged half a glass by mopping it up with a hand towel, then decided against it and drove his coupé round to the gaslighted hallway through which Mr. Speck Hayes supplied his retail trade. He went up the steps and knocked on a thin gray door that blocked the staircase.

"Hello, Mr. Hill. Come right in, sir."

"Hello, Speck. How the rabbits jumpin'?"

"Pretty good, Mr. Hill. What you know?"

"I've just finished dropping my God-damned bottle on the bathroom floor."

"Aw!"

"That was all the liquor I had to get me over Sunday."

"But I got plenty liquor, Mr. Hill."

"You haven't got any liquor like that. That stuff had been mellowing in a charred keg for nearly a month."

"Wait a minute!" said Mr. Hayes in a challenging tone, partly closing one eye. "Just wait a minute, Mr. Hill. Joe, answer the door." He went into another room.

"Evenin', Mr. Rountree," said Joe to a stoutish bareheaded young man, whose hair was getting thin on top.

"Is Speck here?"

"He'll be back in a minute."

"Hey, Lee."

"Hey, Jack."

"Have a drink."

"Be glad to."

Joe poured them drinks.

"I just stopped by to pick up a gallon of corn. We've got a gang going down to the farm."

"Who's going?"

"Last week when we were down there Farrow got so drunk

319

his wife had to hold him up while he said his prayers! I thought I'd die!"

"Who's going?"

"You want to go?"

"Sure."

"All right."

"All right."

"An old girl of yours was coming but her husband went away and she left us flat."

"Who's that?"

"Maybelle."

"Where'd Branch go?"

"I don't know."

"Look here, Jack, I can't go down there with you-all. I just remembered—"

"All right, Lee."

"Is that all right?"

"Sure."

"Have another drink."

"All right. . . . Say, Joe, tell Speck to let me have a gallon of that corn."

"You want to take it with you or drink it here?" said Joe.

"I been laughin' at that, Joe, since 1925."

Mr. Hill lifted his glass and said, "Well."

In a minute Joe came back with a gallon jug in a brown paper bag.

"You ready, Lee?"

"I can't make it tonight, Jack."

"All right."

"Is that all right?"

"Sure."

Joe opened the door to let him out and waited a minute while two men in their shirt sleeves finished the climb and entered in silence. One wore a taxi-driver's cap on the back of his head, the other was bareheaded, with his hair unkempt, as if they had been driving in the wind.

"Sit down over here, Mr. Mobley," the taxi-driver said, leading him to an empty table near the radio.

Mr. Mobley flopped down in a chair and ran his fingers through his black hair; the chauffeur came up to the bar and ordered two drinks.

"What's the matter with him?" said Lee Hill.

"His name's Mobley. He's in a tough spot."

Mr. Hill looked at him over his shoulder. "You need a doctor?"

"No. She's got a doctor."

The driver carried the drinks over to the table and talked to Mr. Mobley in an undertone. Mr. Mobley took down his drink in one swallow.

"I had to siphon it out of the keg," said Mr. Speck Hayes, apologizing for taking so long. "You want to try it?"

Lee Hill unscrewed the bottle cap and applied a professional nostril; he poured himself a drink and tasted it.

"Like to use your telephone," said the taxi-driver.

"Help yourself."

"Four one hundred," said the chauffeur, as if he had the number by heart. "Give me the maternity ward, please, ma'am.— Hello? Hello? Has anything happened to Mrs. Mobley yet? Mobley.—All right. Thank you, ma'am." He held up his hand and shook it negatively at Mr. Mobley. "She's been at it twenty-two hours. It's underminin' him."

Mr. Mobley pushed his glass suggestively across the table and rumpled his hair.

"Come over and talk to him, cheer him up a little."

"I've got to telephone," said Lee Hill, looking at his watch; it was about nine-thirty.

"I'm scared I'm gonna have trouble gettin' him out of here."

Lee Hill left him, moved down to the end of the bar and opened the greasy directory: Wheaton, L. Branch, 273 Davis Road, 7014. She would answer it without the slightest evidence of human understanding, without the slightest hint that she belonged to the human race, probably raise the pitch of her voice as if overcome by surprise, fumbling round all the time for some sort of cloak of banalities in which to bundle herself up to her ears. Candor of soul! Great God, all the candor of soul in five hundred miles wouldn't be enough to fecundate one puerile snicker! For we here Live on tough roots and stubs, to thirst inured More than the camel and to drink go far, Men to much misery and hardship born. He wanted to talk a little, that was all he wanted. Write it in water. 7014. Call it, call it. Maybe he was wrong about Southern womanhood. Yes, maybe the moon was Philadelphia cheese. Maybe the world was flat. Hell, it was flat. Flat, stale, and—God, how unprofitable—

"Seveno one four."

There's something wrong with this country down here. You can't produce candor down here. It won't grow. Won't anything grow but a kind of histrionic gentility. Candor of soul. Christ! They wouldn't even know what you were talking about. To thirst inured more than—

"I'd like to speak to Mrs. Wheaton."

"She ain' here."

"Not there? Well, where is she?"

"I think she gone to a party down to Mrs. Moke's."

He hung up. . . . Well, all right. All right. She'd gone to a party down to Mrs. Moke's. Let her go. He didn't care. To thirst inured more than the camel. They were porous, like the soil. No bottom, nothing to hold the heavenly rain—

"Joe, see if you can get together a light drink back there."

He took the drink over to the table where Mr. Mobley and the taxi-driver were sprawled on their elbows.

"I'm trying to get him to go home," said the taxi-driver. "I can't do anything with him."

Mr. Mobley stared at his empty glass.

"Don't you think we better get out of here. chief?"

"I ain' rea'y to get out."

"You don't work for him, do you?" said Lee Hill.

"Never laid eyes on him before. I was parked at the depot and he came by and asked me to drive his car for him. I didn't think he ought to drive, so I got in. We been everywhere—"

"You been everywhere," said Mr. Hill, sitting down. "Well, that's a good thing. People will tell you you ought to stay home; you ought to stay where you were born. But don't you believe 'em. Some places are better for what you want than other places. If you want a sea lion there ain't any sense in hunting for him in the Congaree River. He ain't in the Congaree River. The Congaree River just don't suit him, that's all. It ain't congenial to him. If you want a sea lion you got to go somewhere else. Now I hear you object that because he wasn't born there it proves he don't belong there. You say he belongs where he was born and the reason you don't find him in the Congaree River is because he's got sense enough to stay home—"

"Let's get to hell out of here," said Mr. Mobley.

"But I tell you the reason you don't find him in the Congaree River is because he just don't like the Congaree River. And I don't blame him because I don't like it either."

"What to hell's wrong wit' the Congaree River?" said the taxi-driver.

"Let me out!" Mr. Mobley stood up.

"Wait a minute, chief."

"Let me out!"

"That's the men's room, sir."

"Where's the front door?"

"If I didn't have to trail this bird I'd stay here and tell you some things that're wrong with you."

"Spare me, comrade, spare me!"

They went out and Mr. Hill looked up Moke in the telephone book.

"Six seven one five. . . . Spare me here a little, while as yet 'tis early morn, Spare me here— Is Mrs. Wheaton there?" He rested his head on the receiver pensively. "Spare me here and when you want me— Hello, Maybelle."

"Who's this?"

"This is that old patron of arts and letters, Lee Hill."

"Why, hello, there."

"How are you, Maybelle?"

"Just fine. How are you?"

There was something a little disappointing about it; it wasn't exactly a flinging wide the arms.

"I was thinking I'd drop by tonight and see you and Branch for a little while, but when I called up the house somebody said you-all weren't there."

"That was Carrie. She's going to spend the night. Branch had to go away."

"Oh, really? Branch gone away? Well,—how you going to get home?"

"Oh, I don't know. George—"

"I tell you what, Maybelle. I'm going to be out that way; I'll come by there when you're ready and give you a ride home."

"Why,—all right, Lee. That would be fine."

"You be ready soon?"

"I'm about ready now."

That sounded confidential; maybe after all—

He had Joe pour him another drink. She wasn't interested, though. They were immature, all of them. Some people blamed the Baptists and the Presbyterians. That wasn't it. That didn't do it. Graustark did it, and The Prisoner of Zenda and The Chocolate Soldier. It wasn't Puritanism; it was sentimentality. For all their corn whiskey they were pink. Watteau. The background was different, but the souls were still by Watteau. . . . And yet—

He put the bottle under his arm and went down the stairs, testing his eye by trying to walk on the unpainted centers of the treads where a runner had once been. Marbury and Green was a stop corner, but that seemed like an infringement of personal liberty and he passed it by. He wanted to talk. Maybe she would talk. Maybe they could go somewhere and have a candid talk; maybe there was one candid soul in Alabama. . . .

He opened the door and saluted the living room with his usual Saturday-night gesture recalling that of a wrestler entering the ring: "Hey, y'all!"

324

Maybelle gave him a restrained but he thought subtle smile.

"Hello, Maybelle."

"Hey, there."

"Ready to go?"

"Am I ready!"

The candor of this warmed him like a drink: "Let's go. You don't belong among this artificiality."

She patted him on the hand. "Wait a minute."

He was wrong about these girls. Wrong! It was the corn. Cold sober, he liked them, he liked the South, he liked Georgetown. That was the truth. There might be truth in wine, but corn whiskey was different. With a little corn, he got steamed up about it all. And there was nothing to get steamed up about. It was a beautiful place. The girls were beautiful. All Southern girls were beautiful; they were pink, but it wasn't Watteau's pink, it was Rubens's pink.

She came back with a girl named Carol.

"Hello, Carol," he said with some foreboding.

"Carol's spending the night with me," she said with a guileless smile. "Shall we go?"

He escorted them with abandoned courtesy to his car, drove them straight to 723 Davis Road, and escorted them with abandoned courtesy to the door.

"Thank you so much, Lee."

"Thanks heaps, Lee."

"Ladies, I assure you the pleasure was all mine."

"Good night, Lee."

"Good night, Lee."

"Ladies, I trust your rest will be undisturbed."

He drove along the street at fifteen miles an hour. It was the quality of that smile that worried him. Was that guilelessness? Or was it guile?

He steered the car with one hand, turned up the quart bottle with the other, and went through an old privet hedge into the soft white sand of a vacant lot. He looked out of the window in considerable surprise for a minute, then tried to back out; the

325

wheels spun. When he smelled scorched rubber he turned off the motor, locked it, and walked two blocks to the car line. He sat under a tree on the ground with the bottle beside him until the car came.

When he got aboard he saw there were two people inside. He was about to take his hat off to the woman, who looked familiar, but he realized suddenly that the other passenger was more familiar still. The man was sitting by the window with a spare tire propped up on the seat beside him.

"Pardon me, sir," said Lee Hill, "but haven't I had the pleasure of meeting you before?"

"I don't think so," said the man, "but my name's Mobley, Jefferson Mobley. I've lost my automobile—"

There was a quick buzz and the woman got up and went to the door.

A few minutes before ten that night the Reverend Riley All put on his alpaca coat and smiled at the sudden turmoil of excitement this caused in his fox terrier; the dog scampered down the hall and stood up against the screen door. Dr. All folded tomorrow's sermon, which he had been working on, and put it in his pocket; the people across the street had just turned on the radio and he thought he would go over to his study in the church where it was quiet. He was anxious to have the sermon just right; Brother Dice was arriving in Georgetown maybe next week and would probably see the report of it in the paper. He had hoped he would have more news to give him; when he looked back now over the twelve months Dice had been away there seemed to be hardly any news. Nothing very important had happened; it had seemed at the time to be passing very slowly, but now he hardly knew where the year had gone. A few funerals, a few christenings, a few new members (very few), nothing else. He had hoped there might be something to tell Brother Dice; he had hoped Miss Tannahill—but God, in His infinite wisdom, knew best. He walked out and strolled down the sidewalk, his hat in his hands behind him.

326

He crossed the car track and went back in the dark angle of the church to his study. He liked the smell as you entered the Sunday School door, the smell of the pamphlets and catechisms in the wooden cabinet, the smell on Saturday night of the damp bare floor scrubbed that morning. He unlocked the door of his study, went inside, and punched a button on the wall which simultaneously turned on his desk lamp and a fan; he laid the sermon on his desk, hung his coat on a rack in the corner, and sat down, wiping the moisture off his face. He opened his soft leather Bible to the text of his sermon and began reading aloud in a quiet voice, a handkerchief in his hand with which now and then he mopped his face: "Put on the whole armor of God, that ye may be able to stand against the wiles of the devil. For we wrestle not against flesh and blood, but against principalities—"

He read on for some time; he enjoyed the beautiful song of the words. After a while he closed the book and read his sermon, making some changes now and then with a pen and blotting them carefully. When he had finished that, he rested his head against the back of the high chair for a minute, then lifted his Bible in his two hands and let it fall open at random; he often did that when he was perplexed and again and again the revelation of Divine guidance amazed him.

It fell open at the twelfth chapter of Second Corinthians and his eye stopped upon the twenty-first verse: "And lest, when I come again, my God will humble me among you, and that I shall bewail many which have sinned already, and have not repented of the uncleanness and fornication and lasciviousness which they have committed."

He closed the book and knelt in front of his chair: "Almighty and everlasting God, Thou who comfortest the sick, who guidest the strong, Thou who lookest down upon Thy children in their sinfulness, comfort and guide Thy erring daughter. Guide her out of the wilderness of temptation, lead her beside the still waters of peace, restore her soul. Lead her out of the clutches of evil and out of the shadows of darkness; lead her, O Lord, into the light of Thy countenance. Be with her tonight and guide her in Thine own good time to Thee. We ask it in the name of Thy Son, our Lord. . . ."

For two years after that, when he went up to the summer colony of Baptists in North Carolina for his holiday he delivered special talks telling about that night; he had had other instances of Divine intervention but none so miraculous as this.

He locked the door of the Sunday School and listened for a second to one of those nerve-racking street cars getting under way from the station above the church; he thought of himself on Sunday in the midst of prayer drowned out by this heavy crescendo of steel on steel.

He strolled out to the sidewalk, turned up toward home, and walked straight into that wayward young woman, tears of repentance streaming down her face. She tried to brush past him, tried to free herself from him, not knowing who he was; then he spoke to her and she ceased resisting.

He led her back to his study, she sobbing in a kind of delirium. For a long time she did not speak. He held her hand and told her how God had answered his prayers for her, how at the very moment that he was asking God to guide her she was coming home to God, the prodigal daughter at last voluntarily coming home to God. He told her how God needed her, how nothing in her past life mattered if she would only trust and follow Him.

"My child," he said, "great will be the rejoicing in Heaven tonight. I do not know how God made Himself manifest to you. It may be that you do not know either. He moves in a mysterious way to answer our prayers. But I do know that your life is beginning again with this hour. You have been born again. You will know happiness now such as you have never known before."

She broke down at last amidst a flood of tears and dedicated her life to Christ.

"I do feel a sort of peace," she said.

328

7. Country Doctor

IT was about seven o'clock when Dr. Abercorn swung his skinny legs weakly out of bed; the electric fan buzzed in low gear on the floor by the fireplace, giving a slow ripple to the warm white hem of his nightshirt. There was no rest in nights like these. He felt as weak as a kitten. He wasn't sure he could stand up. Dear Governor, Decided to try the big city for a while; will keep you posted—hell!

What was really the matter with himself, anyhow? He felt worse than before he had had those teeth pulled out. He was sorry he had done it. Before, he had got round really well enough. He ought to have been satisfied. Now he could hardly walk to the door. Something was the matter. Shake hands, doc, with the executioner. Dr. Abercorn, this is the executioner. Pleased to meet you, sir. He thought he had a little fever. The truth about it was that the boy just didn't like it; he hadn't been happy there. Things had been a little slow for him. And why should he expect the boy to be happy coming down there and going into partnership with a country doctor; that was what he was, just a country doctor, an honest, sympathetic, conservative country doctor. If he could see himself with the boy's eyes he would probably find he was pretty stodgy. Oh, life—life was an incurable disease. Life, that malignant epidemic. What the medical profession needed was more wisdom; it had plenty of tools, plenty of nimble fingers. It was like one of these painters with technique but not much genius. Wisdom. You went under at just about the time you were getting a little wisdom. Or maybe that wasn't so; maybe wisdom was just a slowing up. When everything was functioning well you went in for the dramatic things like love and war and surgery; when you slowed up a little bit you tried to justify it by telling yourself you were getting wisdom. You were really getting a little bit infirm. Maybe

329

wisdom was largely infirmity. If so, he ought to be pretty wise; he could hardly stand up. There was nothing the matter with him; he was just in a blue funk because the boy—nonsense.

He steadied himself at the bedpost then shuffled loosely across the bare floor to the hall. He unlocked the screen door, went out on the front porch and got the morning paper. It seemed very light. The world must have slowed up too; the only headline on the front page was a two-column thing up in the right-hand corner. God, but it was hot. Fever? Maybe. The whole world was running a temperature. Maybe the world had had too many of its teeth out. Maybe the war had pulled too many of its teeth out. That wasn't what was the matter with him; it was something else. That was what the world had: something else; nobody knew what. Georgetown was certainly running a temperature; 99° yesterday. He laughed a little and sank down on the bed. How long was all this going to last, anyhow?

He was lying with his eyes closed when he heard the familiar step downstairs of Julia Cope's white shoes. It was funny about that. It was hard to understand that that was Julia Cope, that that was the same foot he had guided into a crevice in the old brick wall round Saint Paul's Churchyard, the same foot that had jumped lightly down in the grass;—and that slightly hoarse voice which after a while would be saying, "Good morning, doctor," was the same voice that had murmured so beautifully once about the night and the moon and the trees.—And now you felt nothing. Nothing. All that just a shell; the soul had moved on, moved on to—Lucian. Strange how a current of love and pride and satisfaction and all that, ran through your body looking upon your son. Nothing at all now when you looked at Julia Cope, but looking at your son— When was he going to look at his son? His son had gone. Oh, sometime. Leave the boy alone; he'll come back sometime. But in the meanwhile—?

He went into the bathroom, drew a tub of cool water and got in it. When he came out Julia Cope was standing there with his breakfast tray.

330

"Good morning, doctor," she said with a smile. "How do you feel now?"

"Cleaner," said Dr. Abercorn.

8. What an Army of Us Died for Helen!

AUSTIN drove them out to the airport. He hardly knew how he felt, physically, but sentimentally he knew he felt decidedly wretched. She was after all, then, no different from the rest. He was wrong. His theory of beauty didn't work. She was a perfect test,—beauty untainted by training. She should have fallen on his neck. And she was just another Penelope,—neither assenting to the wooers nor sending them away. Penelope in Helen's girdle. And, dear Lord! how they depended on that girdle! And how they could mold their forms to fit it! They could deceive the hosts about Troy. Could? Did it every day.

And yet even now, was he sure? As they drove out she sat in the middle and he could feel the warm pressure of her shoulder through his linen coat, and it reminded him of the warmth of her eyes the first day he saw her. Had it all been due, perhaps, to Eliot? There was no dodging Eliot; he was just there, if not physically there, there in the minds of both of them. She may have tried to get away from him; how could he tell? For all these weeks when she and Eliot had left him at night she had said to him with her eyes that tonight was the night. He had slept for all these weeks on the side of his double bed away from the hall door, his heart burning with hospitality. Once or twice he had got up and walked out into the creaking hall; he had said to them several times that they would find it cooler if they left their door open for the draught, adding however, with a sort of

331

weak Parisian gayety, that of course he couldn't guarantee to answer for the consequences. But their door was always closed. When he saw her in the middle of the morning her eyes would say as plainly as words that she was sorry but it couldn't have been helped. Once toward the end, when Eliot had left them for a moment on the dark porch, he had taken her hand and said, "Tonight?" She had squeezed his fingers and turned her eyes on him for an instant before lowering them. . . . She would have come if she could.

And yet he knew at heart he didn't believe that; she hadn't had the faintest intention of coming. She was like all the rest, using every device known to modern and ancient man to disguise the innate purity of their souls.

"Well, when are you coming up to Phily, old fellow?" said Eliot, watching the boy on top of the wings with the nozzle of the gasoline hose; he wasn't really interested.

Austin glanced at Gwendolyn; he thought the way in which she pulled off her hat and shook her hair had more style in it than all the gestures of all feminine Georgetown put together. A pang of unalterable disappointment traveled slowly down his spine and torso and into his legs.

"You must come, Austin," she said. "I'll find you a girl."

He studied her deep eyes with a not particularly self-possessed grin, pondering for the long moment that she looked back at him on how he would have made the same mistake again today that he had made the first time he saw her. Her disguise was practically perfect; not one man in a thousand would have guessed her true innocence.—Greater scorn, he thought, hath no man than this: that the woman you love should offer to supply you with a substitute.

He thought he would ignore it. "You must come back to see me," he said. "The front door's always open."

"I've heard a lot about Southern hospitality," said Eliot, "but yours really sets a new high."

"You have been my most notable contribution to civic welfare," he laughed.

332

"Well, so long, old boy."

"So long, Austin," she said. "We've had a perfectly grand time."

He shook hands with both of them.

"Which way do we go, anyhow?" she said.

"In there," said Eliot. "Northeast."

"Straight over the reservoir," said Austin, "and across the golf course."

A different look came into her eyes, then she closed them and pulled her helmet on from the front like a bathing cap. . . .

He played golf that afternoon then drove slowly back to town in the warm twilight. He shucked off his cotton trousers, wet with perspiration, and turned on the high shower in the old bathroom. It was a large room; the fixtures seemed to take up no space at all; he remembered when it had been made into a bathroom. The windows looked out into the upper branches of two water oaks growing at the corner; through one of them he could see the levee and part of the pink river. A dry breeze fanned in one of the windows as he got out of the shower, giving him a moment of spring as it evaporated the water on his skin. He usually liked that hour in the warm empty house, dark below as he climbed the stairs, still light in his west room, the sense of tired muscles, the touch of clean linen freshly folded from a drawer, of smooth shoes against his bare feet, the prospect of the long glass of corn whiskey and ginger ale, of Oregon's broiled chicken in the ice box. What had become of that slumbrous peace that had once enveloped it like a summer drought? . . . Not one man in a thousand—

He caught sight in the bathroom cabinet of the little bottle of indigestion pills which he hadn't seen for so long; he had almost forgotten about them. When he started down stairs he paused on the landing, thought for a moment, then came back up and dropped the little bottle into his trousers pocket. He wasn't feeling very well. He stopped by an open window, held up his wrist to the fading light, and counted his pulse. He thought it seemed a little weak. . . .

333

Austin set out the next morning at about a quarter to eleven to keep an appointment. Nobody in the world but he knew the real reason of his appointment and he tried to summon for his own justification a deprecating smile, hoping to pull himself up above the sentimentality of it more or less by his own boot straps. But it was a wan smile; he was rather miserable. "The glass slipper you left with me when you went away—"

He backed his roadster across the creaking floor of the brick stable, turned hard to the left over the cement depression outside with the drain in the middle where Oregon had once washed the red mud off the tall wheels of his mother's Victoria, went forward cautiously through the carriage gate, and swung uptown.

The curb was full in front of the Cotton States Building and he had to park his car a block farther on and walk back, but the skyscraper was three blocks from his house, so he saved himself a walk of two.

He felt an unusual sort of defiance toward the world; he didn't care whether anybody liked him or not. He walked along through the vivid September haze of sunlight, his eyes on the white sidewalk ahead of him, his left hand in his trousers pocket fingering some kitchen matches, not caring whom he failed to speak to or what they thought of him; he knew pretty well what she thought of him and that was enough. "Love, you have tempered the cold night of my soul."

As a matter of fact, though, *did* he know what she thought of him? He could think of innumerable details suggesting indifference, hate, and love. It seemed to depend on the day or the hour or the humidity or the wind; the prevailing wind was—

"Hello, Mr. Austin."

Austin jumped.

"Hello, hello, there." Who was this boy? Knew his face, played golf, very good golf, Meigs. "Dub" Meigs. "How are you, 'Dub'?"

"All right, I reckon, thank you, sir. Er—have you got a minute or two, Mr. Austin?"

334

"Sure, I guess so."

"Er—will you have a dope?"

"I'm afraid I haven't got time. I've got a date at eleven."

"Maybe I oughtn't to keep you. It's really nothing at all."

They went to a shady corner under the portico of the Cotton States Building.

"That's all right. How's your golf?"

"Oh, I don't know. I haven't been playing much lately."

"I thought you'd be practicing up for the State."

"Well, you see—no, sir."

"You're entering, aren't you?"

"I don't know, sir."

"You don't seem very keen about it; what's the matter?"

Elbert laughed a little, shifting his feet. "I haven't been playing much lately."

Austin glanced at the Western Union clock in the hall.

"Everybody liked your visitors, sir."

"Did they?"

"I liked Mr. Owens a lot."

"Yes," said Austin. "Fine fellow."

"They live up in Philadelphia, don't they?"

"Yes.—More or less."

"You don't know their address, do you? I was thinking maybe I'd send Mr. Owens a postcard sometime."

"I think his father's law office would get him. Owens, Scott, Wharton."

"I see."

"They're in the Pennsylvania Trust Company Building, I think."

"I see.—You don't know their home address, do you?"

"Oh, Owens, Scott, Wharton, Philadelphia, would get him."

"I see. Well,—thank you very much, sir."

"Not at all."

"I hope I haven't made you late."

"Oh, no. But I guess I *had* better be pushing along."

"Th-thank you, sir."

335

Austin went up in the elevator to the fifteenth floor and walked into Dr. Troupe's waiting room. He sat down in a wooden rocking chair and looked about him: there she stood, half sitting against the table, pulling off her Leghorn hat.—"Oh, the bonds of love are ill to loose."

He got up and moved to the table. A lump suddenly rose into his throat: there was the April *Screenland!* There lay the identical pages that she had thumbed.

He turned away quickly and rang the lowest of the three bells on the door frame. . . . "What an army of us died for Helen!"

9. You've Seen the Worst

Tuesday, September 1

WHEN Mrs. Eubanks's September envelope appeared discreetly beneath Mr. Applewhite's green-slatted door, he realized specifically that the end of a chapter was at hand; now was a good time to close this soporific book and go back to that tight little hole in the wall looking south from Fortieth Street that he called home. He had done everything he could for Nora; it hadn't amounted to anything, but he had tried and, anyhow, there was nothing further he could do. It would be getting dark by dinner time now; he thought he would just gather himself together and go.

As a matter of fact, Nora had done more for him than he had for her. He had learned a good deal in those three months. He felt quite different about the place. He was a little like those Roman armies invading Britain, settling, and being absorbed by the native population. He had come down with a purpose, sentimental, foolish perhaps, but still a purpose, and that purpose had changed itself completely, had completely reversed itself; he had

336

come down to save his niece from the baleful influence of the home town, to get her away at any cost, and now he was ready to confess, if somebody pushed him, his more mature concept that staying in the home town was the best thing that could happen to her.

And it had been she that had showed him that. His attitude had been a little too romantic, impetuous, a little too radical and selfish and adolescent; hers had some of the wisdom of the earth and the seasons. Here he was, down from the great concentration point of artificialities and his attitude was artificial. It seemed a little trivial to have advised her to break away, to have said to her, in effect, that her only hope of happiness was in getting away from these people and their pettiness. "Go away; make a name for yourself." "I've got a name." She was right. He saw it now. One person's life didn't make any difference; it was a little cheap and spectacular to act as if it did. What mattered was a person's family, and the best way to strengthen a person's family was to stay put. There was something good somehow about being familiar with the appearance of that corner of grass beside your father and mother where you would be buried. You felt somehow that you were playing your part then, you fitted into the scheme of things; you had added one cubit more to your family stature. He hadn't paid much attention to the long-run things like family and tradition; he had been living in the heart of New York and got a little out of touch with things.

But that was a mature wisdom, an old man's wisdom; what was a girl of twenty-four doing with such foresight? Warm blood was usually such a foe of wisdom.

He put on his hat and walked up the hill in the damp September sunlight; he would go tell her that she was right. Her vision had been clearer than his. Maybe the younger generation had a clearer vision. It was a fine thing when a young person could see beyond the temptation of romance, of the spectacular, to the true dignity of life.

The front door was open and he walked into the hall. As he laid his hat on a settee Nora came out of a door from the pantry

337

with a handful of freshly-ironed clothes. She put them on a table and ran to meet him, her cheeks flushed.

"I've been trying to telephone you," she said. "I'm going."

"Wh-where are you going?" He felt, however, that this was more of an exclamation than a question; he knew what had happened: she had changed her mind.

"Where!" she said. " 'Vienna.' "

All he could say for a minute was, "Well, well."

"Maybe you're surprised." She looked down quickly at her hands, then up again with a somewhat forlorn smile. "I've been thinking it over."

"I thought—I thought you'd thought it over."

"I thought you'd be glad."

"Well, I hardly—"

"Oh, please be glad." She laughed when she said it, then she suddenly turned away and felt in the waist of her cotton dress for a handkerchief.

"Goodness me!" said Mr. Applewhite, considerably bewildered. He took her hand and led her out on the garden porch. "Of course I'm—I'm glad. Haven't—haven't I been trying to persuade you to do that all summer?"

That was all he got out of her; she had changed her mind. She had thought it all over and changed her mind. He stayed there talking to her for some time, but that was all he got. He told her that he was going, that if she was not particularly anxious to ride to New York alone they could go together. Then she could come to his apartment while they looked over a few ships. He thought she didn't seem particularly happy about going but he took it for nervousness and didn't press her.

"Have you got your ticket?" she said to him after awhile.

They drove downtown in her mother's car and bought their tickets.

"You know, I have a strange feeling of friendliness for this place," said Mr. Applewhite honestly. "I feel a personal interest in so many of these people. In New York you never know very much about anybody. You never see them from more than one

338

direction, your own. Here you get everybody's slant on them,—but, Lord! I believe you were the one saying that last. We seem to have exchanged camps."

"You aren't in a hurry, are you?" she said, interrupting him.

"God save me from such heresy."

"I'll leave them a full tank of gas to remember me by."

They drove over the sidewalk into the shade of Mr. Lee Hill's filling station. He came out of the shelter bareheaded and did something to one of the pumps.

"Hello, Nora. How's everything? How you, sir? The paper said you left last week, sir."

"Did it really? I'm going tomorrow as a matter of fact."

"You've seen the worst of it. It's going to be getting cooler from now on."

Mr. Applewhite laughed: "It must be only about ninety-five today."

"He ought to come to see us in January, oughtn't he, Nora? If you like weather, that's weather. . . . Fill her up, Nora?"

"Will you please, Lee?"

"I see where your friend, Pavinovsky's gone, too," said Mr. Hill from behind the car.

"I didn't know he had gone."

"Yeah, everybody's gone. Lucian Abercorn's gone. The managing editor of the *News*, McFarlane, he's gone—"

"When did Pavinovsky leave?"

"Two or three days ago. That's what the paper says. I'm not sure but what you and he went together. . . . Look here, sir, are you going to drive up by any chance? The reason I ask you, there's a young fellow in here trying to get a lift in the direction of Philadelphia, good boy, I mean I know him, all right,—maybe you know him. Young Meigs. Nora knows him."

Nora came out of a reverie with a start and smiled at him vaguely.

"We're going by train," said Mr. Applewhite.

"Check your oil, Nora?"

"Will you please, Lee?"

339

"If you hear anybody driving up, this fellow's been hanging round here three days trying to get a lift."

Nora signed a ticket and they drove off.

She dropped him at his boarding house. . . .

When he reached the top step of the porch Maybelle came out of the hall. He glanced at her absently; Nora had upset his ideas; he didn't quite know which end was up. He jumped a little when she spoke:

"Miss Annie says you're leaving."

"It's—it's about time, don't you think?" he said, collecting himself.

"We'll miss you. . . . I came to tell you good-by."

They sat down in the shade at one end of the white porch.

"How's your husband?" he said to her in a few minutes.

"Fine. His vacation begins next week."

"Are you going on a trip?"

"I was hoping you would ask me that. Yes, we're going on a trip."

"Good."

"We're going to take a canoe and paddle down the Congaree River."

"My God! . . . I just mean how perfectly impossible that would be for me. And I mean, too, that I envy you very much."

"We're going to catch fish and sleep on the bank. We've got a pup tent—"

In some way that he couldn't quite describe, she seemed different. He even wondered if he might be imagining it. It was more her manner than what she said,—and yet "manner" wasn't the right word because there was, if anything, a lack of manner now. He wondered if there wasn't a deeper contentment in her face than had been there. He thought it was a little like the first paling of the stars in the East and you hardly knew whether you saw it or not.—

10. Sabbatical

AFTER the first hurried words of greeting, a sort of nervous silence fell between Dr. All and Dr. Alexander; the same thing was obviously uppermost in both their minds: the metamorphosis that travel had brought about in Dr. Alexander. His manner was different; the expression of his face lacked some of the old assurance. He had somewhat the aspect of one who has looked over the edge; there was in him a certain trace of possible regret that he had seen what he had, but also a certain positiveness that what had happened was unalterable.

"I reckon you had a wonderful trip."

"I did, Riley. A wonderful trip. I never dreamed there were such things in the world."

"I want to hear all about it."

Dr. Alexander did not reply for a moment.

"It must feel good to get home again."

"I did a lot of thinking while I was on this trip."

Dr. All glanced at him with some trepidation.

"I did a lot of thinking."

"Wh-what about, Dice?"

"I saw people of all kinds and degrees. I went to all kinds and degrees of churches. I went to churches in China, in Japan, in the Malay Peninsula, in—in Burma, in—the Lord knows where some of those churches were. It set me to thinking."

"I gathered from your letters you had something on your mind."

"It set me to thinking, Riley. Thinking about our religion, our Baptist religion."

"What do you mean, Dice?"

"The idea struck me over there in China somewhere. I didn't pay much attention to it. But the more things I saw, the more this idea kept coming back."

341

"Y-you don't mean you doubt any—any—"

"Riley, that's just exactly what I mean."

"God forgive you!"

"After seeing all these heathen people, Riley, all these heathen religions, I just can't go on believing that it makes any difference to a man's immortal soul whether he's been baptized by complete immersion or by a few drops of water sprinkled on his head. In the sight of God, Riley, it don't matter what kind of baptism a man's had; the only thing matters is that he's been baptized somehow. God don't care how it's done so long's it's done—"

11. *Air de Ballet*

Thursday, September 3

PAVINOVSKY went into the telegraph office. He hadn't shaved in two days and his eyes were pink.

"Can you get an answer from New York by noon?" he said to the man behind the counter.

"Twelve o'clock! Sure. It's just eleven."

Pavinovsky picked up a blank and a pencil and wrote a message, quickly as if he had already arranged it in his mind. He pushed it over the counter.

The man pointed at the words with a pen and read them aloud: "Antonio Bertonelli, New York *Times,* New York. Wired yesterday no answer if you care wire by noon. No signature?"

"No."

"Unsigned," he said, writing it down. "That'll be seventy-three cents and tax—"

Pavinovsky laid down a dollar bill. "Please get that off at once."

342

"What's your address—for the answer?"

"I'm going to just wait here if you don't mind."

"Help yourself."

"My name's Pavinovsky. If you get a message for me just call me."

"How do you spell that name?"

He told him and turned away to the chair in front of a desk in a corner. He didn't feel very much of anything. The whole thing was becoming more and more unreal, muffled. Shapes and colors moved back and forth beyond the window-glass, blurred spots, de-personalized, bacteria under a microscope, a bright light behind them, floating in the fluid of street noises. Two men in shirt sleeves, a man in a white suit, three girls recently dressed going to the movie that had just started, the movie had just started, a policeman in a blue shirt marking the tires of the parked cars with chalk, cars creeping by in the traffic, everything in a glaring twilight, muffled, wrapped in inconsequence. His fingernails needed filing. The third one on his left hand seemed always to have a line of black beneath it, like a splinter lying sideways. The letters on the window, N O I N U, the Ns backwards, oh, yes, UNION. The glass top of the writing table was warm.—

He pulled his watch out from beneath his belt and set it by the clock on the wall; it was twenty-three minutes past eleven. Who was he waiting for? Oh. . . . He lifted the splinter of dirt out from under his fingernail. All clean now; all clear. A good noise behind him, clicking clattering chattering breaking chattering, wooden metallic, telephone bell, typewriter keys, the tight rubber thump of the cap on the pneumatic tube, all swimming in a sea of chatter break break chatter.

Everything was becoming more and more unreal. It reminded him of a night many years ago when he had fainted on the stage. It was a hot night in a little theater in Chicago. He was doing chorus work. He had held a pose for hours, hours; he hadn't been feeling well anyhow. Then quietly, with a strange matter-of-factness, everything had begun to become more and more

343

dream-like and he had fallen. He had hardly thought of it since, but there now was that half-conscious instant of falling, as fresh in his memory now as when it had been buried there, that absence of any feeling of falling, that absence of any surprise or alarm at seeing the floor drawing steadily closer to his eyes. No more instinct to catch himself than if he had been walking up to a wall to look at a picture. Then just as he was thinking he had come close enough, a deafening sort of explosion inside his head.

He looked out through the plate glass window at the world now with the same hypnotic calmness; the nerves of hope were dead; no mental pain could get through.

He watched the hands of the wall clock close in their V, with somewhat the same undramatic detachment that you might watch a train crossing a long bridge or watch the moon sinking behind a chimney. When it was twelve o'clock he got up quietly and walked out into the sun. He stumbled slightly stepping down to the sidewalk, as if he hadn't perceived the change of level, but he caught himself and a moment later the sunlight enveloped him.

12. Local Page

Friday, September 4

GRAND JURY FINDS
"NO BILL" AGAINST
BULLOCH CO. MAN
BEN GRAY OF DUE WEST
GA. FREE; "UNAVOIDABLE
ACCIDENT," SAYS FOREMAN—

*TWO BOUND OVER
ON PROHI CHARGE—*

344

LOCAL BOY FOUND
DROWNED IN 1ST
LEVEL OF CANAL

SERGEY PAVINOVSKY

ACCIDENTALLY DIES

IN UNFORTUNATE FALL

The body of Sergey Pavinovsky, son of the
late—

TOTAL OF $8,421 IN
BUILDING PERMITS
ISSUED LAST MONTH—

GRACEWOOD GA. CITIZEN
OBSERVES 90TH BIRTHDAY

SEER OF HAMILTON COUNTY—

345